Unhappy the Land

Paul Spradbery

For Jan,

with all good wishes,

Paul Spradbery.

Blot Publishing
2002

A catalogue record for this book is available from the British Library.

Disclaimer
The opinions expressed in this novel are those of the author and do not necessarily represent the views of the publisher.

ISBN 1 900929 06 6

Layout by
Blot Publishing: www.blot.co.uk

Printed by
Plumridge & Co., 41 High Street, Linton, Cambridgeshire

To my daughters, Philippa, Phoebe, and the memory of their late sister, Emma, who on Tuesday, 12th May, 1997, fought with nature, and lost. There is no shame in that, my love, no shame at all.

'The great are only great because we are on our knees.'

Pierre Joseph Proudhon (1809-65)

I

**'Travel, in the younger sort, is a part of education;
in the elder, a part of experience.'**

Francis Bacon (1561-1626)
Essays, Of Travel

'Worship and idolatry, Philip,' my mother never tired of telling me, 'are the twin pillars at the entrance to the temple of insanity.'

According to her, no individual could ever be worthy of such exaggerated regard. Historical figures, national leaders, military commanders, cultural icons, saints and sinners alike, were no different from the rest of us: unquestionably flawed and never exempt from the omnipotent, unyielding laws of nature. I had not the faintest idea as to the quote's origin, but I was certain that it was not a product of her own mind. Such a strange metaphor was, in my opinion, way beyond the imagination of a woman of her unsophisticated status. The only logical explanations were that she had either read it in a book or inherited it passively from the previous generation.

Her most scathing outbursts, not surprisingly, tended to be reserved for the advocates of Christianity.

'They won't even accept that their own hero is dead two thousand years after he was born! They're mad - every one of them!'

As far as I could ever see, such a damnation seemed difficult to dispute, but even if tangible contradictory evidence had existed, I would have hesitated before confronting her with it. Tolerating dissent from her son was never her forte. Hypocrisy, on the other hand, often was. Ironically, she all but worshipped my father, who was nothing more than a woefully underpaid, semi-literate Liverpool dockworker whose main purpose in life, as he himself would openly admit, was to make up the numbers. From the age of fifteen onwards he played the thankless rôle of proletarian carthorse, years that were punctuated only by spells of unemployment and ill health. Even when chronic alcoholism fuelled violent rages in his early forties, my mother's devotion was unwavering, much to her detriment as well as, on occasions, my own.

Both died in the months leading up to my eighteenth birthday - my father due to the inevitable cirrhosis of his liver, and my mother several weeks later for a reason equally tragic, and unsurprising, to all who knew them.

Fortunately for me, there were consolations. The humble Gainsborough family home - a peculiar, whitewashed, gable-end cottage which stood about fifty yards from the riverside - became my own; although, after nine years spent living by myself, I had been able to make but few improvements to its drab, memory-haunted interior.

The other blessing was Tim McKee: a loyal friend from schooldays with whom I shared the same birthday, and whose parents were kind enough to regard me as their own. Tim's father was the hard-working proprietor of a small furniture warehouse situated on the western outskirts of the city, and it was no secret that, after twenty years of selfless graft, his sole ambition was to break even, thus providing him with the necessary ammunition to submit one glorious final instruction to his reptilian bank manager. He was convinced it was no coincidence that the bank's logo vaguely resembled a swastika. I took up full-time employment with Mr. McKee the day after leaving school.

Tim himself subscribed to his parents' simplistic view that a university qualification, of any colour, would be his passport to a more comfortable life. He duly graduated with a well-earned degree in Clinical Psychology, or something similar, and accepted a coveted post at the main teaching hospital, thus going some way towards proving their point. From an early age we were generally considered to be of comparable academic ability, but Tim was far more focused and his self-discipline emulated that of his father. Mine, on the other hand, emulated that of mine.

To his credit, the transition from an essentially shy sixth-form pupil to an articulate undergraduate did not suppress the friendship we had cultivated since we were small. In the light of the sudden deaths of my parents, he endeavoured to include me in his exciting new circles, often introducing me to people with whom I had embarrassingly little in common.

The most notable example was Lindsey Corker, a tall, indisputably good-looking freshman, born and bred in rural Nottinghamshire. My first memory of him was listening as he reminisced about growing up in a close-knit mining village, where the streets and alleyways reeked of a distinctive mixture of fried fish and coal dust.

Three years younger than Tim and myself, Lindsey was without doubt the most infuriating individual I had ever encountered. He happened also to be the most intelligent, and seemed well-equipped to make a mockery of a four-year course in Applied Mathematics upon which he had just embarked. His arrogance, often coupled with a disgustingly cynical sense of humour, annoyed me to an extraordinary extent. After spending evenings with him, usually in claustrophobic city pubs, I would lie awake in bed fantasizing about putting my fist in his face. Gratuitous references to *Oliver Twist* and the supposed 'charm' of the Victorian workhouse era so starkly depicted in Dickens's novel, were simply beyond the pale. Never in my life had I shown a disposition towards violence - my scrawny physique rendered such actions potentially dangerous - which served to highlight the intensity of my newly-awakened anger. Indeed, even the sound of raised voices made me feel uneasy, which Tim conjectured was the inevitable consequence of having spent most of my teenage years living in a small house that echoed to the sound of my father's frequent vitriolic outbursts.

Tim, on the other hand, was far less sensitive to Lindsey's torments, and creditably managed a smile when, one morning, on walking into the men's lavatory at the university refectory, he noticed the words: 'Arts and Social Science Degrees. Please take one', scrawled in familiar handwriting across the toilet paper dispenser. I could not help but laugh, despite the fact that no one could have been less qualified to do so. From that day, 'toilet-paper degrees' became a campus cliché, such was the influence of the young Mr. Corker.

Not altogether unsurprisingly, it transpired that a strict routine of lectures, tutorials and perpetual assessments interested Lindsey as much as it would have appealed to someone like myself. His participation lasted only eighteen months, and it was widely rumoured that the course staff were far from sorry to see him depart. Disruptive from the outset, he openly accused lecturers of lacking knowledge of their own specialist subjects, and once had the audacity to walk out halfway through an end-of-term examination, convinced that his responses to the first part alone would lead to a satisfac- · tory pass. Nevertheless, this blatant, almost irrational self-confidence never seemed to be misplaced, which annoyed me all the more.

Since his departure, despite working only on a casual basis in a small watch-repairer's shop, which he thoroughly enjoyed, I never knew him to be short of money. I looked constantly for a logical explanation, at times considering far-fetched notions such as covert drug-dealing or having had money bequeathed to him in the wills of grandparents. Alas, neither theory possessed even the flimsiest scrap of evidence - and he was not one to show his cards.

One facet of his character, however, overshadowed all the others with ease: he was an unshakeable atheist. There were occasions when it would be impossible to hold a conversation without a hatred of religious doctrine spewing from his mouth. Naturally, he loved my mother's poetic maxim about the folly of worship and idolatry, reciting and interpreting it for the benefit of anyone who would listen; although unlike her, he was acutely familiar with the intricacies of both science and philosophy, often quoting the likes of Voltaire, Hume and Darwin with unequivocal respect for their 'beautifully-reasoned heresies'.

Having disliked but tolerated his caustic and unpredictable behaviour for almost two years, he earned my respect within the space of fifteen minutes one evening at a popular city nightclub. For a reason unknown to either of us, a drunken, speed-fuelled lout walked through the crowd and stubbed out a cigarette on my bare wrist. Lindsey snapped. He grabbed the man's hair and punched him full in the mouth, causing him to fall awkwardly over a stool and smack the side of his head against a wall. In an instant, we became surrounded by six or seven of his crazed accomplices, and I soon found myself lying on the dirty floor being kicked relentlessly from all sides. Within seconds, my hair and clothes were splattered with blood and fragments of broken glass.

After what seemed like half an hour, the onslaught was interrupted by a different set of thugs: three unsympathetic doormen dragged us to our feet and ejected us head first into a damp, litter-infested alley. It appeared that we had been found exclusively guilty of perpetrating the entire incident.

I managed to struggle to my feet, light-headed and shaking uncontrollably, and noticed Lindsey leaning against a wall, dabbing his mouth which was frothing with bloody saliva. We looked at each other in silence. He had instigated violence, the inevitable consequences of which he must have been painfully aware from the start, in an attempt to save his friend from further humiliation. As we walked away, side by side, his arrogance drowned in a tsunami of loyalty and courage.

Predictably, that evening reinforced his negative view of my home city, even though he appreciated as well as anyone that such incidents were commonplace everywhere else. Despite the strength of his feelings, though, not once did he give serious consideration to returning to his native Midlands. He viewed the option as a defeatist, retrograde step, which therefore had to be avoided, even if the alternative were to bring him only hardship and loneliness. Other people, however, had their own ideas.

Every year since I was at primary school, the first of September was, with the exception of Christmas, the most significant day of the year. It was almost a day of mourning, simultaneously marking the end of summer and the onset of a long and generally depressing winter. Every year followed the same basic pattern. When I reached my twenty-fifth birthday, however, my determination to delay the arrival of the bleak winter months had become overwhelming.

An eighteen-day trip around the world was Lindsey's brainchild. After less than a minute's deliberation, I agreed to his idea, as did Tim, on the condition that the air tickets would cost no more than a thousand pounds each. The booking was finalized at the beginning of March, more than six months prior to our scheduled departure.

It was to be only my second trip abroad, the other being a dismal weekend sightseeing in a very foggy Dublin which had been organized, albeit rather abominably, by the school. More significantly, I had not been away from home since my parents had died.

Consequently, I spent the entire summer consumed by nervous excitement, and became a regular visitor to the central library, researching whatever I could regarding our intended ports of call. The reputations of Bangkok, Los Angeles and Hong Kong soon became well known to all three of us, as did that of New York City where, conveniently, Lindsey's sister owned a fashionable apartment on Manhattan's Upper West Side.

'Nova won't mind suffering us for a few nights,' he would say, in his customarily complacent manner. 'Besides, it'll save us a fortune.'

That year, the evening of September the fifteenth arrived after I had spent six long months beyond distraction.

The three of us, dressed like overzealous mountaineers, sat slovenly on a damp wooden baggage trolley at Lime Street station, resting our feet on a pile of bulging rucksacks and bags and waiting in silence to board the nine thirty train which would take us to London. Lindsey's only item of luggage was an old canvas bag, similar to those used by newspaper boys and almost as ragged. Its distinguishing feature was a reflective 'Jesus is Lord' sticker, which he claimed to have stolen from a Christian bookstall in Norwich and then craftily defaced with a black marker pen so that it became: 'Jesus is Dead'.

'Nietzsche's words,' he would repeat, 'not mine.'

Tim echoed my own feelings on the matter. 'Who else would think to do such a thing?'

A cold rush of wind funnelled down the platform and into our faces as we shuffled past the other baggage trolleys to the second-class carriages which, typically, were situated furthest away. The train departed on time. The only other passengers in the carriage were three excitable teenage girls seated at the far end and a strange, middle-aged couple squashed behind us next to the luggage racks. The young girls were travelling light, so I guessed they would not be venturing far, unlike ourselves, who would be covering in excess of twenty thousand miles before once again breathing the river-scented Mersey air.

'Phil ... I'm talking to you!'

'Sorry. I wasn't listening. What did you say?'

'I was just curious as to why you're looking so apprehensive,' said Tim.

'I was thinking about the cottage, that's all.'

'In case you've left the back door unlocked?'

Lindsey sat up sharply. 'Perhaps burglars are ransacking the place right this minute.'

'That's enough,' I said.

It was a nauseating suggestion, although not a wholly unrealistic one. For one thing, the enclosed yard at the rear would provide excellent cover for any wicked opportunists, as it had done on two previous occasions.

Admittedly, I possessed nothing of great monetary value, but the set of family photographs on the fireplace were the only ones of their kind, and the shabby, porcelain ornament of St. Paul's Cathedral had been my mother's pride and joy since her wedding day. Every Saturday morning without fail she used to lift it carefully onto the kitchen table and spend at least a quarter of an hour dusting and polishing every tiny fissure, as if she had been tricked into believing it to be priceless. Even when the dome had lost most of its silver-coloured paint, she was truly blind to the blemishes. Nevertheless, as a sentimental token of respect, I continued to take care of it and, for some inexplicable reason, its shoddy condition made me treasure it all the more.

As the city was replaced by dreary suburbs, then by endless countryside, Lindsey stared out of the nearside window into the infinite darkness.

'I remember returning from the States four years ago,' he recalled, almost hypnotized by his own thoughts. 'Took the tube from Heathrow and arrived at Euston at about eleven in the evening, but the last northwest-bound train had already left its blocks.'

'What did you do?' I felt obliged to ask him.

'I spent the night on the station concourse. But I couldn't afford to fall asleep in case some thief waltzed off with my bag.'

'There were other people in there, too?'

'Too right. Tramps ... alcoholics ... pavement princesses,' he mused, 'and one or two normal souls scattered about here and there. I spent the whole night talking politics with a tax inspector from Wrexham. We were glad to have some sane company - assuming, of course, that tax inspectors are sane.' He then smiled dreamily. 'Some of them were screaming at each other and smashing bottles. Eventually, a couple of officers from the Transport Police Unit arrived on the scene and threw out anyone who didn't have a ticket. Now, whenever I pass through Euston, even if the place is heaving with commuters during rush hour, I think back to that night of madness.'

'You might be able to renew some old acquaintances tonight,' said Tim. 'What if they recognize you?'

'Ha, I doubt they'd recognize their own mothers.'

We had envisaged arriving at the airport just after one in the morning, and realized, therefore, that if we wanted to sleep, we would have to make do with whatever seating was available in the departures area. On our budget, the luxury of a palatial airport hotel was out of the equation entirely.

Only the sound of the rhythmical rattling of the train wheels disturbed the silence. The old couple remained tight-lipped, staring ahead as if they were strangers to one another. Lindsey rested the side of his head against the window, his eyes moving smoothly from right to left, following the roads and farmhouses until they were no longer in his field of view.

'Excuse me, young man. Would you mind if I closed that window above your head?' whispered a soft voice from behind me. It was the old man who had temporarily left his seat.

'Not at all,' Tim replied, before promptly standing up and closing it himself.

'Thank you.'

The man sat down without making another sound. His accent was North American but, to my undiscerning ears, the dialect of a Texan, a New Yorker and a Californian would probably have been indistinguishable.

'Are you from the US?' Tim asked him.

'Canada.'

'Hope I didn't offend you.'

'No more than everyone else we've met over here.'

'Have you been touring Scotland?'

'All weekend long. We're now heading for London before doing France and Germany next week.'

Doing France and Germany, I thought to myself. I realized that, being from the largest country in the world, where the nearest town could have been thirty or more miles from his home, he viewed Britain and continental Europe in a different light. I was half-expecting Lindsey to ask if they were planning to do Switzerland and Belgium in an afternoon.

'What about you guys?' the man inquired.

'Thailand, first of all,' said Tim, 'then Hong Kong, across the Pacific to Los Angeles, Toronto and New York, before returning home at the beginning of October.'

His casual, almost flippant manner masked the fact that, like myself, he had spent the majority of his holidays confined to Britain.

Lindsey, on the other hand, was different. He had travelled extensively abroad. His frenetic, one-city-per-day *InterRail* tour of western Europe as a seventeen-year-old provided him with a wide range of weird anecdotes which he would dress up and inject into a conversation with only the slightest encouragement. His sister had moved to New York City a few years previously, along with her fiancé, Jacques, from whom she had become inseparable since their undergraduate days together in Newcastle-upon-Tyne. Consequently, Lindsey made transatlantic trips almost at will, and quickly became as familiar with Manhattan as he seemed to be with most other places. I had met Nova and Jacques on several occasions before they emigrated, and they had stressed repeatedly that we would be welcome to call on them, even at short notice - which, from Lindsey, was all anyone ever got.

Our polite, if somewhat tired, conversation with the Canadian couple passed the time well, before the train slowed right down and crawled the final few miles into the vast abyss of London Euston.

The concourse, with its vending machines and neat, laminated timetable boards, was practically deserted. Nothing but discarded food wrappers and soft drink cartons remained from the chaotic bustle of a typical day. Lindsey smiled to himself as we headed for the escalator leading down to the tube labyrinth; he was probably drifting back to the night he had spent among the drunks and debris.

The tube station was equally lifeless. We spent several minutes perusing the colourful platform wall tapestries which comprised anything from movie advertisements to World War Two posters, financial information to abortion advice. I found London fascinating and unsettling in equal measures. It appeared as foreign to me as any city I was expecting to witness abroad.

A cool, stiff draught preceded the clanking din from an old grey train, which rose like the anarchic orchestral crescendo at the end of the Beatles' *A Day in the Life*. We climbed inside and tossed all the bags onto one of the many unoccupied seats. Along the carriage were two or three expressionless faces, each with a pair of glazed eyes which seemed not to notice us, or even that the train had actually opened its doors. Lindsey scanned them in turn, but the longer he stared the more determined they were to avoid making eye contact. Lifeless souls they were, going nowhere.

Before we had settled ourselves, the lights of the next station flashed through the windows. A gaunt, grey-haired man, about fifty years of age and obviously drunk, stumbled into the carriage carrying a dilapidated polythene carrier bag in one hand and an opened can of beer in the other. He grunted, almost painfully, as he slumped onto the adjacent seat, then finished the last drops of his drink and fixed his eyes on Lindsey in an attempt to coax him into speaking.

Lindsey grinned at him. 'Grand night out?'

'Ah, yes!' came the slurred but courteous reply. 'Started out at Earl's Court and somehow found myself roaming around Kings Cross! And not for the first time!'

He was from the north-east, possibly Tyneside, and was clearly harmless.

'Merseyside!' he exclaimed, on discovering where we were from. 'I had my honeymoon there, on a caravan site not far from Southport. She was a beautiful lass, I'm telling you. Beautiful.'

We remained attentive; it was obvious that he was being truthful.

'Aye, it was the first time me and the wife had slept together, you know. You couldn't do it before you were wed in those days.'

'I hope you recovered the lost ground,' Lindsey remarked with a lascivious smirk.

'Aye, I remember it better than yesterday. We climbed into bed and she said to me: "Why don't you open the window?" You know, in case it got all sweaty and that. So I grabbed the handle and pushed it, and you'll never believe it, I pushed the window right out of its frame and it landed in the long grass outside!'

Tim and I looked at each other and smiled, albeit briefly so as not to disturb his recollections. Lindsey made a sarcastic comment about what might have followed, secure in the knowledge that it would not cause offence.

'She sat up, looked out of the gaping hole in the caravan wall and said to me: "Well, you'd better go and retrieve it, man." So, without bothering to put on my boots, I went round the back of the caravan, in total darkness, and you know what? Full o' *nettles!*' he said despairingly. 'She spent the rest of the night rubbing my poor legs with leaves.'

Lindsey laughed aloud, fully aware, as were Tim and I, that this was no tale contrived by an imaginative storyteller. It was merely a colourful tile from the haphazard mosaic that was his life. He had probably confronted every one of his unavoidable disasters with consistent indifference. Or so I guessed.

The man's expression changed suddenly, as if having experienced an acute stabbing pain in his chest.

'I loved that girl, I'm telling you. I did,' he moaned, 'I doted on her for sixteen years.'

His story ceased to be hilarious. The woman, whoever she was, assuming she actually existed, had walked out of his life and rendered him emotionally bankrupt. What had he done, I asked myself, to deserve such a painful descent into oblivion, apart from having been possessed by such powerful feelings in the first place?

The train came to a halt at Earl's Court. The man got to his feet, said goodnight and disappeared forever. I wondered where he might have been heading, what his home life was like, and whether he had any family or not. In truth, there was no way of knowing for certain, which might have been just as well.

Tim glanced at his watch the moment we reached the bright lights of Heathrow. 'Twenty minutes to one. We board ten hours from now. I hope there'll be a cafe open somewhere.'

'There will be,' Lindsey assured him. 'Up on the top floor. I remember it.'

We walked up the escalator and into the terminal building. A couple of porters, one carrying huge yellow refuse sacks, the other holding a bucket and brush, noticed us enter but said nothing. Both looked as vacant as the tube passengers.

We found the open-plan cafe at the end of the hall on the first floor. In a corner next to the window lay a blond-haired youth, fast asleep, his ruck-sack employed as a pillow; and passing the time over tepid cups of tea were two old men who looked like regulars with nowhere else to go. Already,

Liverpool belonged to a different era. Time had expanded during the first two hundred miles.

I paused to scan the departures information on the overhead monitor which displayed a catalogue of flights for the new day. By sunrise, thousands of travellers would be passing through the now deathly-still lounge and heading for their own preferred corner of the globe. Flight 917 was scheduled for eleven o'clock, and would not arrive in Bangkok until six the following morning.

II

'Only the strong shall thrive ...
Only the fit survive.'

Robert W. Service (1874-1958)
Law of the Yukon

We remained awake throughout the twelve-hour flight and saw the sun explode over what I assumed to be eastern Burma.

'Good morning, ladies and gentlemen,' came a gentle, soothing female voice through the speakers. 'We are about to begin our descent into Bangkok, Don Muang. Ground temperature is thirty-one Celsius, eighty-eight degrees Fahrenheit. Estimated time of arrival is zero six-thirty hours ... thank you.'

I craned my neck to observe the land below as we descended into a dense, homogeneous haze which was invisibly suspended above square mile after square mile of unchecked urban sprawl.

'I wonder what this place holds for us,' mumbled Tim, the second we bumped onto the runway.

'Something memorable?' I suggested, optimistically.

We stepped out of the air-conditioned hall into a wall of tropical heat. The sheltered parking bays were packed with different types of taxi, each patrolled by a sharp-eyed driver waiting for the exit doors to slide open.

'Sukhumvit Four!' barked Lindsey at the nearest one.

The driver, a small, wrinkled man with a gracious smile, strode across to us and relieved Tim of some of the bags before forcing them awkwardly into the boot of his vehicle.

Lindsey climbed into the passenger's seat and turned his head to face Tim and me in the back.

'There's a place on Sukhumvit Road where my cousin stayed last year. Twelve pounds per night.'

'Sounds reasonable.'

'It doesn't have proper air-con but each room has its own fan. Not perfect, I know, but what else can we afford?'

Shortly after we had filtered on to the expressway, we hit the infamous, impenetrable mass of Bangkok traffic. The exhaust fumes from hundreds of vehicles, coupled with dust from the road, formed a thick cloud which obscured the blue morning sky. Parallel to the road was a long row of partially built, hi-tech office complexes, together with construction supplies and battered trucks, scattered around, apparently abandoned.

I looked across at Tim, who seemed impressed by the sheer diversity of our new surroundings. 'Anything goes,' he muttered, 'but hardly anything moves.'

He was right. Western and oriental cultures had coalesced to form a hybrid way of life for the city's millions. Business executives in Japanese sports cars crawled alongside rusty pick-up trucks on which dozens of malnourished peasants sat cradling sacks of perishable goods in the open air. Decrepit, wooden shacks cowered in the shadows of glass and concrete skyscrapers, and elegant Buddhist temples stood out like jewels against a wild backdrop of trees and muddy streams.

Almost a full hour passed before we turned off the expressway and meandered into the city along dusty back roads which were lined with endless rows of tiny shops and wooden stalls, selling anything from motor spares to rice and vegetables.

We got out and retrieved the bags once we had arrived at the central Sukhumvit district. The main road itself consisted of seven lanes, every one of them packed with flatulent vehicles - cars, buses and motorcycles - all jockeying for position as they nudged impatiently through the downtown smog. It looked like a Grand Prix in slow motion. We wandered along to the junction of Soi 4, continually stepping into the filthy gutter to walk around gossiping street vendors and makeshift pavement cafes. Cheerful young girls manned metal ice-buckets containing chilled soft drinks, and huge, blackened woks in which smelly meat cubes and chestnuts sizzled under the noses of pedestrians. Never in my life had my eyes been so desperate to see so much so soon, but the rest of my body, drained from the journey, demanded otherwise and overruled.

'Here it is!' said Lindsey emphatically, his forehead glistening with sweat. 'The aforementioned Condo!'

A bony, middle-aged woman, who could barely speak English, shepherded us to a large, square room on the fourth floor of a plain block of apartments. To our relief, the lift, although old and deteriorating, was fully operational. Two large mattresses lay covered with only a single, clean sheet on the polished wooden floor, and perched on a corner table was a small, whirring fan, oscillating in a sweeping arc like a lone searchlight. It was still only eight thirty.

As soon as she had closed the door behind her, we dropped everything and collapsed onto the makeshift beds, our shirts and hair already saturated with perspiration.

None of us came round until one o'clock that afternoon, waking to find the room pleasantly cool and smelling of scented candles. I thought of

London, which already seemed like a week ago, and Liverpool, which seemed like two or three.

After a much-needed change of clothes, we stuffed bundles of Thai currency into our trouser pockets and headed back down to the street.

'*Sawat-dii khrup! Rao pen khon angkrit!*' Lindsey hollered to the maid who was sitting in the cramped reception kiosk with two other women dressed in identical overalls. She smiled at him and nodded in acknowledgement.

'What does that mean?' I asked him, as we set off at an unadvisedly brisk pace along Soi 4 towards the main road.

'It's Thai.'

'We gathered that,' said Tim. 'Were you making a pass at the old girl?'

'Just being polite. I read the phrases in the back of your pocket travel guide while you were sleeping. I hope she understood. I don't want to spend a whole week here speaking English. What's more, she's not my type.'

We reached the main road and turned left towards what looked like the heart of the city. A continuous stretch of chrome-and-glass hotels and oddly-named boutiques comprised the block between the junctions of Sois 4 and 2, and on the pavement between the bus shelters were mobile stalls offering cheap imitation T-shirts, shoes and leather goods to tourists. We stopped and sat down at a battered old table at the end of Soi 2 and ordered food from one of the many vendors.

'Alfresco!' Lindsey enthused.

'Is it safe to eat here?' said Tim, cautiously.

'Probably not,' said Lindsey, 'but I'm sure it won't cost much.'

'Botulism never does. Still, your cousin survived. That's something.'

Flies and bugs swarmed around each of the tables and dust flew up into our faces whenever taxis or motorcycles sped recklessly past. After a few minutes, a young girl, no older than fourteen, arrived carrying plates of food: three identical mountains of chicken fried rice with shreds of spring onions, chilli peppers, a slice of lime, and a fried egg on top of each one. Regardless of where it had come from, we devoured every morsel without a second's hesitation. I was beginning to get the feel of the place.

We continued walking along Sukhumvit and reached an illuminated sign which read: *Bangkok Night Plaza* - a wide, undulating path leading to a row of timber-framed outdoor bars, almost underneath the expressway and backing onto an exposed railway line.

'At nine o'clock tonight, that place will erupt.' Lindsey remarked, pointing as we strolled past. 'Just wait and see.'

'Erupt with what?'

'Decadence - if our luck is in.'

He was already making provisional plans although, conveniently, the

Plaza was less than two hundred yards from the Condo and therefore well within staggering distance were the inevitable to happen.

We sauntered, aimlessly but contentedly, past shopping malls and hotels - some five-star, some no-star - stopping only at busy road junctions where traffic policemen stood amid the chaos with large white handkerchieves covering their noses and mouths. At the imposing World Trade Centre, we turned into Thanon Ratchadamri: a wide boulevard running between a race-track and a long row of bookshops and more hotels.

After approximately two miles, we arrived at Lumpini Park: a vast square of grass and woodland with two lakes, one of which was full of sailing boats of every colour. We hired a couple of blankets from one of the park attendants and flaked out in the shade of a cluster of small trees.

Hundreds of locals were lazing about in the early afternoon heat although, strangely, the temperature seemed to have fallen a little. I rested my head on the parched ground and gazed up at the gently-swaying branches, the myriad shades of green changing slightly with each breath of wind. I focused briefly on the uppermost branches of the nearest tree and created different sets of surroundings inside my head. Relaxation was now complete.

'Are you still hungry, Phil?'

I looked down from the sky, and noticed Tim sitting next to a small boy, about ten years of age, who was selling fruit from an ice-filled basket.

'What is there?'

'*Nee arai?*' inquired Lindsey, pointing to some plastic bags containing long, skinless segments of pale green fruit.

I presumed he was asking what was in the basket, but I could not imagine how he would be able to understand the boy's reply.

'*Aloi mai?*'

The boy nodded enthusiastically. '*Aloi dii!*'

The moment we had paid him with a handful of tiny coins, he hoisted the harness of the cumbersome basket onto his bare shoulders, and made his way towards the next group of people who were lying side by side, reading books.

We picked cautiously at the different scraps of fruit, the likes of which I had never seen before. Lindsey looked up and spoke with his mouth full.

'I wonder if Central Park in New York will be as peaceful as this.'

'We'll soon find out,' I said, 'a fortnight from now.'

'Nova says that Central Park is at its most beautiful around this time of year.' he added. 'I've only ever seen it at the zenith of summer. Now, the leaves will be at the point of changing colour, and most of the holidaymakers will have crawled back into the woodwork. I think it must remind her of home.'

He stopped eating and looked thoughtfully over my shoulder towards the boats. He appeared to be on the verge of saying something profound.

'I once had sex in Central Park,' he exclaimed, eventually.

'You've done it in every park,' Tim quickly retorted, 'or so you claim.'

'It was late at night so we weren't noticed. I mean, nobody in his right mind goes in there after dark.'

'You did.'

There was a pause. 'She made me do it.'

I laughed at the absurdity of his protest and lay down again, listening as the two of them battled to outwit each other. Their persistent verbal sparring usually ended with one hitting the other right in the balls, with a remark so wonderfully sarcastic that I would be sniggering to myself for days.

At five in the afternoon, following another brief doze, we rolled up the blankets and handed them in on our way out of the park. Lindsey stepped on to the road and flagged down a 'taxi' - an odd, three-wheeled contraption which made a noise like a petrol-driven lawnmower, only much louder. After haggling with the driver for a minute, he signalled for us to climb inside, and we spent the next five or ten minutes scooting along narrow, winding side-streets, and in and out of dusty thoroughfares, before arriving in one piece back at Sukhumvit at the junction of Soi 4.

It was dark by the time we ventured out for the second time, at seven thirty. We headed in the same direction as before: on to Sukhumvit, past the junction of Soi 2, over the single railway line, but this time turning left into the Plaza, which had already sprung to life, well before Lindsey had predicted.

Each three-walled bar occupied no more than a hundred square feet, every one with its own music, albeit of the same type, booming out of powerful speakers which were fastened to the rear walls. The other walls were plastered with photographs, odd souvenirs from different parts of the world, and tapes and compact discs piled precariously on wooden shelves.

We had walked only a short way along the path when we were noticed by six or seven fresh-faced young Thai girls who were loitering by the third or fourth bar.

'Hello, Mister!' came the shouts in broken but well-practised English. 'Hello, handsome man! Hello! Hello-o!'

The sight of three young, white boys seemed to have them covertly rubbing their hands. Soon we were being rounded up like stray sheep and led to a row of battered bamboo stools at the open end of one of the bars.

'Help!' Lindsey called out, laughing. 'I've been arrested!'

His carefree optimism contrasted with the apprehensive expression on Tim's face. 'I hope this is not going to cost us another month's pay, Phil.'

I shared his reservations. This was, after all, a foreign world and, Lindsey's few tourist phrases apart, we could neither speak nor understand a word of their native language.

Nonetheless, we managed to order a round of drinks and endeavoured to communicate with the girls amid the din from the hi-fi. Tim looked increasingly uneasy; he was looking for the catch, regardless of the girls' innocent demeanour. There had to be a catch. There just had to be.

'What-your-name?' piped the slender teenage waif who had led me to my seat.

'Phi-lip,' I told her, slowly and deliberately.

'Where-you-come-from, Phi-nip?'

'Li-ver-pool.'

'Ah, Li-wa-ploo!' she echoed, nodding her head, having evidently never heard of the place.

'That's right. In England. We are all from England,' I stressed, pointing at Tim who was seated next to me, and Lindsey, who was communicating slightly better with a very dark-skinned girl, as stunning as any I had ever seen.

The only other man in the bar was a balding, pot-bellied character sitting at the opposite end, and wearing long khaki shorts and a sleeveless white T-shirt. One of the girls was stroking his tanned, hairy neck whilst another had perched herself on his lap, like an attentive young child seeking favour. I acknowledged him with a slight nod and he grinned knowingly.

'I only came in for a quiet beer!' he protested, in an unmistakable Australian accent.

I looked again at my hostess who by now was sitting as comfortably as she could, with her back to me, on the bit of stool exposed between my legs. Waves of long, shiny black hair cascaded over her bare shoulders and thin straps of a tight orange dress. I rested my chin over her right shoulder and clasped my arms around her tiny waist, resigned to the fact that further attempts at conversation would probably prove futile.

'Is this different, or what?' screeched Lindsey, now standing behind the bar with the dark-skinned girl who, likewise, was giggling uncontrollably.

The explosions of wild laughter from the two of them gradually became louder and more frequent. It was as if he were actually a Plaza regular, changing the music on the hi-fi and joining in the girls' raucous chorus, beckoning to any other westerners who were sufficiently curious as to look in our general direction. In view of the language barrier, I wondered how he was able to captivate the girl so completely.

Back out on the thoroughfare, more and more westerners were beginning to stroll up and down in twos and threes in search of a cosy nest for the evening. Most looked like international businessmen, probably in town for a week or two and glad to be unwinding after a long day's trading and negotiating. The girls' repetitive cries echoed around the bars as they tried to entice into their own particular web anyone who looked to have money to spend.

Tim attracted the attention of a young boy, lethargically pedalling a big old tricycle with an array of seafood scraps hanging from a delicate wooden lattice in the basket over the front wheel. He handed over three or four worthless coins in exchange for a few pieces of strange-looking fish and a bag of sticky white rice. He ripped open the bag, grabbed a piece between thumb and forefinger, and examined it meticulously, possibly uncertain as to whether or not it was still alive.

'You ought really to avoid eating those things, mate!' shouted the Australian, now drinking alone. 'Otherwise you'll be faced with *The Ted Stanley Dilemma!*'

'What's that?' asked Tim, politely.

'You won't be able to decide which end to put over the lavatory bowl!'

'Really?'

'God's honest truth.'

'And who's Ted Stanley?'

'That's me,' he boasted. 'I ate some last Friday. Splashing and farting all weekend.'

'Ach, who cares?' said Tim under his breath. He was now noticeably less uptight. After putting the piece into his mouth and chewing it somewhat gingerly, he offered the bag to the girls, all of whom politely refused. I did likewise, trusting their judgement far more than his.

Half an hour later, I glanced across at Lindsey again. He and the girl had now reversed roles: she was sitting on his stool and he was standing behind her, massaging her neck and shoulders with one hand, and holding a bottle of beer in the other. Aware that he was being watched, he turned and looked at me, then walked over, pulling the girl by the hand.

'Maalii wants to know whether we'd like to go to Patpong for a couple of hours. Apparently, there's a nightclub there that stays open until late.'

Maalii was evidently the girl's name, but how he had been able to ascertain the rest of the information from her, I had not the first clue. She was much shorter than Lindsey, and had a smooth, doll's face which was partially hidden by wild black hair.

'Well, what's the verdict?' he said, impatiently. 'Shall we go?'

I looked at Tim, only to discover that he was looking back at me with the same hesitant expression. I wanted him to make the decision.

Within a minute, we were strolling with three foreign girls back towards Sukhumvit Road which was still swarming with motorcycles and those odd tuk-tuk taxis. Many of them were being driven to their limits by blinkered, kamikaze hoodlums, changing lanes without warning whilst trying to out-honk one another with their horns. We crammed into the back of one of them with the girls squashed onto our laps. I could not even see where we were heading.

'How far is it?' asked Tim, turning to Lindsey as we bumped and swerved along the road.

'No more than a mile or two.' He stroked the inside of the girl's bare thigh and then purred: 'Not that there's any great urgency.'

'Isn't that the park?' I said, leaning as far forward as the cramped conditions would allow.

It was in complete darkness. At the main entrance stood a large Buddhist monument to which the girls bowed in synchronicity and raised their hands to their heads, as if in solemn prayer. Even during a carefree, impromptu night in the city with three strangers, they spared a moment to show a little respect for their culture. Lindsey, aware of the gesture's origin, pretended not to notice and, for everyone's benefit, offered no comment.

We scooted across a busy junction and pulled up unexpectedly at the side of the road. I paid the driver and we squeezed out on to the pavement like squashed tomatoes slopping out of a can. This was Patpong, the notoriously X-rated Patpong, to which an entire chapter of the travel guide had been devoted. The reasons were obvious.

We wandered between the stalls, past dimly-lit bars inside which fully naked go-go dancers could be seen through the open doorways, all of which were being efficiently patrolled by slim young men in brilliant white cotton shirts. They addressed anyone who came into their sights including, quite incredibly, men walking arm-in-arm with their partners. What was on offer in some of the establishments amounted to some kind of freak show: girls who could smoke cigarettes, shoot ping-pong balls, crack nuts and wolf-whistle - using a part of their anatomy which I had always assumed was meant for other purposes. So little I knew.

Westerners bartered with stallholders for cheap summer clothes and Thai oddities - mainly Buddha images - and scruffy youngsters sat about on boxes and plastic crates, gorging takeaway food with chopsticks and washing it down with cans of beer.

After turning several corners, and thereby losing our bearings, we came to a flight of stairs which led to a small, poorly air-conditioned nightclub. Inside, every recess was packed full of Thais and tourists, dancing, drinking beer straight from bottles and watching satellite sports action on huge video screens. The fact that we were barely able to hear each other over the music was made irrelevant by the language barrier. It had become a great leveller, as the girls must have been aware.

For over two hours we drank and danced energetically between tables and stools. On several occasions, Maalii shamelessly threw her arms around Lindsey's neck, as if begging him, a complete stranger, never to leave.

'Why don't we lose our passports?' I bellowed in his ear.

He smiled and raised his eyebrows. 'It's tempting. At least, in this place, it's unlikely that we'll be attacked indiscriminately and then thrown out into the street to spend the rest of the night spitting blood.'

I thought back to that traumatic night in Liverpool and recalled his actions, either brave or foolish. I told myself yet again that, whenever I felt offended by the occasional venomous insult, I ought, instead, to remember the altruistic nature of those actions.

We left at two-thirty in the morning, stumbling back down the stairs and back on to the Patpong strip. Our hair was congealed with sweat and the night air remained stiflingly close. We wandered among the empty shops and bars to a small all-night food store, then made our way back to the main junction carrying bottles of chilled water. In short, we just followed the girls. After all, this fortuitous escapade had been of their design entirely, and they had so far proved themselves to be worthy of our trust. What may have been a typical night out for them had become memorably unique to ourselves.

After crossing the wide road, we arrived back at the entrance to Lumpini Park where we had idled away the afternoon. In the shadow of the imposing Buddha figure was an open patch of grass where twenty or thirty of the city's peasants, presumably homeless, had settled down for the night. The girls led us to the steps at the foot of the statue and we rested silently, peering into the darkness of the park.

'I never realized there was such a thing as an outdoor hotel,' Lindsey remarked, observing the lifeless bodies which were curled up on mats and newspaper with their heads resting upon their paltry belongings. 'The Hotel Buddha!' he added with mild incredulity.

The traffic had vanished but for the occasional taxi cruising alone along Ratchadamri Road to and from the central district. We finished our drinks and got to our feet, suddenly feeling quite exhausted. The girls stopped a tuk-tuk at the roadside and, once again, we squeezed on board and headed back to Sukhumvit, tearing noisily through the mostly deserted streets.

Just when I thought we were totally lost, we stopped in front of a row of old wooden shacks which I could see were situated between the Plaza and Soi 2, parallel to the railway line.

The girls clambered out. 'He take you Condo,' Maalii explained to Lindsey, pointing to the driver, who had not spoken since we flagged him down. 'You go bar tomorrow?' she then pleaded.

Lindsey smiled and nodded to her before we waved goodbye and disappeared into the warm, sticky night.

'There,' he said, 'I told you we could trust them.'

Tim articulated my own view. 'The simple fact that we weren't swindled out of our money is reason enough to be satisfied.'

'That was never a possibility,' Lindsey argued.

'Of course it was. We took a chance and got lucky, that's all.'

'You're just embarrassed by your initial hesitancy. Did you honestly believe those girls had either the capacity or the inclination to dupe us?'

'Maybe.' Tim asserted. 'They exist in a competitive world with no real safety net. You, of all people, should appreciate the Darwinian element running through their lives. Available work at the Plaza is probably scarce. Their survival is no accident.'

At four in the morning, we finally reached our room. The whole building was silent, apart from the noise of the overworked fan, and some insomniac Moroccan dopehead in the adjacent room playing a flute out of his window.

Lindsey switched off the light and groaned as he lay down. 'As far as I'm concerned, the temples, shops and river markets,' he said softly, 'can wait.'

III

**'Men's natures are alike;
it is their habits that carry them far apart.'**

Confucious (551-479BC)
Analects

For the second consecutive day, we resurfaced at one in the afternoon, the hyperactivity of the previous night - indeed, of the previous forty-eight hours - having taken its toll equally upon us all. Our enthusiasm for the place had, however, only intensified. We emerged into the Sukhumvit heat and hopped nonchalantly into a tuk-tuk in order to return to the placidity of Lumpini Park.

The attendant, a slight, bespectacled man who looked startlingly similar to Mahatma Gandhi, smiled a toothless smile when I handed him fifty baht for blanket hire.

'Thank you,' I said, hoping he would understand.

'Tank *you*,' he responded, tilting his head slightly, as everyone seemed to do, as subconsciously as smiling.

We spread the blankets in exactly the same spot, lay down and devised our plans for the day - or, more accurately, what remained of it.

'I said we'd meet the girls at the Plaza at four o'clock,' said Lindsey, apparently offering Tim and myself no say in the matter. 'Any objections?'

'None whatsoever,' I said, quite happy to while away the preceding hours lazing under a tree.

A light breeze tickled our faces every ten seconds or so, with roughly the same strength as the draught from the fan. I thought of the girls, despite being unable to picture their faces, but could not convince myself completely that no ulterior motives lay behind their adoring smiles.

We were disturbed by two fair-haired girls, about twelve years old, who walked over to us and knelt on the edge of Tim's blanket. The taller one seemed content to remain silent and allow her more confident counterpart to command our attention.

'Are you American?' she asked in a courteous, mid-Atlantic voice. She had in her hand a large polythene bag containing books and papers.

'No, British,' replied Tim with a confused half-smile. 'We don't live here. We're on holiday.'

She then looked at me. 'Are you British, too?'

'We all are,' I answered, sensing that Lindsey was reluctant to speak for himself.

Watching them from the shade of the adjacent cluster of trees was a tall black man, carrying more bags which were bulging with leaflets. I prepared myself for the inevitable request for a donation towards some obscure humanitarian cause.

'Are you staying near here?' she continued.

'Yes,' said Tim, now also very curious as to why such young children should have approached us without invitation.

'Where are you staying?'

'In a small apartment block on one of the lanes leading from Sukhumvit Road.'

'Which one?'

'Soi 4 - by the Don Muang Expressway.'

'We live in Prakhanong. We go to school there. Are you Christians?'

Lindsey fixed his eyes on the man in the distance, who must have been a tutor of some kind, and became silently enraged.

Tim stuttered a little. 'Well, I suppose–'

'May I give you some of these?' she said, barely waiting for his reply. She delved into the bag and produced two sheets of bright yellow paper, on which were printed biblical drawings along with verses in fancy italics. 'This is the Lord Jesus Christ, breaking the bread at the Last Supper, and this is a picture of what happened on Ascension Day. These two are my favourite ones,' she admitted humbly. 'May we leave them with you?'

Immediately, they both stood up and said goodbye. Lindsey continued to stare at the man, who acknowledged us with a tentative wave. He turned his back as soon as his young apprentices had caught up, and the three of them walked cheerfully across the grass towards a group of youngsters on bicycles.

Lindsey broke his silence: 'Religion is so congenital.'

'Leave it out,' said Tim. 'They're kids. They're harmless.'

'True, but he isn't. Those girls are being programmed like computers. Freedom of thought, my eye.'

I was unable to contradict his typically blunt assertion, for the same reason that I could never doubt my mother's. But the old fuse had been lit. As we lay there, waiting for the next gentle gust of wind, Lindsey continued to savage 'hereditary beliefs' from every conceivable angle, although we had heard his tirade on numerous other occasions, to the point of being able to anticipate each contemptuous remark.

Before finally rolling up the blankets, we waited for the young boy with the fruit basket to make his way round to us. We ordered a portion of practically every kind of fruit he had, and paid him a little extra in recognition of his tireless, and possibly thankless, daily work.

By three thirty, we were careering through the streets in another noisy tuk-tuk on our way back to the Plaza. The bars were virtually empty. Only three girls, none of whom we recognized, were sitting inside the fourth bar, loading cans and bottles into ice buckets and counting money from shallow, plywood trays. Lindsey attracted the attention of one of them, an unusually plump girl, no older than eighteen.

'Where is Maalii?' he asked.

'Maalii? Maalii Pasi? Ah, she come bar!' The girl pointed to the figure four on her watch and nodded enthusiastically. 'Maalii come bar. You stay, she come.'

We parked ourselves on the rickety bamboo stools and ordered drinks while we waited.

'I used to have this terrifying dream when I was about twelve years old,' mused Lindsey. 'I had variations of it for almost a year.'

'Variations of what?' I asked.

'I was a junior doctor in a maternity hospital.'

Tim nudged me surreptitiously. 'This should be interesting.'

'I used to find myself in the process of delivering a baby. The woman, whoever she was, would be sweating, panting and screaming in agony while I was doing all I could to ensure the safe arrival of her child ... not that I understood the first thing about obstetrics or midwifery–'

'You're digressing,' Tim reminded him. 'Get to the point, will you?'

'At the bedside was a priest–'

Tim laughed. 'I might have guessed!'

'He was standing there like a possessed demon, menacingly waving a huge syringe, ready to inject his own brand of faith solution into the helpless creature's flesh the moment it drew breath.'

He was obviously still quite agitated about the encounter in the park, and had probably thought of nothing else since our departure.

He began to gesticulate wildly. 'It was unbearable. As the woman cried in pain, I would be trying simultaneously to comfort her, carry out the delivery and push the priest away! It would then degenerate into one almighty struggle, each of us blinded by our own desperation!'

'Are you making this up, Corker?'

Lindsey looked at him. 'I wish.' He began to gesticulate again. 'I used to be terrified, though, in case the needle slipped and the stuff was accidentally injected into me. I used to wake up screaming, as if the damned bed was on fire!' He gulped what was left of his drink and wiped his mouth aggressively with his forearm.

Tim threw a sceptical glance at him, evidently convinced that the parable had been fabricated in either the park or the tuk-tuk. The detection of lies did, after all, constitute a notable aspect of his work at the hospital.

I felt a pair of childlike arms clasp around my neck and a wave of soft, perfumed hair brush the side of my face. I turned around. It was the girl with whom I had spent the previous evening. She was dressed in a baggy black T-shirt bearing a picture of Ella Fitzgerald alongside the words '*Ella, Elle l'a!*' and light, faded jeans. Of all the possible ways of spending the afternoon, she had chosen to be with me. As I smiled gratefully, a loud burst of laughter boomed across the bar. It was Lindsey and Maalii, resuming where they had left off in the middle of the night.

After only a minute or two we paid the bar tab and walked to the far end of the Plaza, then across the railway line and up to Soi Phasuk where they lived. Their 'home' consisted of a wooden, single-room shack, no more spacious than the bar in which they worked. The bed, a large but uncomfortably thin mattress, occupied at least a quarter of the lino-covered floor. Their only other belongings were several ineptly-framed photographs which were hanging from the door and walls, and numerous articles of colourful clothing draped over the backs of two broken chairs. I could not help but feel ashamed, not of the girls' impoverished state, but of myself. I had been born and raised in a relatively prosperous country, was dissatisfied with the perceived inadequacy of my wages, and more often than not blamed the government for life's shortcomings, real or imagined. A lesson was there to be learned.

For the rest of the afternoon we were content to sit peacefully, sharing the benefit of the fan and making a determined effort to overcome the highly amusing communication problem. Lindsey and Maalii browsed through an old photograph album of hers, laughing, kissing, and mocking the occasional picture that invited ridicule. The rest of us fought amicably over Tim's well-thumbed phrase book, thus dragging our broken conversation down to the level of a noisy game of charades.

At seven, we returned to the fourth bar the way we had come: down the grassy bank on to the railway line and over the fence to the Plaza. Alongside the bar, collapsible tables, loaded with Thai food, paper plates and plastic cutlery, stood in a long row. The other girls had probably spent most of the afternoon preparing it all.

'What's the reason for all this?' I wondered aloud.

Lindsey smiled approvingly. 'You know, I don't think there is one.'

Very soon the bars were full, unlike the previous evening. Australians, Norwegians, as well as other Britons and dozens of Americans, were packed into every niche, some sharing the same stool, others standing outside or sitting on wooden beer crates.

'How are you doing?' said one of them as he squeezed between us.

'Fine.'

'I'm Joel.' He held out his hand. 'Haven't seen you guys here before.'

'On holiday.'

'From England?'

I nodded. 'Liverpool.'

'Is that right? I'm from Liverpool's twin city - New York, New York!'

'Pleased to meet you, Joel.'

'Yeah, I work for the US military, as do a lot of the other guys in here. This exquisite little crap-hole has practically become one of our bases!'

On the back wall, behind the bar and barely visible from the entrance, was a small watercolour painting of a tranquil tropical valley ruined by a swarm of double-bladed Chinook helicopters and B-52 bombers ploughing across a flaming sky. Underneath was the emotive slogan: *Prisoners of War/Missing in Action - You are not forgotten.*

'New York?' Tim interrupted. 'We'll be staying there for a few days at the end of the month.'

He dragged his stool noisily across the uneven floorboards and joined us for a drink. It was not long before Tim and I were listening to horrific, but utterly credible, tales of war-plagued Vietnam and the incalculable effect upon the collective American psyche. We gabbled enthusiastically, perhaps subconsciously compensating for the fact that we had spent the afternoon struggling to compile phrases consisting of more than two words. The girls sat quietly with us, unable to contribute to the conversation, but nevertheless glad of our company and a steady supply of drinks.

Tim described our night in Patpong, which Joel confirmed was the infamously seedy area of the ever-expanding metropolis.

'Be very careful down there,' he advised. 'Don't go with any of the girls.'

'No?'

'I'm not joking, they've got diseases out here that you won't even have heard of. You'd also lose a shitload of money and end up getting angry with someone.'

'Diseases such as what?' I asked, pointedly.

He began to count on his fingers: 'Skin fungi, crabs the size of maggots, virulent strains of gonorrhoea ... you name it, they got it in spades.'

'Are you speaking from experience?' asked Tim in jest.

'Shit, no! But a guy I used to know, who was clearing landmines somewhere out in northern Cambodia, caught God-only-knows-what from a young woman and was in agony for weeks. End of his goddam piston turned black!'

'Jesus!'

'Cost him a fortune in medical bills too.' He cackled as he took a drink of beer. 'Hey, I guess you could say that his bank balance and his dick swapped colours!'

'What about these girls?' I asked, knowing that neither of them would be aware of the subject we were discussing.

'Oh, these are decent girls. They're not local.'

'Really?'

'No, most of them are from country villages where there just ain't enough work. Having said that, don't play the odds. You understand me?'

We understood perfectly well. I looked around for Lindsey. He was standing out on the Plaza, entertaining not only Maalii but also three or four other girls, all of whom were doubtless curious as to how he was picking up their language so effortlessly.

Joel finished his drink, dropped a few hundred baht onto the bar and stood up to leave. 'I'll be back home next week, but for no more than a month. Why don't you give me a call? Maybe we can get together. I know all the best dives in Manhattan.'

'Sounds good, Joel,' said Tim, with a noticeable American edge to his voice. He took the paper napkin on which Joel had scrawled his address and telephone number, and stuffed it into the pocket of his jeans. In truth, however, neither of us was thinking that far ahead.

Balancing a plate of rice and vegetables in one hand and clasping the inevitable bottle of beer in the other, Lindsey walked over and sat on the stool that Joel had just vacated. Maalii, quickly noticing that he was no longer standing next to her, followed and jumped onto his lap.

'Do we have any set plans for tomorrow?' he asked.

'I don't believe so,' I replied, looking blankly at Tim.

'Well, Maalii is going home for the day. She wants us to go with her.'

'All of us?'

'Why not? She returns periodically in order to give money to her parents.'

'Where does she live? And how far is it?'

'How would we get there?' said Tim, sounding quite agreeable.

'By train. She comes from a village called Krasang, about forty miles west of the Cambodian border. The journey takes approximately ten hours.'

'Ten!' exclaimed Tim, remembering his restlessness during the marathon flight from London.

Lindsey said nothing more. The two of us paused for a moment's deliberation before agreeing that, however arduous the slow, cross-country trek might prove to be, we would probably savour every moment. Besides, it would be different. And different meant desirable.

Within a matter of minutes, we were quietly ecstatic, squeezing out of Lindsey everything Maalii had supposedly told him, unconcerned about the possibility of some of it having been lost or distorted in the translation.

'The railway station is about a mile from here. We passed it on our way from the airport,' he explained, in between being fed bits of food by his attentive hostess. 'There's only one train, though. We shall have to get ourselves out of bed by ten o'clock tomorrow morning. It leaves at eleven.'

'And arrives when?'

'Just after nine in the evening. We shall be returning the following night, arriving back here in the early hours of Saturday morning.'

Again, we were allowing ourselves to be led into the unknown. Maalii leaned across Lindsey and kissed me gently on the cheek, grateful that I had not objected to the proposal.

'You, tired,' she then said. 'You want go sleep?'

I nodded and reached into my pocket for some cash to settle the bar tab.

'You go Condo,' she instructed, then whispered briefly to the girl with whom I had spent the afternoon.

I turned to Tim. 'Where are you two going?'

He clasped his girl's hand and smiled nefariously. 'Back to their place on Soi Phasuk. Heaven beckons.'

A tuk-tuk pulled up opposite the bar. To my momentary surprise, Lindsey and Maalii climbed inside.

'And where are you two disappearing to?' I called out.

'Patpong!' he bawled. 'Sin tends to be addictive! Make sure you wake up on time tomorrow! We'll meet you back here at a quarter past ten, then make our way to the station!' The driver began to move off. 'Have fun, old fruit!'

I watched them vanish from the open end of the Plaza on to Sukhumvit. Maalii's energy seemed as limitless as his own.

The girl led me back to Soi 4 at midnight. The Sukhumvit pavement had at last been cleared of its stalls and general clutter. For the first time, we were alone, but still incapable of communicating by word of mouth. However, as we took the lift in embarrassed silence to the fourth floor of the Condo, we both understood that the universal nature of certain acts rendered the spoken word superfluous.

IV

'A very stately palace before him,
the name of which was Beautiful.'

John Bunyan (1628-88)
The Pilgrim's Progress

I awoke before nine the following morning to the sound of a porter's trolley being wheeled clumsily along the carpetless corridor. It made a change from hearing the Kasbah Kid in the next room blowing on his confounded flute, and it was almost as tuneful. The girl, whose name I had forgotten, lay still next to me. Her silky, untangled hair covered my neck and shoulder. Distant sounds from the Sukhumvit traffic drifted intermittently through the small window. She opened her eyes and sighed gently with a look of helplessness, perhaps hoping she had found someone who might just be able to deliver her from a life of perpetual insecurity. In me, she had drawn a blank.

At the Plaza, Maalii was looking strangely dishevelled, wearing the previous day's clothes, as was Lindsey, although I found that far less surprising.

'You look rough,' I told him.

'Indeed I do. We shall both need to get changed and collect our bags from Soi Phasuk.'

'Don't worry about that. Tim said he'd collect them for you.'

'Good of him.'

'Where the hell did you get to?'

'Back to the nightclub for an hour, then on to some joint overlooking the river.'

'What was it called?'

'I didn't notice.'

'When did you get back?'

'Well, we spent nearly all the money we had between us. I had only twenty baht left and we couldn't even afford a tuk-tuk. We ended up being ferried back to Patpong, *pisto absoluto*, on the back of a truck!'

'And you walked from there?'

'Oh no, we crashed out near Patpong.'

'Where?'

'The Hotel Buddha!'

'Outside?' I laughed in astonishment. 'You mean, on the grass next to the park?'

'Right at the foot of the statue! It was after three o'clock, we were too exhausted and too damned drunk. She's game for anything, you know,' he said, shaking his head. I had no doubt of it.

Tim showed up at five minutes past ten, clean and looking considerably more alert. The four of us crammed into a tuk-tuk, this time cradling our bags instead of the other two girls, but there was still no room to move around. Fortunately, Makkasan station - a vast, concrete monolith, evidently designed by some ego-tripping architect - was no more than a few dusty streets away, north of Sukhumvit. Everything about it looked foreign, and there were no other westerners anywhere in sight. We hopped out one by one and marched briskly in single file through the crowd towards the ticket office. Amazingly, four one-way fares from Bangkok to Krasang cost only two hundred and sixty baht.

'That's two pounds each for a ten-hour journey!' I remarked.

Lindsey remained suspicious. 'We haven't seen the train yet.'

After struggling with the bags up the vertical flight of steps onto the train, we found a half-empty carriage and sprawled out, ready to head across the south-east plateau in the direction of Cambodia. The air-conditioning, for which we had paid a fraction extra, consisted of a series of tiny ceiling fans, rotating in different directions and droning noisily like a swarm of angry bees.

The train departed on schedule and stretched out towards the flat, open country. Tim and I sat side by side and gazed attentively upon the passing scenery. There were numerous dirt tracks lined with ramshackle huts, peasant farmers carting heavy boxes on their bony, worn-out shoulders, and women and young children pushing dilapidated wheelbarrows over rough wasteland. It was like watching the same loop of cine-film again and again...

We slowed to a halt after about forty minutes.

'Don Muang,' said Tim. 'The airport.'

I sat up suddenly. 'The airport is due north of Bangkok, and Krasang is due east.'

'So?'

'Are you sure we're on the right train?'

'Of course we are,' Lindsey insisted.

I looked across at him. He was lying full-length on one of the longer seats, reading a book with his head nestled in Maalii's lap.

'How do you know we won't end up in Laos, or China?'

He let the book fall onto his chest and stared up at the ceiling. 'The line doesn't have to be dead straight, does it? I'm sure the Romans didn't build it. Check the book, if you must.' His blunt, condescending assurance was sufficient to allay my anxiety.

The hours, and the quaint, rural stations - Saraburi, Kaeng Khoi, Muaklek and Pak Chong - passed by in slow motion, until we arrived at Nakhon Ratchasima, known locally as Khorat, where most of the remaining passengers quietly disembarked and went their separate ways. The sun began to set soon after we left, and for the remaining four hours we saw nothing other than our own ghostly reflections in the windows.

At nine fifteen in the evening we finally reached Krasang station: a somewhat flattering description of a place consisting of a single concrete platform a few inches in height, alongside which stood a small wooden ticket office, closed and in darkness.

The train disappeared into the night, leaving us apparently stranded under the dim light of a few buzzing sodium vapour lamps. Half a dozen stunned locals watched as we stepped across the single track to a row of old tuk-tuks - so old that I considered the possibility that they were clapped-out cast-offs from the big city. It was the equivalent of coming across old-style London buses in former British colonies. It was obvious what the locals were thinking: who were we, and, more fundamentally, why had we spent all day travelling to such a secluded outpost? In fact, I did wonder whether they had seen any Caucasians at all, or even realized that such people existed.

We tossed the bags onto the back of a pick-up truck and climbed onto the makeshift benches which ran parallel along either flank. Even so late in the evening the intense humidity remained.

The old vehicle bumped noisily along unlit dirt tracks and narrow, winding lanes for several minutes before arriving at an isolated wooden shack which stood at the edge of a ricefield. Outside, I could see the silhouettes of several small children who were running around, practically naked, in the light of a solitary uncovered bulb which hung loosely from a cable attached to the roof. The house itself did not even have a door, just a gaping hole in the front wall with only mosquito nets separating its interior from the yard.

Maalii jumped out, leaving us to collect the bags and pay the driver. The children looked at us with polite curiosity when we approached the entrance. There were four of them, all barefoot, the eldest being about twelve years of age, the youngest no older than six. They were, unquestionably, the shabbiest children I had ever come across. I felt anxious in case one of them inadvertently brushed against me.

Inside, an old couple were sitting upon a blue lino mat, washing and peeling vegetables with their work-calloused hands.

Maalii signalled discreetly to us.

'*Sawat-dii khrup*,' we said, one after another, and bowed our heads respectfully.

It went without saying that they were her parents, much older than I had anticipated, or perhaps they just appeared that way, and just as emaciated as the children outside. We sat cross-legged on the floor and spoke only when Maalii addressed us.

The youngest of the children sat down beside Lindsey and held out his small hand.

'Hel-lo, *farang!*' he squeaked, revealing two splendid rows of attritted brown milk teeth.

Lindsey turned hesitantly to Maalii. 'Hello what?'

'*Farang*,' she said. 'You, *farang.*'

Lindsey rooted through the bags and pulled out the phrase book. 'Ah, westerner!' he read, then shook the little boy's hand. 'What is your name? *Khun chiu arai?*'

'Chek!' he replied, proudly jabbing his chest with his thumb. '*Chiu* Chek!'

'Hello there, Chek.'

Once the introduction had been made, the boy began to chase around the room, showing off and offering to shake Lindsey's hand over and over again, each time more vigorously than the last. Maalii turned to us and explained, in a mixture of oddly-pronounced words and graceful gesticulations, who the children were. The eldest three were her younger brothers, whose mouths she and her sister had to feed, as their father had become too debilitated with arthritis to work in the paddies. Chek, on the other hand, was her cousin's child - the unwanted outcome of a prolonged on-off affair with a local opium-addict who, during the summer, had shot himself in the head right where I was sitting. Consequently, Maalii had been left with no option but to move to Bangkok and work for a pittance in one of the small fringe bars. I felt genuinely guilty: her ageing parents would arguably have sacrificed everything, what remained of their lives included, in order for their children to enjoy the lifestyle that I had come upon by chance. Indeed, I was beginning to convince myself that every scrap of good fortune I had experienced in life had been completely unmerited.

Perched on a wooden box behind where Tim was sitting was an old monochrome television set - the type my grandparents had had when I was small - its hazy picture distorted and sound muffled almost beyond comprehension.

Maalii looked at me, perhaps trying bravely to cope with her obvious embarrassment. The sadness in the depths of the eyes was now more noticeable. The small area in the corner of the room, partitioned off by another flimsy mosquito net, was probably where her cousin had given birth to Chek - the pains of a lonely midnight labour alleviated only by the shaky belief that she would somehow survive them. She noticed me observe it, and then smiled sweetly, which may have been her way of offering me an apology in case I chose, quite absurdly, to blame her for the family's predicament.

The old couple retired quietly to bed, leaving us at the mercy of the children. Tim had fallen asleep on the floor, in spite of the crackling noise from the television and, of course, Chek's persistent shrieking and giggling.

Maalii stood up and gestured to Lindsey. '*Pai amnam*,' she whispered. 'We go shower.'

The two of them disappeared round to the back of the house and, before long, the sounds of distant laughter and splashing water began to echo into the room. Chek came over and sat calmly next to me, begging to be entertained. Bereft of ideas, I took out my crisp, new passport from the bag and handed it to him. He took it carefully in his hands, which were covered with septic bites and grazes, and looked thoughtfully through its empty pages. I could tell immediately that he had no idea of its purpose and, tragically, it seemed quite possible that he never would.

Lindsey reappeared several minutes later, looking both refreshed and amused. 'That feels infinitely better!' He threw a towel to me across the room. 'Your turn, Phil. By the way, when you get dressed afterwards, be sure to shake all the cockroaches out of your clothes.'

Knowing that he was not lying, I walked somewhat anxiously into a smaller room round the back. Its damp walls were built haphazardly from leftover chunks of concrete block, although the detail in which I could see them was limited, which was probably just as well. The only flicker of light came from the television and a small lamp under which most of the children were sitting. The washroom door was a battered and irregularly-shaped sheet of corrugated iron which scraped noisily along the ground when I forced it to one side. Inside, the concrete floor was cold and slippery, and I could just make out a large trough in which were floating two plastic bowls. The water itself appeared quite black, as if I were peering down into a bottomless well. Maybe I was.

I ducked one of the bowls into the water, tipped it over my head, and then stopped believing that water could not exist in a liquid state below zero. It could, and it did. I gasped and arched my back as the molten ice ran down my legs and splashed onto the floor. I could hear Lindsey laughing to himself on the other side of the wall, and could at once understand why there had been so much hilarity when he and Maalii were in there.

True to my warning, the walls were covered with insects and spiders, scuttling in and out of the cracks in the blocks. Visible for a second, and then gone.

'Lindsey!' I called out.

'You don't need to tell me about the multi-legged residents,' he said. 'Damned things kept dropping from the ceiling into my hair! Incidentally, I think one of the spiders might be a tarantula!'

'A what?'

'As big as my hand!'

'Where?'

'On the floor!'

I hopped up and down several times, slipping on the wet concrete, then grabbed my clothes and quickly jumped out, straight into what I could see to be the kitchen area. Fortunately, nobody was there to witness my compromised dignity. More laughter followed, of course, when I re-entered the main room, still dripping wet, with only the towel wrapped around my waist.

'I wasn't serious about the tarantula,' he eventually confessed.

'You didn't need to be, you bastard.'

'Most of them are just woodlice and cockroaches.'

'Is that all?'

'Having said that, the presence of the creepy-crawlies was incidental,' he teased. 'It's the dark that frightens you.'

I said nothing. He stopped laughing and looked at me semi-sympathetically. I could not bring myself to dispute what he already knew to be true, although I had never admitted as much either to him or anyone else. The phobia originated from my childhood when, every single night, my father, drunk or not, would insist upon closing my bedroom door long before I had fallen asleep. What difference it made to him, I never found out. Perhaps he simply derived pleasure from such petty, indiscriminate torments, doing to his son what he believed the world was doing to him. As a result, I learned from experience just how easily the imagination of a small child could transform itself into the enemy within.

'Here,' said Lindsey, getting to his feet, 'take some of this.'

He threw a large tub of Maalii's talcum powder onto my clothes. Chek scampered across the floor, removed the cap and rubbed a handful of it into his own face, leaving only his eyes and teeth showing through the blotchy white mess.

'Chek, *farang!*' said Lindsey. 'Chek, white man!'

Without delay, he poured an even bigger heap onto his hand and this time patted it onto the top of his head, then again, and again. He quickly became enveloped from head to foot in a thick, white cloud. The other boys - who I realized were more or less his uncles - giggled energetically and encouraged him to continue until there was none left.

'Why don't we disappear for a while?' said Lindsey. 'Chek can then make his snowstorms in peace.'

Taking care not to disturb Tim, who had still not stirred, we slipped out, leaving the children whooping and chasing each other around the floodlit yard.

'Chek *baa!*' said Maalii, as the three of us headed back on foot towards Krasang village.

'She says Chek is mad,' Lindsey explained. 'She's convinced it's part of his genetic make-up and therefore not his fault - and not curable either.'

'Poor creature,' I said.

'I'm not feeling sorry for him. He'll probably spend his days of whatever blissfully happy, which is more than most people are destined to achieve.'

We wandered for about a mile and came across an open roadside bar, which was nothing more than another three-sided wooden hut, similar to those at the Plaza, with an untidy collection of bottles standing upon a large, sagging table. In attendance were three villagers, all of whom spoke casually to Maalii. One of them, a leather-skinned man of about forty, wasted no time in offering drinks to Lindsey and myself. Most of the bottles were filthy, as was the man himself, who appeared to have spent the whole day labouring in a muddy field. I assumed that his two assistants were his wife and daughter, both of whom were relatively well-groomed, and somewhat excited by our presence.

I pointed to the bottles and looked quizzically at Maalii.

'*Arak*,' she said, approvingly.

Lindsey unscrewed a bottle, which appeared to have been sealed for a hundred years, and confidently took a mouthful. 'Reasonably potent,' he said, eyes watering. He then shuddered and shook his head before taking another gulp of the stuff straight away.

'What is it?'

'I think it's some sort of rice brandy,' he said. 'They have it in Malaysia and Indonesia too.'

I took a sip, and it all but set the back of my throat alight. 'It's disgusting!'

The young girl laughed to herself after seeing me grimace.

'It'll get better,' Lindsey reassured me, 'if you drink enough of it.'

I glanced at my watch: it was eleven thirty, and the temperature had cooled to perfection. For the first time, I had no need to wipe the sweat constantly from my face. To soak up the drink, we tucked into small bags of rice containing shrivelled cuttlefish and scraps of meat, which were ominously similar to the ones Tim had unwisely consumed at the Plaza.

For over an hour, Maalii gabbled incessantly with the young girl and her mother, leaving Lindsey and myself to become as drunk as we had ever been.

'If the pubs in Liverpool sold this stuff,' he prophesied, inverting the bottle so that every last drop went the same way as the previous ones, 'then beer would become obsolete overnight. How privileged we are, Phil.'

Eventually, we paid the man for his potions and stood up to leave. The girl kissed Maalii and clasped her hands, as if she were wishing her friend luck.

The road back to the house was completely deserted; there were no street lights or passing vehicles, and only the raucous laughter from a pair of appallingly intoxicated *farangs* disturbed the peace of the midnight hour.

We left the main road and headed up the lane where we could just make out the ghostly outline of the shack on the horizon. A stray, flea-bitten mongrel wandered on to the road and began to bark persistently.

'Did you have a rabies injection, Phil?'

'I didn't think it was necessary.'

'Well, I doubt that the dogs round these parts are particularly domesticated.'

The dog followed us closely. Impetuously, I removed one of my shoes and let fly with as much force as I possessed. The animal jumped back but, before I could retrieve it, picked it up in its dirty mouth.

Lindsey laughed loudly. 'Poor mutt! It'll probably drop dead due to foot odour!'

I swore and hopped towards it. Lindsey and Maalii then collapsed into hysteria as the dog retreated into the ricefield with my shoe still stuck inside its foaming mouth. I hobbled after it, trying hard not to fall over, and collected the shoe which was now coated with a thick film of sticky saliva.

Lindsey fell silent, and then exclaimed: 'Stand very still! Remember what Joel told you! Rice paddies are full of landmines!'

In an instant, my sobriety returned. A shiver shot like an electric current up to the back of my neck. I clenched my teeth and hopped quickly back to the track. For the second time, the two of them howled with laughter at my expense. I had been fooled again.

On reaching the darkness of the shack, we quietened down. Even the children were now sleeping, doubtless having exhausted themselves as thoroughly as the tub of talcum powder. We crept inside, following Maalii to a small, bamboo-framed extension, on the floor of which was a large inflatable mattress. We neither washed nor undressed before lying down.

In the adjacent fields, dogs were barking.

'I hope they don't yap all ruddy night long,' I muttered.

'Maalii says they invariably do.'

'Marvellous. Why doesn't somebody shoot them?'

He tried to stifle an explosion of laughter. 'Apparently, the locals believe the dogs bark across the fields at night to their ancestors, so they are left alone, out of respect.'

I turned my head and looked at him, even though it was too dark to see even his outline. 'Barking to their ancestors?'

'That's right.'

'Barking to their bloody ancestors? That's insane.'

'They are simply incapable of differentiating truth from myth,' he said, in a sleepy, drawn-out tone. 'They are no more deluded than some other people I could mention.'

'Who?'

'Your own next-door neighbours, for example.'

'Which ones?'

'Those born-again happy-clappies at number five,' he chuckled deri-sively. 'Evangelical worshippers always remind me of the characters in *One Flew Over The Cuckoo's Nest*.'

I closed my eyes and immediately pictured a hall full of rowdy psychi-atric patients, some howling like banshees, others expressing themselves in equally bizarre ways. I could appreciate his point, sarcastic though it was.

We continued mumbling until we could neither hear each other nor muster sufficient effort to speak coherently. Finally, and in spite of the canine seance, I succeeded in drifting off into a peaceful, uninterrupted sleep. The day had been as long and as unpredictable as the previous one.

V

'But I, being poor, have only my dreams.'

W.B. Yeats (1865-1939)
He Wishes for the Cloths of Heaven

Day four began to the unusual sound of children's laughter. It was nine o'clock and I had slept for longer than I could have hoped. Lindsey was sitting at the foot of the bed, shaving with the aid of a bowl of cold water.

'Where's Maalii?' I croaked, rubbing my eyes vigorously.

'She's in the washroom ... either getting washed or trying to identify one or two new species of insect.'

The mosquito nets parted and an already-dirty face appeared along with the fierce morning sunlight. Chek jumped inside and dived under the sheet - wearing Lindsey's spare shirt.

'Take that off and put it back!' Lindsey told him, not caring that his command would not be understood. He shook his head incredulously. 'The little rat has been rummaging in my bag!'

Lindsey finished shaving and began to tickle the little boy's feet. I crawled out and walked round to the yard where Tim was sitting with the other children on a broad wooden bench, writing postcards which he had bought from a Sukhumvit news-stand in Bangkok.

'What happened to you last night?'

'For a start, we stayed awake,' I replied, 'unlike you.'

'I was dog-tired.' His head jerked back and he screwed up his face. 'Mary, mother of whoever! Your breath smells like a petrol tank!'

'Something I drank. Sorry.'

'What?'

'*Arak.*'

'*Arak?* Is that the Thai word for rocket fuel?'

From a respectful distance, I explained where we had gone, and then heard how he had awoken in the dead of night to find Chek curled up alongside him.

After a few minutes in the open air, I began once more to feel uncomfortably hot, to the extent that I had an urge to change out of the clothes I had just put on. Lindsey appeared, carrying his bowl of frothy water which he poured carefully into a malodorous, open drain in the corner of the yard.

'Maalii and I are going to the market square. Will you two be coming with us?'

'I suppose so.'

'There's a small cafe where we can have lunch, then Maalii wants to visit one of her sisters in Surin. Are you up for it?'

I shrugged my shoulders agreeably. 'Why not?'

'That's the spirit.'

I picked up the travel book and turned to the provincial maps. Surin was just another nondescript town, approximately five miles east of Krasang. Its railway station was at the very end of the south-east line.

I turned my head to see Lindsey holding Chek upside down by his ankles and threatening to duck the boy's head into a barrel of filthy rainwater. The youngster was loving the extra attention. Tim reached for the camera and took several quick-fire photographs of the two of them cavorting together. Not for the first time, the language barrier had become immaterial. It appeared to me that juvenile fun was just another universal human construct, triumphantly independent of race, creed or culture. It was as perennial as hospitality or visiting relatives, courtship or love itself.

'Lindsey, when does tonight's train leave?'

'Nine thirty!' he yelled, in an attempt to make himself heard above Chek's shrieks. 'We might need to get there early, though. According to Maalii, the overnight train is usually crammed, presumably because it's cheaper than the day train.' He put Chek back onto his feet and washed his hands and face in the barrel. 'We might have to stand all the way back to Bangkok.'

Back home to Bangkok, I thought - back to familiarity. We would have only two more days to relax in Lumpini Park, or run wild at the Plaza and Patpong, then it would be time to say our prescribed goodbyes.

Maalii appeared. Her damp hair was tied back tidily, which made her look even more like one of the children. She and Lindsey looked at each other and grinned simultaneously, evidently amused by something only they understood. The bashful expression on Maalii's face made me think that they had perhaps spent the whole night engaged in a rampant, sweaty sex session as I slept beside them.

On the ground next to my feet lay what I assumed to be one of the children's toys. It consisted of a block of wood, roughly cuboid, its dimensions being comparable to those of a shoe box. Attached to its four corners were circular plywood discs which constituted wheels, and at one end a bent nail around which was fastened a length of string to enable it to be pulled along the ground. As I scrutinized it more closely, however, I noticed that each of the discs was fixed rigidly to the block with more than one nail, thus making rotation impossible. All in all, it was the poorest, most pitiful imitation of a child's toy truck that I could ever have imagined. I thought of computer games and other modern-day gizmos at the opposite end of the spectrum which western parents bought for their children without a second thought. I glanced up at Tim who also had noticed it.

'I've just given the eldest one a hundred baht,' he explained, touchingly. 'Now they'll be able to play with something better.'

The four of us left the children to entertain themselves in the yard and made our way along the dirt track towards the main road, where Lindsey and I had been larking around during the night. As we passed the edge of the ricefield, I became slightly tense, hoping that Lindsey would not think to refer to the embarrassing episode with the dog. It was too much to expect.

'Those are Phil's footprints,' he said, pointing over the fence. 'Bare footprints, no less. He chucked his shoe at a stray dog!'

I then had the pleasure of hearing an exaggerated version of it told for the benefit of Tim, all the way into the village. The locals peered inquisitively at a well-known young girl, strolling conspicuously along the roadside with three *farangs*. I wanted to know what they were thinking.

The market square consisted of a dense network of semi-covered, wooden stalls displaying food and clothes. Wrinkled old peasants bartered for eggs and meat, and bare-chested teenage boys unloaded heavy boxes from vans and pick-up trucks. We walked around the periphery to a corner stall which was overladen with fruit. Hundreds of tangerines, some still green, were piled impossibly high on tables covered with fresh newspaper. Maalii greeted the stallholder with an affectionate hug.

'That must be her elder sister,' Lindsey whispered discreetly.

We took turns in giving our well-practised formal greeting: hands together, raised to the chin. She scanned us one after another and offered each of us two or three of the ripest oranges. After we had sat down, Maalii stood behind Lindsey and massaged his shoulders, as she had done on our initial visit to the Plaza.

A group of schoolchildren filtered past us after half an hour or so, all smartly dressed in identical white shirts or blouses with the school emblem embroidered onto the breast pocket, along with navy blue shorts or culottes. These immaculate youngsters were the traders' children, generally impoverished, and yet both clean and dignified. One of the older girls jogged straight across to the stall and leaned over to kiss Maalii. It was her younger sister.

'Hello. How are you?' she said with surprising fluency.

'Very well, thank you.'

'Where you come from?'

'Liverpool, England.'

'My name is Auy. I go school Krasang. I learn speak English two years now.'

'You speak it very well.'

'Tank you.'

She looked about sixteen years of age and was obviously both intelligent and eager to educate herself as thoroughly as her restricted circumstances would permit.

She walked with us across the square to the solitary cafe, where Lindsey ordered lunch - our first meal since leaving Bangkok. She was a shade taller than Maalii, and very slender, almost unhealthily so. I watched her for a while; she was the epitome of virginal perfection. As far as I could see, all her life's major pathways had yet to be mapped out. It was all up for grabs - apparently.

Lindsey was smiling to himself. 'You're wondering what the world holds for her, aren't you?'

'How did you know that?'

'Simple observation. Your eyes have been following her every move since she arrived at the stall.' He waved his fork at me. 'You can't deny it, old fruit.'

'I don't.'

'First of all, you undressed her.'

'What?'

'Didn't you?'

'No.'

'You did. Admit it. You noticed that she wasn't wearing a bra under her blouse and your eyes clouded over for about five minutes. Then, your lustful thoughts were superseded by more respectable ones. You can't deny that either.' He took a drink and slapped the empty glass down onto the table, almost causing the stem to shatter. 'If you ask me, she'll be out of school within a year and looking for either a husband or a menial job somewhere.'

If his confident prediction were to prove accurate, it would be a tragedy. She possessed that rare combination of high intelligence and a stunning physical shape, but I had to accept that Lindsey was probably right: the chances of her realizing her potential seemed unjustly slim.

By four o'clock, the frenetic activity in the market had subsided. We climbed into a tuk-tuk and made the twenty-minute journey to Surin, home of Maalii's elder sister's family. After we had jumped out onto the bank of a stagnant stream, about seven or eight metres in width, we noticed a wooden barn surrounded by trees - on the other side.

Tim, who for some reason had not spoken for hours, looked at Maalii and pointed across the water. 'Is that it?'

'Yes! We go!' she affirmed, and led us down the dusty bank.

We arrived at what we discovered to be the crossing point: two upright metal poles, one firmly embedded in each bank, with a rope connecting them across the stream and a wooden raft partially submerged in the muddy water.

Maalii grasped the waist-high rope with one hand and stepped onto the raft, carefully maintaining her balance with her feet apart. Tim and her sister joined her and the three of them proceeded to float across the water, with Maalii pulling on the rope in order to allow their combined weight to move the raft. I had never seen anyone display such slick control in a situation which had the potential to be hilarious.

'She's a genius!' Lindsey marvelled, equally impressed by what was, in all fairness, a simple innovation, albeit utilized with breathtaking expertise.

On reaching the opposite bank, Tim turned to us and smiled, relieved that he and his clothes were still dry.

'I wouldn't like to attempt this at night,' he said.

Lindsey laughed again. 'You'll have to, old fruit. It'll be dark by the time we get back!'

Maalii remained on the raft and returned to collect Lindsey and myself, her tiny hands moving nimbly along the rope and not for a second losing either her grip or her balance. Clinging both to Maalii and very firmly to each other, we stepped onto it as carefully as possible and drifted smoothly to the other side.

'Perhaps, one day, someone out here will construct a bridge,' said Lindsey, helping Maalii on to the bank. 'But I hope not.'

In front of the house, several hammocks had been suspended between the walls and the most convenient trees. The house itself was much the same as Maalii's parents' place, only larger and having slightly more in the way of material comforts: electric lights, running water, and an old-fashioned stereo system crackling softly to itself in a shaded corner. Maalii introduced us in turn to her brother-in-law, nieces and nephews, most of whom looked understandably bewildered by the unannounced arrival of three alien creatures - tall, pale-skinned things with round eyes and enormous noses. How odd we must have looked to them. Fortunately, the children were far less boisterous and demanding than Chek. We sat on the polished wooden floor, unable to take part in the conversation, but perfectly content to be once more sitting in novel surroundings. That was what counted.

We stayed for over an hour and took several photographs of ourselves swinging like simpletons on the hammocks with Maalii's obliging, albeit thoroughly bemused, family. By the time we had found our way back through the mosquito-infested undergrowth to the stream, the sun had set behind the trees and only the merest hint of light reflected up from the dirty water. We made the crossing in exactly the same fashion as before, balancing cautiously on the raft which was now barely visible below us.

For the second consecutive evening, we arrived at Maalii's house in a tuk-tuk to find the children in the yard. On this occasion, however, they were playing with a brand new blue and orange football, which they had bought from the market square with Tim's money. We packed our belongings and, after having suffered the relentless heat for a whole day, a cold wash in total darkness was strangely bearable.

Before leaving, each of us gave five hundred baht to Maalii's old mother - a token of gratitude for allowing us to stay, and a contribution to the humble family coffers in order to make their predicament marginally less desperate.

And so it was, at eight o'clock, that we decided we could not delay the inevitable any longer. We waved goodbye to four downtrodden young children who stood to attention at the side of the lane. For once, Chek's toothy smile was missing; he looked as thoroughly dejected as the old couple. His three new playmates were leaving after barely a day, and he knew full well that we would never be returning; whereas we would have our everlasting colour photographs sitting in leather-bound albums on polished shelves, he would be left with only fading childhood memories. We had said hello to his small world then, almost in the same breath, bid it farewell.

When we reached the main road I looked back and waved for the last time. The children were now only just visible, and Lindsey took one final photograph of an inadequate wooden hovel that none of us would be able to forget.

The railway platform was crowded and full of noise. It was as if the entire population of Krasang was about to embark upon the ten-hour trip to the distant capital. Again, we could not avoid the attention of hundreds of pairs of curious eyes as we dropped our bags onto the platform and waited in silence for the westbound train.

We boarded ten minutes late and could find only two vacant seats for the four of us. Maalii and Lindsey sat down, bags beneath their feet, leaving Tim sitting uncomfortably cross-legged on the dusty floor, and myself standing in what little space remained. The smell of stale tobacco pervaded the humid air.

I was startled by a knock on the window just before we departed. I looked out and noticed a small figure jumping about on the platform. It was Chek, who had followed us on his tricycle and managed to reach the station just in time. Lindsey pulled himself to his feet and peered through the glass. Chek smiled for him and held out his hand. Lindsey quickly reached out of the small window and took what Chek was holding, just as the train began to move off. We both looked back and watched in silence as a small boy, and a Spartan village, were swallowed up by the darkness.

Lindsey resumed his seat and opened his hand to reveal a small pebble which had the Thai equivalent of the letter 'L' scratched boldly onto its flattest surface. He cleaned the stone on his shirt and tied the string around his neck. Maalii squeezed his hand and smiled peacefully. The gift did not look out of place.

I gazed out of the open window as we rattled along the track, not that there was anything to observe. Lindsey and Maalii immediately rested their heads against each other and closed their eyes, knowing that we would not reach the city until dawn. Krasang had been the most haunting place I had ever visited, and I was already certain that its images, equally beautiful and disturbing, would remain indelibly etched upon the walls of my memory.

It was not until we reached Khorat at one in the morning that a significant number of passengers alighted, thus enabling Tim and me to complete the journey in relative comfort.

The train crawled to a halt at Makkasan station just after six in the morning, leaving us to plod wearily across the concourse to a vacant tuk-tuk which shuttled us directly back to Maalii's room on Soi Phasuk. As we were on the brink of collapse, the city was slowly reawakening.

Predictably, it came to life without us. I did not lift my head until early afternoon.

Tim was already dressed. He grinned, apparently amused by the fact that I had contrived to sleep so heavily.

'Where's Lindsey?' I yawned.

'At some bookshop at the World Trade Centre. He left about half an hour ago. Promised he'd be back at two thirty, but I wouldn't count on it.'

'The World Trade Centre?'

'That's right.'

'On Pl ...'

'Ploenchit Road.'

'Why has he gone there?'

'He wanted a book on the Burma-Thailand Railway. *Bridge on the River Kwai* and all that.'

'Does that mean he wants to see it before we leave for Hong Kong?'

'What do you think?'

'So we'll be going today?'

He nodded. 'One night's cheap accommodation shouldn't be too difficult to arrange, then we can see the place properly tomorrow. So pack your things, Passepartout.'

VI

'And trains all night groan on the rails
To men that die at morn.'

A.E. Housman (1859-1936)
A Shropshire Lad

Our next moves were being planned before I had recovered properly from the Krasang trip, but I felt way too relaxed to be objectionable. This was the essence of Lindsey: getting his own way without coercion or provoking suspicion. There had, however, been one or two occasions during the previous months when following Lindsey impulsively had been unwise to say the least. One of them had occurred during our annual summer break in Edinburgh. We had spent a long weekend with his cousin, revelling in the Festival Fringe during the afternoons and pub-crawling along the busy Lothian Road after dark.

Late on the Sunday evening, we had taken a short train ride to North Queensferry in order to admire what Lindsey considered to be the sole wonder of the civilized world: the Forth Bridge.

'Magnificent!' he proclaimed, balancing on the platform's edge, holding a half-empty bottle of 'seventy shilling'. His dramatic reaction was such that one could have been forgiven for wondering if he had built the thing himself. 'Every Englishman should take the time to appreciate this before he dies.' He looked across the water, before clambering down onto the railway line.

'What do you think you're doing?' his cousin asked him.

'Taking a closer look. Come on.'

Half drunk, he proposed that we all walk back along the track, over the bridge itself, then catch the return train from the station through which we had just passed. Impetuously, we all agreed. We slid clumsily down the bank and walked on the gravel between the tracks towards the illuminated super-structure. The reflections from the bridge's piercing lights danced in the gently undulating water below as we wandered negligently through its vast steel web.

Tim, uncharacteristically, was exuberant. 'What would happen if a train came along?'

'Strangely enough, you're about to find out,' said Lindsey calmly.

We all laughed. In such a frivolous frame of mind, the notion of a train hurtling at us out of the darkness seemed too comical to warrant serious consideration.

'Believe me,' he insisted. 'I checked the timetable at Haymarket. The last train to Aberdeen was due out at twenty-one forty-five.' He glanced at his watch. 'It should show its face in a minute or two.'

The laughter ceased. The rest of us froze and fixed our eyes on the south end of the bridge. A bright headlight, like a colossal eye, was gradually increasing in size, while contemplating a few insignificant figures in its path. The apprehensive silence yielded to a frantic scrambling to the barriers which ran close to the northbound track.

Lindsey stood his ground. 'What's your problem?' he taunted. 'Scared or something?'

'Corker, you're so drunk!' his cousin yelled authoritatively.

'That I am!'

'So get your bones off the track while you still can!'

The eye moved closer. Lindsey returned its stare with a mixture of admiration and smug defiance. I thought of Buchan's *The Thirty-nine Steps*, where the protagonist had risked his life by jumping onto the bridge in order to escape from custody. But that was merely fiction.

The beast began to growl as its momentum increased. Lindsey raised his voice so that we could hear him.

'Think about it! The train will remain on the rails, will it not?'

He then proceeded to lie down, flat on his back, between the tracks. At that moment, I realized just what he was trying to prove, and nothing would dissuade him.

The din steadily approached its inevitable climax.

'Corker! Get up!' his cousin shouted. 'No! Too late now! Stay there! Stay there!'

'Just think about it logically!' he screamed, lying motionless with his hands clasped firmly behind his head. 'Horror films! Bungee jumps! Roller coasters! No danger, therefore no fear! *Woooooeeeeee!*'

His cry was drowned as the furious beast stormed past us with a bone-shattering roar. We fixed ourselves rigidly to the barrier until the noise subsided, then immediately turned our heads to see Lindsey lying in the same prostrate position, blatantly high on his own intrepidity.

'You mad bastard!' his cousin barked suddenly. 'You could have been sucked underneath it!'

'Ah, cool off. I was perfectly safe.'

'What if the driver saw us? He might be on the phone to the police right this minute!'

'They could be waiting for us at the end of the bridge,' Tim added, seriously.

Lindsey remained unconcerned. 'We could claim to have got lost hitch-hiking to Glasgow.'

It was no longer funny. The prospect of spending the night in an Edinburgh police cell followed by a court appearance did not appeal to us. We reached the south bank out of breath, but continued walking all the way to Dalmeny station which was, to our relief, deserted. Lindsey had proved his point: cold logic had triumphed over everything, as he knew it would. My last recollection of that mad evening was hearing him fantasize about 'the ultimate thrill': lying between two trains travelling in opposite directions.

The door opened and Lindsey walked in carrying a couple of pristine paperbacks.

'Shit! It's like a sauna out there!'

Maalii jumped to her feet and threw him a clean hand towel.

'I only walked half a mile! By the time I reached the mall, I was sweating like a gravedigger!' He wiped his face which was dripping profusely. Noticing that I was now fully awake, he pointed to the front cover of one of the books. 'What do you think?' he asked.

'How would we get there?'

'Tuk-tuk to Sai Tai, first of all.'

'Where's that?'

'No idea, but there's a bus leaving for Kanchanaburi at four o'clock.'

'Well, you know what you're doing ...'

He opened the smaller of the two books:

'*The recent history of the Kwai Valley serves to remind us of the horrific depths of malicious savagery to which our species, and ours alone, is capable of sinking. Sixty thousand prisoners of war, along with an even greater number of conscripted Thais, were forced to build a railway from Kanchanaburi to Thanbuyzayat in Burma. Many died from exhaustion, disease and even physical torture at the hands of their Japanese and Korean captors.*'

He began to flick through the pages. Maalii took the towel from him and scanned the book's pictures over his shoulder.

'It disturbs me to think that people can be conditioned to be so vicious towards those whom, under different circumstances, they might love instead. Some are even prepared to lay down their lives as a consequence of indoctrination.' He clapped the book shut and tossed them both into the bag. 'Dreadful.'

After spending a quarter of an hour all getting washed in the same water, and packing spare shirts at the Condo, we put on our shoes - striped canvas articles which we had bought for next to nothing - and walked to Soi 2 for a late lunch. The four of us sat around one of the battered, fat-splattered pavement tables in the shade of a row of shops, perusing Lindsey's new books and devising a provisional timetable for the next twenty-four-hour stint. Maalii sat in silence, unable to take part in the discussion. She had temporarily become a stranger in her own land. In fact, Lindsey seemed almost oblivious to her very presence, which made me want to grab him by the throat and express my disgust at his appalling lack of manners. For a moment, I hated him again.

I picked up one of the books and opened it so that Maalii could see the map. She sat up sharply, surprised that anyone had taken the trouble to include her. I ran my index finger along a black calibrated line which began at Bangkok and meandered in a north-westerly direction towards the Burmese border. I tapped the end of my finger on a small red circle, along-side which was printed the word 'Kanchanaburi' in both English and Thai scripts. She shrugged her shoulders and smiled awkwardly. I knew straight away that her knowledge of the Kwai Valley was no better than my own.

We finished eating and returned to Sukhumvit.

'*Sai Tai!*' barked Lindsey at a tuk-tuk driver. '*Pai Sai Tai*, old fruit!'

We crowded round the vehicle, ready to hop on board once the brief, and largely pointless, haggling ritual had run its circular course. We bumped along the traffic-choked city roads and arrived at the bus terminal only minutes prior to our scheduled departure. Tim hastily handed five or six hundred baht to Maalii who scampered inside the ticket office and booked four seats for the outward journey.

Within a minute of boarding, we had left the terminal and were crawling patiently through the city's western outskirts - which looked every bit as chaotic as those to the east and north. Lindsey quickly immersed himself in the larger of his two books, the harrowing effects of war atrocities manifesting themselves in his facial expressions. Maalii rested her head against his shoulder and tried to sleep. He held the book in his right hand and stroked her hair lovingly with the left. It all looked so comfortable. The thought of them exchanging goodbyes within a matter of days now seemed inconceivable. In fact, Lindsey being ruled by his heart even a little seemed inconceivable.

Outside, in the heat we could no longer feel, the rural scenes looked indistinguishable from the ones we had witnessed *en route* to Krasang: peasants hawking their wares along dusty dirt tracks, and small children, mostly shoeless, chasing each other in the shadows of tall trees and wooden shacks. I glanced repeatedly at Maalii, sincerely wishing that she would not eventually be condemned to a similar fate.

Nearly three hours on the open road was quite enough both for my stomach and my eyes. We reached Kanchanaburi - a smaller version of Khorat - just before sunset. Behind the bus station noticeboards, teenage touts were lurking like cheetahs in the undergrowth, sizing up their prey and preparing to pounce. As soon as we emerged, the inevitable confrontation began. Maalii and Lindsey were instantly apprehended by a taxi driver - a greasy, overweight local with an unpronounceable name - who was holding a plastic concertina wallet containing business cards for nearby hotels. Maalii took hold of it and compared their respective tariffs which had been pencilled onto the backs of the cards. We then followed her on to the back of the man's rusty pick-up truck and quickly disappeared into the rich countryside.

A mile or two along the road, the driver ground his noisy vehicle to an abrupt halt, stalling the engine in the process.

'San's Place! This is good hotel!' he shouted through the broken glass partition. 'Good hotel!'

In the middle of a dense, jungle-like mass of liana and mangrove trees was a series of bamboo huts on wooden stilts, with the River Kwai flowing directly underneath.

'This is unreal!' Lindsey marvelled, arms outstretched, standing back to view the complex in its entirety. 'I wonder if Tarzan is at home.'

Tim and I were equally impressed by Maalii's choice of place to spend our one night, although it was far more expensive than we had anticipated. It consisted of an outdoor bar where a group of seven or eight westerners were huddled around drinks and barbecued snacks, and about ten separate chalets which were connected by a wooden walkway suspended by ropes above marshy foliage.

'Be sure to keep your doors closed,' said Lindsey, stepping cautiously from the swaying walkway towards the corner chalet which he and Maalii were to be sharing. 'You wouldn't want your bedroom to be swarming with mosquitoes.'

'Nor crawling with spiders,' I retorted, referring to the washroom in Krasang.

Inside the chalet itself, everything was made of bamboo: the furniture, the bed, and even the walls which constituted vast playing fields for dozens of scurrying geckos. Between the cracks in the floorboards I could see the flowing river, and standing alongside the bed was a sturdy chest of drawers with an intricate tropical landscape carved onto the front of each one. Through the rear window I noticed an old fishing boat which had been attached to the main structure and ingeniously converted into an extra chalet, despite having been moored at a considerable angle to the horizontal. The shower consisted of an old copper tap connected to a short length of green, garden hosepipe. Naturally, cold water was all there was, but, having twice paddled among the cockroaches in Krasang, it amounted to relative luxury.

I drew the blind and collapsed onto the bed, still fatigued after the series of late nights and perpetual travelling. I listened carefully to the water splashing against the chalet's wooden supports and imagined for a moment that I was actually lying in a weathered old fishing boat, similar to the one outside, drifting peacefully downriver, away from life's tribulations.

At sunset we emerged from our respective rooms and found a quiet niche under a meticulously woven bamboo canopy next to the bar. Tim scribbled a second batch of postcards, to his parents and both sets of grandparents in Belfast, all of whom were eager to hear of our day-to-day progress. Lindsey remained still, resting his arm around a sleepy Maalii, painfully aware that Kanchanaburi would be their final escapade together. I watched him as he gazed pensively across the darkening valley into infinity.

'What do you see?' I asked him, thereby breaking the silence.

'Darkness.'

'Anything else?'

'No, just darkness. Darkness everywhere.' He yawned restlessly and stretched his legs under the table. 'We shall discover what's out there when tomorrow dawns.'

'What if it doesn't?' I persisted, confident that he would not scoff at such an odd question.

'Then I'd be content to admit that I couldn't possibly know ... unlike some, who would invent things purely to fill the void.'

It was as predictable a reply as I could have reasonably expected. He then proceeded to philosophize about 'man's childish tendency' to fabricate simplistic, and often fantastic, explanations for the mysteries of nature. I had heard it all before, usually on occasions when either something or someone was perplexing him.

The bar closed its shutters at midnight, leaving us to retreat quietly along the wooden suspension bridges to our respective rooms.

I stirred shortly after nine the following morning to see piercing rays of sunlight filtering through the tiny but numerous cracks in the walls. The noise from the river was louder; somehow I felt closer to it. I showered and vacated the room, but not before I had taken a photograph of the skew boat outside. I knew I would never see such an odd modification again; and without proof of it I knew no one would believe I ever had.

We left all the bags behind the reception desk and waited until the driver arrived in his noisy, exhaust-pipeless pick-up truck to ferry us around the locality.

'Hey, Mithter! We go Kwai Bridge?' he called, in his deep, gravelly voice, and leered at Maalii as she walked to the back of the vehicle, doubtless wishing he had been the one sharing her bed.

We shot off towards town with a welcome breeze blowing in our faces. As we did so, I noticed that the driver was spending almost as much time staring at Tim in the rear-view mirror as watching the road ahead.

'What's the matter?' said Tim.

'Hey, you do the jiggy-jiggy, yes?'

Tim leaned forward so that he could hear above the racket from the engine and looked quizzically at the man's dirty, grinning face. 'Jiggy-jiggy?' he chortled. 'What the hell is that?'

'No idea,' I said.

'Sex!' Lindsey explained. 'He's probably just a complete pervert.' He then smiled, and nodded politely to the driver, knowing that his understanding of English, particularly when spoken with an uncompromising Nottinghamshire accent, was sufficiently poor. 'I expect he wants you to give him a detailed account of your sordid activities in bed last night.'

'I was sleeping alone,' said Tim.

'What difference does that make?'

We turned on to a dirt track and arrived near to the bank of a different stretch of the river, where a few dozen tourists, most of them elderly, were wandering around, taking photographs and waiting for the stragglers to catch up.

'This is it,' said Lindsey, almost in awe. 'The bridge over the River Kwai.'

Maalii looked at it inquisitively, unaware of its wartime significance. It was rather like a Polish Jew not knowing the history of Auschwitz. The reason was obvious, and quite sad: she was a native, not of Thailand, but of a mere fraction of it, and the remainder was just another foreign land.

We jumped down from the back of the truck, leaving the driver to spend a few minutes trying to figure out who had spent the night with whom.

'Lindsey, ask him if he'd mind taking our picture, would you?'

Without waiting to be asked, the driver hopped out and was more than willing to oblige, probably believing we would pay him more as a result of his enthusiastic compliance. We huddled together under a painted wooden sign-post which bore the words: *River Kwai Bridge*, in both English and Thai.

He steadied himself for a moment and clicked the shutter button with his tobacco-stained finger. 'No prom-blem,' he grunted again and again, before handing over the camera and plodding back to his vehicle.

We followed the railway line and walked onto the bridge itself: a black metal construction which spanned the muddy river. Boats, kayaks and float-ing restaurants adorned the water's surface and, on the opposite bank, a dense area of luxuriant woodland stretched as far as the horizon.

Lindsey walked on ahead and stopped halfway across the bridge. 'This central portion was bombed to hell during the war,' he pointed out, 'which is why it looks different from the rest of it. The wooden bridge was smashed beyond repair.' He shook his head thoughtfully and walked a little further. 'Isn't it ironic that allied servicemen destroyed a bridge which their own troops had been forced to construct? And isn't it absurd that it has now become a holiday attraction for their grandchildren?'

He continued to assume the rôle of tourist guide, explaining, with the aid of his books, how the war in Asia had unfolded. In short, the concept of hell had been redefined over and over again. Every day, thousands of pris-oners had lived and breathed it. We, on the other hand, simply by accidental virtue of having been born in a different age, were in a position to walk away whenever we had seen enough.

'Is the bridge still in use?' I asked him, in an attempt to divert his thoughts away from the grotesque cruelty that had taken place during Japanese occupation.

'Looks that way to me,' said Tim. 'Why don't we all lie down next to the track? You never know what might come along.'

Lindsey smiled but said nothing. We headed towards the floating open-air restaurant which was moored to the opposite bank by a series of ropes, each of them as thick as a man's arm. The whole valley possessed an indefinable tranquillity, much like that of a cemetery, which was, therefore, disturbingly appropriate. However, the contrast between what lay before our eyes and the disease-ridden labour camps so vividly portrayed in Lindsey's books was beyond all decent contemplation.

At the other side, we climbed down the steps to the riverbank and sat at a table in the nearest floating restaurant. This was the first time we had eaten or even seen western food since our long night at Heathrow.

Lindsey sat with his back to the bridge and stared over my shoulder for several minutes, oblivious to the rest of us.

'Are you all right?' I asked.

For a moment I thought he was ignoring me. 'Will you look at that?' he said incredulously, and then began to laugh.

I turned my head and looked into the trees. In a small clearing, a group of four men were offering rides on an elephant to any passing tourists who happened to be frustrated mahouts. Two stout, horizontal branches from one of the trees had been employed to support a small wooden platform which stood at a convenient height for willing participants to climb onto the elephant's back. Additionally, a broad plank with incremental wooden strips was being used as a ramp to gain access to it. A plump gentleman, wearing a brilliant white lounge suit and a huge stetson, had walked the plank up to the platform and was waiting impatiently for the hapless men to lure the animal into position. Frustratingly for them, however, the elephant was having none of it. The man stood conspicuously on the rickety shelf, cocking his leg like a dog at a gatepost whenever the elephant appeared to be moving within reach. I could visualize him mis-timing his step and falling out of the tree altogether.

'Jump!' Lindsey called out to him. 'Go on, jump!'

It was not long before everyone in the restaurant was on his feet, watching the farce develop.

'Just look at the fat old fool,' said Lindsey quietly. 'I only hope Nellie's knees don't buckle when he eventually mounts her ... should he be so lucky.'

After five minutes of pure slapstick entertainment, the man succeeded in placing himself squarely onto the elephant's back, and we watched him disappear into the forest like some sort of tropical cowboy. Lindsey proceeded to imitate the man's undignified, and very comical, movements for the benefit of Maalii, lifting his leg repeatedly, causing her to giggle helplessly in that idiosyncratic, twittering manner of hers.

An hour later, we emerged from the fan-cooled restaurant into the overwhelming heat and climbed back up onto the bridge. The joking and mimicry quickly subsided. We returned to the truck in silence, out of subconscious respect for men and women no different from ourselves - British, American, Dutch, Thai and Australian - who had endured such appalling degradation during the war years.

The driver was waiting for us on a bench nearby, passing the time of day and sharing a marijuana joint with a couple of locals. Half stoned, he drove leisurely away towards the town of Kanchanaburi and I watched the bridge disappear behind us.

'Patpong this evening?' I suggested, as cheerfully as I could.

'Patpong?' said Maalii. 'We go Patpong, *wan nii?*'

'One last fling before we leave,' Lindsey agreed. He put his arm around Maalii's shoulder and kissed the top of her head, as he would a child, his thoughts becoming more private by the hour.

On the main road we passed the elegant gateway to Kanchanaburi War Cemetery. Hundreds of polished headstones stood in identical rows of carefully-tended flower beds. Less than one square mile had been set aside to remind the populace of a wasted generation. At least the sun was shining on them - a pathetic, solitary consolation.

En route back to San's, we stopped off at an imposing temple at the brow of a hill.

'You take picture here!' called the driver, who knew instinctively that Tim was eager to capture the natural beauty of the valley from as flattering a position as possible. We climbed one flight of steps after another, wiping the sweat from our faces, until the entire tropical panorama exploded into unobscured view. Tim pivoted smoothly and clicked the camera in all directions.

'Where is she?' said Lindsey, looking around.

'Over there.' I pointed to a glittering, golden Buddha statue at the foot of which Maalii had knelt in solemn reflection. 'I wonder what she's praying for,' I whispered. 'Money? Food for her family? A *farang* for a husband, perhaps?' I then braced myself for his reply.

'What does it matter?' he replied, derisively, and looked across at Maalii with the same sorrowful expression that he had cast upon the war graves. He must have realized that he could not endow her with his own brand of truth any more easily than he could inject life back into the wretched souls rotting in the cemetery. 'There's nothing to be gained from dropping to one's knees in hope,' he added, with humble resignation. 'History has proved it. People shouldn't degrade themselves like that. It annihilates self-respect.'

'Desperate predicaments bring about desperate measures,' I said, thoughtfully.

'You're right. Did I ever tell you how my grandmother died?'

'No.'

'She had a heart attack in church - during prayers!'

'That's absurd.'

'Well, God does have a sense of humour.' He looked at me and shook his head slowly. 'If only my mother had got the message ...' He walked away before I had time to ask him for an explanation.

We collected the bags at half past two in the afternoon and headed for the bus terminal. On arrival, I handed the driver a fistful of baht - more than he could have hoped to earn in a typical day - in appreciation of his patience, lewd humour and extensive local knowledge. Tim took one last picture of him, sitting proudly in his driver's seat, and waving like a lunatic out of the window.

Once more we had found ourselves in a strange provincial settlement, waiting to return to the city. Here, though, the locals seemed generally indifferent to the sight of *farangs*, whereas in Krasang, the intense but reserved curiosity of the villagers had been apparent the whole time.

I caught the eye of a raw-boned young girl as she was stepping out of the crowded ticket office, on her own and looking rather lost. I smiled with a hint of uncertainty.

'Excuse me, do you speak English?' she asked, with an unexpected London accent.

'We *are* English,' I responded, helpfully. I assumed that she wanted directions.

'Are you going to Bangkok?'

'Yes, any minute now.'

'Really?' She seemed pleased, as well as relieved. 'May I ask you an enormous favour?' She smiled painfully. Her teeth were dirty and protruded down over her lower lip, and her clothes were as shoddy as they were ill-fitting. 'I must get this parcel to Bangkok by tonight. Would you possibly be willing to take it for me ... please?'

Lindsey snapped at her. 'What do you take us for?'

He scowled for a few seconds before turning away and placing his hand protectively on Maalii's shoulder. The girl walked despondently away, having probably anticipated the negative response.

'What do you suppose she was carrying?' said Tim, who had discreetly observed the encounter. 'Drugs? A gun?'

'Who can say?' said Lindsey, shaking his head. 'Although I'm sure the police would be interested to find out.'

We boarded the bus on schedule at a quarter past four, grateful to be back inside an air-conditioned space. I thought of the bedraggled girl, wandering gloomily around the bus terminal, shamelessly begging complete strangers to take responsibility for a suspect item in a foreign country. The poison in the chalice was narcotic. I could just sense it. As for the girl herself: rather like the prisoners of war, she may have been trapped inside an unspeakably evil sphere from which she could not escape.

VII

'Each man is the architect of his own fate.'

Appius Caecus (4th-3rd century BC)
De Civilate, Book 1

Most of the passengers were asleep when we arrived back at Sai Tai in Bangkok, including Tim, who had been in a state of chronic exhaustion ever since our arrival in Krasang. The station was much quieter than during the previous afternoon when we had left; just three or four lethargic travellers were waiting anonymously to board the last buses out of the city to God knows where.

Lindsey and Maalii skipped across the bus bays to an unoccupied tuk-tuk. Our flight to Hong Kong was now less than fifteen hours away. Six days together had already woven several colourful patterns into each of their life-tapestries; and that mutual pleasure, effortless and uncomplicated, was about to slip through their hands which were clasped so tightly together.

The tuk-tuk driver, as predictably as ever, slalomed like a daredevil between the cars and buses on Ploenchit and Sukhumvit Roads before passing under the expressway bridge and bumping over the open railway line. At the entrance to the Plaza, the blue, red, green and orange lights sparkled in the dusk. On Soi Phasuk, a group of six or seven shoeless children were playing with an old football on the grass verge opposite the shacks, oblivious to the nightfall. For once, they continued playing, having doubtless become accustomed to seeing the four of us come and go at various times of day.

Inside, Maalii plugged in the small fan and we lay side by side on the hard floor, cooling off and preparing ourselves mentally for our intended finale on the Patpong strip.

One of the young girls from the adjacent room opened the door and brought in a cardboard box containing some of our clothes which she had kindly washed in our absence. Lindsey stood up and proffered two fifty-baht notes which she reluctantly accepted.

I followed Tim outside, thereby giving Lindsey some time to be alone with Maalii. We strode across the grass and climbed onto the fence next to the railway line. Above the traffic noise, a mixture of thumping music and wild laughter reverberated from the Plaza on the other side of the track. It was just another extravagant night gradually descending into anarchy.

'Do you think he'll miss her?' I wondered.

'That goes without saying, which in itself is incredible, although I'm not sure he'll admit it to you and me.'

'Why not?'

'He isn't the type. He'll vent his frustration only when his resistance reaches breaking point. Should that happen, I just hope it manifests itself in the form of gradual leaks rather than an almighty explosion.'

After a short while spent hypothesizing about Lindsey's frame of mind, he levered himself off the fence and lay down on his back in the long grass, resting his head against a discarded car tyre.

'It's ironic,' he yawned.

'What is?'

'I'd been looking forward to visiting Hong Kong more than anywhere else, but now I couldn't care less.' He closed his eyes and said nothing more. He did not need to.

Over on the opposite side of the expressway I could see the silhouette of a towering crane standing alongside three skeletal concrete office blocks - a powerful reminder of the city's burgeoning prosperity. In comparison, the necrotic, wooden huts in the foreground, which comprised the Plaza, looked dangerously on the verge of being trampled underfoot as the merciless capitalist stampede gathered momentum.

A large apple core landed at Tim's feet, causing him to sit up sharply. We looked round at the young boys who were still playing football.

'Hey!' called a voice from along the railway line. It was Lindsey, walking on the track, and laden with the remainder of our luggage which he had gone to collect from the Condo on nearby Soi 4.

'Have it back!' Tim replied, picking up the core and throwing it from a sitting position as hard as he could.

Lindsey waded through the knee-high grass, dropped the heavy bags onto Tim's lap and jumped onto the fence beside me.

'I've paid the landlady,' he puffed. 'It cost us next to nothing.'

'How much, exactly?'

'Eight thousand baht.'

'*Each?*' I shrieked.

'No, you dimwit - for the three of us.' He gazed down the undeviating track, away from Sukhumvit and into the hazy sunset. 'Where do you suppose that leads?'

'Well, there's a railway line that runs the entire length of the Malay peninsula from here to Singapore,' I said. 'This may be it.'

'You've been reading my books.' He looked at me with an annoying smirk, fully aware that there was no other way I could possibly have known such a fact. 'Perhaps, one day, it will be possible to travel by rail from London to New York.'

'Across the Atlantic?'

'No, through Europe and Russia, then across Siberia, Alaska and Canada. Remember where you heard it first.'

We sat contemplatively for a few minutes before picking up the bags and returning to Maalii's room. She was sitting cross-legged in front of the humming fan, effortlessly dragging a brush through her thick, black hair. Lindsey bent over her and they kissed lovingly, resigned to the fact that these would be their final few hours in each other's company. In spite of having packed so much into the week, our arrival at Don Muang now seemed barely an hour ago.

For the very last time, we strolled the short distance along Soi Phasuk on to the floodlit Sukhumvit, then across the railway line to the Plaza, where all the usual girls were loitering with a few bronzed, beer-drinking *farangs*. Maalii led us to some of her friends at the fourth bar. The smallest of them, who looked no older than sixteen, even with a liberal plastering of make-up, perched herself on the adjacent stool.

'Maalii say you go tomorrow,' she piped, making sure I could hear her above the mellow sound of *Crowded House* singing the appropriately titled *Don't Dream It's Over*.

'Yes, we go Hong Kong,' I replied, in the usual overpronounced manner.

'You say goodbye *Pra-thet Thai?*'

I forced a tight-lipped smile and nodded to her. Maalii turned to Lindsey and rested her head on his shoulder, not wishing to hear any talk of our impending departure. Indeed, she had become increasingly withdrawn through-out the course of the afternoon, gradually surrendering to the inevitable, but still hopelessly unable to suppress feelings for a man she barely knew.

I waited until she had momentarily left his side then moved across to speak to him.

'How is she?' I inquired gently. 'I assume she would rather we remained here.'

Lindsey shrugged. 'I wish we could, too. But circumstances dictate otherwise.'

There was an awkward silence.

'And is that it?'

'We live five thousand miles apart, Phil. What am I supposed to be able to do about that?'

'I don't know. I don't have your brains.'

'The hurdle is practically insurmountable.' He made a point of appearing disconsolate, eyes staring down at the dusty floorboards beneath our feet.

'I'm sure you could do *something*.'

He raised his head and threw a sideways glance as he took another drink. It was a familiar expression, one of icy self-confidence, and it fuelled the curiosity I already possessed and was struggling to control.

At ten o'clock we stood up to leave and spent at least fifteen minutes saying our goodbyes to the ten or twelve people with whom we had become acquainted in spite of the language difficulties, and whose genial faces we would never see again. On reaching Sukhumvit Road, I turned to look at the Plaza - yet another magical part of the world for which I would always have to depend upon only photographs and memories.

Lindsey stood on the edge of the pavement, waiting for a tuk-tuk to emerge from the mass of darting headlights and thicker-than-usual exhaust fumes. I had even grown fond of the Sukhumvit smog.

'She looks choked,' Tim whispered to me, 'if you'll forgive the bad pun.'

'I agree. Do you think Lindsey might be plotting something we don't yet know about?'

He raised his eyebrows. 'Think? I'm sure of it.'

'Really?'

'Frankly, it wouldn't surprise me if he'd actually arranged for her to come with us to Hong Kong.'

'We shall see, soon enough.'

Before we could continue our covert conversation, a tuk-tuk careered across three lanes of traffic to where Lindsey was standing, almost crushing his toes in the process, and we climbed inside for our last ride down to Patpong. The tiny vehicle screeched through the now-familiar streets of Ploenchit and Ratchadamri, none of us uttering a word. It was a time only for reflection - a few minutes' contemplation of a week's events which had been as unique as they had been utterly fortuitous.

Patpong was going crazy. Groups of *farangs* in multicoloured T-shirts and shorts packed the marketplace and walkways, to the delight of the street vendors who were competing vociferously for what they knew was a finite amount of throwaway cash. We strode briskly between the stalls, aware that stopping to inspect any of the items on show would automatically engage us in a full-blown negotiation in which none of us was remotely interested.

We arrived at the entrance to the same club we had visited on our first night, and climbed the steps to the cool, strobe-lit hall. Inside, it was barely possible even to turn around without an unwanted clash of elbows and, despite the air-conditioning, there was a distinct smell of perfumed perspiration lingering in the air. At least two hundred energetic revellers of all nationalities were packed tightly together, untroubled, perhaps even turned on, by the acute shortage of space.

'We can forget about sitting down!' Lindsey yelled as we shuffled patiently through the crowd to the edge of the dance floor.

We stopped directly underneath one of three enormous ceiling fans, which resembled helicopter rotor blades. Maalii waved enthusiastically to someone she evidently knew. I recognized her immediately: she, too, worked at the Plaza, but at a different bar. The girl called out and ploughed across the room towards us. As they began to bellow at each other above the racket, I noticed the occasional sympathetic gesture being thrown in Lindsey's direction. They were discussing our imminent departure.

Several minutes later, the girl turned to me with a sorrowful gaze. 'You go tomorrow, yes?'

'In the morning.'

'Good luck, I say to you,' she replied, before leaning forward to kiss me on the cheek. I smiled politely and watched her disappear back into the thickening crowd.

As I turned around, I noticed that Tim and Lindsey, as well as two of the bar staff, were leaning over Maalii who was standing against the back wall, weeping uncontrollably. Everyone who looked at her seemed to know the reason. It was as if they had seen it all too many times to remember: a love that could have been, if only, if only ...

Lindsey looked mildly embarrassed and seemed incapable of consoling her. The hideous sight of such a naturally cheerful girl in such a state of grief alarmed me, even more than I could have expected.

Tim left her side and walked towards me, hopelessly shaking his head. 'I'm dreading tomorrow. She'll be hysterical at the airport. I know she will. Who the hell put Liverpool and Bangkok on opposite sides of the globe?'

'He won't leave her like that,' I insisted.

Eventually, Maalii recomposed herself, and seemed comforted by whatever Lindsey had been trying to explain.

'She's fine,' he assured us, unconvincingly. 'Everything is just fine.'

Tim leaned across once again and shouted in my ear the second Lindsey's back was turned: 'Can't you sense what he's doing?'

'No, what?'

'She'll be coming with us to Hong Kong,' he said, categorically.

'Has he told you so?'

'No, but it wouldn't surprise me.'

Bodies continued to pour in from outside. There was scarcely enough air to breathe. Lindsey turned to us and pointed to the door. We followed him back down to the alleyway which was almost as congested as the club itself.

'Perhaps that wasn't such a bright idea,' said Tim. 'Why don't we find a quiet cafe instead?'

Maalii led us back to where we had climbed out of the tuk-tuk. I watched her body language closely. She appeared less tense now than at any time since we were back in Kanchanaburi, embracing Lindsey spontaneously as they walked along the pavement, and occasionally resting her tired head against his shoulder. On the opposite side of Surawong - a wide boulevard screaming with high-powered motorcycles - was a small, unpretentious cafe, empty and inviting.

'Is everything OK?' I asked him, once we had sat down.

'The obstacle will be overcome,' he said, 'but don't ask me how.'

Departure was now only twelve hours away. I visualized the surreal image of Maalii bursting out of Lindsey's bag at the hotel in Hong Kong.

The waiter - a stocky, sullen man who had what looked like blood smeared down the front of his once-white apron - walked over and wiped the soiled pine table with a damp cloth which stank of disinfectant.

'Cow-pat,' said Lindsey suddenly. 'Sii cow-pat!'

The man nodded his head sternly and walked away without saying a word.

'Cow-pat?' said Tim incredulously.

'Yes, cow-pat. It's Thai for chicken fried rice.'

'In that case, I just hope he didn't think you were ordering in English.'

The tension eased as Lindsey listed the names of several other dishes which were open to outrageous misinterpretation in various parts of the world.

'If you said "'ell fire!" to a waiter in Germany, you'd get eleven eggs.'

Within minutes, the food had arrived and he was proved right, as I knew he would be.

'There, I told you. Four succulent cow-pats.'

The mood continued to lighten over dinner. We sat at the open end of the cafe for more than an hour, telling jokes and playing the fool over a steady supply of cheap Thai beer, whilst observing the frenetic comings and goings on Surawong which showed no signs of waning. I had been astounded by the street's complete metamorphosis as day faded into night. Every day at dusk, dormant walkways erupted into illuminated foci of hyperactivity. In effect, the streets constituted two different cities superimposed upon one another - one thriving as the other slept.

At midnight we dawdled along to the end of Surawong - Lindsey and Maalii holding hands twenty yards ahead - past Lumpini Park where we had idled away our first two afternoons, and headed back to Maalii's room, this time on foot.

The Plaza was in total darkness, and deserted, with the exception of three or four neglected street children, who were roaming aimlessly from one boarded-up bar to the next, probably in search of food scraps. At least we had somewhere to lay our heads, and our stomachs were full.

We crossed the railway track and made the familiar right turn on to the unlit Soi Phasuk. Our day had begun in one bare, wooden shack and was about to end in another. Maalii switched on the fan as we collapsed simultaneously onto the mattress for our final night's rest.

Lindsey whispered across the darkened room: 'I don't know why I'm lying here. I won't sleep.'

VIII

'Upon your journey of so many days,
Without a single kiss or goodbye?'

Coventry Patmore (1823-96)
The Unknown Eros, Book 1

I shuffled restlessly back and forth throughout the small hours of the morning, unable to keep cool and managing to doze for no longer than half an hour at a time. I noticed that Tim was awake, resting his head awkwardly against the flat side of his rucksack and staring vacantly up at the dilapidated ceiling.

'What time is it?' I whispered.

'Six thirty,' came the muffled response.

'Is that all?'

I was now aching for a long night's sleep. We lay there in silence, listening to the build-up of the Sukhumvit traffic, as well as the occasional tuk-tuk scooting down Soi Phasuk towards the market at nearby Klong Toey.

Tim struggled to his feet, opened the door carefully and stepped outside on to the pavement. I rolled on to my side and looked at Lindsey and Maalii, huddled together on the uncushioned floor. If the noise from the creaking door failed to disturb them, then the incoming daylight certainly would. Maalii stirred and opened her eyes for a few seconds, then wrapped her arm around Lindsey's bare midriff, almost subconsciously, and held him securely.

Tim came back inside, leaving the door wide open. 'It's raining,' he said, 'and heavily too.'

'How appropriate,' Lindsey muttered.

He and Maalii sat up together, and with equal reluctance. He looked affectionately into her sleepy eyes and caressed her smooth face with his hands. Her head dropped despondently. Gently, he lifted her chin with his little finger until she was looking straight at him once more. Her solemn expression gradually gave way to a broad, loving smile. His silent reassurance seemed to have been accepted.

After washing and changing we picked up all the bags and ventured out into the continuing downpour. The grass strip, which separated Soi Phasuk from the railway line, lay saturated and undisturbed, and muddy puddles had formed in a neat row at the foot of the fence. It was as if the young boys we had seen playing football never actually existed. I could not understand why things of no real importance had become so thought-provoking.

'We could have breakfast at that cafe at the end of Soi 4,' Lindsey suggested, characteristically unconcerned about the state of his hair and clothes. 'Agreed?'

'Provided it has a roof,' said Tim. 'I'll join you in five minutes. If I take the film rolls to the pharmacy, we'll be able to see the photographs before we leave. Processing won't take more than fifteen minutes.'

We burst through the cafe's double doors, thereby attracting the attention of all the other customers, who were reading newspapers and sipping cups of coffee. Maalii looked at Lindsey and myself and giggled under her breath.

'What's so funny?' I wondered.

'We are,' he said. '*Farangs* always look a mess in this climate, rain or shine. I think she finds our inability to cope amusing.'

We settled ourselves at a conspicuous window table where she immediately wiped Lindsey's forehead and face with a clean napkin, as if it were obligatory. Tim barged in, minutes later, his cotton shirt clinging uncomfortably to his stout torso. Maalii looked up and began to laugh once more. She now seemed inexplicably relaxed.

'This is just like being at home,' said Tim, blowing drops of rainwater from the end of his nose on to the tablecloth. 'The pictures will be ready before we've finished breakfast.'

The hilarity gradually subsided as the thought of exchanging goodbyes reoccupied our minds. We drank fresh fruit juice from glasses the size of thimbles and nibbled at pieces of buttered toast until the rain finally stopped. I hated times like these; only when we had boarded the aircraft would it be possible to relax.

At nine fifteen, we paid the bill and strolled to the end of Soi 4 while Tim called to collect his prints. For the very last time, Lindsey waited at the Sukhumvit roadside and, almost immediately, a hungry vehicle muscled its way across the road and spluttered to a standstill right in front of him.

'Do you want to go on ahead?' I called to him, anticipating his wish to spend the remaining precious minutes alone with Maalii.

'All right,' he said, gratefully.

'I'll wait here for Tim.'

He followed her, not into a tuk-tuk, but on to the back seat of an air-conditioned taxi and then rolled down the window halfway while she gave the simplest of instructions to the driver.

'You won't have any difficulty finding another taxi,' he added.

I put my head to the window. 'I know that. A *farang* has only to stand on the pavement looking lost and one seems to pop up out of a hole in the road.'

'Either a taxi,' he replied, 'or half a dozen pimps.' He looked over my shoulder. 'Here comes Sigmund.'

I turned to see Tim walking towards us with his eyes fixed on the glossy photographs in his hands. Luckily for him there were no holes in the pavement either. Lindsey slapped me on the shoulder before they moved off and took their place in the congested procession.

Tim handed over the crisp packet just as a second taxi applied its brakes. We jumped inside and I began to peruse the pictures: the three of us lounging on a blanket in Lumpini Park; a Sukhumvit traffic jam at sunset; a haggard old peasant on the train to Krasang; Chek shrouded in talcum powder; Tim balancing nervously on the raft in Surin; and the two lovers kissing on the Kwai Bridge - each one a story of too many words to recount.

I sat back and observed the never-ending stream of cars in the other carriageway, privately wishing that I could have been inside one of them, returning to the city to relive it all a second time. After spending an hour limping along in second gear, we arrived at the entrance to the departures building where we immediately noticed Lindsey and Maalii frolicking around under the flights information monitor.

'She doesn't appear to be too distraught,' Tim remarked, stepping onto the forecourt.

'Maybe she *will* be travelling with us.'

It was not to be. We checked in and walked submissively across the packed hall towards the dreaded Passport Control partition. The moment had arrived. I smiled at Maalii and kissed her tentatively.

'I no forget you,' she said, with palpable sincerity.

When Tim had wished her well, in that clinical way of his, we waited anxiously, not wishing to hurry the parting. I watched the two of them furtively. She reached up and stroked his wet hair with her childlike fingers. He held her for all too brief a moment and whispered a few words before kissing her forehead. She smiled again, almost excitedly, then stepped away from the barrier, as she knew was inevitable. Just before we finally disappeared from her sight, a brown-suited immigration official frisked Lindsey from head to foot. As he stood motionless with his arms outstretched like the archetypal scarecrow, she began to laugh once again. It was precisely how I wanted to remember her.

We trudged to Gate 8, relieved that there had been no tears - from either of them.

'Well, what did you say to her?' asked Tim, who was in one of his heightened states of curiosity.

Lindsey was nonchalant. 'Nothing much.'

'Bullshit. You *must* have.'

'Why?'

'She was too calm.'

'I just told her that I would write from Hong Kong.'

'Write? In English?'

'No, in Thai.'

'Thai? You?'

'Why not? We have a dictionary. It may not turn out to be grammatically perfect, but it will be both legible and intelligible. After all, every known language is based upon subject-verb-object. We all speak variations of the same theme. That will be as much help as I shall need.'

'How is she going to reply?'

'In the same way - provided she keeps it simple. I gave her Nova's address, so when we arrive in New York ... let's see ... ten days from now, there should be something waiting for me.'

He was deliberately making everything sound so straightforward; I was almost convinced that, had we stayed an extra week or two, he would have been speaking the language as well as any native Bangkokian.

We made our way down the escalator where, outside, we could see the colossal 747 aircraft dwarfing the baggage vehicles and shuttle buses which, in comparison, were swarming around on the steaming concrete like remote-controlled toys.

Tim sat down, took out the photographs and handed them to Lindsey who sifted through them and replayed each scenario within the secret confines of his head.

'Keep the negatives, if you wish,' Tim told him. 'You can have duplicates printed in Hong Kong.'

'Thanks, but photography preserves next to nothing,' he said forlornly, 'however skilfully it may have been executed.'

'Perhaps your turbocharged imagination will be able to compensate for my lack of expertise.'

Lindsey said nothing more. He was keeping something to himself.

As it turned out, the aircraft was barely half-full. We shot along the runway and soared into the hazy sky, craning our stiff necks to steal one final glimpse of the haphazard skyline of a city which had captivated us all so comprehensively.

'I've spent my last ten nights in ten different places,' said Lindsey, closing his eyes gently. 'That could explain why I've been waking up in the mornings wondering where the hell I am.'

'Would you have it any other way?' I asked him.

Predictably, he shook his head. I, too, closed my eyes, and returned to Krasang: the winding lane leading to the railway station; the overloaded fruit stalls at the marketplace; and a few small children playing barefoot outside a broken-down shack. I knew that it would be impossible to forget Krasang, but I realized also that there would be no possibility of my ever returning. I dreamed of Chek, so obviously happy, playing football with Lindsey between the trees at the side of the lane. I hoped he would remember me, if only for a week or two.

I lifted my head and peered out. It was dark, apart from a sprinkling of distant lights below.

'We shall be arriving at Kai Tak in forty-five minutes,' said Lindsey, who was sitting in an upright position, reading one of his new books.

'I must have been tired,' I said, stretching my arms and legs simultaneously.

He grinned, which made me wonder whether I had been talking gibberish in my sleep and he had stayed awake in order to listen.

Over on the opposite side of the plane, Tim was lying face down across three seats.

'Look at Sigmund over there,' he remarked. 'He hasn't so much as twitched for over four hours.'

'No?'

'Perhaps he's dead.'

'And you?' I said, still yawning. 'Have you been sleeping?'

'No, reading.'

'What?'

'This - *Contemporary Asian History*.'

'One bloody conflict after another, right?'

'More or less. Each oppressive regime is invariably usurped by one that develops into something even more horrendous. Communism, in particular, seemed to destroy the lives of the very people it was designed to protect. Still, the word *revolution* does imply a full circle, does it not? Remember *Animal Farm*?' He closed the book and stuffed it disrespectfully into his jacket pocket. 'The free market is a callous beast, you know. Socialists, such as yourself, believe, quite naively, that it can be harnessed for collective benefit. Conservatives, on the other hand, such as Tim and his tribe, rightly accept that it cannot, but seem to care little for the consequences. I'm not sure whose views are the more contemptible.'

The mammoth aircraft banked one way and then the other as we began our descent towards mainland Hong Kong. I could make out the sparkling lights of the Kowloon skyscrapers standing tall like a hundred Christmas trees packed into a tiny garden. Meanwhile, Lindsey's evangelistic ramblings made the natural progression from politics to religion, and he was still in full flow long after we had landed.

I wound my watch forward by one hour. It was six o'clock in the evening, local time.

'We have every chance of being out on the streets by seven thirty,' he said.

'What about your letter?' I said, gently, not wishing to make him feel under any obligation.

'That can wait until tomorrow. I've already exceeded my thinking quota for today.'

We turned off the runway at Kai Tak in total darkness. Sadly, I could not feel even the faintest spark of excitement. We had arrived in Hong Kong but my mind was still roaming around Thailand, digesting it thoroughly, reluctant to catch up. We plodded through the usual airport formalities and made straight for the taxi rank where a couple of predatory young men descended upon us in an instant.

'Hell-o! Where you go?' said one of them in a loud, clipped voice, rather like that of an army drill sergeant.

'Causeway Bay,' Lindsey called back, and the three of us squeezed into the back of yet another air-conditioned taxi, this one smelling of cheap after shave.

'Where you go?' he repeated, having been told only twenty seconds beforehand.

'*Causeway Bay.*'

'Ah, *Tung lo wan! Tung lo wan!*'

He started the engine and bolted along the airport underpass with the controlled urgency of an ambulance driver.

Lindsey looked out inquisitively. 'So this is the clitoris of the Far East, is it?'

'It doesn't look very British,' replied Tim, with a hint of dismay.

'I thought that was the whole point. If we'd wanted to see Britain, we could have stayed at home.'

After half an hour of swerving, swooping and sudden braking, the driver stopped and flicked the button to open the boot.

'This, Causeway Bay,' he announced.

I relinquished the first of the crisp Hong Kong dollars that I had obtained back in Liverpool, and stepped out onto the roadside to collect the bags.

'There it is,' said Lindsey, pointing across the busy dual carriageway.

'Looks quite smart,' I said, carefully.

'And therefore expensive,' he snapped. 'Just as well we shan't be here long.'

We muscled through the revolving doors into a spotless foyer and looked around. Observing us from behind the reception desk was a young woman, immaculately groomed in a matching emerald green skirt and jacket, and with black bobbed hair which was combed to absolute perfection. She looked slightly stunned: her cocktail party had just been gatecrashed by three tramps.

'Your name plea,' she demanded, in a courteous, but distinctly formal tone.

I assumed she was addressing all of us; English, as spoken by the Chinese, always sounded to me like a language with more vowels than consonants.

'McKee, Gainsborough and Corker,' said Tim, obediently. 'We're booked to stay for two nights.'

She flicked through the files, scrutinized our passports with the pedantry of a paranoid immigration official, then directed us to our room on the second floor. Once safely inside, Lindsey dropped his bag onto the waxed mahogany desk and sprawled at full length on one of the three beds without first bothering to remove his shoes. He was just making a point.

'This place is so fucking *stiff*. At least in Thailand the people smiled.' He sat back up. 'Perhaps that overstrung bitch downstairs detests the likes of us because of the imperialistic instincts of our great-grandfathers - whom we never even knew. Very rational.'

I glanced across the room at Tim who was standing at the window with his back to the room. Neither of us was going to object to Lindsey's irritability.

IX

'Absence is to love what wind is to fire:
it extinguishes the small, it inflames the great.'

Bussy-Rabutin (1618-93)
Histoire amoreuse des Gaules

Outside, hoards of shoppers and preoccupied business executives were dashing in and out of sterile malls, and above us was a complex network of overhead walkways and dazzling shop signs, almost all of which were written in Cantonese. We had landed in the ultimate downtown jungle, and a very alien one at that. British it was most definitely not.

The MTR station was especially sterile: clean and modern, but totally lacking in any of that hip, subterranean artistry which adorned the decaying London Underground. In fact, everything in sight reeked of automated efficiency.

The automatic carriage doors opened without a sound, and we hopped on board the Kowloon-bound commuter train.

'Where do we get out?' I asked, after scanning the colour-coded map above the doors.

Lindsey seemed uninterested. 'I don't suppose it matters.'

'Get it together, Lindsey,' said Tim, with as much impatience as he dared to express. 'Phil and I are right behind you as far as Maalii is concerned, but you're in danger of letting the next fortnight pass you by. We're in Hong Kong, for Christ's sake!'

'Fair comment,' he conceded, 'but try to make your point without stabbing me with it, please.'

After several stops, we climbed out and emerged halfway along Nathan Road at the stroke of seven thirty. Directly opposite the MTR exit, a group of elegantly-attired Chinese ladies, assisted by men in tuxedos, stepped out of polished black limousines onto the pavement. Images of Krasang flashed across my mind and my flesh was consumed by an irrepressible surge of adrenaline. Further along, a contrasting array of ostentatious restaurants and casinos were waiting impatiently for the evening's money to start flooding in, which it surely would. I could literally smell the district's renowned affluence and, when I pictured Chek's toy truck, it almost made me nauseous.

Lindsey continued to complain. 'I'm hungry.'

'That's understandable,' I said. 'You haven't eaten since we had break-fast at that joint in Bangkok.'

'Didn't you eat anything on the plane?' asked Tim, with mild incredulity.

'It tasted like shit,' he scoffed. 'I suspect it was recycled waste from the previous flight.'

We eventually wandered into a narrow side-street and came across a rundown old cafe which looked about half-full. We opened the door without needing to reach any verbal consensus.

The cafe's interior reminded me of a place at the heart of Liverpool's old Chinatown, which I had frequented with Tim's family in the days when I would do anything to avoid going home.

On the wall opposite the bar was a series of large, square photographs of the harbour, taken at different angles, altitudes and times of day. At one of the adjacent tables were two male clones, sipping white wine like gentlemen, picking at dollops of chow mein like animals, whilst at the same time conducting separate conversations on their mobile phones. In spite of their being together, it appeared that neither of them possessed sufficient patience to conclude one meeting before planning the next. Perhaps they had no alternative, I thought. I could accept that their behaviour was an accurate reflection of the city's hyperdisciplined work ethic on a wider scale.

'Six beers, please!' Lindsey called out with great intent.

'Six?'

'Two each. It's a start.' He turned to the waiter again. 'And bring us the menus, would you?'

One of the clones concluded his call, closed his phone and left without a word to his counterpart, pausing only to acknowledge him with a slight nod and drop some cash onto the table.

It was not long before we reached a comfortable, semi-drunken state, gulping down king prawns and crispy duck, pausing occasionally to take a breath.

'Remind me to give my sister a call while we're here,' said Lindsey with his mouth full. 'She doesn't know that we'll be travelling from Toronto to New York by coach.'

Tim and I looked at each other. 'Neither did we.'

He feigned surprise. 'Did I not tell you?'

'You know you didn't.'

'It will enable us to stop off halfway and see Niagara Falls.'

'Corker, I hope you know what you're doing.'

'Trust me.'

Once we had emptied our troughs, we spent the rest of the evening listening to Lindsey's recollections of wild antics with former girlfriends in

Nottingham. Most of his conquests beggared belief, particularly his claim to have deflowered one of his schoolteachers in a telephone box on the bank of the Trent. Nevertheless, I was pleased that he had stopped daydreaming about Maalii, even if his alcohol-inspired exuberance was destined to be short-lived.

By eleven o'clock I was almost too dizzy to stand, and when I tried to put on my jacket one of the armholes had disappeared. We stumbled out into the street and flapped our arms at every passing vehicle, knowing that sooner or later one of them would turn out to be a taxi.

'Where you want to go?' called the driver with the short straw.

Lindsey leaned forward. 'Bangkok, old fruit! Soi Phasuk!' He then opened the door, tripped over the sill, and fell face first between the seats, shaking and jerking with laughter.

'He means Causeway Bay,' I explained, and we managed to climb inside, giggling like schoolgirls and fighting for space on the back seat.

The driver moved off at a leisurely speed.

'You enjoy Hong Kong?' he inquired, untroubled by our appalling condition.

'Loving it,' I replied.

Lindsey turned his head and spluttered in my ear: 'He's exactly like the waiter in the cafe! I told you they all looked the same!'

'They might be brothers,' I responded, rather stupidly.

The driver smiled enthusiastically. 'You like heavy metal?' he shouted.

Without waiting for a reply, he took his eyes off the road, reached forward and inserted a tape into the machine.

'Waaaaaaaah!'

The sudden noise from the four speakers shook my brain.

'Waaaaaaaah! Waaaah wok-a-hoowah! Wok-a-wok-a-wooh!'

Lindsey shrieked hysterically. '*Chinese* heavy metal!'

The harsh sound of crashing cymbals and fuzz-box guitars began to thunder through our already-abused heads.

Tim wound down the window. 'He's going to blow the doors off the vehicle.'

'You like?' bellowed the driver, thrusting his head back and forth like a chicken.

'Some day!' I said, turning to Tim, who had protruded his own head out of the nearside window. 'From the streets of Bangkok in the early hours of the morning to this!'

We pulled up outside the hotel and stuffed a considerable tip into the driver's grateful hands.

The hotel foyer emitted the silent hum of a village library. We walked, as normally as we could, to the desk, at which the same stuffy receptionist was leafing assiduously through the telephone directory. She looked at us coldly:

same tramps, she was doubtless thinking to herself, but now obliterated by alcohol to boot.

Lindsey took the key from her. 'Go on, smile,' he taunted, and made a ridiculous face. 'Go on, we won't report you to the manager, I promise.'

She maintained her constipated expression for a further few seconds before breaking into an uninhibited grin, of which I had assumed her to be congenitally incapable.

'Thank you,' he whispered to her.

She quickly recomposed herself, probably ashamed to have been made to abandon her pretence by an inebriated foreigner. Lindsey smiled to himself as we waited for the lift, amused by his success in removing her veneer of formality, if only for a few precious seconds.

It was hardly surprising that the next day - our only full day in Hong Kong - did not even begin until five o'clock in the afternoon. Lifeless and almost fatally hungover, I sat up and strained to focus my eyes. Tim was lying on the adjacent bed, fully dressed, listening to music on his personal hi-fi, and 'singing along'. It appeared for a moment that Lindsey was not even in the room, until I noticed a large bulge in the pale green curtains. He was sitting on a small footstool, using the window sill as a writing surface, and had been thoughtful enough to drape the curtains over his back in order to keep out the bright sunlight.

'The headache tablets are in the bathroom,' he said, without needing to move from behind the curtains to realize how I felt.

'Thanks. What are you doing?'

He paused for a while. 'Just scribbling.'

Tim removed his earplugs. 'You've been sitting there for three hours already! Are you sending her your autobiography?'

'If you give me another twenty seconds, I can write yours too.'

I stood up and almost blacked out. I managed to drag myself across to the window and threw back the curtains. The ledge was completely covered with books, scraps of notepaper and even a length of toilet roll, on which he had been practising writing Thai characters. Every single piece had been filled from top to bottom with strange loops, dashes and squiggles, some with only the subtlest of differences.

He picked up the finished article, which consisted of a solitary sheet, and held it up to the light.

'*Et voila!* Where's the nearest mailbox?'

I shook my head. 'I wouldn't even know what one looked like.'

He sealed the letter inside a pale blue envelope and put on his old leather jacket.

'I shall be back in half an hour.'

He closed the door quietly on leaving, as if Tim and I were still asleep. I gathered the remainder of his notes, placed them in a neat pile on his unmade bed and sat down on the window ledge. We watched as he set off along the busy pavement opposite Victoria Park, moving against the general flow, as he tended to do in most other aspects of life.

He did not return for well over an hour. He eventually wandered back in carrying a crumpled picture postcard of the New Territories and, at first, offered no explanation as to where he had been.

'Good news,' he said, belatedly. 'I've just spoken to Nova.'

'What time is it in New York?' Tim asked.

'Six in the morning.'

'Idiot. Did you miscalculate the time difference?'

'No, they invariably get up early. Most days, Jacques is at the office before seven. This is the best time to call.'

'So tell us the good tidings,' I said.

'Jacques will be flying out to LA on business tomorrow morning. He said he'd be at the airport to meet us when we arrive.'

'Is his trip purely a coincidence?'

'Probably not. As far as work goes, Jacques does exactly as he pleases.'

'And writes his own pay cheques too, I expect.'

'That's not all. A colleague of his lives a few miles north of the city, and Jacques reckons he'd be happy to put us up.' His eyes shone with immoral excitement. 'Just think of all those hotel expenses we won't be paying!'

He handed the postcard to Tim and sat down on the window sill, resting his feet on the stool.

'Adam van Bergen.'

'He and Jacques work for the same company,' Lindsey explained, 'but are currently based on opposite sides of the continent.'

'What's this guy like?' I asked, with a detectable trace of suspicion.

'Decent. Square, but decent.'

None of us possessed sufficient energy to venture far from the hotel, let alone attempt a repeat performance of the previous night. By the time we stepped outside for our first breaths of fresh air it was almost dark, which seemed both laughable and mildly tragic. We slipped past the receptionist without uttering a word either to her or amongst ourselves. She watched us in silence: it now appeared that, after prowling the streets at night, the tramps slept during the day, rather like vampires. Whatever she was thinking, her face stank of disapproval.

As we set off, I thought again of Krasang. I could see the silhouette of a malnourished young boy, perched alone on the wooden fence surrounding the yard, gazing down the lane at dusk, waiting undeterred for his *farang* friends to return. In my own world, at least, he would be sitting there forever.

We ambled aimlessly along Yee Wo Street and embarked upon a gentle exploration of the Wanchai district, which turned out to be a diluted version of Patpong. Nubile teenage girls leered at us from neon-lit doorways in the hope that, being pop-eyed tourists, we might be tempted to cross the threshold. Sadly for them, we could see beyond it, and none of us was about to be taken in.

From the ferry pier, we sauntered back along the waterfront, thinking aloud and observing the river traffic, as we so often did in Liverpool. The squalid, wooden houseboats, which belonged to the local fishermen, looked uncannily similar to the Soi Phasuk shanties, and were packed so tightly together that some did not appear to be in contact with the water. Behind them, separated by an invisible but impenetrable demarcation line, was an equally dense collection of majestic white yachts - toys as opposed to homes.

By the following morning, Lindsey had become totally preoccupied, to the extent that he did not even pass comment on the receptionist's newly-acquired politeness.

'Did you notice? She smiled at us!' I remarked as we were returning to Kai Tak.

'You sound surprised,' he growled. 'Sunday worshippers invariably smile at the priest for a similar reason as they file out of church. It's all to do with direction of travel.' He had nothing further to say, which was just as well.

Surprisingly, our brief stay in Hong Kong had been a non-event, and it seemed reasonable to predict that, if Lindsey's lethargy continued, Los Angeles would be no better.

After enduring three hours of silent boredom in the departures lounge, followed by another two in transit at Narita, Tokyo, we made our intended connection, sleepy and somewhat disorientated, on to the transpacific flight to the thriving west coast of North America. A new day had dawned, and with it, a renaissance of the optimism we had left behind in Bangkok.

X

'A truth that's told with bad intent
Beats all the lies you can invent.'

William Blake (1757-1827)
Auguries of Innocence

Jacques Pardeau, BSc, MSc, PhD, was born in the Montparnasse district of Paris. His father, a studious engineer, had secured a lucrative position with an international electronics company in the north of England, and left France - as it turned out, for good - with his young wife and son, then aged six. Within months of the upheaval, the young Jacques was able to speak English as fluently as any of his new school friends, and wasted no time in occupying a class of his own when confronted with anything remotely scientific. His intellect, coupled with unwavering self-motivation, led inevitably to years of academic excellence, even surpassing that achieved by his father; consequently, everything else in his life seemed to land exactly where he wanted it - in the palms of his hands.

'When his mother was a child,' Nova had once told me, 'she was forced to stand and watch Nazi tanks roll down the Champs Elysées, but refused even to consider the possibility of eventual defeat. Jacques has the same obsession with independence. It must be in his blood.'

As we emerged into a packed arrivals hall in Los Angeles, I noticed a tall, muscular man in a dark suit, waiting quietly behind the barrier, all by himself. This was Jacques, the same unmissable figure, with wiry black hair and a thick moustache, whom I had not seen for almost two years.

'What's happening, Jacques?' Lindsey called from one end of the hall to the other.

We walked over to him, pushing two autonomous baggage trolleys.

'This is Tim McKee, my friend from university, and you remember Phil, don't you?'

We shook hands vigorously. His appearance was no different, but I could not fail to notice the latest change in his indecipherable accent.

'By the way, Jacques, I do love your suit,' said Lindsey as we made our way to the car park.

'Very threatening, don't you think?'

'I never realized airports over here employed bouncers.'

'Blame your sister - she chose it.'

'Had you been waiting long?'

'Less then five minutes. I had a meeting downtown. I wasn't sure I'd make it on time. Traffic was a bitch.'

Jacques packed our luggage into the 'trunk' of the car he had hired for his short stay in the city.

'Are you sure your friend won't mind having the pleasure of our company for a couple of nights?'

'Adam? No, not at all. I spoke to him only an hour ago. He's very obliging. You guys could turn up on his doorstep, explain who you were, and he would be happy to have you stay ... provided, of course, that you didn't trash the place.'

'We'll do our best not to.'

Once more we proceeded to crawl along a busy highway in air-conditioned comfort. I looked out at the surrounding area with a shameful feeling of indifference. Even the imposing Los Angeles skyline looked anything but extraordinary. I could see nothing to differentiate it from either Hong Kong Island or that other 'City of Angels' - Bangkok.

'Is your vacation living up to expectations?' asked Jacques, just as we were turning off towards the northern suburbs.

Tim spoke frankly. 'Lindsey hit the jackpot with a girl in Bangkok.'

'I know. He told me on the phone.' Jacques looked inquisitively at Lindsey in the rear-view mirror. 'I got the impression that you wanted to bring her along, am I right?'

Lindsey smiled, but all too briefly, then quickly diverted the discourse. 'What time do you have to leave tomorrow, Jacques?'

'Eleven thirty sharp. I shall probably be above the clouds by the time you three bums are fully conscious, and Adam will be at a meeting.'

'On a Sunday?'

'Occasionally, yes. His office is downtown, which is where he'll be for most of the day, but he won't mind you just coming and going as you please.'

'It really is kind of him. Is anything planned for tonight?'

'Well, as you're in town for only a few days, Nova proposed that I should take you all out for a bite to eat. Adam knows a new restaurant not far from where he lives. Do you like Italian food?'

'Yes, we all do.'

'Adam's sister might be joining us. Apparently she's keen to meet you.'

'Really?'

'She's currently studying at one of the universities here in LA, but don't ask me which one.'

'What is she like?'

Jacques paused before answering. 'I've only met her twice. Once was at a party in town, but I was so steaming drunk I couldn't remember a thing. The other time was at our place while she was on vacation with her Gatsby-esque cronies out on Long Island. She's attractive, intelligent, about nineteen or twenty. Adam *adores* her. The age gap between them is about fourteen years so, to be truthful, I guess he tends to be a little overprotective.'

We arrived at a broad, tree-lined driveway. Prestigious cars were dotted around outside six large detached houses - a reflection of life's big competition.

'Is this it?' Lindsey cooed, gazing into the street and, for once, stuck for sarcasm.

'This one right here. Each of these houses is as grand as a mansion but the actual plots are relatively tiny. I've seen bigger gardens on tenement balconies back in Newcastle.'

'What's the reasoning behind it?'

'These folks would have no time to tend big gardens because they are all way too busy working their tits off to pay the mortgages on their big houses. There's probably some sense in there somewhere, but you would have to ask someone else to find it for you.'

'You don't have a garden at all,' Lindsey reminded him.

'Yes I do. It's called *Central Park*.'

'But you don't have to pay for its upkeep.'

'I can assure you that I do.'

We parked at the end of the driveway and got out, leaving our bags in the boot. A short, bulky man opened the front door and walked a few steps towards us across the sun-lit lawn.

'Hello there,' he said in a soft, relaxed tone. 'Is everything OK?'

'Adam, this is my brother-in-law, Lindsey.'

'Happy to meet.'

'This is Tim ... and Phil, the resident daydreamer.'

He reached out and shook my hand firmly and sincerely. His shirt sleeves were rolled up to his elbows, and two bulging blue eyes peered with intent over a pair of rectangular, chrome-rimmed spectacles. A strong and resource-ful character, I thought to myself, accustomed to doing business with others and, more often than not, getting his own way.

'Welcome to LA, fellas. I have a case of beer waiting for you round the back. You must be quite thirsty.'

We followed him into his silently air-conditioned hallway, which had a polished wooden floor and old black and white portraits, presumably of illus-trious forebears, in elegant frames on the walls. Was his wealth self-created, I wondered, or simply inherited? According to Jacques, the entire neighbour-hood, and dozens just like it, had sprouted from the foundations of 'old' money.

Tim and I scanned the pictures and ornaments in turn. On one of the shelves stood an imposing marble bust of the pioneering industrialist Henry Ford, and through in the sitting room I noticed a strange chess set with hideously-shaped pinewood pieces.

'A shade different from Krasang,' Tim remarked quietly.

I reflected for a moment; the contrast could barely have been more exaggerated.

We followed our host through a large sliding door at the rear and sat in the open air on garden chairs at a square oak table. The next hour was, not surprisingly, spent discussing our frenetic exploits in Thailand and Hong Kong.

'Where next?' Adam asked. '*Sam Frank's Disco?* Vegas?'

'Not enough time,' Lindsey replied, somewhat curtly. 'We'll be flying to Toronto the day after tomorrow, then travelling across upstate New York to stay with Jacques and my sister for a few days. After that, we go home.' He stood up, finished his beer and returned to the car for the bags.

'I expect you'll be pretty deflated when you get back to the old country, Phil,' said Adam with a little sympathy.

'Lindsey already is - well, not deflated, but certainly withdrawn.'

Tim agreed. 'He misses Maalii more than he will admit.'

'He'll come to terms sooner or later,' said Jacques, optimistically. 'But I did notice that he was slightly subdued. He hasn't been shooting his mouth off as much as usual. Still, as I say, he'll come to terms.'

Tim was not convinced. 'I'm not so sure. If he were resigned to the fact that he'd seen her for the last time, then he wouldn't still be walking around in a dream. If you listen carefully enough, you can hear his brain cogs rotating.'

A silence descended when Lindsey reappeared with most of the luggage slung awkwardly over both shoulders. He knew instantly that we had been talking about him, but seemed not to care.

Adam jumped up and took hold of some of the bags. 'Feel free to put your belongings upstairs. The three of you will be sleeping in the same room, I'm afraid, but there's no shortage of space in there.'

'That's hardly a problem,' Lindsey replied, on his way back into the house. 'We've been sharing single rooms ever since we set out.'

The alcohol slowly took effect. I now felt abnormally relaxed, lounging like an idle aristocrat under the cloudless Californian sky. The monotony of home life had become just a vague memory, but I realized that the escape would very soon seem equally abnormal in its brevity, like a flicker of candle-light in the dead of night.

Adam reappeared at the door. 'Are any of your clothes dirty, guys?'

'Yes, all of them.'

'That's fine,' he chuckled. 'If you throw them into this basket when you get changed, they'll be laundered for when you leave on Monday.'

'Thank you.'

'How about we leave in an hour? The restaurant is only two or three kilometres from here. Erin, my sister, will be on her way over by now.'

We climbed the stairs to the room that had been set aside for us: an exquisitely decorated home office-cum-bedroom with a few carpeted steps dividing it into two levels. For once, the air-conditioning was perfect, unlike either the system in the Hong Kong hotel, which worked only during daytime, or the solitary, oscillating fan at Soi Phasuk which had been as useless as an open window.

Lindsey threw off his shirt, stood bare-chested at the window and shook his head slowly. 'Luxury,' he drooled. 'I feel that I'm indulging myself.'

'How come?'

He sat down and wiped his face which I noticed for the first time had become quite tanned. 'I feel uncomfortable lazing about in a place like this.'

'Why?'

'Maalii is sweating in the heat, sleeping on a mat and being forced to wash her clothes by hand. The contrast is embarrassing.'

'Her way of life is all she has ever known,' said Tim, correcting him, but in a supportive, non-patronizing kind of way.

'He's right,' I dared to add. 'She can't compare her lifestyle with one she has never experienced.'

I could now sense what he had really been feeling since leaving Bangkok. Unusually, his hard-nosed logic was becoming distorted by his emotions, and he needed no confirmation of it from Tim, me or anyone else.

'I'm sorry,' he sighed. 'It's getting to me a little. When we arrived in Hong Kong I managed to distract myself for a while, but as the days pass I can't seem to focus on anything else.' He looked up at us. 'That's the truth.'

'We can tell.'

'You can?'

'Sure, but we thought it would be wiser to leave you to your dreams. Jacques noticed straight away.'

'Anyway,' he said, in a slightly louder, restless voice, 'none of us knows how it will all unfold.'

Tim opened the bags. 'Come on, let's get ourselves sorted out. We need to be away in twenty minutes.'

Lindsey was no longer listening. 'This must be her,' he said, looking out of the front window.

'Who?'

'Adam's sister. What's her name?'

'Erin.'

He eyed her for a few seconds. 'She looks too well-heeled to be a student.'

I looked out inquisitively over the driveway. She was more attractive than Jacques had described: slightly taller than her brother, with fair, shoulder-length hair and wearing black jeans with an immaculate cream blouse tucked in at a trim waist.

A minute later we could hear her laughing with Jacques and Adam downstairs. As we changed our clothes, Tim looked into the large oval wall mirror and combed his hair with his fingers.

Lindsey returned to his normal self. 'Let's go. She won't fall for a basket-case like you.'

'That doesn't bother me,' said Tim.

Lindsey laughed. 'No? You hardly ever comb your hair.'

'Neither do you, which is why it resembles a lavatory brush.'

'But I'm not the one who's acting out of character.'

We walked outside and there she was, standing proud with her hands in her pockets. Again, Jacques politely introduced us in turn. Her voice seemed artificially high-pitched, and she spoke through a fixed smile.

'You must be Dr. Pardeau's brother-in-law,' she said, turning finally to Lindsey.

'Who gave you the description?' he joked.

'I saw your photograph in your sister's apartment last year.'

'I wasn't aware she had one.'

'An apartment?'

'No, a photograph.'

'You were standing on the Rialto Bridge in Venice, watching all the gondolas on the Grand Canal. You could easily have passed for an Italian.'

'I don't remember that being taken.'

'Your hair looks much longer now - and not as tidy, if I may say so.'

Tim smirked. 'You ought to see it on a bad day, when he doesn't wash it.'

The six of us returned to the front of the house and climbed into one of Adam's cars - an elongated station wagon with three rows of seats. Erin said nothing further, but watched Lindsey intently. The photograph had come to life, and with it, the partial fulfilment of her curiosity.

'Six in a car this size is much more comfortable than six in a tuk-tuk,' I remarked quietly to Lindsey.

He threw back his head as if about to laugh, but kept his thoughts to himself. I had unwittingly reminded him of Bangkok which made him stare blankly on to the street. The cogs were turning.

The short ride in such a large vehicle took me back to when Tim and I were small. Our Sunday afternoons had often been spent driving out to sprawling country parks in his family's ungainly estate car - affectionately nicknamed 'The Tank' - with his parents in the front, grandparents in the back and the two of us squashed behind them with footballs, tennis racquets and a hyperanimated Labrador who was not fussy about his sexual partners. Sometimes, as late as eight-thirty on a summer's evening, we would be miles from home, sitting on a rustic bench outside some remote pub, drinking lemonade and sharing packets of peanuts. This was innocence that had died long ago.

My patchy recollections were interrupted after five or ten minutes. We stopped at a small plaza surrounded by trees with leafy branches swaying lazily in all directions. The others, with the exception of Tim, had been deep in conversation since leaving the house, although I had no idea about what they had been discussing.

'OK, everybody, this is *La Serenissima*,' said Adam, opening his door.

We filed out and followed him to the restaurant which formed the gable-end of a prefabricated block of six identical units.

'So, tell me about your travels, Philip,' said Erin, as we perched ourselves on a row of immovable bar stools. 'Good fun so far?'

'Undoubtedly.'

'In that case, I hope nothing spoils it for you.'

I told her how we had met Maalii at the Plaza, and then spent the entire week with her, at Lindsey's request, trailing around the country, barely pausing for breath.

'The proverbial holiday romance, right?'

'More than that,' I protested. 'She and Lindsey became quite attached.'

She looked bemused, even a little sickened. 'Really?' she said, before eventually focusing on Lindsey who nodded thoughtfully. 'How could you communicate?' she then asked him. 'Could she speak English?'

'I picked up a little Thai,' he replied modestly, maintaining only minimal eye contact.

'Yes, in more ways than one.' She began to look even more puzzled, as well as wary, and seemed in no mood to let it drop. 'You didn't give her money, did you?'

'Yes. Yes, I did.'

'Don't you think you were being a little naive, maybe?'

Lindsey sat up and raised his eyebrows in a gesture of objection. 'Naive? In what way?'

'I didn't mean to offend you, but ...'

'But what?'

'Well, a few guys I know, who spent their vacation in Thailand, fell in over their heads with some cheap little oriental sex kittens and ended up drowning in a sea of debt. All they seemed to want was money, money and more money, and they knew that western holidaymakers have it to blow away.' She took a drink from a tall glass of grapefruit juice. 'Those girls operated with the efficiency of piranha fish and, take my word for it, they could be every bit as ruthless.'

She stood up and followed Adam, Jacques and Tim, who were conversing freely, to a long table in the far corner.

I hung around with Lindsey at the bar for a while longer. He shrugged his shoulders and smiled indifferently.

'Out with it,' he said.

'Who does she think she is?' I asked, incredulously. Without giving him time to open his mouth, I answered my own question. 'I get it: Adam has been kind enough to let us doss at his beautiful home, so you decided to bite your tongue. Is that about right?'

'I suppose it is.'

'I know, but even so-'

He interrupted without raising his voice. 'Did I ever tell you about my grandfather, back in Nottingham?'

'Which one, the coal miner?'

'That's right, my mum's father. He had this unaccountable ability to let crass remarks sail right over his head. Don't misunderstand me, he knew a fool when he encountered one, but would rarely be drawn into making his displeasure known.'

'But you're nothing like that,' I persisted.

'Perhaps not,' he admitted, belatedly, 'but I can aspire to it, can't I?'

'That's up to you.'

'Quite correct.' He patted me affectionately on the back. 'Let it pass, Phil,' he whispered, 'let it pass.'

We wandered across to our table which was decorated with ornamental green, white and red tricolours. Tim continued to relay tales of our Thailand days to the others who listened attentively and flicked through our books of photographs.

'Is this Maalii right here?' asked Jacques.

Lindsey leaned forward. 'Let me see ... yes, that's her.'

'She's pretty.'

'I know.'

'Where the hell was the picture taken?'

'Krasang,' Tim explained. 'That's where her parents live. It's about two hundred miles east of Bangkok.'

The pictures circulated in both directions around the table. Jacques seemed both fascinated and impressed, unlike Erin, who seemed to be thinking to herself that only those with a serious common-sense deficiency would voluntarily spend time in such a meagre place.

Lindsey spoke only occasionally, and stopped to smile at a picture of Maalii and himself, creased with laughter at the Plaza. Whatever Erin had to say, he was refusing to let go. Indeed, there must have been an overwhelming temptation for him to stay behind in Bangkok, thus aborting his own circumnavigation at the very first port of call.

'How's university life, Erin?' asked Jacques, who was now looking far less stressed than when we had met him at the airport. 'Are you setting the place alight? You certainly were looking forward to it.'

'I'm loving every minute of it,' she replied, evidently pleased that someone had raised the issue. 'It sure is hard work, as you well know, but it'll be worth it in the long term.'

'What are you studying?' Tim inquired respectfully.

'See if you can guess.'

'I have absolutely no idea.'

'Try.'

'No, really-'

'Go on, try.'

'Very well. Literature?'

'No.'

'Physics?'

'Not Physics,' said Lindsey quietly. He looked up at her without raising his head.

'How can you be so sure?' she wondered.

'You're not a scientist. I can tell.'

'So what am I studying?'

'I would say History.'

'Who told you?'

'No one.'

'Someone must have.'

'Not necessarily.'

'Was it Nova?'

'No.'

'Then how did you know?'

'I didn't.'

'But you did.'

'I was just guessing.'

'Medieval History and Theology,' she explained.

'Sounds about right.'

'And you? What did you do?'

'Mathematics - for a while.'

'What are you saying?'

'I completed the first year and a half of the course, got bored and quit.'

'You *quit*,' she laughed. 'Why did you do that?'

'I was bored.'

'Did you find the work too difficult.'

Lindsey smiled. I took over as he paused for thought.

'He's an idle genius,' I explained.

'So what made you give in?'

'I didn't give in - I gave *up*.'

'OK, you gave up. Why?'

'I was *bored*,' he pointed out for a third time.

'That is amazing,' she scoffed. 'Don't you regret it?'

'Not for a minute. Been perfectly happy ever since.'

She turned away, bewildered by his indifference, just as Tim and I had been at the time he announced his decision.

'What about you, Tim?'

'I have a degree in Behavioural Science. I work at one of our local hospitals.'

'Fascinating.'

'Sometimes it is. I'm hoping to specialize in Criminology. You know, forensics and so on.'

'I didn't attend college at all,' I admitted, before being asked. 'I just don't have the brains for it!'

She smiled. 'Very few of us do - and fewer still have the stamina to see it through.'

'That's another of my shortcomings,' I said.

To my relief, the prickly tension at the table evaporated. I could see that Erin had formed premature conclusions about Lindsey and was, more worryingly, prepared to air them in front of everyone else.

We returned to the house at eight o'clock, trying to ignore the fact that our third long-haul flight in ten days had knocked the life out of us. We spent the rest of the evening in Adam's converted basement, watching baseball on television - Cleveland Indians versus Chicago White Sox, although I must have spent half an hour trying to determine which was which.

Erin returned to campus, while Jacques and Adam sat at the kitchen table discussing the implications of their afternoon conference, using advanced in-house phrases such as 'corporate intranets', 'problem resolutions' and 'incompetent assholes'.

Tim broke the silence, as I knew he would. 'I hope she didn't annoy you.'

Lindsey, aware that Tim was fishing, smiled tentatively without taking his eyes off the game. 'Of course not. How could she?'

Tim jumped forward. 'She implied that Maalii was a prostitute. Did that not rankle?'

'Let's not forget where we are. If she were being tactless-'

'Tactless? She was being blatantly and unnecessarily offensive.'

'Perhaps so, but it wasn't my place to object.'

'Adam could have said something.'

'Yes, but he didn't.'

I could see that Tim was becoming increasingly perturbed, as much as a result of Lindsey's reticence as of Erin's lack of civility. 'Adam evidently thinks she can do no wrong. I can't think why.'

'Never mind. We shall be out of here the day after tomorrow, then she'll be just like her toilet-paper degree course - history.'

There the conversation ended, and Lindsey fell asleep in his armchair.

XI

**'What is food to one man
is bitter poison to others.'**

Lucretius (c99-55BC)
On the Nature of the Universe

Jacques breezed in at ten thirty.

'I'll see you in Manhattan, fellas. Nova has been looking forward to your visit for months.'

Tim and I stood up and shook his hand again.

'The Port Authority Terminal is on West 42nd Street,' he explained. 'If you want a lift to our place, call us when you get off the bus. If, on the other hand, you prefer to walk, then head straight up Eighth Avenue to Columbus Circle and along Central Park West. Lindsey knows his way around in case you forget.'

'He's asleep,' I whispered, after scribbling his directions on the back of an envelope.

'Yes, I thought it was quiet down here. Anyhow, leave him where he is. He's been looking jaded all evening. He probably needs all the shuteye he can get.'

'Don't think that's the reason he hasn't been his usual self,' I tried to point out. 'He spends most of his time thinking about Maalii. He's as frustrated as hell that she's so far away.'

'I gathered that too. I don't suppose Erin made him feel any better.'

'You're right, but he won't admit it. I wasn't sure you'd noticed.'

'Noticed? It was as plain as the dirt in his hair. To be honest, though, Nova couldn't stand the sight of her, either. She can be so thoughtless. Well, have a good time in Canada.'

Tim smiled. 'We will.'

We saw him to his car and watched as he set off back to his downtown hotel. It was impossible not to admire Jacques. He oozed can-do. Friendship between someone like him and myself was almost an honour - in my favour.

'OK, guys, it's time for me to hit the hay,' said Adam, walking back along the driveway towards the front door. 'Stay downstairs and watch TV, if you like. I have cable - not that I have ever made much of it.'

'Thanks.'

'Another thing, I have to be away early tomorrow and I won't be home until seven in the evening. You'll find a spare door key in your room, so feel free to do whatever you wish, and I'll catch up with you in the evening.'

'Goodnight.'

Back down in the basement, Lindsey was still asleep in exactly the same position, in spite of the frequent eruptions of noise emanating from the sports commentary.

'Let's leave him,' Tim suggested.

He switched off the television and all but one of the lights, and we spent the midnight hours playing cribbage and knocking back bottled beer at the kitchen table.

'I don't honestly know how he managed to keep his lid on,' he muttered, referring to Erin's tactless provocations.

'Neither do I.'

'Believe it or not, Phil, I think she liked you.'

I sat back, uneasily. 'How could you tell?'

'By her body language, and the way she was looking at you over dinner.' A teasing grin spread itself across his face.

'You've had too much to drink.'

'I'm *telling* you,' he protested, still smiling. 'Ask Lindsey in the morning. He'll back me up.'

I thought of what she had said about poor Maalii. 'Well, it's not reciprocated.'

'Why not?'

'Her manners are non-existent and ... and she's just not my type.'

'But isn't she a picture?' he went on.

'Yes - in depth,' came a quiet voice from behind me.

I looked over my shoulder and saw Lindsey standing in the doorway. He looked utterly exhausted, and his hair was even less tidy than usual, rats' tails hanging over his squinting eyes which he was shielding from the bright, fluorescent kitchen lights.

'We thought you were out for the night,' said Tim.

'I hoped I would be. Were you discussing Her Ladyship?'

'Briefly.'

'I'll bet.'

'Do you think she took a shine to Phil?'

'No. She was too obvious. Sorry, old fruit.'

'No harm done.'

Lindsey poured himself a glass of chilled apple juice. 'I'm going to sleep in the chair. It's more comfortable than most beds I've tried out.'

'Very well. See you in the morning.'

'Goodnight.'

The door closed and the stairs creaked slightly as he returned to the basement.

'Did you notice his eyes?' were Tim's next words.

'What about them?'

'They look like death.'

We crept upstairs and crashed out on the spare beds that Adam had provided. All was silent. I could not even hear the sound of passing cars. Undisturbed, I mulled things over inside my head: after all the travelling had been consigned to the inevitable past, I would return to life's routine and probably become even more depressed than usual. In the light of everything I had experienced in less than a fortnight, I was rapidly arriving at the conclusion that every one of my twenty-six years had been essentially empty.

I thought of Krasang once again - in particular, the roadside shack, which I could picture almost as vividly as my own cottage.

I awoke several times during the night as bullets of rain hammered against the windows and, consequently, I felt even more drowsy in the morning. To hell with California, I was thinking. I needed to rest. If Tim and Lindsey had disappeared without me, I would not have objected.

As it turned out, they had not. I rolled over and peered across the room to where Tim was lying, motionless and half-dressed, his bare feet uncovered. I staggered sluggishly across the room to look outside. Rain poured relentlessly from a grey, almost blackened, sky. I had assumed that it never rained in California.

'I'm knackered,' Tim groaned in a hypnotic whisper. 'And my head feels as big as a pumpkin. I don't think I can be bothered going anywhere.'

He got up and rubbed his eyes. I sat down next to him and picked up his watch from the carpet. It was almost midday. We had only another twenty-four hours in which to explore what we could of LA, and we were becoming resigned to seeing even less of it than we had of Hong Kong. The fact that neither of us cared was probably the result of having already experienced so much. Our sensory faculties seemed to be approaching saturation point.

'I can't keep my eyes open,' he yawned. 'Let's go down and find out what Lindsey is doing.'

'You can sprawl out on the couch.'

'Provided he isn't on it.'

We shuffled downstairs and entered the spacious front room where Lindsey was reading a newspaper with the lights on and the curtains still drawn. If Tim and I looked haggard, Lindsey was far worse. He had not shaved since leaving Hong Kong which made him look particularly dishevelled, and his eyes were slightly bloodshot.

'How about we do absolutely nothing?' he suggested.

'Agreed. You must have read our minds.'

'Besides, the weather will probably be better than this in Toronto.'

'How do you know?'

'I've just seen the forecast on TV in the basement. Seventy degrees and sunny across the entire southern part of Ontario.'

Tim became restless. 'I feel that we're nothing more than squatters in this place.'

'Sit down. You'll get used to it. I have.'

'I know Adam doesn't mind but, nevertheless, I feel we ought to have gone elsewhere. When Erin was here yesterday, she must have seen us as three total strangers descending into her brother's space, without a proper invitation, almost like parasites.'

Lindsey shook his head. 'Your conscience dominates you to an unhealthy extent. Did they teach you that in *shrink school*?'

Tim answered back. 'I could just sense that she thought we were using him!'

'We are.'

'Personally, I couldn't care less what Erin might think,' I said. '*Screw* Erin.'

Lindsey sprang up from his chair. 'Well, here's your opportunity,' he said, peering through the front window.

'For what?'

'She's here.'

'She must know that Adam is out,' said Tim, in mild annoyance. 'What on earth does she want with us?'

As the key turned in the lock, I began to feel distinctly uneasy, and immediately appreciated what Tim had just said about our having effectively invaded the place. I noticed also just how untidy the room looked: Lindsey had scattered newspapers, books and saucerless coffee cups all over the table and carpet.

'Hello,' I said.

Unsurprisingly, she looked surprised. 'Aren't you guys going out sometime today?' She had certainly not expected to find us inside her brother's house at one thirty in the afternoon.

'We were rather tired after yesterday.'

'Yes, we've just this minute rolled out of bed,' Lindsey interrupted, 'although not the same one, you know.'

'That's something,' she said, unimpressed by his reference to the ridiculous notion that the three of us were sexually involved.

'You look very smart,' Lindsey then remarked, with as much courtesy as he could muster. 'Where are you headed?'

'Nowhere now. I've just been to church. That is what Sundays are for, in case you didn't know.'

'Grovelling on my hands and knees doesn't appeal to me, I'm afraid.'

She exhaled angrily. 'You ought to open your mind sometime. You might learn something.'

Tim was looking very edgy but did not speak.

'Don't you have faith in God?' she asked, dismissively.

'No, why should I?' He was inviting her to strike the first blow, as was his way.

She rose to it squarely. 'So you doubt the intellectual value of religion, do you? That's rich, coming from a drop-out who has to scrape a living mending watches.'

'Could you mend a watch?' he challenged her. 'You wouldn't understand the graceful workings of a watch any better than you would the workings of your own brain - comparable though they may be, in terms of size.'

I tried desperately to stifle a burst of laughter.

'Besides,' he added, 'I don't repair just watches.'

'No?'

'I do clocks too.'

'Clocks! You do *clocks*! Oh, I apologize for underestimating you!'

'Accepted. So tell me - how come you're so certain that there's a god?'

'God is everywhere. I can feel a presence inside me right now.'

Lindsey's eyes widened. '*Inside* you? Are you wet between your legs?'

'That is disgusting! I meant inside my *head*.'

'You hear things inside your head? That smacks of schizophrenia.'

'How come?'

'Can you prove, not to us, but to yourself, that your god is more than just a figment of a twisted imagination? Can you? Can you prove it to *yourself*?'

'Listen, I don't need to do that in order to satisfy someone like you.'

'Of course you don't. Doubting would be too dangerous.'

She sat down on the coffee table, right opposite him, fully prepared for the exchange of gratuitous insults to continue. I glanced repeatedly towards the front door, hoping that Adam would not return home unannounced.

'Perhaps if you had completed your university course,' she taunted him, 'you might have pondered the very basic question: who made us?'

'I knew the answer to that before I even applied for my place. Billions of years of blind, purposeless evolution.'

'And how does so much beauty in nature come about without a mind to conceive it?'

'If you don't know, then you ought to reserve your judgement.'

'You are so arrogant!' she exclaimed. 'Are other people not permitted to hold a different opinion? Is yours somehow more valid than mine?'

'It appears so. How can an uneducated mind be capable of making an educated judgement? You are the arrogant one: you form conclusions on a subject that you barely comprehend.'

'So who do you suppose Jesus Christ was? Was he a figment of many more *twisted imaginations*?'

'I'll tell you who Jesus Christ was. He was a lowly man who contrived to exert influence upon his contemporaries. In their ignorance, the masses have made an art form of elevating their heroes and leaders to supernatural status. They still do.' He paused for a moment. 'Worship and idolatry are the twin pillars at the entrance to the temple of insanity.'

'Really? And which unpoetic moron said that? Some two-dollar village atheist?'

'Phil's mother, actually. Dead these last few years.'

Such was her mood, she could not bring herself to turn her head and offer me even the merest hint of an apology. For that reason, I began to relish every cutting remark that Lindsey was throwing at her.

There followed an awkward silence. I tried to make myself as small as possible, anxious to avoid being dragged into an argument that I did not even fully understand.

'I'm sure you quote your own mother's opinions, Erin,' he persisted. 'After all, religious myths are inherited almost as faithfully as the genetic data that make it possible. Children take it in with their mother's breast milk. Is that not what you did?'

Her lower lip began to quiver slightly. 'My mother died last month.'

My anxiety intensified. But at least she now knew the pain an insult to the memory of one's mother could cause. It served her right.

Lindsey's offensive drove onward. 'You haven't answered my question,' he rasped. 'Did your mother force-feed you with God? Did she rape your mind when you were a little girl?'

'*Stop it!*' she snarled. 'Don't you dare speak of my mother in such a disrespectful manner!'

'Why not? She can't hear anything.'

The row escalated to a level reminiscent of the days when my father was alive. Tim and I stood up and, without a word to either of them, sloped off into the basement and switched on the television in order to distract ourselves.

'I could envisage this happening,' he said, once we were safely out of earshot. 'She has been provoking him ever since they met.'

'But why?'

He shrugged. 'It seems she had something or other to prove. Either that or she was extraordinarily jealous of Maalii.'

'Whatever her motives, she's sure to tell Adam when he arrives home. He won't take kindly to a total stranger fighting with his precious kid sister.'

After half an hour, we began to hear Erin's raised voice echoing ominously down the stairs. In truth, all shouting matches trashed my nerves, thanks again to my dear father. My reaction to aggressive arguments had almost acquired the status of a so-called 'conditioned reflex', just as Pavlov's dog had salivated at the sound of a bell before being fed.

'But in his case,' Tim had once pointed out, 'what transpired actually brought the creature a modicum of satisfaction.'

The two of us tried unsuccessfully to concentrate on the television programme - a drab cowboy film from the forties or fifties. The dispute, I kept telling myself, had nothing to do with us.

She began to rant venomously, although her exact words were unclear.

Tim got to his feet. 'This is no use,' he said restlessly. 'Adam is going to explode when he finds out. Why don't we get lost?'

I considered what he had said. 'Are you serious?'

He began to pace up and down in front of the television. 'Our flight to Toronto is tomorrow, so we could check into an airport hotel this evening.'

'They don't come cheap.'

'What the hell? What's the alternative? I don't want to be here when Adam walks in.'

'You're right. Let's get back upstairs.'

Lindsey was sitting in the same place on the couch. Newspapers covered the carpet. Erin was holding her face in her hands, crying to herself, because of herself, and in spite of herself. The moment we opened the door, she moved her hands and looked straight into my eyes. Her face was red and streaked with half an hour's tears. It was impossible not to feel sorry for her, but I could not entirely forgive her for having been so heartless towards both my mother and my loyal friend.

Lindsey spoke very calmly, as if they had, in our absence, somehow reconciled their differences. 'Death is irreversible, Erin. You won't ever see your mother again for the same reason that I'll never see my father. The concept of heaven is just another foundationless but well-propagated myth.'

Her crying became hysterical, and she began to shake from head to foot.

Lindsey waxed philosophical, in his own strange style. 'The process of logical reasoning runs like a train across a vast archipelago, linking together only the islands of truth. Heaven isn't one of them. There is no afterlife.'

'Just shut up!'

He did not. 'The flesh of our bodies, buried in the earth, is consumed by our own ravenous bacteria. What do you think of that?'

'I've had enough of this bullshit!' she screamed. 'I only came here to collect some photographs. I did not intend to sit here and be lectured to by someone as *vicious* as you!'

Lindsey remained where he was, and smiled disdainfully. 'Get off your knees, Erin. Get off your knees. Your prayers are futile.'

She ran across to the door. 'Fuck you! Pope Pius the Twelfth said that man is great *only* when he is kneeling!'

Lindsey stood up. 'Well he would! If you get off your knees, you lame bitch, you might discover that you can walk!'

'Why don't you just disappear back to your little island and play with your broken watches?'

'Why don't *you* go and join your mother?'

'Go *fuck yourself! Hard!*'

She stormed out, slamming her brother's front door. None of us uttered a sound as she started the engine and sped recklessly down the road. Lindsey stumbled into the kitchen. He still looked hungover, and an even layer of dark stubble now covered the lower half of his face.

A minute later, he reappeared and began to tidy the newspapers and cups.

'I'm sorry,' he said softly, without looking directly at either of us. 'I lost control of myself. I should have known better than to do that.'

'That's all right,' I said, uneasily. 'I don't know why she had to be so obnoxious towards you in the first place.'

'Still no excuse, Phil, especially as she will doubtless relay the entire story, or at least her version of it, to Adam ... assuming, of course, that she isn't already in the process of doing so.'

'True. She must have a phone in a car like that. Shall we clear out before we are thrown out?'

Lindsey blew out his cheeks and sighed loudly. 'It would seem sensible. But we ought to straighten the place up a little, otherwise Adam will be furious with Jacques for having vouched for us.'

Lindsey cleared the mess from the coffee table while Tim and I shot upstairs to pack the bags. My heart hammered uncomfortably against the inside of my ribcage. In an instant, I felt that we had become trespassers, burglars even, dashing frantically to and fro in the knowledge that the slightest delay could wreck our devious plan.

'I knew it, Phil.'

'Knew what?'

'I felt uneasy about coming here from the outset.'

'You never said anything at the time.'

'Only because you didn't, either.'

Lindsey barged in, carrying his books and the shoes we had left in the basement the previous night.

'Where are the passports?' I asked.

'I have them here,' he replied.

'I've brought too much baggage,' said Tim.

'I told you that in Liverpool - twice at home then again at the station. Now, surprise, surprise, you find you can't get the guts back inside the belly. Here, we'll be needing these.' He handed Tim the air tickets for the following day.

It was not long before our bags were packed and the bedroom looked exactly as it had done when we had first opened its door - as if no one ever came into the place.

'Don't forget the stuff in the bathroom!' called Tim, now on all fours, checking for anything that might have rolled under the bed - the one which Lindsey had not even touched.

We stuffed toothbrushes, shampoo and shaving foam bottles into the bags, not caring where they came to rest.

'Right!' I puffed. 'That's it. Are you sure there's nothing else? If there is, I don't imagine it will be getting sent on.'

We stood still for a few seconds. Tim appeared easily the most anxious; Lindsey merely looked like a man who had not slept for a week, which was not far from the truth.

'We can phone for a taxi from the shopping plaza down the road. It won't take more than a few minutes.'

The sound of the front door being opened seemed to send a tremor through the entire house.

'She's back!' Tim exclaimed. 'What the hell does she want now?'

Lindsey dragged his hair back with his fingers and stepped across to the window. We looked at him in nervous anticipation.

'It's Adam.'

'Shit! You are joking!' Tim gasped, running to the window to see for himself.

'No I'm not. See?'

'What is he doing back?'

'He lives here - remember?'

'He said he'd be out until seven!'

'She must have told him everything,' I surmised. 'Now what?'

'Well, we can't stay up here forever.'

We crept sheepishly downstairs. On reaching the kitchen, however, there was no sign of anyone. The back door was still locked, and the only sound we could hear was the continuous humming noise from the freezer.

'There you are!' came a harassed voice from the top of the basement stairs.

Tim jumped and turned around quickly.

'I assumed you guys would be out cruising Sunset Boulevard. I didn't expect to find you here just yet.'

Likewise, I thought. 'We were too exhausted to go out today,' I admitted, 'not to mention the good old English weather.'

'The rest will have done us good,' Tim added.

'Well, that's important, I guess. Have you eaten yet?'

'We've had breakfast.'

'Is that all? No lunch?'

'We did get up rather late.'

Adam removed his jacket and hung it on the top of the kitchen door.

'I have an idea,' he said brightly. 'I'll drive down to Pedro's, which is about a mile from here, and bring us back a take-out. You all like Tex-Mex?'

'Yes ... yes, anything like that,' Tim replied nervously. 'Here, we'll give you some money.'

'No, this is my treat, guys. Save your greenbacks for when you arrive in New York City. There'll be heaps of stuff you'll want to spend it on over there.' He grabbed his keys from the table. 'OK, give me a few minutes.'

We stood rooted to the kitchen floor as he slipped back out and closed the door behind him.

XII

'The cruellest lies are often told in silence.'

Robert Louis Stevenson (1850-94)
Virginibus Puerisque

The nervous silence returned. Tim looked at me and sighed.

'So he doesn't know,' he stated, then shook his head pensively. 'I feel extremely guilty about all this.'

'I was the villain. Why should you feel guilty?' said Lindsey, mocking and reassuring him simultaneously. 'I'm not asking you to empathize.'

'I wasn't. I feel bad about the sheer deceit, of which we are all now culpable. Here we are, in his house, soon to be eating food that he has bought, and drinking beer from his fridge. He'll almost certainly discover what happened before we leave tomorrow. Then what?'

'Shall we disappear now, while he is out?' I interrupted.

'Not now he has gone to buy our dinner.' I could detect the helplessness in his voice.

'He's right, Phil,' Lindsey added calmly. 'We ought to stay until tomorrow. If, heaven forbid, we get thrown out in the middle of the night, then we can head for the airport and crash out in the departures lounge. Still, I don't believe it'll come to that.'

We waited downstairs. I could not even bring myself to sit down. Tim picked up a newspaper in an attempt to compose himself. I could see that he was not digesting a single word of it, only staring blankly at the requisite pretty face on the front page while his mind conjured up possible outcomes of the remaining hours to be spent in a place we were now desperate to leave.

'I almost wish I'd stayed at home,' I said, jokingly.

'I wish I'd stayed at Soi Phasuk,' Lindsey replied, totally earnestly, under his breath, while gazing through the kitchen window at the waterlogged garden.

Tim placed the newspaper neatly on the coffee table and said nothing more. I walked over to Lindsey and looked outside. The cloudburst had finally run its course, leaving a saturated lawn and heavy foliage dripping in the early evening haze.

'Does it remind you of home?' I asked him.

'Not quite Sherwood Forest,' he remarked, 'but it's green and pleasant.'

'Home in nine days.'

'Don't be so negative!' he spluttered, and turned to look at me with an expression that belied his obvious fatigue. 'There's no limit to the fun we can have in that time.' He gazed upon the garden again. 'Once we're out of here, that is.' His emerald eyes, normally sharp and darting, were heavily glazed, like those of an ailing old dog.

The unnerving rattle of key in lock preceded the reappearance of Adam in the hallway, this time bearing plastic bags and polystyrene cartons which contained our evening meal. It was yet another act of generosity for the benefit of his three parasites. I was beginning to think with Tim's ready sense of shame.

'OK, here it is,' he said quietly. 'There should be another case of beer in the basement. Could one of you go down and collect it?'

'I'll go,' I was quick to say.

I made my way down the basement stairs and walked over to a small corner room which contained a huge freezer, and a washing machine full of our clothes. Had we disappeared, they would have been left behind.

I loitered there for a minute, silent and still - the slightest excuse to escape the awkward exchanges taking place in the kitchen. Adam was certainly an intelligent, perceptive man; I found it difficult to believe that he would be unable to deduce that something was not what it seemed.

Reluctantly, I picked up the cardboard box, which contained twelve bottles of ice-cold American beer, and returned to the kitchen, where the parasites' banquet of ribs, fajitas and a mountain of fries covered the table. No expense had been spared, which simply compounded my discomfort.

Lindsey and Adam had already settled themselves in the sitting room and were devouring their food while conversing about trivialities so trivial that, in less polite company, they might have fallen asleep.

Tim picked hesitantly at what was laid out on the table.

'Don't you feel guilty?' he whispered.

'A little,' I replied, helping myself to liberal quantities of food.

'I don't think he does,' he said, glancing through the open doorway at an inappropriately-relaxed Lindsey.

'He must feel some degree of regret.'

'I'm not convinced, Phil. Sometimes he just doesn't care. One of my colleagues at the hospital reckons he bears the hallmarks of a socialized psychopath!'

'But psychopaths are evil.'

'True, but some contrive to disguise it with astounding ingenuity.' He looked at me quizzically. 'Don't you blame him for what happened earlier?'

'No, he was justified in standing his ground.'

Tim shook his head thoughtfully but refrained from prolonging his evident disapproval of my expression of solidarity.

'Are you eating yours out there?' Lindsey called.

'Let's go,' I said. 'He's facing it on his own.'

We entered the front room, carrying our piles of food and placed them on the coffee table which, only a couple of hours previously, had been strewn with newspapers and dirty cups.

Lindsey feigned interest in Adam's work arrangements, nodding in agreement and occasionally sounding surprised on learning of all the places he covered.

'I guess I do get around a little,' Adam confessed modestly, in between enormous mouthfuls of food. 'Thirty flights last month alone, most of them between here and other cities in or near California. San Diego, Seattle, Phoenix. It has become as much a way of life as getting into the goddam car every morning!'

The telephone rang. I looked at Tim. He immediately stopped eating. Adam continued his painfully superficial conversation with Lindsey as he pushed himself out of his armchair and walked over to answer it.

'I should be spending the next week or two here in LA, as far as I know.' He picked up the handset. 'Hello.'

I held my breath.

'Yes. Yes, they're still here.'

He turned, telephone pressed to his ear, and looked at us blankly. None of us, not even Lindsey, seemed able to move. I looked down at all the food and beer, which had been provided for us in ignorance. I could sense Tim's frayed nerves as acutely as my own.

The silence lasted a minute before we heard another word.

'Yes ... OK. Call it twelve, then. Provided nothing else blows up in the meantime. Fine. See you tomorrow.' He replaced the handset and returned to his chair.

'Everything all right?' Lindsey probed, politely.

'Sure. That was one of the sales directors from the office. He never stops.'

The relief was overwhelming.

'I told him yesterday that I'd be giving you guys a lift to LAX tomorrow and, therefore, I wouldn't be at the office until lunchtime.'

'You didn't have to-'

'No big deal, really. What time is your flight?'

'Eleven thirty.'

'OK, so if we leave here just before nine, that ought to give you plenty of time to check in. It's a busy airport.'

'Thanks very much,' said Tim with a sickly smile.

Escape delayed even further, I thought. I never imagined that our much-anticipated adventure could have me wishing away the time, especially when so little of it remained. Only when Adam had left the room did the three of us make eye contact with each other.

'I thought that was Erin calling!' said Tim, leaning across the table, eyes wide open.

'So did I,' I said.

Lindsey put down his beer bottle. 'Never mind the phone,' he interrupted. 'How would you feel if she called in?'

'She won't do that.'

'Oh won't she?'

'No. There's no way she'll show up while we're still here.'

Lindsey opened another bottle just as Adam reappeared. 'We shall see.'

He sounded disturbingly confident that his antagonist would return prior to our departure. Had she told him as much, I wondered, or did that annoying intuition of his stretch further than I realized?

We finished eating and stacked the empty plates and dishes on top of the table.

'Thanks, Adam,' I said. 'Very kind of you.'

'My pleasure. You know, it's good to have some company other than tiresome dweebs from the office talking nothing but share prices and profit margins.'

I jumped into the air when the telephone rang a second time, filling me with foreboding, as if it were an air-raid siren or something. We sat in silence once more as Adam answered the call.

'Hello.'

Twice lucky, I wondered?

'Oh, hi, kid. What are you up to?'

This time there was no doubt as to the caller's identity. We listened intently, clinging to every nuance and trying hopelessly to speculate about what Erin might have been saying at the other end of the line. Characteristically, she proceeded to do most of the talking, whereas Adam remained as expressionless as he had during the previous call, giving only his usual concise, businesslike replies.

'No, that won't be a problem, Erin. Yes. Yes, I'll see that it all gets sorted out.'

Lindsey casually picked up the plates and empty bottles, and carried them into the kitchen. Meanwhile, the conversation showed no signs of coming to a swift end.

'Erin, are you sure you're OK?'

There was another pause. I glanced towards the kitchen where I could see Lindsey tidying the waste paper and dirty dishes, now apparently unconcerned.

'You don't sound fine to me. Come on, Erin, what's eating you?'

Yet another tense silence overwhelmed the room, this time lasting much longer.

'Of course you can,' he continued, in a soft, fatherly voice. 'What time do you want to come over?'

Again, I looked into the kitchen. Lindsey, in a show of pure *sangfroid*, peered through the doorway and nonchalantly pointed a finger at me. 'I told you so!' he mouthed.

'All right, I'll see you at eight thirty tomorrow. And take it easy - do you hear me?'

As he said a tender goodnight to her and replaced the handset, Lindsey reappeared with his fourth or fifth bottle of beer, sat down with his legs outstretched onto the rug and tapped his fingertips rhythmically on the chair arms.

'Was that Erin?' he asked innocently.

'It was.'

'Is she all right?'

I could barely believe what I was hearing; I just wanted him to keep quiet. Adam sat down opposite and looked straight at him. I prepared myself for the worst.

'She'll be fine,' he replied, unconvincingly. 'Our mother passed away only five weeks ago. Brain tumour. Three unsuccessful operations. Gave her three years of living hell. Erin has been having a real hard time ever since the burial. Some days she copes, others she gets terribly depressed. The slightest thing that reminds her of mom sets her off. Still, she's a tough old egg. Everything will be back on the level pretty soon.'

'I'm sure.'

'She's going skiing ten days from now. That ought to pick her up.'

'Where's she going?'

'Banff, Alberta. She goes up there about twice a year.'

'We had no idea that it had happened so recently,' Tim explained apologetically. 'Had we known of your bereavement, particularly with it being your mother, we wouldn't have imposed upon you.'

'It's really not a problem. As I said, it's not every day I get visitors, certainly not from London!'

His geographical *faux pas* went uncorrected. I began to feel marginally less tense, and I could see that Tim was trying his utmost to defuse the device which was still, in his view, destined to explode.

'Did you say you'd been here *all* day?'

'Yes, we were tired,' Tim reiterated.

Adam looked puzzled. 'That's strange. Erin said she came round to collect some old portraits of mom which she intends to frame for her new apartment. It would have been about one thirty in the afternoon. I'm surprised you didn't see her. Were you all still sleeping?'

I looked at Tim, hoping he would once again find the right words.

'We did see her,' said Lindsey casually, 'but she didn't stay long.'

Considering that she viewed Adam as a parent figure, I was amazed that she had not told him what - or rather who - had exacerbated the pain in her already badly-resolving wound.

'Oh. So you have seen her, right? You never said. I assumed you hadn't.' He peeked over the top of his spectacles. 'Did she look OK to you?'

Tim gulped. 'I guess so.'

'She did seem rather stressed,' Lindsey added, 'and incredibly uptight.'

Tim interrupted again. 'Although we had no idea why.'

'Well, I expect you'll be seeing her tomorrow morning. Then, after I've dropped you guys at the airport, I'll take her to the *Phoneys' Nest* for breakfast.'

'I assume that's a cafe of some sort.'

'Of some sort, most definitely. It's about six or seven blocks west of here - mostly full of amnesic old bullshitters bragging to each other about stuff they've never done. To hear this one guy tell it, you'd swear he won the war all by himself. It's nothing swanky, but it is relaxed, and homely. I ought to be able to pick her brains a little.'

The relief was immense. At least, by then, we would be on our way to Toronto, never to return. I glanced at the large mahogany clock standing proudly on one of the shelves above the back of Lindsey's chair: less than eleven hours remained, most of which were to be spent sleeping, but the feeling of liberation was being all but neutralized by the prospect of coming face to face with Erin in the morning.

Adam left the room and began to clear what remained of the mess in the kitchen.

'He doesn't know!' said Tim in disbelief. 'She hasn't told him!'

'She will,' Lindsey muttered. 'Give her time. I think she views breaking down in front of her brother as a weakness, particularly as we are still here. But believe me, she'll squeal eventually.' He then smirked mischievously. 'And as far as her precious faith is concerned, the seeds of doubt will already be taking root.'

He was sounding increasingly unsympathetic. Tim was right: his sole regret was having lost his composure, rather than the actual things he had said.

'Don't forget your clothes, guys!' Adam called from the kitchen. 'I put them in the machine this morning before I went out. They should be clean and dry by now.'

Tim stood up and walked towards the doorway. 'Thanks. I'll get them, then we can pack.' He looked at Lindsey and me in turn, then signalled discreetly for us to go upstairs. Any excuse to get out of the way seemed sensible. After all, every second we spent making polite, if vacuous, conversation with our host was now a display of audacious deceit, every word spoken a cruel charade.

'I love your chess pieces, Adam!' enthused Lindsey who, to Tim's displeasure, seemed determined to remain where he was.

'Beautifully grotesque, wouldn't you say?' came the delayed reply. Adam walked in, wiping his hands vigorously on a towel. 'The set used to belong to my father. He brought it back from Tanzania, hence the pieces' distinctive facial morphology. Every one of them was hand-carved, no less.'

'That explains why some of the pawns are bigger than others.'

He lifted the heavy board and placed it carefully on the coffee table to enable Lindsey to take a closer look. 'Do you play?' he then asked.

'Yes, do you?'

'Sure I do. Would you like a game?'

'On one condition.'

'Uh-oh. You're sounding like Erin. She generally insists on playing with two queens.'

'Nothing quite so unfair.'

'Go on.'

'Resignation is not permitted. We have to play right to the death.'

Adam looked confused, as well he might. 'Would that not become somewhat futile?'

'Perhaps.' Lindsey leaned forward, almost menacingly. 'I like to pick off my opponent's pieces one by one, then force the defenceless king into a corner. A lame fox about to be ripped apart by a pack of rabid hounds.'

'A chess-playing sadist, huh? Well, as you wish!'

Adam evidently assumed that the proposal had been made in jest. I myself was not certain, but I knew who would win the contest.

Adam returned to the kitchen to put away the towel before settling down to play. Lindsey laughed surreptitiously while he was out of the room.

'A *chess-playing sadist*, he called me. I thought, given the immeasurable amount of suffering that characterizes the animal kingdom, he was referring to the Great Architect himself.'

I returned to the bedroom without replying to his blasphemous diatribe. Encouragement was the last thing he needed. Tim appeared a couple of minutes later, carrying our clean clothes which had never smelled quite so fresh. I continued to count the hours until departure.

'He's pushing his luck,' said Tim angrily. 'You know, I wouldn't be surprised if he actually confesses to Adam what happened ... and thinks nothing of it.'

'He won't,' I said. 'He's not stupid.'

'I never said he was. I just don't think he feels guilt. Some of the things he said about their mother were as repugnant as anything I have ever heard.'

We spent what remained of the evening leafing through tattered travel guides and the books Lindsey had bought in Bangkok. At eleven o'clock, he barged in, leaving the door open behind him.

'He's got a nerve, you know!'

'Keep your voice down!' Tim told him.

'I won the first game easily, the second had barely taken shape when he decided he'd had enough, and shall I tell you what he said? Shall I tell you? "One game each." Can you believe that?'

'Keep your voice down!'

'He said we'd have to play a decider some time. I'm not joking, some people just can't accept the inevitable. *Canute* van Bergen!'

'Stop droning, will you? And why are you looking so bloody relaxed, apart from the obvious reason?'

Lindsey sprawled on the bed, clasped his hands behind his head, and put on a silly grin - the sort only a drunk is ever capable of wearing.

'How did you know Erin would be coming round in the morning?'

'Instinct.'

I smiled at him. He looked a wreck. Not only had he neither washed nor shaved all day but, having waded through umpteen bottles of beer, he was now barely able to lift his eyelids.

'So you knew *instinctively* that she'd return, did you?' said Tim. 'Where's your crystal ball?'

Lindsey paused for a moment, presumably to refocus his eyes. 'Crystal balls are for the intellectually myopic, old fruit,' he scoffed, and began to chuckle to himself.

Tim shook his head impatiently, probably wishing there were a length of rope at hand with which he could throttle some anxiety into his annoying companion. 'Don't you care about what happened earlier?'

'No.'

'Don't you feel any remorse? Any regret?'

'No.'

'Well you should!'

Lindsey opened his eyes and looked across at him without raising his head from the pillow. 'Really? Well, *Mr. Rent-a-conscience*, if you think back to yesterday evening in the basement, you were imploring me to object to her dreadful manners.' His eyes closed again. 'Don't scold me for taking your advice.'

'I, personally, wouldn't have taken it quite so far. But never mind about that. How come you were so bloody convinced that she'd come back?'

'Simple. Because she thinks that, on reflection, showing her face again would make me feel uneasy.'

'And don't you? No, of course you don't.'

'She doesn't know that, though,' Lindsey replied, as if sharing an important secret. 'Still, if, like her brother, she enjoys games, we'll carry on playing.'

At two o'clock in the morning neither Tim nor I had succeeded in disconnecting our thoughts from the events of an afternoon which had been derailed. We lay wide awake in our parallel beds, only a few rays of light from outside disturbing the darkness of the night. Lindsey had been sound asleep for almost three hours, the occasional stir from the far end of the room reminding us of his presence. Adam, presumably, was in the other front room on the first floor, still completely oblivious to the altercation which had dominated our day.

'Just think,' Tim whispered to me. 'Supposing Erin can't sleep and cracks up in the middle of the night and drives over here! She might bang on the door any second now!'

I sat up. 'Listen, you won't get to sleep, either, if your imagination is churning out plots like that. You're making yourself worse.'

'Maybe I am. Isn't it typical that *he* is sleeping like the dead? I expect he'll have forgotten about it by tomorrow. In fact, I wouldn't be surprised if those lumps in his duvet were a pile of pillows. He may have crept out for a night on the town.'

I laughed at the absurdity of his suggestion. 'If he felt the urge to deceive us, I'm sure it wouldn't tax his brain too much. He is there, by the way - I can hear his breathing.'

'I wonder what he's dreaming about.'

'I can guess.'

There was a complete silence for several seconds. 'In Bangkok, the bars at the Plaza will be in full cry, and Maalii will be all alone. Do you think she loves him, honestly?'

'Of course she does,' I said. 'And vice-versa.'

'Do you think so?'

'I love him, too,' I admitted.

'What?'

'I love him, in a jealous sort of way. I struggle to cope with as mundane an existence as a man could have, worrying like hell about problems that may never arise. But him? He finds ways round *everything*.'

'Until now,' he went on. 'That's the reason he flared up this afternoon - frustration at not being able to get what he wants.'

Eventually, I managed to shut down. I dreamt of home, walking through Vale Park with some mysterious, almost faceless, young girl. The rest of the world had ceased to exist. The two of us were strolling alone in the shadows of the tall, unbending trees, breathing the salty air, aware of, but untroubled by, our solitude. Neither of us uttered a word the whole time, preferring to communicate our love by thought alone. I held her hand tightly, feeling every contour of every finger, and knew that letting go, even for the briefest moment, would resurrect the unwanted world around us.

I was awoken by the light. Tim had thrown back the curtains and was in the process of packing the remainder of his clothes. So vivid was the dream that I was momentarily surprised to have returned to my senses in the same place. Lindsey lay still in his bed, with an arm wrapped around one of his pillows. Perhaps my dream had been inspired by his days with Maalii. It seemed simplistic, but plausible nonetheless.

'It's a quarter to eight,' said Tim. 'Time the two of you got yourselves organized.'

'Is he still asleep?' I replied, nodding my head towards Lindsey, who had remained motionless in spite of the bright sunlight which had flooded the room. 'He must have been shattered. That's almost ten hours.'

'Five, to be exact,' Lindsey groaned, and sat up slowly, looking as cadaverous as he had done throughout the previous day.

'Five? Why five?'

'How could I possibly get to sleep while you two were gossiping like fishwives?'

'You never said anything,' I remarked.

'I preferred to listen.' He then began to laugh. 'It's reassuring to know that you love me, Phil!'

I picked up a pillow and slung it at him across the room. Adam put his head round the door just as the pillow thudded against the wall.

'Good morning, guys. Just making sure you were awake.'

'Thanks, but no need.'

'I'll see you downstairs,' he added. 'Erin should be here soon. I think she wants to see you off.'

The door closed.

'I expect she does,' Lindsey agreed, rolling out of bed and making his way sluggishly towards the bathroom.

I stood up and helped Tim to tidy the beds. 'How are you feeling?' I asked him.

'Better. In a day or two, we'll look at yesterday's unwelcome little episode as a mere hiccup. And by the time we arrive home, it will be all but forgotten.'

In the court, the sound of a car engine grew louder before smoothly cutting out.

'I wonder who that could be,' I said.

We rushed to the window and stole a very brief glimpse so as not to be noticed from the driveway. She had arrived, possibly to erect one final hurdle on the road back to freedom.

Lindsey was watching me from the bathroom. 'I know,' he said softly. He had shaved, washed and changed, and consequently looked much healthier.

Again, we slipped stealthily downstairs and dropped our bags next to the front door which was wide open. I could see Adam leaning into the passenger's side of the car, clearing out papers and box files in order to provide extra space for our luggage.

I stepped into the cavernous front room and there she was, sitting nervously on the edge of the couch.

'Hello,' I said, tentatively.

'Good morning, Philip.'

Her face looked featureless, apart from her eyes which were still red and puffy, as though she had not stopped crying since leaving the previous afternoon. Her expression changed as she looked through me and saw the person she held responsible for her tears. There followed an excruciating silence which was appreciatively disturbed when Adam returned from outside.

'OK, guys,' he said quietly, not wishing to rush us. 'Car's ready when you are.'

Erin got up from the couch and we all made our way to the front door.

'Enjoy what remains of your vacation,' she said calmly.

I could detect an uneasy sincerity in her platitude. I shook her hand and stood aside, allowing Tim to do the same. He said nothing. I then watched as Lindsey dropped his bag onto the doormat and stepped towards her. She was unable to look at his face. He placed his hand around the back of her neck and kissed her cheek, softly and silently. She closed her eyes until she could no longer feel his skin next to her own. I turned away and followed Tim outside. Lindsey whispered a few words to her but I was too far away to hear. She did not respond.

We tossed most of the bags into the spacious boot of Adam's station wagon and jumped into the middle row of seats along with the rest. As he reversed carefully on to the road I glanced momentarily at a young girl standing alone in front of his splendid house. I raised my hand and waved to her as we drove away, humbly grateful that she had kept her brother in the dark. After all, he could hardly have failed to notice her swollen eyes and lack of vitality. He had clearly put it down to her continuing difficulty in coming to terms with their mother's death and, to my great relief, nothing more.

At home, we had planned to see so much in Los Angeles; and yet, in reality, we had seen nothing, even less than we had seen of Hong Kong. Nevertheless, the knowledge that we would be in New York with Jacques and Nova within four days provided us all with more than adequate compensation for the days we had lost.

Conversation *en route* to LAX was an obsequious chore. As Adam had predicted, the airport was already crowded with cars, taxis and coaches when we pulled up outside the terminal.

'I won't be able to park here for long, guys, so grab your bags out of the trunk.'

We jumped out and shook hands with our unknowing host through the driver's window.

'Many thanks for taking the trouble, Adam,' Tim shouted above the traffic noise, which was reverberating around the fume-filled parking bays.

'It's been a pleasure,' he replied. 'I apologize for Erin's state of mind. I'm sure you can all appreciate why she's been so upset.'

'Of course.'

'Look after yourselves, and be sure to give my regards to Jacques and your sister, Lindsey.'

'I'll do that.'

'And don't forget that you and I still have a game to finish!'

Lindsey smiled unconvincingly and tapped on the car roof as Adam wound up his window and drove out of sight and out of our lives.

'What did I tell you?' Lindsey said, finally. 'I said there'd be nothing for us to worry about.'

XIII

'I never expect a soldier to think.'

George Bernard Shaw (1856-1950)
The Devil's Disciple, III

We first saw the welcoming runway lights of Lester B. Pearson International Airport at seven thirty in the evening. After the anticlimaxes that were Hong Kong and Los Angeles, I had decided in advance that Toronto - 'meeting place' - would be as mind-blowing as Bangkok had been. We were now two thousand miles from a distraught Erin van Bergen but, sadly, Lindsey had become two thousand miles further away from another girl he had encountered for the first time only a few days beforehand. Perhaps, in that guarded mind of his, he was taking the optimist's view that, as the earth was roughly spherical, our flight across North America had actually brought him and Maalii closer together.

We boarded the shuttle bus and left for the city. None of us made even the vaguest reference to Lindsey's fight with Erin; prolonging the memory was as unsettling as it was unnecessary.

After half an hour spent cruising along the multi-laned 401 Highway, the illuminated city towers appeared in front of us - yet another collection of overgrown Christmas trees reaching for the night sky.

'We can afford to stay in a decent hotel for our two nights here,' Lindsey pointed out, quite unexpectedly. 'We haven't had to spend much in recent days.' He did not need to extrapolate.

'Where shall we go?' I asked him.

'I'll call Jacques when we get out. He has attended dozens of conferences and seminars at the universities here. He ought to know.'

'Royal York!' hollered the driver, braking smoothly at the corner of a busy downtown junction.

'What's that?' I wondered.

'A hotel,' Lindsey pointed out. '*The* hotel, so I've been told, and therefore far too classy for irredeemable trash like us. We can still get out here, though. Come on.'

We alighted from the bus and waited until it had moved off.

Lindsey pointed to a large stone building across the road, which was reminiscent of the Walker Art Gallery back in Liverpool. 'That's *Union*, the main station. There must be a phone in there somewhere.'

To our right, it was impossible not to notice the stupendous Canadian National Tower, soaring with ease above all the neighbouring buildings. Lindsey strode across the wide concourse to a vacant kiosk, dialled New York City, and waited.

'Hello ...' There was a long pause. 'Nova?' He smiled contentedly. 'Yes, we're fine ... Toronto! Just this minute arrived!'

The evening was surprisingly cool. I wandered around for a few minutes, observing both the grand architecture of the Victorian station and groups of travellers who were carting luggage up and down the steps.

As we waited for Lindsey's money to run out, I noticed a man, possibly Spanish, wearing a surgical collar, standing nervously at the adjacent telephone. In his free hand were several large black and white photographs of what looked like the bodies of mutilated soldiers, lying face down in their own blood on an open road. The man looked up at my bewildered face then turned his back to guard his privacy.

Lindsey replaced the handset. 'He says there's a comfortable place halfway along Victoria Street. It's not far.'

'How's your sister?' I asked.

'Very well. Jacques arrived home yesterday morning. From the way she speaks about him, you would think he'd been away for a year!'

'Is there any mail waiting there for you?'

He smiled bravely. 'Not yet.'

I glanced again at the gruesome pictures as we headed for the exit. It appeared that the man was describing them in meticulous detail down the telephone. He stared at me again, and this time scowled in protest. I looked away. He did not look the type to issue subsequent warnings.

The hotel was only a short distance from the station. In its foyer was a sweeping array of leafy rubber plants, and an illuminated ornamental fountain opposite the lifts. Every minute or so, the background lights would change, making the water appear to switch from blue, to green, to red, then back again to blue, before repeating the primary-colour cycle.

'Oh, good choice, Jacques, good choice,' Lindsey uttered, either approvingly or sarcastically. He glanced across the reception desk at the clock. 'Nine fifteen.' I knew what he was thinking: we had plenty of time left to scour the streets.

We had the unusual luxury of separate rooms. Even more strangely, the receptionist attended to us with a smile - a forced one, as if she were showing off her teeth, but it was better than the alternative that 'greeted' us in Hong Kong.

'Meet downstairs in an hour?' said Tim, once we had reached the second floor.

I closed my door, collapsed onto the cool, freshly-made bed and contemplated for a moment in the dark. As far as I was aware, neither Tim nor Lindsey had seen the injured man's photographs, and I was too tired to supply them with a description. I wondered about the man's identity. Was he a former soldier himself, I pondered, or an eager journalist, or just a common thief? For all I knew, he could have been all three. One fact, however, was indisputable: in some terrifying corner of the world, a band of young men had gambled with their lives, perhaps not entirely voluntarily, in pursuit of a supposedly noble cause, and had paid the ultimate price. I could not decide which was more disturbing: being compelled by a higher authority to risk suffering a violent death, or being brainwashed so successfully that such orders were superfluous.

'Definitely the latter,' Lindsey would have brazenly insisted, before expanding the theme for the sole purpose of making one of his vituperative assaults upon what he saw as a wicked form of psychological abuse. It was another good reason not to mention what I had seen.

I showered, and changed into the clothes that had been washed, conditioned and tumble-dried in Adam's basement. I then dug out my baseball jacket, which had been squashed at the bottom of my bag since leaving London, slung it over my shoulder and returned to the foyer where the others were already waiting.

It was after ten by the time we ventured on to Yonge - the city's bustling equivalent of Sukhumvit. This street, too, was infinitely long, bisecting the entire metropolis, but in a north-south direction as opposed to east-west. I quickly noticed that most of the other streets that crossed its path ran either parallel or at right angles to it, thus slicing the central district into a gigantic tessellation of unique rectangles. Marvelling at the street life we headed north, crossing the numerous intersections: Adelaide, Temperance, Richmond, Queen, and Dundas, where a couple of gangs of idle youths were loafing around the entrance to the subway station.

Lindsey suddenly became acutely bad-tempered. 'I need a fucking drink,' he growled, walking two or three steps ahead.

'Let's go in here, then,' I suggested, pointing to the nearest bar on the left side.

He turned to inspect its flashy exterior and shook his head. 'How desperate do you think I am?'

'You tell me.'

'The typical character in that sort of joint is a pretentious nonentity with a thick wad of gold cards and a brain the size of a walnut. I propose we give it a swerve.'

'If you feel so strongly about it ...'

Fortunately, and only after listening to him brooding for a few minutes, we came across somewhere more to his taste. It was a small bar with a low ceiling, very dark, and full of people of our own age. Young Afro-Americans in shiny suits and gaudy jewellery had taken centre stage and two denim-clad Latinos were trying, in vain, to charm a gaggle of painted girls in tight microskirts. In every other corner, more and more hyperconfident pretenders were begging to be noticed. Ironically, the nature of the place was exactly what Lindsey had claimed to despise. Either he had been desperate after all, or had concluded that there were likely to be no better options. Nothing but the Plaza in Bangkok would have truly sufficed.

I abstained from the conversation and skydived into my own small world. Again, time had expanded as a result of yet another long flight. The fact that we had left Adam's house that same day seemed implausible. Moreover, I could barely remember anything about Hong Kong, and Thailand felt like six years ago, rather than the six days that had proved insufficient time even for Maalii's expected letter to reach New York.

Lindsey's irritability was extinguished by his first few drinks, but the taciturnity and preoccupied expression remained.

'You're dreaming again,' I remarked.

'Wouldn't you be?'

'I wasn't being critical. What are your plans?'

'I'll wait until I've read her letter. Assuming she didn't misspell Nova's address and write *New Orleans* or *New Brighton* instead of *New York*, it should arrive tomorrow morning.'

I had an idea. 'You could telephone Nova again and, if it has arrived, ask her to read it to you.'

He looked at me, quite irascibly. 'Read *That*? Where's your head, Phil?'

'Oh, of course. I forgot. Well, you can at least be sure that she won't steam open the envelope in order to take a sneaky look.'

'My sister would never do that. And it wouldn't bother me if she did.'

Tim looked thoughtfully at him with a studious expression, one he had acquired from his experience of unlocking the confused minds of psychiatric patients.

'When we arrived at the airport earlier, Phil and I were half-expecting Maalii to be there to meet you. Similarly when we landed at both LAX and Kai Tak.'

Lindsey withstood his stare. 'What the hell made you think that?'

Tim was unequivocal. 'Because you've been plotting!'

Such bluntness generally came about as a consequence of excess alcohol swimming around inside his blood vessels, and tended to increase in direct proportion.

'Plotting what?'

'I'm not exactly sure.'

Lindsey sighed with mild petulance. 'In order to relieve you of further curiosity, don't expect her to be waiting in New York either, because she won't!'

'All right, keep your clothes on.'

'Besides, how do you think I could have procured the money for her flight?'

'Your question invites one of a similar nature.'

'It also invites an answer.'

'What I'm saying is-'

'What you're saying is, you haven't the first clue.'

'That's true, yes. Nor can I quite work out how you managed to raise a thousand pounds for your *own* flights.'

Lindsey smiled. 'Has that been bugging you since March?'

'You're not answering my question.'

'Nor you mine.'

Lindsey leaned back in his chair, thereby truncating the entire conversation. Despite Tim's tenacity, he was not going to be cajoled, tricked, or even threatened, into making a premature declaration of his motives and intentions.

By closing time, whatever time that was, the bar was packed from wall to wall, and almost from floor to ceiling. It reminded me of the Patpong nightclub back in Bangkok: twenty-somethings from all parts of the world communicating in the common language of midnight excess.

We returned to the street and quickly lost ourselves in the downtown maze, wandering aimlessly and carelessly along any street bright enough to catch our clouded eyes. Inevitably, we stumbled into the red-light district, somewhere south of Bloor Street.

Tim stole my exact words. 'We gravitate towards sleaze. I'm beginning to think one of us has inbuilt radar.'

A loud explosion of drunken laughter burst simultaneously from each of us, and the conversation rapidly sank into a prolonged recital of crude, sexual anecdotes.

We walked for about half an hour, trying, as well as our condition would permit, to maintain a mental note of our general direction. At one in the morning we found a small square verge at the junction of Bay Street and Dundas Street West.

Lindsey slumped down on a conspicuous patch of grass. 'I think that's the bus terminal,' he said, focusing on the corner building across the junction. 'That's where we catch the bus to Niagara Falls on Wednesday morning. It can't be more than two hours from here, so departures ought to be quite frequent.' He lay flat on his back and gazed between the towers up into the darkened heavens. 'Where are you, girl?' he pleaded dreamily. 'Why can't you be here?'

Tim, no longer irritated by Lindsey's secrecy, sat down next to him. 'I don't think she could be further away, could she?'

'Let me think ... the time difference between here and Liverpool is five hours, and there's another seven between Liverpool and Bangkok. Twelve in total. We are in opposite hemispheres, too. So I suppose not.'

'Nevertheless,' I added, 'it does mean that as soon as we board that bus, you'll be getting closer.'

'Since when have you been an optimist, Phil?'

'It's late,' said Tim. 'We did check into a hotel, so we may as well make use of it, rather than stay out here at Toronto's answer to the *Hotel Buddha* and catch hypothermia.'

It took no longer than a couple of minutes to walk eastward along Dundas then south on Yonge to the hotel. I switched off the bedside lamp at two fifteen and listened to the muffled, and infrequent, traffic noise from the street below. It had been yet another elongated day. I was becoming convinced that twenty-four hours constituted merely a day of average length which stood to be augmented by travel. At the same time the previous day, I had been lying awake in a different bed, two thousand miles west of here, discussing with Tim a situation which, in keeping with his prediction, had now begun to drain from our tired heads.

XIV

**'Tempt not the stars, young man, thou canst not play
With the severity of fate.'**

John Ford (c.1586-c.1640)
***The Broken Heart*, I:3**

Day thirteen was initiated by an aggressive knock on the bedroom door.

'Are you staying in the sack all bloody day?' It was Tim, impatient as ever.

'What time is it?'

'Just after ten thirty. See you downstairs at eleven?'

'I'll do my best,' I groaned, and reached over to switch on the main lights. 'By the way, where's Lindsey?'

'You'll never believe it.'

I opened the door. 'Try me.'

'He's sitting in a quiet corner of the foyer bar, which is where he has been for most of the night.'

'Doing what, drinking the place dry?'

'Playing poker - with a group of Japanese businessmen.'

'And relieving them of their dollars, no doubt.'

'He did seem rather pleased with himself.'

'Did he not get tired?'

'Well, I don't imagine he would have become tired of taking their money, if that's what you're implying.'

I laughed. 'No, I suppose not.'

'Who knows? We might even be able to travel down to Niagara in a stretched limo.'

'I didn't know gambling was allowed just anywhere.'

'It's not. Don't take too long.'

I closed the door and changed as quickly as I could. Already my room resembled a riot scene, almost to the point where I felt obliged, out of shame, to tidy it myself before the chambermaids began their daily rounds.

Lindsey, surprisingly, looked quite fresh when I stepped out of the lift into the foyer, where the coloured fountain lights were no longer switched on.

'So you had a wild night, did you?' I called, eager for him to fill in the details.

He winked at me. 'A profitable one.'

'How profitable?'

'Seven hundred.'

'*Dollars?*'

He laughed mischievously. 'There were three of the suckers, none of whom realized I was conning them! I licked them out good and proper!'

'So I see,' said Tim, pointing to his bulging wallet. 'What are you going to do with the money, you unscrupulous being?'

'Nothing outrageous. I'll pay for us to go up the CN Tower, and mail some of it to Maalii.' He paused pensively, rubbing his eyes. 'Her need is far greater than ours.'

Outside, we could see the heart of Toronto in full daylight for the first time. The sun's rays bounced energetically off the glass-fronted office blocks and car windscreens on to the immaculate streets. Parked opposite the Royal York was a chrome-panelled bus, considerably larger than the airport shuttle, and about to embark upon a far more ambitious trek: along the lakeshore all the way to Montreal and Quebec City.

Lindsey located the apex of the tower in the sky and we began walking towards it, like the three mythical gift-bearers following the star to Bethlehem.

'The tower is more than half a mile from here,' he said brightly, 'and yet we're looking at the top of it at an angle of about thirty degrees to the ground.'

'Is that so?' came Tim's predictably sarcastic reply.

'It must be almost a third of a mile in height.'

'That can't be right.'

'It has to be.'

It was, too. It took almost a minute for the lift cage to hoist us up to the tower's observation deck. We gazed out towards the hazy blue horizon where Lake Ontario blended perfectly with the sky, miles in the distance. Small, coloured planes were taking off from the island's airport, like exotic birds leaving their nests; and wide boulevards - lined with trees which we could hardly see for all the multinationals' gigantic billboards - stretched out towards the smart, western suburbs.

Lindsey was looking much happier, more talkative, hyperactive almost, which was remarkable in view of his nocturnal activities.

'How many jumpers do you think come up here?' he said.

'*Jumpers?*' I repeated.

'Suicide cases. Would it not be the ultimate way to bow out?'

'In terms of mess, it probably would.'

'It's the nearest one could get to flying,' he said, as if he might be tempted one day to consider it. 'Imagine being in the air for over ten seconds before reaching an impact speed of 120 miles per hour.'

'You really are sick,' Tim told him.

The discussion became increasingly banal. Eventually, having spent half an hour gasping at the view and talking typical post-hangover nonsense, we took the statutory photographs, ticked the mental checklist and returned inside.

'How do you expect to die, Lindsey?' I asked him, for some reason.

'Young.'

'Why?'

'It's my own Pascalian wager, in the hope of being pleasantly surprised. But I can assure you of one thing - I won't die on my knees in a church, as my grandmother did.'

Tim laughed to himself. Lindsey had somehow managed to divert yet another abstract, and perfectly meaningless, conversation towards the usual goal: his aversion from all things religious. Like water inside a funnel, our discussions and debates had a gravitational tendency to disappear down the same old hole.

'Worship is utter folly,' he would repeat. 'Your mum was right, Phil. Few morals could be more profound.'

We returned to earth just as the altitude, and Lindsey's ramblings, were beginning to make me dizzy.

'Lunch is on me,' he said, casually.

Tim was surprised - and suspicious. 'Thanks. Do I detect an ounce of guilt?'

'For what?'

'For having spent all night swindling some of our fellow guests.'

'I didn't force them to play.'

'Nor did they force you to cheat.'

'They, too, might have cheated, or at least were intent upon doing so.'

'You don't know that.'

'It stands to reason. Two of them were lawyers. They are trained to swindle people.'

Anyway, we soon discovered that his act of generosity was not as exceptional as it had initially sounded. We dawdled along Bay Street, gobbling salsa-soaked hot dogs and sharing cans of coke which he had bought with his loose change from a street vendor at the foot of the tower.

'Four dollars for a slimy hot dog,' he complained. 'Now who's been swindled?'

We arrived unintentionally at Nathan Philip Square, where neat concrete artefacts lay awkwardly in the shadows of some oddly-designed arches opposite the ornate city hall. Sitting alone on a bench next to the noisy water fountains was an elderly gentleman. His grey overcoat was buttoned right to the top, and wrapped securely around his neck was a brown and maroon checked cravat.

'Would you mind if we sat here?' I asked, politely.

'Not at all,' he replied, in an articulate but throaty voice. He sounded English, and bore the appearance of a typical retired gentleman making the most of the pleasant afternoon air, as so many did back home.

We squeezed onto the bench, finished eating, and spent a lazy half-hour sharing ideas. Lindsey said something to the old man which escaped me.

'Have you been here long?' the man inquired.

'We arrived only yesterday - from Los Angeles.'

'Really? You sound like an Englishman.'

'So do you,' Lindsey respectfully pointed out.

The old man suppressed a laugh. 'I'm from Oxfordshire.'

'Do you live over here?'

'Eighteen years this Christmas.' He paused for breath, then pointed to the sky. 'Did the view from the tower impress you as much as you had hoped?'

Lindsey looked silently astounded. 'How did you know we'd been up there?'

The old man looked at him as he would a precocious young grandson. 'I'm sorry. I could not help but overhear you earlier. Skyscrapers seem to fascinate you.'

'Is that not true of most visitors from England?'

'Have you been to New York City? Or Chicago? The architecture in the windy city is second to none, I'll have you know.'

They began to look at each other with mutual fondness.

'May I ask what your occupation was?'

'I used to lecture at one of the universities.'

'In which subject?'

'Pathology. Medicine for the dead, as we used to call it.'

'You were educated in England, though, weren't you?'

'Scotland. I was an undergraduate at Edinburgh before the world declared war upon itself. I then served with the Indian Imperial Police in Rangoon. Following that, I lectured in and around London until my dear wife passed away in 1974. She was forty-nine.' He looked blankly into the fountains. 'That's why I moved out here. Even the fondest of memories can be traumatic, you know.'

'How long did you work at the university here?'

'Three years.'

'That means you retired early.'

Now it was the old man's turn to look quizzically at Lindsey. 'How did you know that?'

'If you had been a student in the late thirties, as you just said, then you shouldn't have been scheduled to retire until about 1980.'

'Your young brain is very sharp!' he said warmly.

'I try to give it plenty of exercise.'

'Well, before you ask, I was diagnosed as having a terminal illness.'

'Fifteen years ago? What are you, well, doing here?'

'Learning how to die.'

'I understand,' said Lindsey, carefully contemplating the man's frank reply. 'You can be a dreadfully slow learner when it suits you.'

The old man laughed, as heartily as his tired lungs would permit. 'You could phrase it like that! Every hour of every day is potentially the last, and its probability of being so is forever increasing. Some days I feel as fit as I ever did. Others are something of a strain. I try to approach each of them with the same degree of caution; and if I am able to see the sun in the sky, and can watch young people like yourselves walking across the square with smiles on their faces, then life is still worthwhile. It is as much as I can hope to enjoy.'

'Do you sit here every day?'

'Only on Tuesdays. I meet an old friend, a former colleague of mine, and we have tea at a small cafe just off University Avenue, up by the US Consulate. If I come in on an earlier GO train, however, I get to steal an extra hour or so sitting here.'

'We leave in the morning. Next stop, Niagara Falls, then New York City, where my sister lives.'

'How was Thailand?'

Once again, Lindsey looked startled. 'Thailand was fun. How did you-'

The two of them looked at each other without either saying a word. The old man reached out his arthritic hand and touched the pebble which had been draped around Lindsey's neck on a piece of string since our departure from Krasang. He had spotted the character that Chek had scratched onto its surface, and recognized the peculiar script to which it belonged. I began to wonder what else he had the ability to see.

'I visited Thailand, albeit briefly, in 1946, after the Japanese had finally surrendered. I was one of the fortunate ones. Some of my closest friends are buried there.'

'We saw the war graves at Kanchanaburi,' I explained, in an attempt to show some respect.

The old man was visibly moved, as we had been during our brief stay. 'Did you visit the railway?'

Lindsey pulled out a crumpled photograph from his jacket pocket and passed it to him. The old man held it at arm's length and focused on the image of Lindsey standing behind Maalii, arms wrapped around her waist, on the Kwai Bridge.

'Is the young lady your girlfriend?'

'Yes.'

'She is very beautiful, even for a Thai. You must miss her terribly.'

'I do.'

'That's understandable. When I was stationed in Burma, I had a girlfriend back in Oxford. We were apart for well over a year - and that's a long time to be living for letters. Torture by hope. I wouldn't like that to happen to you.'

'I won't let it.' Lindsey looked at his watch, not wishing to monopolize the old man's time. 'At what time do you normally meet your friend?'

'As a rule, half past two.'

'Would you mind if I asked you one last question? It's not often we come across people with your education and life experience.'

'Not at all.'

'Do you believe in a god?'

The old man smiled, causing his ruddy face to wrinkle further. 'You appear to be asking for reassurance, which I find somewhat odd. You don't strike me as being riddled with self-doubt.'

'You're right. I'm not.'

'You yourself sound like a typical atheist.'

'I am, yes,' said Lindsey, unashamedly.

The old man breathed deeply. 'In my view, atheism is an asymptote. Do you understand what I mean by that?'

'I've studied Mathematics.'

'As each of my last days moves from future to past, I approach atheism asymptotically, that is, moving ever closer, but my mind has to remain open, if only very slightly. Therefore, it is a position I shall never reach.'

'I've already reached it,' Lindsey admitted, as if, absurdly, he were making a confession to a priest.

'Well, I suppose that is a more honourable, and more intellectually tenable, position than those at the opposite end of the spectrum, but that's just my own personal feeling.'

'I agree with you. Would you mind if I wrote to you when I arrive home?'

'A letter? Not at all. I should be very happy to read an account of your travels.' He wrote his name and address on the back of the Kwai Bridge photograph. 'Do write legibly, though. I'm afraid my near sight is atrocious.'

'So is my handwriting,' said Lindsey, 'but I shall make extra effort.'

The old man handed the picture back to him.

'Thank you,' said Lindsey, as if having just received a coveted autograph.

'Do enjoy the rest of your journey,' said the old man, getting to his feet. 'Treat it as if it were going to be your last.'

We watched him walk away, stooping slightly, and within a few seconds he had turned the corner and was gone - forever.

'So sane an individual,' Lindsey drooled, 'alone and inconspicuous in a corner of the global asylum. Nobody takes any notice of an old man like him although, I admit, he did seem full of inward pity.'

'That's one of the consequences of losing a loved one,' said Tim, very sarcastically.

'What's his name?' I asked.

'Mr. King.'

'What's his first name?'

'Wang.'

'Very witty.'

'Samuel.'

'Didn't he write his title, or qualifications?'

'I don't suppose he had anything to prove to the likes of us.'

'Perhaps there was insufficient space on the photograph on which to list them. He lives in Oakville, wherever that is. Out of town, I presume.'

'When do you intend to write to him?'

Lindsey frowned. 'Jesus, you're full of questions. I'll write when I get home.' He then smiled to himself. 'By then I shall be in a position to put his mind at rest.'

XV

'Revenge, at first though sweet,
Bitter ere long back on itself recoils.'

John Milton (1608-74)
Paradise Lost, Bk. IX

We took to the street once more. I glanced back at the square, knowing that, should I be fortunate enough to return, I would automatically visualize the unlikely image of young and old, sitting together exchanging thoughts with the frankness of lifelong friends. Perhaps the old man had been like Lindsey in *la belle époque* between the wars, riding the waves of life with inexplicable ease; although, in a reciprocal sense, I hoped that Lindsey would not wind up dreaming away his own twilight days, plagued by his own thoughts, broken and alone in a distant land.

We headed north along Bay Street and arrived at the grass verge where we had rested in a semi-stupor in the middle of the night. Strangely different in broad daylight, and being viewed by eyes which were no longer operating independently of one another, it had become a delightful suntrap. Office workers were sitting around, chilled drinks in hand, conversing in small clusters, apparently oblivious to their overbearing, concrete environment.

'Why don't we buy our tickets for tomorrow?' Tim suggested, in his typically cautious manner.

'Good idea. When do we need to arrive in Niagara?'

'Lunchtime, say?'

We all agreed before darting across the busy road.

Lindsey looked around the terminal's interior like a child in a colossal toy shop. 'I can't help but feel excited whenever I walk into places like this.'

'Bus stations?'

'Gateways to freedom, old fruit. Just look at the size of that timetable board. We could go anywhere from here - Montreal, Edmonton, Philadelphia ...'

'Back to LA?'

'Bottom of the list.'

'To you, putting down roots represents stagnation,' Tim asserted. 'That's why you'll never settle. Not in Liverpool, nor in any other place, regardless of what gets left in your wake.'

Lindsey, for once, did not dispute what had been conjectured. 'Back in the bad old days,' he recalled, 'when I was still at university, I used to walk down to Lime Street station and just hang around for an hour or so, observing all the weirdos and studying the timetable board. Therapeutic, you see.'

'For what?'

'Restlessness. I used to peer past the checkpoint on to the platform like a prisoner gazing through the bars of his cell. Liberty was both visible and imaginable but, at that moment in time, temporarily unattainable.'

'Did you really hate it that much?'

'No, I was simply acknowledging that student life had ceased to interest me. It would have been pointless pretending otherwise.'

'Three one-way tickets to Niagara Falls for tomorrow morning, please,' Tim requested.

'Departing nine thirty,' said the woman perched behind the tidy booking desk, in robotic monotone. 'Is that OK for you?'

'It's perfect. Secondly, could we book the same number of tickets for the overnight service from there to New York, arriving Friday morning?'

There was a brief pause as she raked through the availability details. I had never seen anyone look quite so bored by what she was doing. Perhaps she was on the threshold of acute depression; or maybe she was sitting there naked from the waist down and deriving a huge thrill from everyone's unawareness.

'Departing Niagara Falls at eight o'clock on Thursday evening, changing at Buffalo, and arriving in New York City at seven the following morning.'

'I'll phone Nova this evening,' Lindsey whispered, as the clerk typed the finalized itinerary into her computer terminal. 'We should arrive at her place just in time for breakfast. I'll have to remind her to buy some black pudding, or *blood sausage*, or *Jamaican's dick*, or whatever the Yanks call it.'

'She might have a letter for you.'

Tim collected the vast wad of tickets and slipped them into his jacket pocket. 'Now what?' I said.

Tim turned to Lindsey. 'We can stay here a while longer if it would make you happy. I'm sure there will be one or two weirdos strolling around somewhere.'

Lindsey laughed to himself. 'Did I ever tell you about that strange girl I met at the old *Rigby One* bus station in Blackpool when I'd just finished my 'A' levels?'

We left the terminal building and walked further uptown along Bay Street, eager as ever to hear the explicit details of another one of his absurd chance encounters, regardless of its relationship to the truth.

'I was on my way to Pitlochry in Scotland. My cousin had a summer job at a guest house up there and managed to fix me up with a weekend's free accommodation.'

'Legitimately?'

'Not exactly.'

'What about the girl?'

'It was about one in the morning. We'd been waiting in torrential rain for over an hour before the bus finally appeared.' A puzzled expression dawned on his face. 'She was the most peculiar-looking creature I'd ever seen.'

'In what way?'

'Her eyes were too big for their sockets. Damned things looked like poached eggs.'

'Exophthalmous.'

'I don't remember her name.'

'I meant the condition.'

'I know what you meant. She looked frightfully odd, but in a sexy kind of way.'

'Don't tell us *she* wasn't actually female.'

'No, nothing like that.' His eyes sparkled. 'There were no other passengers on the bus. We had it to ourselves for six and a half hours.'

Tim and I stopped walking, having loosely deduced what must have transpired.

'And did you?'

He laughed aloud. 'We were going at it like orang-utans on the back seat all the way from Preston to Stirling! The bus didn't stop so neither did we!'

'Did the driver notice?'

'Possibly. We tried to be discreet, but after a while she started moaning. You know how it is: once you get into a rhythm, nothing matters.'

'Did she go with you to Pitlochry?'

'No, she got out at Perth and I never saw her again. There she was, a total stranger, straddling me with her knickers off and wet skirt hitched up round her waist, hammering away at full throttle. I thought her eyes were going to pop out altogether and hit me in the face!' In an instant, the licentious grin evaporated. 'Anyhow, those days are over.'

We wandered all around the sedate northern reaches of the city, twice inadvertently retracing our steps, and eventually returned to the hotel along the broad, sun-drenched University Avenue.

'Any ideas for this evening?' I said.

'A repeat of yesterday?' Lindsey, now in excellent spirits, was quick to suggest.

I was glad to be able to lie down in my room for a while before going out again. We had trekked at least five miles, shuffling randomly north, east, south and west, like animated characters in a child's computer game.

Tim walked in before I had become fatally relaxed, and slouched in the armchair next to the bedside table. He looked as exhausted as I felt. His bloated face was quite flushed and a film of congealed sweat had stuck his blond hair to his forehead.

'Do you think Lindsey's Japanese buddies will still be in town?' he muttered.

'If so, I expect they'll have gone to a bank in order to replenish their wallets.'

'That's assuming they managed to find their way back from the cleaners.'

We both laughed, with what little energy we possessed.

'Let's hope they don't belong to some organized gang of homicidal maniacs and decide to come up to his room to teach him a lesson!'

'Come up to *my* room?' Lindsey interrupted, leaving the door wide open behind him. 'Why would they do that, when I gave them the number to yours and told them my name was Tim?'

Fooled, Tim sat up. 'You did what?'

'I'm only joking. Besides, those guys had dollar bills leaking out of every orifice.' He sat down on the window ledge and gazed upon Victoria Street below. 'I wish you'd been there. I wrung them out like dishcloths.'

'You cheated,' Tim insisted. 'Are you going to be down there again tonight?'

'And forfeit another night's sleep? Of course!'

Tim shook his head in light-hearted despair. 'You've no bloody conscience at all.'

Lindsey turned on him without warning. 'Let me tell you what I *do* have.'

'Spare us, please.'

'I have a girlfriend on the opposite side of the world who, through no fault of her own, has barely sufficient money to feed and clothe herself. Is that not an example of compassion?'

'*Selective* compassion.'

'It was simply a minor exercise in wealth redistribution,' he explained in a softer voice. 'Robin Hood was from Nottinghamshire, too, don't forget.'

'So tell us, then, how generous a proportion of your ill-gotten spoils do you intend to post to Maid Marion?'

Lindsey swung his legs round and leaned back against the window. 'I don't know. I shall get an international money order from one of the banks in Manhattan. She should have received it by the time we arrive back in London.'

A week today, I thought. Never before had I felt quite so detached from the reality of my sad, solitary existence at home. The sheer fluidity of life on the move was infinitely more satisfying; but there was no escaping the fact that, unlike the celebrated 'beats' in Jack Kerouac's novels, I had neither the funds, nor the self-confidence, nor the energy to sustain it.

Without another word, Lindsey levered himself from the window sill and left the room, this time taking care to close the door quietly behind him.

'Where is he going now?' I wondered.

Tim shrugged his tired shoulders. 'Don't ask me.' He lay across the bottom of my bed, resting his head on my feet, and closed his eyes. 'Consider the events of the past fortnight.'

'What about them?'

'He has got himself - and us - embroiled in all kinds of situations we could never have foreseen. There's no predicting what he might do next. I shall be happy to make it home alive.'

'You worry about him too much,' I replied.

'And you're beginning to trust him too readily.'

It would have been difficult to disagree, although I could not recall a single case of naive judgement on Lindsey's part, with the exception of the nightclub incident in Liverpool which was, in essence, nothing but a demonstration of brave loyalty - whatever anyone said to the contrary.

He returned several minutes later.

'Where have you been?' I said, requesting what he seemed reluctant to share.

'Down to the foyer.'

There was a silence.

'What *for?*' said Tim.

'I noticed some tourist information leaflets on the front desk this morning, and thought there might be one for Niagara Falls. There was, and I've made reservations at a motel. Any more questions?'

He and Tim glared at each other momentarily. The friction growing between them was becoming more palpable by the day. Lindsey sat down again on the window ledge and surveyed whatever was still happening out on the now-shaded street.

'Are you going to phone Nova?' I asked, in an attempt to provide a much-needed distraction.

'You can call her,' he said, without taking his eyes of what he was looking at. 'Tell her we shall be arriving in the *rotten apple* between seven and eight o'clock on Friday morning.'

I stretched across the bed and picked up the phone.

'Don't forget to reverse the charges,' he added, indifferently.

'Hello,' said a gentle voice.

'Nova?'

'This is Nova.' She sounded nearby.

'It's Phil, calling from Toronto.'

'Where?'

'Phil-'

'Oh, *English* Phil!'

'That's right.'

'I apologize. For a second, I thought you were Phil Bramson from Jacques's office.'

'He's in Toronto, too, is he?'

'Actually, no. Believe it or not, he's in a Brooklyn hospital being treated for something rather unpleasant. Jacques has been telling people that it's a combination of haemorrhoids and rectal gonorrhoea!'

'If that's true, he's welcome to it - and whatever treatment he's getting.'

'Wire brush and bleach, if Jacques had his way. The guy's a liability.'

I told her when to expect us.

'Seven thirty? That's fine. I shall be here, but I'm not sure about Jacques. He had to leave for Baltimore this afternoon. In fact ... he should be landing there any time now.'

'Won't he be back before the weekend?'

'I don't know, and neither does he. Would you like me to meet you at the bus terminal? It would be no trouble.'

'No, we can walk, thanks.'

'Are you *sure*?'

'Jacques said it wasn't too far.'

'As you wish. Finding your way will be relatively easy. All the midtown junctions are numbered like co-ordinates on a graph. Avenues run north to south, streets west to east.'

'Very mathematical.'

'It is. Fifth Avenue represents the y-axis - East Side positive, West Side negative.'

'I'm not sure I understand that, but I know someone who will.'

'By the way, a letter addressed to Lindsey arrived this morning, post-marked *Phra-kha-nong*. It appears to be from his Siamese girl. *Maa-lii Pa-si* - have I pronounced that correctly?'

'Yes, you have. That's her.' I looked up at Lindsey who was smiling to himself.

'Well, it's more a package than a letter,' she explained.

'A package?'

'Tell him it's here waiting.'

'That won't be necessary. He has figured out what you have said.'

'Oh, is he there with you?'

'Would you like a word?'

'If you wouldn't mind.'

I handed the phone to him and he sprawled out on the bed, playfully rubbing his bare, and very smelly, feet in Tim's face, causing him to snap out of his brief snooze.

He listened concentratedly for a few seconds and then began to chat amicably with his sister for about twenty minutes. I had always been impressed by their intimacy and mutual kindness, so often lacking in sibling relationships. There was no disputing who his most valued friend was, always at hand and never betraying the trust he generally found so difficult to bestow. She was altruism personified. He certainly spoke to her in an uncharacteristically deferential manner, free of all that sarcasm and smugness, almost as if he were addressing a relative one or two generations older than himself.

After a while, he turned his back and returned to the window, stepping over the trailing telephone cable.

'When was that?' he asked, in a relaxed but curious tone. There was another silence. 'Let me explain on Friday.' He scraped his upper teeth repeatedly over his lower lip and looked at Tim, who had forced himself into a sitting position. 'Don't worry, will you? I'll see you in a few days ... yes, all right ... look after yourself. Over and out.'

He hung up and took a large mouthful of his drink. 'You'll never guess.'

'Then tell us,' Tim urged.

'Adam phoned her this morning.'

'Are you surprised?'

'Apparently Erin has become quite depressed since we left.'

'Maybe she misses your charming conversation.'

Lindsey remained impassive. 'She was hysterical last night. Adam could neither calm her down nor even deduce what had triggered off her latest bout of grief.'

'What made him think to call Nova?'

'He wanted to know whether Erin had mentioned anything unusual, or whether one of us had unknowingly upset her.'

Tim stood up and began to pace up and down at the foot of the bed. 'Why didn't you tell Nova what happened?'

'In case he calls again,' Lindsey replied, calculatedly.

'That's so unfair of you.'

'No it's not. Why should I put my sister in a position where she has to tell lies in order to protect me, particularly as he might be able to see through them? I could never do that to her. No, better if it is explained to her on Friday. She'll understand.'

'Adam is on the brink of uncovering the truth, though, isn't he?'

'I realize that. Didn't I say she would squeal? It won't be long now before he phones again.'

I felt relieved that Los Angeles and New York were so far apart, although Lindsey, typically, looked as if he could not have cared less. To him, Erin van

Bergen never really existed. His only hint of concern seemed to be for his sister, who had been interrogated regarding a matter to which she was oblivious. Such stony indifference was the hallmark of a man who knew how to disappear and reinvent himself whenever necessity called. It was no coincidence that our accommodation in Toronto, and Niagara Falls, had been arranged only after leaving LA.

We changed our clothes and prepared to return to the downtown streets which now lay exhausted beneath a black, cloudless sky. Images of awkward exchanges flashed haphazardly through my head. I could envisage Adam phoning Nova's apartment while we were there, and demanding to confront Lindsey. I quickly realized that, in effect, Los Angeles was not thousands of miles away after all, but merely at a different location on the telephone line, where geographical separation was irrelevant.

XVI

'I forget what I was taught.
I only remember what I've learnt.'

Patrick White (1912-90)
The Solid Mandala, Ch.2

The dry evening chill contrasted sharply with the heat of the previous day, so we were content to venture only a short distance from the hotel. We filed into another seedy, dimly-lit bar just off Yonge with all the brain-dead abandon of addicts in search of their nightly fix. It soon became apparent that some of the other lowlifes had achieved theirs already.

Lindsey, eyes wandering inquisitively, nodded to one of the harassed bar girls then sat down, somewhat cautiously, as if he could sense that we were not welcome.

'They're all obliterated in here,' he said, unusually discreetly, but still making himself heard above the noise.

'We must have found the right place, then,' I concluded, playfully.

'I wasn't implying alcohol.'

The place appeared to have been refurbished only recently, but had been decorated to give it a late sixties look. However, its tawdry decor and utterly artificial image seemed to have gone unnoticed by most of them, assuming they were in a fit enough state to see it at all.

Almost inevitably, an unsavoury creature in a green, double-breasted suit managed to attract our attention before our drinks had been brought over to us.

'Where are you guys from?' he asked in an over-sincere, nasal tone.

'England,' Lindsey replied.

'Where in England?'

'Liverpool.'

'Wow! The Beatles!'

'That's right, pal,' Lindsey continued, in an exaggerated, McCartney-esque voice. 'I'm Paul, this is Ringo, and,' pointing to me, 'that's George.'

I froze for a moment, anxious as to how he would react to such a facetious remark. After a moment, he grinned, as if he had initially believed what he had been told. He shuffled across the seat, sat close to Lindsey, and offered to shake hands with each of us in turn. A hand grip would have been a more accurate description; he clasped our hands tightly, palm facing downward, perhaps to demonstrate his perceived superiority.

'So ... what the hell brings you all the way to a city like this?' he inquired coolly while lighting a hand-rolled cigarette.

Lindsey looked blank, but flinched slightly when puffs of bluish smoke drifted across his face.

'You understand me?' the man slurred. 'You know what I'm saying?'

'We all know perfectly well what you're saying, but what are you *selling*?'

'Hey!' he protested theatrically. 'Who said I was selling anything?'

'I did. Dealers give off a very distinctive odour.'

The man turned to Tim. 'Is your buddy always as paranoid as this?'

'Just overintuitive, sometimes,' Tim stressed politely, in an attempt to maintain the peace.

'If you had nothing to sell,' Lindsey persisted, voice raised, 'you wouldn't have spoken to us. That's generally the way in foreign towns, is it not? There are no other ways in which we could possibly interest you. Elementary, really.'

'Guys!' he called to his associates. 'We got Sherlock Holmes here! We got Sherlock Holmes!' To my relief, he seemed intrigued, rather than offended, by the brick wall into which he had just walked. 'OK, wise-ass English boy, what am I selling?'

'Smoke and amphetamines, I expect. And you could probably get your paws on the really hard stuff quite easily within a matter of minutes.'

The man laughed, thereby fully admitting what had just been surmised.

'Did I meet you guys in here last week?'

Lindsey shook his head. 'I don't think so. And none of us is in the habit of pointing a loaded revolver at our own fucking heads, get it?'

'OK, man, I give up.' He raised his hands in surrender, stepped smartly back from the table and returned to the others.

'Vermin!' Lindsey snapped under his breath, once the man's back was turned.

'For heaven's sake, Corker, mind your nasty tongue!' said Tim. 'If trouble finds us then that would be just too bad, but stop trying to ignite it out of thin air!'

Lindsey was not listening. 'Their strategy is so predictable. Question number one concerns where we're from, in the knowledge that most people are proud to mention their hometowns.'

'Particularly when miles away from it,' I agreed.

I looked around and noticed the same man attempting to initiate a conversation with a couple of peroxide blondes, no older than twenty, who looked as though they were waiting to be picked up anyway. Perhaps he had his own collection of introductory lines and selected them according to the type of potential prey. It all seemed as nauseatingly contrived as the rest of the place, almost clinical, as though he were just some computerized automaton following a tried and tested algorithm. I watched slyly as the two girls, designer labels sewn conspicuously onto their cheap clothes, progressively succumbed to a kind of flattery they mistook for charm. The desire to impress was equal, but the motives were opposite.

Tim's anger eventually subsided. 'Why did you refer to a revolver?'

'A columnist in the local rag stated that the drugs game was the modern-day equivalent of Russian roulette,' Lindsey explained, 'with barrels variable in size and bullets variable in number. Hard drugs represent a small barrel that is almost full, and to bet against such unfavourable odds is as arrogant as it is reckless.'

'Have you ever taken anything?' I asked him. 'Be honest.'

'Never, knowingly.'

'Not even at university?'

His reply remained in the negative.

'Ever smoked?'

'Expensive and unsociable way of screwing my own body. Why should I want to do that?'

Tim was exasperated. 'Jesus, was there ever a time in your life when you weren't so far-sighted?'

'I can't remember.'

'You do have a phenomenal intake of alcohol, though. Doesn't that kill your precious brain cells?'

Lindsey finished his drink. 'You consume almost as much as I do. If that's true, you'll be out of them altogether by the time you hit thirty - not that anyone will notice. Still, at least when your grey matter has degenerated irretrievably, you'll be ripe for a consultancy, especially in your field!'

The dealer glared for a moment in our direction as he stood up to leave, then cursed loudly. Lindsey waited until he had left the bar before speaking.

'Go on, push your filth, and your luck, somewhere else,' he spat, eyes fixed on the closed door. He then opened his right hand with the deliberation of a conjuror, and revealed a set of car keys. 'But you won't get far without these.'

Tim looked at him incredulously. 'You've just ...'

'Picked his jacket pocket - the louse.'

'Get rid of them!'

'Very well. Where's the nearest drain?'

Tim pointed his finger aggressively. 'Just knock it off! You're asking for trouble!'

Lindsey rattled the keys in front of his face. 'I hope he'll be stupid enough to ask the cops for assistance - and then get busted for possession.'

He was now as relaxed as he had been in Bangkok, probably reassured by the knowledge that only two lazy days stood between himself and Maalii's latest outpourings, but no less irritating as far as Tim was concerned.

'Remind me to buy some stamps in the morning,' he said.

'Canadian ones? What for?'

'I'll post them with my letter to Mr. King so, should he decide to reply, he won't have to buy any.'

'Mr. King?'

'The old man in Nathan Philip Square.'

Tim, still in argumentative mode, leaned provocatively forward and rested his elbows on the table. 'Fancy asking a complete stranger whether he believed in a god or not.'

'What's wrong with that?'

'It's inappropriately personal.'

'I knew he wouldn't object. He was very frank, polite, unassuming-'

'And very perceptive, which you found unsettling. You always do.'

'Stop digging, Sigmund. We all endeavour to keep some parts of our lives buried.'

'I don't.'

'That's because you have never experienced trauma.'

'True, but if I had, I wouldn't bottle it up or shovel it under the carpet.'

'How do you know you wouldn't?'

'I treat traumatized patients every day at the hospital. I understand the things that alleviate their pain.'

'Yes, about as well as a virginal midwife can appreciate the agony of natural childbirth.'

I sat back and let them continue toying with each other as we drank ourselves senseless - again. Lindsey avoided being too specific about his supposedly unsettling pre-university years, but we already knew that few tears had been shed when his Merseyside-bound train departed from Nottingham. Tim's long-held belief was that the entire neighbourhood had breathed a day-long sigh of relief when he announced his choice of university - but he did not know specifically why. Lindsey had shed his skin, as it were, and in doing so had been able to assume the guise of a different animal altogether. Tim called it *self-laundering*, and only certain people did it.

For the second consecutive evening, half an hour before midnight, three drunks stumbled pathetically out of an insignificant downtown bar and into the cool darkness. The frivolous sound of spiralling trumpets and moody saxophones spilled out of a first-floor jazz bar and echoed along the street.

'Breathe that noise,' Tim cooed, leaning against me in order to steady himself.

Lindsey's inevitable response was quick. 'Jazz is to music what anarchy is to law and order. Do you get it?'

'No.'

'The former is defined as being the absence of the latter!' He cackled at his own wit. 'On the other hand, perhaps they are just tuning up. Who can tell?'

'I can,' said Tim. 'All that alcohol must have gone to your ears.'

'My ears are fine. Perhaps, then, they are attempting to play Bach but are as polluted as we are.'

The never-ending drunken banter continued all the way back down Yonge to the hotel. For some reason, as we staggered across the foyer towards the lift, I imagined being confronted by the pompous receptionist from Hong Kong, seething under her breath and scowling in disgust, as if half-expecting one of us to urinate into the fountain on our way to bed.

We disappeared into Tim's room on the third floor. I slumped into the black leather armchair and rested my revolving head against the revolving wall. Thoughts of returning home had been resurfacing with increasing frequency throughout the evening; only seven days now remained, and the hours were passing ever faster.

'Stay there if you like,' said a soft voice.

I struggled to open my eyes just before Tim switched off the main light and collapsed onto his bed.

'Where's Lindsey?' I asked him.

'In his room, I think. He left half an hour ago, just after you fell asleep. To be honest, Phil, I'm long past caring.'

I let my head fall back again and sank deeper into the chair. Walking along the corridor to my own room would have required energy that I no longer possessed. Languishing, I replayed memorable clips of our adventure over and over again as my consciousness faded to nothing, like a worn-out battery. For the umpteenth time, I walked across the dusty yard into Maalii's parents' shack in Krasang, although on this occasion no one else was there, not even the little ones. I imagined that I had once lived there, and returned years later to discover the place derelict, the old couple having passed away and the children having grown up and made what they could of their lives elsewhere. In reality, I knew I would never visit the place again, and could therefore preserve it in my dreams exactly as I had seen it, in beautiful, unearthly ruin, and let *Krasang Day*, twentieth of September, live as long as the rest of me.

With what sparse light there was I could just make out the fuzzy silhouette of Tim, curled up asleep on the bed. I listened for a minute or two without moving but could hear absolutely nothing - no distant echoes from the street nor even the sound of his nasal, basal breathing. I guessed that it must have been between three and four o'clock in the morning - the smallest hour of all, even in hotels.

I stood up and crept to the door as lightly as I could so as not to disturb Tim. My head throbbed rhythmically as the blood blasted around inside, resulting in near-blinding pulsations right behind my eyes. I realized that, tragically, I was no further than halfway down the unavoidable path from stupor to hangover. Worse was set to follow.

I stepped out and clicked the door shut behind me, before noticing that I was wearing neither shoes nor socks. Instead of returning to my room, though, I plodded along the darkened corridor and made my way down to the ground floor bar to see whether Lindsey had opted to spend a second night taking his chance with a pack of cards. My suspicions were proved right.

'Christ, Phil, you look like a corpse! And where are your shoes, man?' he exclaimed, looking up from a partially-shaded corner table, which he was sharing with his three oriental adversaries; and judging by the unequal distribution of banknotes, he was in total control of the proceedings.

'I must refrain from taking your advice when it comes to choosing drinks,' I groaned. 'In any case, how are *you*? You ought to be exhausted. You haven't slept properly since we left LA.'

'I shall have to make up for it on the bus.'

'To Niagara Falls? The journey will last barely a couple of hours.'

'Better than none at all.'

One of the Japanese, a bloated, middle-aged man with a disgruntled expression apparently chiselled onto his face, looked at me, raised his eyebrows, then held out his hand, inviting me to join them.

I declined politely, and turned to Lindsey. 'What is this, *Insomniacs Anonymous*?'

'It's only twenty past three. You go and get yourself some sleep. I'll wake you up in time to check out.'

I shuffled back towards the lift, the inside of my skull was taking a relentless battering, like a sea wall at high tide.

Lindsey called after me. 'Make sure you drink plenty of water!'

I returned to my room which was cold from my having inadvertently left the window wide open all afternoon. I did as Lindsey had advised, then closed the window and fizzled out. The very last ounce of energy had finally drained from my body and every single muscle fibre rapidly relieved itself of even the slightest tension.

I came to my senses before he eventually tried to knock down the door at eight thirty. We crammed all my belongings into the bags which seemed to have shrunk. The pulsations inside my head, initially separate and distinct, had merged into one almighty central pain.

'How do you feel?' he inquired gently, but looking noticeably amused. 'As awful as you look?'

'Probably worse.'

'You'll feel much better after you've been sick a few times.'

'That's reassuring. Do you have the headache tablets?'

'I gave them to Tim, although there might not be any left.'

'He's suffering, too, is he?'

'Not to the same extent as you.'

That much was obvious; a worse feeling was frankly unimaginable.

He slung the larger of my bags over his shoulder, clasped the strap of the smaller one in his left hand and I followed him wearily down to the reception desk where Tim was already waiting.

'By the way, how much did you win last night?' I asked, not for a moment considering the possibility of his having come unstuck.

'You were gambling again?' Tim interrupted in disbelief.

'Just for a couple of hours. I didn't fare quite so well.'

Tim looked even more surprised. 'No?'

'No, I don't think I won more than a hundred and fifty dollars.'

'A measly sixty pounds. Is that all?' came the unsympathetic reply.

Tim looked at me and shook his head as Lindsey proceeded to pay his own share of the hotel bill with a fraction of his gains from the two-night poker massacre.

'And some postage stamps, if you will.'

'Certainly, sir,' said the lanky, flame-haired receptionist. 'How many would you like?'

'Ten at seventy-six cents, please.'

He concluded the transaction and smiled innocently. In only two days, he had roamed the city, stayed at a decent hotel, blown a fortune on whisky and beer, and was now about to leave for Niagara Falls having made a net profit.

'The majority of criminals,' Tim had once argued, 'are both unintelligent and uneducated, and because of that, society ought to be grateful. If people with Lindsey's brains were to divert their energies towards crime, then the scope for havoc would be endless.' He was certain Lindsey knew it, too.

XVII

'The original is unfaithful to the translation.'

Jorges Luis Borges (1899-1986)
Vathek Sobre el 'Vathek' de William Beckford

The westbound journey out of Toronto, down the billboard boulevard and along the Queen Elizabeth Way, was both smooth and free from the congestion we had witnessed on our previous bus ride, from Kanchanaburi to Bangkok, which by now felt cloudy and remote almost to the point of non-existence. Time continued its strange expansion. We by-passed the lakeside towns: Mississauga, Oakville - where the old man lived - Burlington and industrial Hamilton, without making a single pickup. I knew that the less stopping, changing of speed and turning of corners I had to endure, the greater the likelihood that the volcanic contents of my poor stomach would remain where they were.

Tim gently closed his eyes as the opening chords of *Bridge Over Troubled Water* drifted out of the coach radio speakers and filled the cooled air like a symphonic hymn flooding the confines of a small church. Oblivious to everything around him, he sat there like a meditating monk, mumbling along out of key, and probably also fantasizing about being able to play the piano.

Indeed, none of us uttered a coherent word until we eventually left the highway and began to navigate the sleepy streets of St. Catharine's to make our first scheduled stop. Rolling slowly through the town's pastoral suburbs gave us our first glimpse of autumn: gardens covered with shrivelled, pale brown leaves, many of which had blown on to the road and accumulated neatly along the gutters. What was more, the tidiness of their simple configuration could almost have fooled the eye into believing they had been placed there with conscious intent. It was art without the artist.

'How are the hieroglyphics coming along?' I muttered to Lindsey through the gap between the seats in front of me.

'Slowly,' he replied, rattling the end of his pencil between his teeth.

He was sitting at right angles to our direction of travel with his back against the window and his long, crossed legs sticking right out into the aisle. I leaned over the seat and scanned the pages of his black notebook on which he had been scribbling more Thai words and phrases, with their phonetic pronunciations and English equivalents in separate columns.

'Is it as intimidating as it looks?'

'Every bit. There are about thirty vowels, five tones, and the grammar is, quite honestly, a law unto its lawless self.'

'I'm sure your linguistic skills will improve very rapidly,' I added supportively.

'I hope so. Otherwise she'll think I'm as dim as you.'

While ignoring the insult, I smiled at his uncharacteristic expression of self-doubt. 'I think not.'

He slotted the long orange pencil down the spine of his book and closed it carefully.

'You know, languages evolve just like animals and religions. Forever undergoing short-term modification which invariably results in strange anomalies that make little sense in terms of overall design.'

'Such as what?' I said.

'Male nipples, for instance.'

'Languages are full of male nipples, are they?'

'Symbolically, yes. Evolution is a one-way street. Imperfection is inevitable. French nouns have gender, for instance. No good comes from it, but who can turn back the clock?'

'And what about religion?'

'Well, there are plenty of *useless tits* in the church!'

Tim sat up and began to laugh. 'Thirty-seven seconds!' he exclaimed. 'I knew it wouldn't be long!'

'What are you talking about?'

'A mere thirty-seven seconds after he stops writing, *Corker the Faithless* starts lambasting religion!'

'I wasn't commenting on the drug itself,' Lindsey corrected him. 'Karl Marx did that. I was mocking the pushers.'

Yet another acerbic repartee followed.

About a third of the passengers alighted at St. Catharine's, but we had to wait a further quarter of an hour because an old Jewish couple were attempting to board with invalid tickets. Once the problem had been resolved, to the satisfaction of neither them nor the driver, we moved off and rejoined the thickening highway traffic.

Lindsey persevered a little longer with his notes.

'I thought you were going to get some sleep,' I remarked.

'I feel fine. How are you?'

'Hungry, more than anything.'

To my surprise, the streets of Niagara Falls were as deserted as those of St. Catharine's. The only logical conclusion I could draw was that the falls themselves had to be a considerable distance from where we were about to be let out.

The driver pulled away, towards an empty crossroad, leaving the three of us apparently stranded at a tiny bus terminal building, inside which I could see only a portly woman puffing on a cigarette behind the snacks counter.

'So this is the place,' said Lindsey, equally puzzled as to why we had been dropped off at the edge of a ghost town.

'Which way?' I wondered.

'Listen for splashing water.'

'We'll have to ask someone,' said Tim.

After scanning the immediate vicinity of the terminal, he came across a young Chinese girl who was hurrying along, carrying a couple of bulging shopping bags.

'Excuse me!' he called to her.

'Straight along that road,' she answered, anticipating his question, without so much as a hint of an oriental accent. 'Then you'll need to take a left down a hill. There's a bank on the opposite corner. You can't miss them.'

'Don't bet on it,' said Tim, ventriloquist-style, under his breath.

Lindsay called out the name of the motel.

'If you arrive at the falls,' she replied, 'you'll have walked right past it.'

She continued on her way, past the terminal and along a quiet side street, having probably recited the exact same words *ad nauseam*. She was a tidy girl with shiny black hair, and from the back looked vaguely similar to Maalii. Lindsey was watching her dreamily.

'Could be, couldn't she?' I said.

'If only.'

She disappeared from view, leaving us to amble along the roadside in search of the motel which Lindsey had supposedly booked in Toronto. There was a calm but vacuous feel to the place, as if, in anticipation of the bleak winter months which I myself so despised, the entire town had been closed down and all the local children kept indoors.

A solitary railway line ran parallel to the road as far as the cloudy horizon, and an even autumnal blanket of dried yellow and red leaves obscured the grassy partition. It was difficult to envisage huge clanking trains passing so near to such a tranquil walkway. I considered, with my daydreamer's optimism, the possibility that the line might be out of use. The notion of passing trucks did seem absurdly inappropriate, as did the fact that the track itself was an exposed extension of the road.

Lindsey walked next to the track, head down, metronomically kicking up clusters of dry leaves into the air with each step. Watching him made me think back to our final evening in Bangkok, when he had casually strolled along the track between Soi Phasuk and the noisy Plaza. In contrast, however, there were now no sounds from either a row of outdoor bars or a dense swarm of cars and motorcycles, or anything else.

After about half a mile, we reached the junction that the young girl had described, and made our way down Clifton Hill. The motel consisted of a reception office strategically positioned at the roadside, and a large car park with a long row of flat-roofed, single-storey chalets dotted around its perimeter. We entered the office, leaving our bags outside on the step.

'Good afternoon,' came a woman's voice from behind the desk.

'We've reserved three single rooms for tonight,' Lindsey explained.

She studied her file, which was as chaotic as Lindsey's notebook. 'Mr. Croker?'

'Corker.'

'Oh, I do beg your pardon. I can't read my own writing here.'

'Never mind, it makes a change from *Cocker*.'

'Well, sir, regrettably, your rooms are still being cleaned. I'm afraid they won't be available for about an hour.'

'That's fine. Does that place next door serve breakfast?'

'It certainly does. All day long.'

'Excellent. We'll return at one.'

Across the road was a lively amusement park where teenage Neanderthals were wandering around in garish T-shirts and shorts so long and baggy that the crotch was at knee level. It was something they would not have had a hope of doing on an October day in England. I could not fathom the reason why, as well as dressing similarly, they all contrived to walk with the same Neanderthal gait.

Down towards the bottom of the hill were more tourist shops, motels and advertisement boards, but still no sign of the falls.

We pushed open the door to the cafe to find it virtually empty, thereby immediately distracting one of the waitresses - a gaunt woman with a black, beehive hairstyle and wearing a smart, pastel-blue apron. Full English and American breakfasts with a pot of tea and an unlimited supply of toast were on offer for only six dollars fifty, although I would have been happy to pay much more, such was my desperation to replenish myself. Poignantly, sitting huddled around a small breakfast table reminded me of our days with Maalii. It was as if our enjoyment had actually been enhanced by our inability to speak the Thai language. It saddened me, knowing how happy she would have been had she been able to travel with us. I could not imagine the intensity of the thoughts that had been pounding Lindsey's head since he kissed Maalii's head at the airport. In fact, the contrasting, but equally charged, exchanges that he had had in such a short space of time, with Maalii and then with Erin, would have stretched my own composure way beyond its limit.

'Do you feel any better?' said Tim, once we had finished eating.

'Much better. Even my head feels more or less normal.'

'Good. You were especially quiet on the bus.'

'I'm sorry. My mind has been wandering.'

'And it invariably ends up wandering around the same place,' said Lindsey knowingly.

'How can you tell?'

'Your face is a reflection of my own. It's like one of those silly word-asso-ciation games that Sigmund and his comrades play, where the subject subconsciously converges upon the same point. All your roads, like mine, lead back to Thailand. Am I right?'

I just nodded in agreement.

For once, he spoke openly: 'I hear a motorbike engine and think of the Sukhumvit traffic,' he said, 'I see a railway line and think of the Kwai Bridge. And when I saw that Chinese girl at the bus terminal ...'

It was all he was going to say. We made breakfast last as long as we could by ordering extra cups of viscous black coffee, then returned to the recep-tion kiosk a few minutes before one o'clock.

'Three, four and twenty-six,' said a different woman at the desk, before handing us three sets of keys, each of them attached to a rectangular piece of red perspex, about the same size as the place mats in the cafe. 'Two of the rooms are adjoining, but I'm afraid the other one is at the opposite end of the block-'

'I'll take number twenty-six,' Lindsey calmly interrupted, 'if it's all the same to you. I need to sleep.'

'You mean, lie down before you fall down.'

'Something like that. Wake me up at five, would you?'

'Very well.'

We carted our bags down the gently sloping car park towards the blocks of identical chalets. Lindsey turned around, shielding his eyes from the powerful midday sun.

'Well, goodnight!' he said, and headed in the opposite direction.

'Excuse me!' came a shrill voice from behind us. 'Excuse me! Which one of you is Mr. Croker?' It was the receptionist, slightly out of breath, having chased us halfway across the car park.

'It's *Corker*. There he is,' I said, 'over there. He took room twenty-six.'

'Ah. I forgot to tell him that a letter arrived for him by fax this morning, at about nine thirty.'

'Thanks. We'll give it to him. It'll save you having to walk all the way down there and back up again.'

'I appreciate that. Thanks very much.'

She handed over the letter which she had sealed inside a motel envelope and written the words: *Croker - arriving today* boldly on the front. We stood exactly where we were and watched as Lindsey unlocked the door to his room and disappeared inside.

'What should we do?' I muttered.

'Let him have it later. He must be exhausted,' said Tim, noticeably unsure of himself. 'He won't mind waiting a few hours, will he?'

'What if it's urgent?'

'How could it be?'

'Who knows we're here? No one.'

He paused for thought and then smiled. 'Nova.'

'How come?'

'Did he not mention the name of this place over the phone yesterday afternoon?'

'I can't remember.'

'I know!' he said, raising his forefinger. 'She has sent him a copy of Maalii's letter.'

'That's possible, but-'

'Just think. If she had mailed the thing, it might not have arrived in time.'

'So that's why she sent it by fax.'

'Come on,' he urged, 'he might not forgive us if we delay delivering it. A week is a long time when Lindsey is being unbearable.'

The door to number twenty-six was ajar. I pushed it open to find Lindsey lying on the bed, reading.

'This arrived for you in reception this morning,' I said, from the shadows of the doorway.

His eyes gleamed, thus supporting Tim's theory. 'Thank you,' he said, and took it without either looking at me or uttering another word.

We closed the door behind us and left him alone. I knew full well that he would read and translate it before finally succumbing to the need to close his overworked eyes.

The rooms were much more spacious than I had anticipated, each with a double bed, twin standard lamps at either side like a pair of goalposts, a large desk, and a combined bath and shower unit partitioned off at the rear.

I strolled with Tim between the cars to the road and turned left towards the foot of the hill. Eventually, the effusive Niagara River came into view and, over on the opposite side, the north-western extremity of the Empire State of New York. We crossed the road and stared over the wall like the couple of inquisitive children we once were, peering over the garden gate. To the left, the fast-flowing river raced between the supports of a lightweight, single-span suspension bridge conspicuously connecting Canada to the United States;

and, to our right, the magnificent horseshoe waterfalls which were partially obscured by an opaque white cloud of spray and vapour. We walked for about half a mile, content to be silent, until we were in line with the edge of the falls, and gazed in wonder at millions of gallons of water falling under tireless gravity. Hundreds of other tourists, mainly bug-eyed Americans, stood in clusters, holding cameras at the wall overlooking the plunging water; and below, one of those small pleasure boats was valiantly fighting its way through the endless waves.

Standing with our backs to the spectacle, we noticed the imposing Skylon Tower, which resembled a giant stonemason's gavel, protruding above a small but dense area of well-established woodland. I watched as its yellow lift cage ran smoothly up the outside of the tower to the observation deck, like an insect crawling up the stem of a sunflower.

Despite the fact that we could not find anything to say to each other, we did not leave the busy viewing area until four thirty. Clouds had begun to invade the sky, to the point where I expected it to rain, but the fall in temperature was barely even noticeable.

My feelings were becoming contradictory. I was not ready to go home, but I could hardly wait to reach Manhattan. I was utterly drained after having travelled for so long, and yet I cherished every single trip - ten-minute tuk-tuk rides as fondly as the gruelling flights.

We returned to the foot of Clifton Hill and made our way slowly back to the motel. From a distance, I could see that the lights were on in room twenty-six but there was no sign of any movement from behind the flimsy green curtains. Perhaps he was sound asleep, I thought to myself, or still reading, or even outside somewhere.

To my surprise, Lindsey opened the door before we reached it.

'Have you slept?' I called.

'A little.'

'What about the letter?' Tim asked. 'Was it from Maalii?'

'Yes. I thought it was strange when Nova asked where we'd be staying. Now I know why.' He shook his head. 'She's so appallingly thoughtful.'

We followed him inside. He picked up the letter from the desk at which he had been working, and passed it to me.

'Have you completed the translation?'

'Just this minute. Amazingly, she managed to write parts of it in English.'

'What about the Thai bits?'

'She did as I suggested and wrote in big letters - as if she were writing for the benefit of a child, I guess. It wasn't overly taxing.'

'May we read it?'

I removed the pages from the envelope and sat down.

From: Nova K. Corker, Manhattan, NY.

October 2nd.

Dear Lindsey,

I hope you don't object to my having opened your package - not that I would be able to decipher much of the letter, even if I tried. I just sensed that, after our conversation yesterday, you would rather not have to wait until Friday, so forgive me if I have done the wrong thing.

There were also several photographs enclosed. She is every bit as stunning as you described. I won't tell you what Jacques said yesterday morning. Unfortunately, he'll be in Baltimore until Sunday afternoon. I can only apologize on his behalf.

Incidentally, Adam van Bergen phoned again. What on earth happened in LA? I couldn't understand why he was shouting at me. What am I supposed to have done? No doubt you will enlighten me in your inimitable style. I shall look forward to it.

Well, our kid, stay out of mischief, if you can. I'll be here waiting for you on Friday morning.

Love, Nova.

'So, Adam has phoned for a second time,' I remarked, not that he needed reminding.

Lindsey nodded. 'I said he would. But if Nova doesn't know the saga, then it follows that Adam hasn't heard it, either. Not yet, anyhow.'

I handed the covering page to Tim and turned to Lindsey's untidily scribbled notes.

28/1, Soi Phasuk,
Sukhumvit Road,
Bangkok 10300.

25 September.

My love,

How are you? Fine, yes? How was your fly to Hong Kong? Please write and tell me anything about you. Any good news will make me happy. I would like only that I could have my dream come true and be near to you.

Right now, I can not concentrate at all. I am ..... always think of you. Want to know what you are doing. Please, please do not disappoint me. I really hope and trust in you. If you disappoint me, I really do not know how my life would/will be.

Lindsey, I do not feel so well. I am ill, not good my health, so I have not worked for several days. Just lay down in bed only looking at your picture. My friends take care me.

I hope you not mind that I write mainly in Thai. I know you are very clever man. I ?admiration for you because of that.

I give you six photographs. Do you like them? My birthday is 12 October. I expect nothing. Except a card, if it is your wish.

Please answer me soon. Remember I (always) do what I promise you. That the truth from my heart.

I love you still. Maalii.

I passed the remaining pages to Tim and looked up at Lindsey, impressed by his translation.

'I shall post my next letter to her in New York,' he said calmly, 'along with a birthday card, a few photographs and of some of the money I won at the hotel.'

If he had harboured even the slightest reservations about her sincerity, they had dissolved in just a few broken phrases. Tim sat down on the edge of the bed and studied every word carefully, as he would if it had been a psychological profile of one of his more impenetrable patients. I looked outside and noticed how dark it had suddenly become. Rain had begun to pour from the grey, overpowering sky we had hoped would not follow us from Los Angeles.

Lindsey became ecstatic. He opened the door and stepped outside. 'Let it rain!' he bellowed theatrically, as if he were on stage, performing for hundreds of people in the car park. 'Let the heavens haemorrhage until they have bled themselves dry! Not a drop will fall on me!'

In a matter of seconds, his hair and shirt were saturated. He stretched out his arms, in the style of an opera singer, and leaned backwards.

'Goodnight, goodnight! Parting is such sweet sorrow, that I shall say-'

'Close the door, you fool,' said Tim restlessly. 'Anyone might be listening.'

He came back inside after a minute, so blatantly pleased with himself, beads of water streaming down his face. I closed the door behind him.

'Perhaps I've been a closet Romeo all my life,' he suggested unconvincingly and, I assumed, jokingly.

Tim scoffed, then stated the obvious: 'You? You're as cynical as anyone I know.'

'About the sexier sex?'

There was a brief pause.

'About most things.'

'Past tense,' he whispered, before heading for the bathroom, singing to himself.

'Past credibility, you mean.'

'In any case, cynicism is just an unpleasant way of saying the truth.'

'Says who?'

'Lillian Hellman.'

'Who?'

'She was an American dramatist, old fruit. Did you not read *The Little Foxes* at school? Did you not read anything at school?'

As he disappeared into the bathroom, Tim sat down on the edge of the huge desk.

'At least he's happy,' I said quietly.

'Yes,' he responded, 'let's hope nothing spoils his picnic when we arrive in New York.'

'Such as what?'

'Such as Adam phoning again.'

'He might not,' I said.

'He will!' Lindsey yelled above the noise of running water from the bathroom.

He had been listening to our conversation. Consequently, neither one of us uttered another word until he reappeared.

'Not only will he continue to pester my sister,' he added, 'but I reckon he will also have been in touch with Jacques.'

'Does that annoy you?' asked Tim.

'Jacques can take care of himself. But if Nova gets upset,' he said, wagging his finger, 'he will *erupt*.'

'That goes without saying.'

'In fact, he's so damned protective, it's almost pathological. At university, some creep from the squash club tried to force himself onto my sister. Jacques stormed in, clasped the guy's balls in one hand ... and lifted him off the ground.' Those emerald eyes filled with a mixture of defiance and pride. '*No one* hurts Nova.'

XVIII

'Conversation has a kind of charm ... an insinuating and insidious
something that elicits secrets from us ...'

Seneca (c.4BC-65AD)
Epistles

I was more reluctant than usual to drag myself out of bed before noon the
next day. The forthcoming night was destined to be spent sitting uncomfortably upright on board a packed coach, which implied that I would most likely
endure eight further hours of sleep deprivation, so I felt an obstinate self-
justification in stealing the extra rest.

As I lay there, searching for human faces in the ceiling's messy plaster-
work, I wondered how Lindsey truly felt, having learned that Maalii was so
unwell. It would have been impossible, even for him, to deduce the extent of
her illness merely from reading her letter; although being confined to bed did
indicate some degree of severity. In a brief moment of nightmarish morbid-
ity, I contemplated the worst predicament imaginable, namely that she had
contracted one of the horrendous diseases to which Joel had referred at the
Plaza. I did not dwell on it for long.

Tim opened the adjoining door. 'Are you up?'

I threw back the blankets and jumped to my feet. 'I am now. Is Lindsey
still in his room?'

'No, he went to the breakfast cafe about a quarter of an hour ago. I said
we'd meet him there.'

'You go on ahead,' I told him, 'I'll be along in five minutes.'

Twenty minutes after Tim had left, I had a quick wash, threw on the last
of my clean clothes and took my bags to the reception desk, ready for our
eventual departure. Outside, the ground was slowly recovering from the
torrents of the previous night, and the air was now as cool as that of a typical autumnal day back in England.

In the cafe, Lindsey was enthusiastically spilling out his latest thoughts to
Maalii on headed notepaper which I presumed he had taken from the bureau
in his room. I sat down next to Tim, who had already devoured his breakfast,
and watched as Lindsey completed his paragraph with impressive fluency.

He leaned back and called to the waitress - the same woman with the
impossible hairstyle who had attended to us the previous day.

'Three more coffees, if you will.'

'And an American breakfast, please,' I added.

'Certainly, sir. Thank you.'

Lindsey folded his incomplete letter and placed it carefully between the pages of his book, *Railway of Death*, which he had purchased in preparation for our trip to Kanchanaburi. It went without saying that he was not learning the language so painstakingly, purely to enable him to write letters; but I knew that bombarding him with further questions would be futile. I still refused to reject Tim's hunch that Maalii, somehow, would be meeting us in New York or, more incredibly, waiting at Heathrow Airport the following Tuesday.

We wandered down the hill again, towards the falls. For once Tim and I knew what lay around the corner, whereas Lindsey did not. The unusual feeling of superiority was as odd as it was amusing. The day's congregation of wide-eyed tourists, most of their faces obscured by either cameras or binoculars, lined the roadside, watching the boats and gazing at people gazing back at them from the opposite bank. A pleasant afternoon was gradually taking shape. It possessed a familiar essence: the fresh smell of damp leaves and grass, and a playful breeze blowing leisurely in from the Niagara River.

After spending two whole hours looking idly down on the world from the observation deck of the Skylon Tower, we returned to *terra firma* in as relaxed and docile a state as we had ever known, listening to Lindsey's tales of life in New York City. Each of us bought another batch of postcards, and several loose bottles of beer which we intended to consume, albeit covertly, on the bus to Buffalo. Additionally, Lindsey paid fifteen dollars for a huge white T-shirt, emblazoned on the front with a bright blue maple leaf, and changed into it at the roadside as casually as fastening a shoelace.

The crowds gradually dispersed and the sun began its descent to mark the closing of day fifteen. The prospect of seeing it re-emerge early the next morning above the equally famous skyline of Manhattan made me think that the best was in fact yet to come.

We collected the bags from the reception area of the motel and called into the cafe for one final meal, possibly my last ever in Canada. I liked the warmth of the cafe. It was a homely sort of place which we had not once seen more than half-full, and the waitresses were happy to let us sit at our window-table writing postcards long after the dirty plates and coffee cups had been cleared away.

'England ... a distant memory,' Lindsey muttered in monotone, whilst scribbling. 'Might return ... some day ...'

'Whose is that?'

'This one's for my mother, although I've written the same words on the others.'

'Very imaginative of you.'

'They'll get the message, I'm sure.'

'How many have you written?'

'Three.'

'Is that all?'

He nodded. 'But I did send a letter to my cousin in London. Six pages.'

'When did you do that?'

'I wrote it in Hong Kong and posted it with my first letter to Maalii.'

'You told your cousin about Maalii?'

'I had to,' he insisted, which puzzled me greatly.

'Why?' asked Tim, who was equally baffled as to why he claimed to have had no choice in the matter and, as ever, unable to contain his curiosity.

Lindsey simply smiled. 'Just keeping him informed.'

'And us in the dark,' Tim sighed, before collecting all the postcards together. 'We can post these tomorrow morning.'

The waitress walked across to us from the counter and slipped the bill discreetly onto the edge of the table.

'Ready?' I said.

We left enough money to cover both the cost of the meal and a sizeable tip, then once more hoisted the bags onto our shoulders, ready for yet another departure.

'Nice meeting you,' called the waitress with a sincere, affectionate smile. 'And have a safe journey back to London.' I knew she meant it, and that alone was worth the tip.

We filed out and laboured with the bags to the brow of Clifton Hill, having walked down it for the very first time only thirty hours previously. The thought of it seemed absurd.

The tranquillity we had witnessed the previous morning returned the moment we took the necessary right turn to head back to the bus terminal. It was as if one of the most peaceful settlements in the whole of North America had been mistakenly selected to exhibit one of nature's most spectacular works.

A middle-aged man came out of the side entrance to one of the timber-framed dwellings opposite the railway track as we walked by. I nodded my head politely in acknowledgement.

'Hello there,' he replied quietly, evidently accustomed to the sight of strangers laden with rucksacks strolling past his veranda, even in October.

He climbed into his vehicle - an ungainly, rusting pick-up truck, similar to the one in which we had toured the Kwai Valley - and set off steadily along the deserted road ahead of us. Long after the truck had disappeared from sight, the noise from its engine lingered, like a haunting musical cadenza - performed by a cellist, perhaps. The subsequent stillness made me ask myself whether I could be certain that it had actually appeared.

Maybe I was more tired than I thought.

Our lonely return walk to the windswept bus terminal took only half as long as I had anticipated. I noticed the narrow side street along which the young oriental girl had walked the previous morning. I could still see her there, striding purposefully with her shopping bags towards a row of small townhouses, her silky hair flowing uncannily like the falling waters that we had travelled so far to see.

Lindsey looked at me out of the corner of his eye and laughed for a moment. 'What is it?' I asked him.

'That street reminded you of the girl we saw yesterday.' I had become hardened to feeling his eyes penetrating my head. 'And you thought of Maalii.' There was a brief but significant pause. 'I know,' he confessed with gentle sincerity, 'I see her everywhere I look.'

'Is that such a problem?'

'A few days ago, it was. But not now.'

'You're doing it *again*,' Tim interrupted with unexpected force.

'Doing what?'

'Inviting questions that you haven't the slightest intention of answering!'

'I was inviting nothing,' Lindsey protested. 'You see things that aren't there.'

'Nonsense.'

'Yes you do. You analyse everything. I'm not joking, you'd analyse your arsehole if you could make eye contact with it.'

I loitered in the shadow of the locked-up terminal building, simultaneously observing what scarce life there was and listening as they launched into yet another duet of mocking each other's perceived foibles. As we waited, two identical buses arrived and then departed, both of them bound for St. Catharine's and Toronto, and both of them full of tired heads propped up against the windows. By eight o'clock darkness had fallen, the Buffalo bus was still nowhere in sight, but the bickering continued in full swing.

'What do we do if it fails to show up?' I said, fumbling for reassurance.

'Don't fret,' said Tim, 'it will.'

Lindsey, typically, disagreed. 'Six years ago, when I visited the States for the very first time, I waited for a bus, alone, at a remote pick-up point outside Ashtabula, Ohio, and the damned thing never appeared. That, too, was supposed to go to Buffalo.'

'What did you do?'

'I gambled.'

'Naturally.'

'My only chance of reaching New York was to head in the opposite direction, to Cleveland, in the hope that from there I could then complete the journey across southern Pennsylvania.'

'Did you make it?'

'With seconds to spare. Had I been late, I would still have been stranded but further away. And I'm telling you, some of the undesirables prowling downtown stations over here make the gutter gang at Euston look about as threatening as a bunch of choirboys.'

Another chrome-panelled bus swung round the corner of the block and pulled up right where we had dropped our bags. To my relief, it was bound for Buffalo before continuing eastward to the state capital, Albany and, finally, Boston. The driver, a baby-faced man who looked no older than Lindsey, jumped down the steps and checked the tickets.

'Go right on in,' he mumbled, with a noticeable Irish accent. 'I'll take care of your belongings.'

We climbed unhesitatingly inside and the bus was soon back on the highway. Within minutes, the myriad lights of downtown Buffalo burst into view and twinkled like tiny crystals through the tinted windows.

'Peace Bridge,' said Lindsey, just before the driver announced that we had reached the well-patrolled border.

The immigration formalities took an eternity but, after re-entering the United States, we arrived at the bus terminal almost immediately. It was considerably smaller than the one at Dundas-Bay in Toronto, but nevertheless full of the usual suspects: two muscle-bound Aryans, loaded with rucksacks the size of military parachutes, staring up at the timetable board; a large family of Negroes sitting peacefully in the furthest corner; and a young Hispanic girl struggling to pacify a tiny baby in a wicker carrycot. The small shop in the centre of the concourse, displaying baseball posters and pennants, was closed for the night; and nothing more than the occasional brief discussion at the booking desk disturbed the desolate atmosphere.

Lindsey ambled around inquisitively. 'This is the place I should have reached when I was nineteen - if only the bus had turned up.'

Tim slumped down next to the bags, folded his arms and closed his eyes. He looked thoroughly bored, and not for the first time. Dramatically, a ferocious argument broke out at the ticket desk. A young black woman, travelling with more luggage than the three of us put together, began shouting and swearing at one of the drivers who, in contrast, defended himself in a whisper audible only to the woman herself. She was heading home to Memphis and had missed her final connection. Whose fault it was, I could not figure out from only one half of the conversation, even though that particular side did account for ninety per cent of both the noise and emotion.

Finally, having presumably gone through every possible combination of expletives, she sat down opposite Tim, still salivating at the prospect of having to wait an hour and a half for the next service, which would be going no further south than Pittsburgh. The other passengers averted their gaze, and Tim feigned sleep in a blatant attempt to distance himself from her unceasing fury.

Lindsey turned his attention away from the timetable board and smiled wryly.

'Three cheers for third-class travel! Where else could you encounter someone like her?' he mumbled, having been thoroughly entertained. 'People of her type don't exist outside bus and railway stations. Do you remember that drunkard on the Underground in London?'

He proceeded to mimic the man's melodic Tyneside accent, eyes half-closed and slurring his speech, exactly like the ataxic, alcoholic wreck the man himself had become. I could not help but think of my father. If only his own pathetic addiction had given rise to a similar display of spontaneous humour and humility, as opposed to the countless episodes of gratuitous aggression and violence. But I realized that the man on the train was the exception - my father the rule.

The Memphis woman stared at Lindsey, doubtless believing that he was a perfect example of one of the 'crack-brained oddballs' to which he had jokingly referred. Foolishly, Tim looked up and inadvertently made eye contact with her.

'Where you goin'?' she asked, jerking her head back impatiently.

'Er ... New York.'

'Manhattan?'

'That's right. The bus leaves at eleven.'

'Ha! You hope it does!'

His door had been forced open. Having engaged him in a conversation that he had tried to avoid, she proceeded to relay the intricacies of her woes regardless of his apparent wish to be left alone. Once again, the rest of us had no choice but to listen to the woman's amplified ramblings of anger and self-pity until, to everyone's relief, the Pittsburgh bus arrived.

By ten thirty, a small but noticeably restless crowd, mostly teenagers, had congested around the departures bay. Some serious chaos was brewing.

'OK, *Noo Yawk Ciddy*! Anyone here for *Noo Yawk Ciddy*?' barked a pot-bellied man in a well-worn blue uniform from the other side of the glass doors. It was lucky for him that the partition was there, otherwise he would probably have been trampled to death.

Inside the coach, few seats were vacant, so we had to sit wherever we could: Lindsey next to an obese man who occupied about two thirds of the space, Tim right at the back next to the toilet cubicle, and myself directly behind the driver's cab. I found it rather transparent when passengers sitting alone on double seats would spread out and pretend to be sound asleep as others made their way down the aisle. In all fairness, however, perhaps they were the only ones who had adequate space in which to make themselves comfortable enough to sleep in the first place, as being squashed next to some other poor soul with the same problem made the task laughably impossible. Some of the desperate, contorted positions I had seen adopted by bus passengers over the years were beyond description.

Predictably, I was unable to sleep, so I remained content to stare silently into the dark wilderness, with only the characteristic green road signs for company. Everyone else appeared to have drifted off. Even when we arrived at Syracuse to pick up two other passengers, there was barely a stir from behind me.

We quickly resumed the journey, rolling on and on through the forgotten, rural wastelands, where young people reputedly spent Friday nights indoors getting better acquainted with their cousins, as oblivious to us as we were to them. I shuffled down to the toilet compartment, stepping over bodies which were lying full length in the aisle, and taking care not to tread on any stray feet. Lindsey, sandwiched securely between the obese man and equally immovable window, was fast asleep, as was Tim, who had managed, incredibly, to fold his legs into the foetal position without disturbing the woman next to him, whose head had lolled forward onto the back of the seat in front. As the bus sped along, her lifeless head wobbled around as if her neck were made of rubber.

The toilet bowl was completely blocked with paper and, to compound the problem, there was a large, punched-out hole in the bottom of the cubicle door where water and vomit had begun to trickle through to the aisle whenever we rounded a bend or hit a bump in the road. The stench struck my face with the force of a sledgehammer, and I knew that it would have diffused through the hole well before our arrival. For that reason alone, I felt relieved to be sitting at the front.

Sure enough, by sunrise, the smell had invaded the entire vehicle, although Lindsey remained asleep and, therefore, totally oblivious to the collective feeling of nausea.

When we arrived at our final pick-up point - Newark, New Jersey - everyone on board was either moaning or making crude comments.

'Sonofabitch!' came a gruff voice from the back. 'Goddam bus has gotten like a ... like a sewage pond on wheels!'

Several hoots of barely-restrained laughter rang out and I turned my head to see small puddles of water, or possibly urine, soaking into the floor. I then heard Lindsey's voice:

'Any more complaints about the smell of piss, and you'll be out on *urea!*'

The laughter escalated, and a perverse sense of camaraderie was born from the realization that every one of us, driver included, was breathing the same pungent air. Another great, heart-warming leveller had just made its mark.

The doors opened after we had come to a halt, and the unluckiest person in the world, a businessman carrying a suit on a coat-hanger, climbed inside. Everything fell ominously silent as he headed towards the only available seat which, tragically for him, was situated right next to the toilet. He could have been forgiven for thinking that this was some tasteless practical joke.

'*Jeeeezus* H. Chrysler,' he mumbled to himself. 'Looks like we got a problem with the bathroom back here.'

The rest of us sniggered in unison at his understated misfortune. *Bathroom*, I thought to myself. If ever a word had been used as an insult to its definition, we had just heard it.

Fortunately, he did not have to suffer for very long. We arrived at the bottleneck entrance to the Lincoln Tunnel at a quarter to seven and resurfaced in midtown Manhattan, the epicentre of New York City, glad to be on the threshold of respiratory freedom.

The three of us stood in front of the Port Authority Bus Terminal at the junction of West 42nd Street and Eighth Avenue, and tried to work out our bearings. Never before had polluted city air acted as such a tonic to my lungs. Typically, we found ourselves at the sleazy end of town, which consisted of the now-familiar array of dazzling red triple-X signs leading to peep shows, sex shops and strip joints, all patrolled by a motley assortment of street-hardened drop-outs who were milling around the corner of the block.

'There was no mention of this little lot in the book!' remarked a stunned Tim. 'It's hell,' he gasped. 'We've finally arrived in hell.'

Lindsey laughed. 'Charming, isn't it?' he said, apparently pleased to have discovered that nothing had really changed since his last visit.

'Come on,' said Tim, 'let's hail a cab. We look too conspicuous to be navigating streets of this nature.' I shared his reservations.

All the streets and avenues were awash with the characteristic yellow taxi cabs, just as Bangkok had been with tuk-tuks. How I was missing Bangkok. I hated the fact that the memories were deteriorating so quickly.

Once we were out of the seedy district, there was hardly anyone in sight, except for the occasional crop of joggers taking the early morning air in Central Park, risking heart attacks in an effort to prevent them. I would have fallen asleep if the ride had lasted more than a few minutes.

We climbed out, a short distance from what I thought was the junction of West 76th and Broadway. Lindsey waved towards the upper storeys of a dark stone building across the street. I looked around but failed to see any movement in the mass of square windows.

'I see that you decided against walking!' called a familiar English voice from behind me. 'I figured you would!'

It was Nova, beaming at us from the entrance to a Gothic apartment block, and looking thoroughly radiant, even at such an early hour. Apart from her above-average height, she looked nothing at all like Lindsey. Indeed, some people found it difficult to believe they were related at all. Her strawberry-blonde hair, which, according to Lindsey, she tended to 'flavour' from time to time, was considerably shorter than during her college years, coiffured into a neat bob, but with the same girlish fringe which all but covered her eyes. She had a thoroughly honest look about her, vulnerable perhaps, and was, in an unconventional, almost indescribable way, quite beautiful.

She greeted Tim and me with a generous kiss on the cheek then hugged her brother dearly, as if they had not seen each other since they were children.

'Good to see that you actually made it.'

'Thanks for letting us stay,' I replied.

'That's not a problem, Phil. I wish you could come over more often.'

We followed her into the foyer - which, being surprisingly modern, looked totally out of keeping with the building's weathered exterior - and took the lift to the third floor. It was evident that they were new to the property, in which they had installed only a minimal quantity of furniture, stylish though it undoubtedly was. It was also the first time Lindsey had seen it.

'What do you think, then?'

'This is a decent apartment,' he affirmed, peering out on to the street.

'And it's much bigger.'

'Great. We won't all have to sleep on top of each other.'

'We practically stole it,' she added, then turned to Tim and me. 'The other place, which we were renting over in Greenwich Village, was falling apart by the day. We were given the option of buying it, but Jacques was determined to move to the Upper West Side. This is where most of our friends live.'

'Wise decision,' said Lindsey, removing Maalii's photographs from his precious package. 'And let's face it, your neighbours down there made the Munsters look normal.'

'That's another reason,' she said. 'Jacques used to tell everyone that they were aliens! More alarmingly, quite a few people in the neighbourhood were prepared to believe him!'

To the accompaniment of laughter, I carted the bags through to the small bedroom at the rear, which I alone had been allocated. I then returned to the living room and sat down wearily on the black leather couch, happy to let the conversation continue without me.

XIX

**'Now I'm dead in the grave with my lips moving
And every schoolboy repeating my words by heart.'**

Osip Mandelstam (1891-1938)
Poems, **No.306**

My irregular sleeping pattern continued. I came round at two o'clock in the afternoon, only to discover that the others had gone. In what was widely reputed to be one of the noisiest cities in the world, there was an unnerving silence, as if I were all alone in it.

I was relieved when the door opened.

'Are you feeling all right, Phil?'

'Fine, thanks, Nova.'

'You were tired.'

'Still am.'

'Were you unable to sleep on the coach?'

'I'm afraid so,' I said, furiously rubbing my eyes. 'Where are Lindsey and Tim?'

'They disappeared about half an hour ago. I said we'd meet them once you'd woken up, if that's all right with you.'

'Where have they gone?'

She looked puzzled. 'Lindsey said you'd know.'

'He did? How?'

'I've no idea. Did he not say anything to you?'

'Nothing at all.'

'Where do you suppose they would have wanted to go?'

The answer eventually came to me. 'Where would they go to get the best view of the city?'

'To the top of the Empire State Building, I guess. That's where most people go.'

'That's it!' I concluded confidently.

'Are you sure?'

'Positive.'

'In that case, Lindsey was right. You *did* know. Do you mind if we walk there?' she then suggested, very casually.

'Not at all. How far is it?'

'A mile or so. We can go across the park if you like. Besides, there's something I really need to discuss with you.'

I knew exactly what she wanted to hear, and I was quite prepared to speak openly with her, but my heart raced nonetheless.

We left the apartment and began to amble back towards Central Park. By now, the streets had come to life, but the grey autumnal air remained stubbornly cool.

'You know what I want to ask about, don't you?'

'I think I do,' I admitted.

We stopped at the kerb.

'Do you promise you'll be frank with me, Phil?' she pleaded.

'Of course.'

She took a deep breath. 'What happened with Erin van Bergen?'

'What do you already know?'

'Precious little. Adam phoned last Tuesday, wanting to know when you'd be arriving. When I asked what was wrong, he stuttered to himself for a minute, hung up, and I was left none the wiser. He called again the following day, sounding even less coherent and extremely impatient. He said, as his sister was already devastated as a consequence of their mother's death, the very last thing she needed was, I quote, "*some atheistic limey know-all twisting the knife*". This time I hung up. I assumed he was referring to my brother.'

'He was, yes.'

She looked even more concerned, for Lindsey's sake rather than her own. 'I don't get it, Phil. What happened?'

We crossed the broad avenue and headed down the entrance path into the park, where dozens of New Yorkers were strolling around the lake. I recalled everything as fairly as I could, beginning with our first day in Los Angeles, in particular Erin's disgraceful remarks about poor Maalii. Nova listened carefully, piecing my recollections together without uttering a word, but I knew that she could easily have anticipated the whole sorry melodrama from beginning to end. The more I explained, the more I seemed able to remember, as if my brain were composed of rows and rows of neural dominoes, but I took care, nonetheless, not to omit anything through carelessness.

She eventually broke her silence. 'It's largely my fault,' she insisted. 'I knew it would resurface. I knew it.'

'I don't follow.'

'I ought to have told Jacques not to mention Adam's offer. She was always going to show up - with her loose tongue and all.'

It was my turn to be curious. 'What are you saying?'

'Last year, about this time as it happens, Erin came to a dinner party one Saturday evening at our old place, and I spent the best part of an hour boasting to her about my brother - his looks, intellect, and the fact that he seems to be able to walk on water. I should have kept my mouth shut.'

'That doesn't make it your fault,' I reassured her.

'It does. Jacques knew instantly that she resented what I was saying, and now, his working relationship with Adam will become restrained to say the least. It could prove costly.'

'You can't blame yourself,' I said, firmly but sympathetically. 'She instigated the whole thing.'

Nova nodded thoughtfully. 'I appreciate what you're telling me, but had she thrown something other than her religion into his face, anything at all, he would never have thought to react.'

'Why is he so aggressive towards Christians and the like? I mean, a couple of days ago he was comparing priests to drug-pushers. What's his problem?'

'His *problem*, Phil, has been festering for years.' She stopped walking and looked at me inquisitively: 'Has he ever told you about the incident at *The Ablutions*?'

'I don't think so.'

'Thought not.'

''I'm not sure I want to know!'

'It was a not-so-affectionate nickname for our Alma Mater,' she explained. 'Most of the corridor walls were covered from floor to ceiling with those hideous, white porcelain tiles. Some wag had once remarked that it looked like a giant urinal.'

'What happened, then?'

'Lindsey was in his first year when I was in my final one. You will keep this to yourself, won't you?'

'Are you serious? He'll know, the second he looks at me.'

She smiled. 'Most probably, but I think you have the right to know.'

I was immediately reminded of what Lindsey had said in Toronto, about the need to bury parts of one's past, and Tim's scepticism about individuals who contrive to rewrite their own histories. As we walked steadily, the magnificent midtown buildings beyond the park's southern perimeter fence did not appear to be getting any nearer, not that I minded. I knew that Nova would become bored of explaining long before I lost my willingness to listen.

'Throughout that year,' she began, 'Lindsey and I used to walk to and from school together every day. It was at least a mile from home and we lived too far from the local bus route. Even then, he could talk about anything. In many ways he was older than I was. He still is!' she added, as an admiring afterthought.

'I know how you feel.'

'I remember this particular walk as vividly as any. It was a typically dull, late winter's day, and he was walking under my umbrella, sheltering from the drizzle. I was much the taller back then, don't forget. Anyway, he stopped suddenly, in the middle of the lane, and asked me why we prayed, apart from the fact that it was a requirement. Standing there, getting wet through, he wanted to know the reason.'

'What did you tell him?'

'What *could* I tell him? I was only fifteen.'

'And he would have been all of eleven.'

She smiled again. 'Back then he was always full of questions, some quite profound, others just plain weird. By the time we had arrived at the school gates, however, we'd gone on to discuss other things. I watched him follow his friends into the classroom and thought nothing more of it.'

Her eyes began to fill. I stopped and placed my hand gently on her shoulder.

'Don't go on if it is distressing you,' I said, although I had no idea why it was.

'I'm fine, really. I've told the story enough times.'

'I'm sure you must have.'

'Every Friday morning, without exception, we had our weekly assembly in the main hall - first and second-year pupils at the front, and so on, with my own class at the back. This particular Friday was no different from any other. We would mumble one or two hymns and listen to the headmaster bleating about whatever was currently annoying him. Finally, before we all dispersed, we had to recite a whole series of prayers. School policy. He insisted on it.' She began to speak dreamily. 'Only this time, one kid, out of six hundred, wouldn't bow his head.'

'Lindsey?'

'I went numb. I started to shiver. He ... he just stared forward, right into the headmaster's eyes, as if he were in a trance. "*You! Head down!*" But still he refused. I knew exactly what was going through his mind.'

'I wouldn't have dared to attempt a stunt like that,' I admitted.

'Nor would I, especially in front of the entire school.'

'What was the head's reaction?'

'He screamed: "*Get here, now!*" The rest of us watched Lindsey climb the steps on to the rostrum and walk over to where the head was standing.' She raised her voice dramatically. 'By now the old fool was incandescent.' It softened once more. 'And our kid just stood there, quietly defiant. I wanted to run out to protect him, not that I could have done anything.' She sighed and then smiled, somewhat apologetically. 'You must think I'm terribly soft where Lindsey is concerned.'

'Just true to your nature.'

She sat down on the grass, freshly cut perhaps for the last time before winter, just as we finally approached the exit into Fifth Avenue, and began to sob a little. Her tears seemed to be born of anger rather than either sadness or pity. I sat at her side and put my arm across her shoulder, stroking her hair, perhaps more than I ought, and said nothing until she spoke again.

'To make an example of him, the head thrust the book into his hands and ordered him to read the so-called *Lord's Prayer*, aloud, presumably to deter other potential miscreants from contemplating any similar acts of dissent. Don't ask me how but, amid the ranting and lecturing, our kid kept his composure.' Her tone softened further. 'Until he saw me. The second he looked into my eyes, his lip began to tremble and the tears began to flow, and I had no choice but to stand there with everyone else and watch.' She glanced up at my expressionless face. 'He looked so small, Phil, up there all alone in his oversized blazer and school tie. He looked as insignificant as a toy soldier.'

'Was he made to recite all of it?'

'Every last word. He could barely speak for crying, and he continually had to wipe the tears from his cheeks with his sleeve. After the old bully was satisfied, he was ordered out and instructed to wait outside the caning chamber.'

'Was he caned?'

'Yes - for "blatant disobedience", which had occurred merely because no one had ever given him a rational reason for worshipping something he couldn't even see.

'Lastly, to make matters worse still, he had to walk back into his classroom midway through the lesson. You know, for weeks and weeks, the school talked of little else: brave little Lindsey Corker, the first-year misfit who'd had the temerity to be true to the few instincts he possessed.'

'Were you proud of him?'

'Immensely. I shall never forget that day.'

'I don't suppose he will, either.'

Her voice broke slightly and she looked into my eyes again, unashamed by her tear-streaked face. 'You don't humiliate a child, Phil. You just don't.'

'I know that.'

She wept silently, shaking her head. 'You don't, Phil. You just *don't*. Not ever!'

I felt strangely honoured. No one, not even my parents, had been this open with me, and my ample affection for her blossomed further.

'What did your mother have to say?'

'She was livid.'

'With the headmaster?'

'With my brother. She's a born-again Christian, you see. She was summoned to school that same day and had the whole embarrassing tale relayed to her. Christian that she is, she gave Lindsey pure hell when he got home, and he has never forgiven her for it.'

'Do you think he ever will?'

'I know for sure he won't ... nor, incidentally, will he forgive her for marrying the village philanderer after Dad died.'

'I'm familiar with that story.'

Her tears dried quickly. 'The saga didn't end there, though. The other kids began to flock to him. I used to watch him leading them round the playground as if he were the Pied Piper of Hamelin, and a gaggle of young girls from the next village used to take turns in coming to the house at weekends.'

'So, in effect, his refusal to show reverence resulted in his becoming the object of it. What could be more ironic than that?'

'The incident also inspired an obsessive interest in atheist literature, even as a school kid. He spent innumerable hours sitting in the library, seeking out kindred spirits - Nietzsche, Sartre and Bertrand Russell - the sort of stuff I still don't understand.'

'Nor do most other people.'

'Maybe that's one of the reasons they still believe there's a god.'

'Out of ignorance came fear, and out of fear came gods.'

'Bull's-eye, Phil.'

'It's rubbing off on me.'

'He would quote all this highbrow stuff in class, often clashing with the teachers, and the other kids relished every minute of it. I'm not exaggerating, they followed his every move like proles hungry for revolution, and Lindsey was perceptive enough to realize that, if he chose to rebel again, the outcome could well be different.'

'And did he?'

She nodded. 'I always knew he would, although he appreciated that timing was everything.'

I was now utterly captivated by her recollections. She could have fed me anything. 'What did he do?' I asked.

'On the Friday prior to his final examinations, they all filed into the hall for morning assembly, the old man demanded that they bow their heads for prayers ...'

'And?'

'More than half of them stood bolt upright in defiance.' She raised her head and gazed contentedly across the park, her delicate eyelashes fluttering like the wings of a butterfly. 'They weren't asked a second time. You see, one pupil had convinced a few hundred others that worship was as demeaning as it was futile, and that was that. You know what school kids are like: if someone presses the right buttons, most of them just follow like sheep. I wish I'd been there to witness it.'

'What did your mother have to say this time?'

'Not a word.'

'Why not?'

'Firstly, no one could actually prove that Lindsey was the instigator, and if she'd turned on him again, he would have come to live with Jacques and me in our flat in Newcastle.'

'Shrewd.'

'As I said, he waited for the optimum moment before declaring his hand.'

'Like any good poker player,' I remarked.

'Exactly. As far as I know, the only other occasion he entered the school grounds was to attend the annual backslapping. He received all his certificates, in the school hall, under the noses of the head and his staff, from *the parish priest!*'

'More ironic still.'

We both lay back on the soft grass and looked up to the sky. Incredibly, I had almost forgotten where I was. She closed her eyes and continued to reminisce. I turned my head and watched her furtively. With each breath, her breasts rose, gently pressing against the inside of her diaphanous blouse, before falling, then rising, then falling again, each time more slowly than the last, as she became more and more relaxed. I wanted to kiss her, nothing else - she was worth so much more than that crude, Bangkokian lust I had worn on my sleeve a fortnight earlier - but, although she was lying less than two feet away, she was way out of reach.

Above us, the treetops swayed lazily in the dry, early afternoon breeze. I thought of Lumpini Park in Bangkok: a similar heavenly green oasis which had successfully resisted the callous dynamics of urban expansion.

'Come on,' she urged, 'they'll be wondering where we are.'

We left the park on the East Side and headed down Fifth Avenue where I caught my first glimpse of the most famous building in the world.

'So there you have it,' she concluded. 'Now you can understand why he showed such scant mercy for Erin van Birdbrain. She mocked him for his lack of faith in front of his friends, and he probably saw her as a reincarnation of that cantankerous old despot back at *The Ablutions.*'

'Even when she mentioned her mother's untimely death, he offered no sympathy.'

'That doesn't surprise me. You and Tim have known for a long time that religion is Lindsey's red rag. He went for it, and the girl had neither the strength to fend him off nor the agility to get out of the way, which was just too bad. Torment the bull and you feel its horns. Period.' She nodded her head purposefully. 'I'll stand by my brother, come what may.'

'I know you will,' I said, with undisguised admiration.

'Loyalty has to be unconditional, Phil, otherwise it is not loyalty at all.'

The moment we entered the foyer of the Empire State Building, we switched subconsciously to lighter subjects, and I had immense pleasure in reliving the seven perfect days that we had enjoyed roaming around Thailand. Of course, she was feverishly curious about Maalii.

'It's just like him to fall for a girl who lives on the opposite side of the planet!' she laughed, as we squeezed into the elevator which would hoist us all the way to the eighty-sixth floor. 'When do you think they'll see each other again?'

'I don't honestly know. He's being quite secretive. Tim is convinced she'll be on holiday in England before long, though, possibly as soon as the New Year.'

We stepped out of the lift, with no visible indication that we were hundreds of feet from street level, and took a second lift to the viewing platform.

'You were right,' she announced. 'There they are.'

'Did you two lose your way?' called Tim, who had been looking down to the tip of the island with the aid of a coin-operated telescope.

'Phil has only just woken up,' Nova confessed, in an attempt to avoid having to mention our lengthy conversation in the park.

'Any sign of the Armada?'

'Not as yet.'

'What about dead bodies floating face-down in the river?'

'So that's what all those things are. Here, see for yourself.'

The view from the south side of the observation deck was awesome. Manhattan's downtown buildings looked like magnified versions of Adam's chess pieces, crammed together in one corner of the board, intricately carved, none the same size or shape, some flat-topped, some pointed, with the twin towers of the World Trade Center appearing to represent the king and queen. I had always believed that the most aesthetically-pleasing objects in our world were those over which man had held least influence, but these striking examples of twentieth-century architecture compelled me to reconsider.

Nova followed Tim round to the north side which overlooked Central Park, Times Square and, on the horizon, the infamous districts of Harlem and South Bronx. I was now alone with Lindsey, and felt an awkward tension - the type born of deceit.

He paused deliberately. 'So now you know,' he said quietly, then smiled with a rare trace of humility. 'I figured all along that she would tell you.'

'That's why you put us together, isn't it?' I surmised.

'Pardon me?'

'That's why you put us together! You and Tim came here by yourselves because you calculated that Nova would ask me about Erin.'

'I know also that she loves to wander through the park, which would have given you plenty of time together.' He brought his face closer to my own.

'For a start, you haven't just woken up. Anyone can see that.'

'I knew that was the reason you left early,' I responded, feeling rather pleased with myself.

'Becoming predictable, am I?'

'Not entirely.'

'Well, someone had to explain why Adam has been bothering her, Phil. My account would naturally have been biased, and Tim tends to get carried away and become all theatrical. You know what he's like.'

'So that left me.'

'Right. You are always impartial, Phil. And Nova's my sister. She deserved no less.'

His compliment was sincere, and it filled me with pride.

'It upset her to talk about your altercation with the headmaster.'

'I know. It cut her more deeply than it did me.'

'Well, your scars don't show *all* the time, in case you were wondering.'

'I wasn't,' he added with indifference. 'I had the last laugh, did I not? Here, let me show you the big, bad apple.'

We walked around the perimeter of the observation platform and he pointed out the world-famous landmarks, which I had seen previously only on television: the Brooklyn Bridge spanning the placid East River, the Statue of Liberty in the insignificant distance, and the supremely elegant Chrysler Building, the top of which sparkled like a chandelier in the sunlight. In fact, there did not seem to be many parts of Manhattan which were unfamiliar to him.

The previous subject of conversation was quickly forgotten and I soon became lost in his tales of reckless adventure, which had begun shortly after Jacques and Nova had emigrated. Whether it was a magical evening at Madison Square Garden, a drunken New Year's Eve romp in Times Square, or merely an early morning ride downtown on the 'A' train, he described what he admitted had been the most thrilling days of his life.

'One evening, in a rancid basement bar somewhere on Seventh, I met an old prostitute called *Allcock*!' he recalled, spluttering with laughter. 'Can you believe that?'

I got the impression that he was even more excited about his sister's choice of adopted city than she herself was. His reasons needed little justification.

Eventually, I said a reluctant goodbye to the chess pieces from the mother of them all, saddened further by the knowledge that yet another first experience could easily turn out to be another last.

I spent what remained of the afternoon tangled up in my own frivolous and chaotic thoughts as we roamed up and down Fifth Avenue, in and out of flashy department stores, and glancing repeatedly towards the tops of towering buildings - confirmation of my tourist status to the endemic muggers and conmen. In fact, so overpowering were the buildings that I felt that we had shrunk to the size of mice and were scurrying between the legs of tables and chairs.

By the time we had trekked the whole distance back across the park to Nova's apartment, my spindly limbs were aching and pulsating with blood, just as my poor head had been on the bus between Toronto and Niagara Falls. Lindsey posted his birthday card and money order to Maalii, exactly as he had intended, but remained reluctant to speak of her, even to his sister, which surprised me. I tried hard not to feel irritated by his ongoing reticence, but I knew he could sense that we were all as keen to learn of his secret plans as he was to keep them to himself.

XX

**'For there is no friend like a sister
In calm or stormy weather.'**

Christina Rossetti (1830-74)
Goblin Market

It was becoming impossible not to dwell upon the deflating prospect of returning home in only three days; and yet, had this been the first day of a three-day trip, such a melancholy attitude would never have entered my over-worked head. It was probably a variation of childhood Sunday doldrums, when every weekend the temporary feeling of liberation was diluted, nullified even, by the imminent prospect of going back to school.

The following day, our third Saturday away, went according to our pre-departure plans, which was unusual. We flitted around negligently, as if the city were a vast fairground crammed with rides and stalls to the extent that there was insufficient time to try them all out. Nova came along with us. I could tell she was lost without Jacques, as well any woman might be; and as she undoubtedly knew Manhattan as intimately as anywhere else, I assumed she was simply happy to have some company during his absence.

From Grand Central to not-so-grand Hell's Kitchen, to Liberty Island and back on a heaving ferry, then across the East River to Brooklyn Heights, we must have spent more on taxi and subway fares than anything else, not that it mattered. In fact, nothing mattered, least of all money.

On arriving back at base at four in the afternoon, we made straight for the refrigerator and grabbed the bottles of beer which had been bought in anticipation of our visit. Nova pressed the 'Play' button on the telephone answering machine.

'*Bonjour*, Slime pants!' came a strong voice from the small speaker. 'Have the reprobates arrived safely? If they have, make sure they don't guzzle all the beer. I'm just calling to let you know that I shall be out of here first thing in the morning, flying into La Guardia for nine thirty. No need for you to meet me there - I shall bum a ride home with Petriona Young. See you tomorrow.'

'*Slime pants?*' said Tim, who was sitting opposite me at the kitchen table. 'Is that what he calls you?'

'Afraid so,' said Nova. 'But ... there are worse nicknames, are there not?'

Tim laughed. 'I'm not sure. Where did it originate?'

'Oh, it all began during a potholing jamboree in the Derbyshire High Peak, just after we'd graduated. It had rained for days and I slipped into a peat bog, to his eternal amusement. He has a photograph somewhere.'

'What do you call him?'

The phone rang again and she answered it before the pre-recorded message had time to play itself.

'Tim, you don't want to know! Hello ...'

'She calls him *Posto*,' Lindsey explained, in a loud, mocking whisper.

'What's that - *Moscow?*'

'*Posto*. It was his nickname at primary school - well, amongst the few kids who dared to mention it to his face. It started when a supposedly dyslexic chum of his - probably just thick - misspelled *Pardeau* on a birthday card.'

'Misspelled it? He mangled it beyond recognition.'

We stopped laughing when Nova began to speak, not that she was saying much. She and Lindsey eyed each other pensively, communicating by telepathy as only siblings know how. Slowly, and somewhat reluctantly, he got to his feet and walked towards her, cautiously maintaining eye contact. She handed over the receiver without uttering a word, and stood in the doorway right in front of him.

'Hello. This is Lindsey.'

Nova looked at me. 'Adam,' she whispered.

Lindsey waited for a while before speaking, brow furrowed and eyes blinking rapidly. 'I'm sorry,' he eventually confessed. 'Yes I am, I'm very sorry. Sorry that you insist upon passing judgement before you–' He listened again, but the calm indifference remained. 'That's fine, then. But if you won't listen to *me*, then you can't honestly expect–'

Inevitably, a moment's silence followed.

'What was that all about?' I said.

He shrugged, replaced the handset and sat down again.

'Don't look so worried,' he said. 'His scorn is not directed at you.'

'What did he say?' asked Nova, nervously.

'Nothing you haven't already heard, I shouldn't imagine. Erin has become haunted by the idea that there might not be life after death for her mother, despite all she has been told. Apparently, she's depressed, can barely sleep, and is even considering cancelling her latest holiday in the Rockies.' He finished his beer and opened a second bottle.

'And Adam now blames you exclusively?'

'It seems so. Regardless of the vitriol his perfect little pixie of a sister poured over me–'

'Without the slightest provocation–' I interjected.

'He insists that it was "an act of pure malevolence to poison her mind in such a way". At least I think those were his exact words - without the expletives, that is.'

'It was what?'

'Furthermore, he said he could scarcely believe my audacity in engaging him in a friendly game of chess, knowing that Erin was crying like a baby on the other side of town. Before he slammed the phone down, he told me that if I thought our little duel was over, then I was "dangerously mistaken".'

Nova looked disgusted. 'Oh, he's being stupid. Juveniles talk like that. It's just a pity your vacation has been blemished.'

'What do you suppose Jacques might say?' I asked.

'Not much. He never has any time for anything petty, which is precisely what this is. Anyway, enough of that. What do you have planned for this evening?'

'Why don't we call Joel?' Tim suggested.

'Who's Joel?'

'A guy from the US military who was staying in Bangkok. He lives in Yorkville.'

'Really? That's straight across the park from here. Feel free to use the phone.'

'Thanks. I'll do that.'

We left the kitchen while Tim figured out how to use the telephone. Lindsey began at last to discuss with his sister the confrontational episode in Los Angeles, so I returned to the back bedroom to change my clothes.

On the wall above the bed were two small, framed photographs of Jacques and Nova which had evidently been taken during their student days. The slightly larger one was a simple snap of the two of them in a rowing boat, laughing to themselves on what looked like an idyllic midsummer's evening. The other showed them wearing their caps and gowns on the day of their graduation ceremony, arms linked like newlyweds in the centre of a shrub-filled campus quadrangle. Six years on, they were living right at the heart of one of the world's most vibrant cities, understandably happy with the extent to which their love had evolved.

'Was Joel at home?' I asked, after rejoining the others in the sitting room.

Tim was upbeat. 'He certainly was. He said he'd meet us on Eighth Avenue at 56th Street, wherever that is. He knows a trendy sidewalk cafe nearby. I told him we'd be there for nine.'

'Would either of you mind if I gave it a swerve and stayed here?' asked Lindsey, very politely.

'No, of course not.'

'Thanks. Big sister and I have some catching-up to do.'

'That's right,' she affirmed. 'A full eighteen months of it. Incidentally, West 56th is just the other side of Columbus Circle, so your best option would be to take a cab ... unless you're especially keen to walk. If that's the case, you'll need either to head straight down Broadway or turn right at the Dakota and walk to the end of the park.'

We dismissed the pedestrian options immediately; both Tim and I felt naturally wary about walking city streets after dark, particularly in a city with a far more frightening reputation than that found in the sleepy suburbs where we had grown up.

I recognized Joel as soon as we stepped out of the taxi. His distinctive blue eyes were abnormally close-set, as if they were trying to hide behind his nose which, as a consequence, looked much bigger than it actually was.

'Yo! How's it going?' he called.

'Fine!'

'Where are you staying?'

'Uptown.'

'West Side?'

'A couple of blocks from the Natural History Museum.'

I explained to him the reason for our being able to stay in a relatively affluent part of town, and described Lindsey.

'Yeah, I remember him. Tall guy with too much hair. He was with Maalii.'

'Do you know her?'

'Not that well. She has only been living in Bangkok for two or three months.' He smiled slyly. 'Ain't she something special?'

'Lindsey thinks so.'

'I bet he does. Most of my buddies over here would sell their wives for a girl as striking as she is. Come to think of it, some might relinquish them for free! And throw in their mothers for good measure!'

We followed him across the street and into a small restaurant near to the corner of the block where we began to listen to tales of Manhattan life from someone who had lived it from birth. Some of the yarns left me wishing I could have grown up in the same neighbourhood, whereas others made me feel positively relieved that I had not.

Frequent eruptions of alcohol-assisted laughter punctuated our casual conversation, thereby falsely indicating to the other diners that Tim and I knew Joel as well as we knew each other. Sadly, however, although this straight-talking New Yorker was potentially a good friend, I realized only too well that we would never see him again. In that context, it all seemed embarrassingly pointless.

'How long will you be staying here?' I asked him.

'Not long. I have to be back in Thailand a fortnight from now and, from what I've been told, I'll be staying out there until Christmas.'

'Do Thais celebrate Christmas?'

'Not officially. But Bangkok is full of visitors who do, so you wouldn't notice.'

As he spoke, I struggled hard to prevent a powerful wave of jealousy spreading from my mind to my face. Joel would be mooching about in summer clothes at the Plaza, whereas I would be bracing myself for the inevitable loneliness brought on by yet another miserable English winter.

'The guy who owns the bar in Bangkok is an old friend of mine,' he went on. 'We used to work together in Hawaii. Detachment Five. Crazy sons of bitches to a man. Not that I see much of him these days. He owns a beach bar down in Koh Samui. Built the goddam thing in a day. That's where he spends most of his time nowadays, and he occasionally condescends to leave me in charge at the Plaza. I earn more for him than I do with the military!'

Joel was interested to learn of the things we had done since leaving Bangkok, and inevitably we got around to explaining the LA incident.

'Yeah, I get it,' he concluded confidently. 'The bitch walked in brandishing the Bible and went away with it jammed up her ass, right?'

'Are all New Yorkers as eloquent as you are, Joel?'

'Of course not,' he joked, 'it takes practice. Having said that, if some West Coast cheerleader had patronized me, I would have torn her a new asshole altogether.'

Once we had stuffed our faces with barbecued salmon steaks and pasta, we left the cafe and disappeared into a smoke-filled basement hole under a porn cinema on Broadway, where we were introduced to several of Joel's tough-looking friends, mostly military personnel, at a corner table. I could not help but conjecture that their admission to the army, and that alone, had diverted them from a seductive life of crime, violence and heaven knows what else besides. Instinctively, I felt the urge to conceal my status – as a gauche, small-town English boy – from the hundreds of penetrating eyes, but realized that it was a deception way beyond my capabilities. Instead, I kept quiet and coolly observed the crowd with the same curiosity with which it appeared to be scrutinizing me.

At midnight, we flagged down one of the innumerable yellow taxis and, for the second time on our travels, said goodbye to Joel.

'Take it easy, guys. Let me know when you're in town again - or in Bangkok! You know where to find me!'

I could hardly bring myself to speak, let alone deceive him with a smile. I knew that the chances of a third meeting, at any time in my life, were extremely remote. We shook hands then headed back uptown to the apartment, letting ourselves in with the keys that Nova had given to us in case we happened to crawl back in, piss-faced and legless, during the small hours of the morning.

After having become accustomed to the relentless din of a midtown bar, the apartment seemed to be buzzing with an uncomfortable silence. Lindsey and Nova were sitting contemplatively at the kitchen table, drinking black coffee, with only the small wall lights switched on. Lindsey sounded strangely curious about Joel, perhaps regretting his decision to stay indoors. He must have been drawn to the fact that we had been in the company of someone who knew Maalii better than he did.

Jacques arrived home at ten thirty the following morning, pleased to have finalized the formalities of his business stitch-up in Maryland, and apologizing repeatedly for his absence.

Lindsey was last out of bed. 'Good morning, dear Posto,' he said, stumbling half-dressed into the kitchen. 'Did you have a comfortable flight?'

'Thank you, yes. I see you have drunk all the beer - as usual.'

'I was worried in case it went stale.'

'Jesus, your liver will be like horse shit.'

We all sat down together for a midday breakfast and brought Jacques up to date with what we had done since he left us in Los Angeles the previous weekend. Nova looked apprehensive, softly stroking her lower lip with her thumb and forefinger.

'Has Adam van Bergen contacted you since you left California, Jacques?'

'Twice,' he answered, without looking up, 'once last Thursday and again yesterday afternoon. I thought he was calling because one of these bums had done something disgusting in his house - like soiled the bed, or puked up all over that Balinese rug, or-'

'What were his exact words?'

Jacques shrugged. 'He just told me that your brother and his sister had butted heads. So what? It happens, you know.'

As Nova had predicted, he was not the least bit concerned. She outlined the rest of the tale very briefly but he seemed to pay more attention to what he was eating.

'Ah, it serves her right,' he said. 'She has been on course for getting her butt kicked for as long as I can remember. I think the principal reason she was so damned eager to show her face was so that she could pick a fight.'

'Thanks for the prior warning!' Lindsey joked in protest.

Jacques replied in earnest. 'How could I have told you? For all I knew, the two of you could have fallen in love and spent the weekend exchanging fluids. We all know how charming you can be.'

'She did take a bit of a shine to Phil,' said Tim mischievously.

'Well, there you are. I had to let you judge her for yourselves.'

Jacques finished his breakfast, leaned back in his chair and folded his muscular arms with the authoritative poise of a judge preparing to pass sentence.

'The truth is,' he began, 'she has been indulged and pampered like a princess for most of her life, not just by Adam, but also by her mother and a whole boatload of other people, I expect. And as you know, victims of religious faith have a long and colourful history of intolerance and hypersensitivity. Many of them consider their irrational and simplistic little superstitions to be beyond dispute. If you ask me, they've no fucking humility when confronted with an objective argument, however it's presented to them.'

Lindsey nodded approvingly. Jacques tended to offer his views in a similar fashion to the way a boxing champion threw punches: forcefully and with effortless precision.

Nova looked at her Gallic *parvenu* with a warm glow.

'Come here, beautiful,' he said, and pulled her backwards until she fell into his lap. 'I've missed you.' His unfaltering strength of character seemed to provide a therapeutic counterbalance to Nova's natural insecurity.

As late as three in the afternoon, we were still lounging around inside the apartment, none of us having devised any grand schemes for the penultimate day. More importantly, this was Jacques's first break from work in over a fortnight so we respected his need to unwind. I remained seated at the table with Tim and Nova, sifting through our recently-acquired multitude of photographs and making more small talk about the vagaries of third-class travel. Lindsey seemed very much at home, wandering in and out of the room, still not fully dressed, sitting down to write letters, then helping to clean up the mess in the kitchen.

Any residual energy I possessed had ebbed away completely by the same time the next day. Oddly enough, I now felt more enthusiastic about arriving home than either the remainder of our final day in Manhattan or the flight back to London. At least when I was safe inside my own home I would be free to sink into melancholy without having to disguise it in front of the others. Tim seemed to be similarly affected by it all, and Lindsey barely spoke a word to anyone, having only a brief conversation with Nova early in the morning.

I stuffed everything randomly into my bags, clean and dirty clothes tangled together, and souvenirs squashed against damp toiletries. To my amazement, I had the equivalent of two hundred pounds in unused traveller's cheques and a plastic bag full of Thai baht, Hong Kong, Canadian and US dollars which brought the total to nearer four hundred.

I carefully removed the framed picture of Jacques and Nova in the rowing boat from the bedroom wall and gazed fondly into it, convincing myself that, if ever I were so fortunate as to find a woman offering such genuine devotion, I would readily sacrifice any other desires and ambitions. But, being neither talented nor lucky, I knew it was destined never to happen.

Before I had time to replace it on the hook, Nova walked in carrying the clothes that she had voluntarily washed and ironed.

'Lindsey took that photograph,' she said brightly.

I looked up. 'Somewhere in England?'

'Scarborough. Peasholm Park. Jacques and I used to meet him there during university holidays, partly because it lies roughly equidistant from Newcastle and Nottingham.'

'Convenient.'

'Have you never been?'

'I don't think so.'

What I did not tell her was that I would have no real wish to visit such a place unless I had my own Nova Corker with whom I could savour the experience. Rowing boats were meant only for lovers.

I returned the picture to its rightful place, making sure that it was not lopsided, then looked around for anything I might have forgotten.

'Just remember,' she said softly, 'you'd be welcome here anytime, with or without Lindsey. The same applies to Tim.'

'That's kind of you. I just wish you weren't so far away.'

She smiled, with the same flawless sincerity that radiated from the photograph. 'And another thing,' she said, 'thanks for being such a loyal friend to my brother. You and Tim are the only allies he has in Liverpool.'

'Does that surprise you?'

'On the contrary. It surprises me that he has any friends at all.'

'What's the obstacle?'

'His own temperament. It's just so unalterably ...'

'Independent? Like Jacques?'

'In part. But Jacques is not an island, whereas Lindsey is.' She looked across the room towards the door which she had left ajar. 'In the beginning, *all* creatures were of a solitary nature. Social behaviour emerged only because many were incapable of self-sufficiency. And now the solitary types, the outsiders, the loners, the glorious misfits, like any other minority, have to suffer a lifetime of discrimination at the hands of the herds. Lindsey used to say it was "an honourable cross to bear".' She then looked at me, somewhat self-consciously, and smiled. 'I think you bear it, too. I think you and he are essentially the same.'

'Maybe we are,' I admitted.

'Anyhow, as I was saying, thanks for your loyalty. It would tear me up if I knew he were all alone.'

'Today I think he *wants* to be alone,' I remarked. 'He has hardly spoken.'

'I expect he's eager to complete the translation of Maalii's letter.'

'He already has. He finished it in a breakfast cafe in Niagara Falls.'

'I meant the one that arrived this morning.'

I was taken aback. 'This morning? Are you sure?'

'I ought to be!' she laughed. 'I picked it out of the mailbox myself!'

'He never-'

'Told you?'

'No.'

'I think I know the reason.'

'What's that?'

'I think the girl might have called the whole thing off.'

'What?'

'That would explain his reluctance to discuss it with anyone. But please don't say anything to him.'

'Of course not.'

She got up and returned to the sitting room. On reflection, there was no lack of logic in her observation.

By four thirty in the afternoon, our luggage was packed and ready to be loaded into the car, along with a polythene carrier bag containing chocolate bars and magazines which Nova had gone out and bought for us from the windswept wooden kiosk on Central Park West.

'Are you coming with us to the airport, Nova?' Jacques called from the bottom of the stairwell.

'There won't be room for me. I don't mind staying here.'

Indeed, once we had squeezed Tim's bags into the vehicle, I was amazed there was enough space for any of us.

Nova hugged Lindsey as we were about to depart, closing her eyes as her face squashed against his jaw.

'Please don't forget to call us when you get home,' she whispered. 'Just let me know you're all right.' She then turned to Tim and me. 'Good to see you both again. As I said, feel free to come over whenever you get the oppor-tunity. We shall still be living here next year.'

'Perhaps you'll be married,' I teased.

'Phil, the day we need a government document to keep us bound together will be the day we have nothing left,' she asserted, then kissed Jacques lovingly as he climbed into the driver's seat. 'In fact, I think Lindsey is more likely to drag his butt up the aisle than we are!'

Jacques stuck his head out of the near-side window. 'Take part in a reli-gious ceremony? *Him?*'

'And why not?' she joked.

'I think he'd rather dip his genitals into an acid bath.'

Nova laughed and shook her head, then stepped back a couple of paces from the kerb. 'Drive carefully, Posto. Don't forget you've got my brother in there.'

'How could I?'

'I'll see you later.'

As she kissed him a second time, I felt that her negative view of the necessity of marriage actually reflected a kind of depth and solidarity of her relationship with Jacques. I found it somewhat reassuring, knowing how inexplicably saddened I would be if ever they decided to part. I looked at her for the last time as I was getting into the back of the car.

'Wedding or no wedding,' I said quietly, 'I'm sure you'll make an admirable wife ... and mother.'

She smiled bashfully, tilting her head to one side, fully aware that I was referring, as sincerely as I knew how, to the selfless way in which she had looked after Lindsey when he was too young to look after himself. As far as I could see, his debt to her was immeasurable, and any trouble that had occurred throughout his life was probably not his fault.

XXI

**'A man travels the world over
In search of what he needs
And returns home to find it.'**

**George Moore (1852-1933)
The Brook Kerith, Ch.11**

We crawled patiently across midtown, then south on Park Avenue which was congested, Sukhumvit-fashion, with stagnant commuter traffic. I thought about Lindsey's letter, and the fact that he had not acknowledged receipt of it to either Tim or myself. Perhaps he thought we had easily sufficient fat of his to chew as it was. Whatever, Nova's theory seemed to be the only credible one. As we sped along the craterous highway through Queens to Kennedy Airport, however, he was surprisingly talkative. A face-saving charade, I thought.

Jacques pulled into a parking bay once we had arrived at Terminal 5, and switched off the engine.

'Well, has it all been worth your while?' he asked, smirking to himself.

'I think so,' Lindsey replied, then looked at him and they both laughed freely.

Busy international airports were becoming as familiar to us as they were to Jacques himself. The cacophony from security machines, conveyor belts and raised voices had degenerated to the barely noticeable level of an old ticking clock. Typically, Jacques helped us cart the bags all the way to the check-in desk, even though he must have known that there would be a considerable charge for even a few minutes' parking, not that it would have crossed his mind. As Nova had said, trivialities never did.

'Thanks for everything, Posto,' said Lindsey. 'I owe you one.'

'Not at all. I'm sorry I wasn't home when you showed up.'

'Any chance of you and Nova coming to England next year?' Tim asked.

'It's a possibility, although it would be helpful if I could chalk up some more *Frequent Flyer* points so that one of us could qualify for free tickets. Ideally, I'd like also to take her to Paris and spend some time with my aunt and uncle. Whatever happens, we shall be in touch.'

'Best of luck, Jacques,' I said and shook his hand. 'Not that you appear to need it.'

He understood my implication without my having to mention Nova by name.

'Believe me,' he said with unquestionable grace, 'there's nothing I'm more constantly aware of.'

My intention, once we had said goodbye to him, was to refrain from pestering Lindsey about the content of his second letter, but I just had to know.

'Have you translated your correspondence yet?'

'I didn't need to,' was his sprightly reply. 'She had it all written in English.'

'By whom?'

'Some friend, also from Krasang. Works in a jewellery shop on Soi 22. Doing well for herself. Speaks English, you see.'

I made no complaint about his decision not to mention it earlier, and he offered no explanation. It was probably subconscious on his part anyway.

Tim was just as predictable. 'How's Maalii? What did she say? Is she feeling any better?'

'She's fine, physically, but desperately short of cash. No one should have to survive on just one proper meal a day. Not to worry, my money order will reach her in a day or two. Problem solved.'

'And she still feels the same way about you?' I probed with playful curiosity.

'That's not in question, old fruit.'

A composite expression of relief and satisfaction spread across my face, which he noticed instantly.

'Why are you looking like that? What did you expect?'

'I don't know.'

'Come on, out with it.'

'I thought you'd kept quiet because of the things she'd written.'

'What things?'

'Things you ... um ... didn't want to read.'

He paused for a moment, then spoke positively. 'Nova told you that, didn't she?'

'She did,' I was forced to admit.

He laughed and leaned back in his seat, causing it to rock onto its back legs and creak under the strain. 'She naturally imagines the worst. Sometimes I think her brain is innately tuned to the wavelength of doom.'

I had been so careful not to mention my conversation with Nova in the small bedroom, but it would have made no difference if I had - he probably knew what had been said.

We boarded the aircraft at seven thirty, knowing that it was well past midnight in England, which meant that we would have to force ourselves to sleep immediately if we were not to feel utterly wasted on arrival at Heathrow. Tim and I endeavoured to detach ourselves from the constant disturbances caused by incontinent passengers filing clumsily up and down the aisle every few minutes and the requisite Cheshire Cat stewardesses handing out thimbles of fruit juice. Lindsey curled up next to the window and spent a few extra minutes flicking through his Thai books, adding notes and doodling in the margins. Never before had I known his mind to be so concentrated, not even when he was studying for exams. Of all the novel events of our three weeks together, I managed, for some reason, to think only of the smelly lavatory cubicle on the bus out of Buffalo, and the comical comments coming from the disgruntled victims of its overpowering stench. Strangely, it made me want to suffer the journey all over again.

I slept for little more than an hour but nevertheless thought I had done well under the circumstances. We ambled lethargically from the aircraft down to the baggage carousels and into the arrivals hall at Heathrow, the sole interruption being when an immigration jobsworth confronted Lindsey after noticing that he had scratched out the word 'European' from the front cover of his passport. In my view, his display of nationalistic protestation was no more surprising than the fact that he had been able to restrain himself from drawing a moustache and spectacles over the out-of-date photograph inside. I agreed with the sentiment, as did the official, but lacked the courage to make it known.

The minute I felt the cold, damp air rush through the Tube station outside Terminal 3, I realized that it was all over. We had finally come home. The same old posters lined the platform walls, the same mixture of faceless travellers waited for the noisy old train to emerge from the dank tunnel, and the outward flight to Bangkok seemed like only yesterday. My thoughts turned to our good friends, Jacques and Nova, now in a different world, and the longer I dwelled upon them, the more distant they became. Such deflating reflections made me reluctant even to consider succumbing to another dose of wanderlust, however well-earned.

The old grey train screeched in and out of the Piccadilly Line stations towards the heart of London and I began to feel sleepy, infuriatingly more so than at any time during the seven-hour-long homeward flight.

As soon as we had pulled out of the third or fourth station, Lindsey sprang to his feet and slung on his jacket.

'What are you doing?' said Tim.

'Well, now that I have finally circumcised the globe, I thought I might take the opportunity to pay my cousin a visit and bore him with the small print.'

Tim was as surprised as I was by his ostensible spontaneity. 'Do you want us to come with you?'

'No, I shan't be staying long. See you back at home.'

When the doors opened at the next station, he grabbed his bag and jumped out without even saying goodbye. Before the doors closed again, he was already out of sight. After having spent every waking hour for almost three weeks being entertained, annoyed and enlightened by him, he was gone.

Tim shrugged his shoulders and sighed. 'When do you suppose he decided to do that?' he said to me.

'About thirty seconds ago?'

'I don't think so.'

'Why not?'

'He's never *truly* impulsive. Even if he sometimes appears to act that way, it's only because his brain beats time faster than everyone else's. And that's not impulsive.'

'Where are we?' I wondered aloud.

'Hammersmith.'

I was now even more puzzled. 'Doesn't his cousin live in Swiss Cottage?'

'St. John's Wood,' he pointed out. 'Up the road from Regent's Park.'

'All the same, that's nowhere near Hammersmith. Why did he get out here?'

Tim twisted himself round in order to peruse the Underground network map on the overhead panel. 'I know. From here he can get onto the Hammersmith and City Line which will take him all the way to Baker Street. Then he can take the grey route, which is ...'

'The Jubilee Line.'

'Straight to St. John's Wood.'

We changed onto the Victoria Line at Green Park and arrived at Euston just after nine o'clock, still unsure of Lindsey's exact motives. As if to underline the fact that our tour was at an end, the morning was depressingly overcast, totally alien to anything we had witnessed abroad, with the exception of the odd, but unforgettable, spells of rain in Bangkok, Los Angeles and Niagara Falls. Our holiday had begun in summer and ended in winter; there had been no gradual transition period from one to the other.

'How long do you think he intends to stay in London?' I asked, somewhat pointlessly.

'I've no idea - but do you remember what he said about his cousin at the cafe in Niagara?'

I pondered for a while. 'Only that he'd written to him from Hong Kong.'

'He said he felt *obliged* to explain about Maalii. Why was that so crucial - and why did he have to be so bloody evasive?'

I tried in vain to recall the precise details of the conversation in the cafe, or even the expression on Lindsey's face when he told us. I felt that he had quite deliberately led us into an elaborately-designed maze, and then abandoned us once we had lost ourselves in it. What was the point of it all?

We left Euston on the Liverpool train which was virtually empty - a sharp contrast to the journey from Krasang to Bangkok, I thought, especially the part we had had to endure on our feet. I rested my head against the pile of bulging bags on the adjacent seat and began to doze again. By now, even Lindsey felt distant, as though he had never actually left New York. Time was everything, distance nothing.

I did not return to my senses until noon but the uncontrollable drowsiness remained. I glanced across to speak to Tim but he, too, had fallen asleep, presumably soon after our departure from London. Looking outside, I could see exactly where we were: the familiar outline of Liverpool's imposing Anglican Cathedral stood conspicuously underneath a mass of angry rain clouds.

When the train slowed down, I woke Tim by prodding him repeatedly on the shoulder, although he did not finish yawning and clearing his throat until we had finally ground to a halt at Lime Street's buffers. On the platform a teenage couple were sitting on a baggage trolley, where our journey had begun, holding hands affectionately. I looked at them with eyes drained and a mind numbed by such incessant travel.

'I'll see you sometime tomorrow,' I said wearily, and watched as Tim climbed into the back of a black cab whilst rubbing the sleep out of his bloodshot eyes.

The air was unexpectedly harsh, but I was unable to summon the necessary energy to root out my jacket from the bottom of my bag. Instead, I struggled down the hill to the bus stop, content to submit to the violent gusts of wind as they blew right through me at will.

It was twenty minutes to two in the afternoon when I finally took out my front-door key and turned it in the lock. As expected, there was nothing to welcome me home but a haphazard pile of local newspapers and advertisement leaflets, none of them remotely interesting, and the cottage itself was as pitilessly cold as the street. Even the fact that the place had not been burgled seemed somehow unimportant.

I dropped both bags onto the armchair and lit the antiquated gas fire which emitted a stale, smouldering smell around the room. On the carpet at the foot of the coffee table lay a small aluminium meat and potato pie carton and an empty can of lemonade which, I remembered, had contained a last rushed snack prior to our departure. I had to stare at the crumpled, crumb-filled carton for almost a minute to dispel the idea that I had spent three weeks in a wild dream. Perhaps I had: the drunken raconteur on the Tube, the young peasant boy in Krasang and the wise old gentleman in Toronto, all heartbroken in their own ways, may have been just inexplicable visual anagrams of days long passed.

Naturally, I thought mostly of Lindsey, doubtless finding plenty of ways to entertain himself at his cousin's place which was, after all, barely a mile from Covent Garden and Leicester Square. I imagined the two of them wandering in and out of Soho pubs, hopping back and forth on the Tube or rolling into one of the multiplex cinemas to soak up a late-night movie. In contrast, I was alone in the same bleak, characterless cottage that I had inhabited since birth, and would have to walk to a corner shop at the brow of a hill simply to buy food for a hot meal. Feelings of self-pity seemed unavoidable. The ironic, and shameful, truth was: I felt deprived without the company of the most irritating human being I had ever known. My imagination continued to work overtime: all the miles, the rough nights, the improvizations, the chance encounters, some consequential, some not, and no sure way of differentiating one from the other. It was all in there, jumbled together without order or meaning, but without doubt there to stay.

I left the house feeling unnecessarily nervous on my first day back at work. I had to remind myself repeatedly that Mr. McKee's warehouse was not an army barracks; I was not returning in disgrace having been absent without leave. In fact, Tim's father was as congenial and flexible an employer as I could have hoped for, even if, at first view, my wages seemed low in light of the long hours I spent taking orders from customers, driving the delivery van and lumbering spine-breaking stock up and down two flights of stairs.

When I arrived, at eight thirty, I was relieved to find that Tim had dropped by on his way to the hospital and had answered most of the standard questions from the other staff regarding what had happened abroad and, of course, why 'that malcontent from the Midlands' had not yet completed the intended circuit. Indeed, by midday I had become channelled into the old routine so completely that I began to wonder whether everyone had forgotten that I had done something out of the ordinary for once. Perhaps I preferred it that way, as being bombarded with the same witless queries over and over again would inevitably have made me long to be elsewhere.

Saturday was just another delivery day on the road with Tim - something we had done together since passing our driving tests at the age of seventeen. There had been no word from Lindsey, either by telephone, which he hardly used even for emergencies, or by postcard which in his case would have taken less time still. I was disappointed in him: he had lied about his intentions and I had to admit, to myself at least, that it hurt. More alarmingly, I found myself spending an increasing amount of time daydreaming about Nova, after she had been so touchingly honest with me as we strolled across

Central Park. I had arrived at the conclusion that if any man did not consider her to be everything he could wish for, then he was simply lacking in both taste and judgement and had only himself to blame for his myopia. I was not envious of Jacques, not as such, nor could I consider myself to be competition for her limitless love. Nevertheless, I lay in bed night after night comforting myself with scenes involving a reciprocation of the affection that she did not know I held for her.

XXII

'Pain of mind is worse than pain of body.'

Publilius Syrus (1st century B.C.)
Sententiae

The days passed. I was too lazy to unpack the nonessential items from my bags, and my remaining foreign notes and traveller's cheques lay discarded on a corner of the kitchen table.

When the following Saturday came around, my thoughts were focused on only the menial task of devising the most parsimonious route for the day's deliveries which had as always been labelled for us and stacked next to the warehouse garage door, ready to go. Tim's father burst in at nine o'clock, just as we were about to start the van. He gesticulated briefly from across the showroom and scrambled towards us, tripping over a box of tools.

'Clumsy old bugger,' Tim muttered to himself, before winding down the driver's window. 'I wonder what the hell he wants now.'

'Here, I've got a present for you two.'

'Bonuses? Already?'

'You're dreaming again, gentlemen.'

He passed a long, pale blue *Airmail* envelope to Tim through the window. Instinctively, I thought of Nova - until I noticed three identical Thai postage stamps which were semi-obliterated by a Bangkok postmark.

'What is it, an invoice from a brothel?' said Mr. McKee.

'It's from the girls at the Plaza!' I exclaimed, and grabbed one corner of it for closer inspection.

Tim spoke calmly: 'That's Lindsey's handwriting.'

'What?'

'Guess where he is.'

'Are you sure it's his writing?'

'Look at it. Who else could write as dreadfully as this?'

'Come on,' his father urged us impatiently. 'Let's get the wagon rolling today, if possible.'

Tim wound the window back up and started the engine. 'OK, Phil, I'll drive, you read.'

'Do we have time?'

'Twenty minutes from here to Woolton. Go for it.'

I slit open one end of the envelope with a pencil as Tim bounced the sluggish pantechnicon from the pavement on to the road and set off across the city.

'"*Dear sphincters ...*"'

'Charming.'

'"*First of all, I owe you both an apology. Allow me to explain a few things, beginning when we were in that sweaty Patpong nightclub. The truth is, the moment I saw Maalii's tears, I knew it could not be farewell. Sorry if that sounds a little sickly. I told her a thousand times, in what little Thai I knew, that I would find a way whereby I could return before the end of October. Phom mar Krung Thep! Phom mar Krung Thep! I come Bangkok!*

There were, however, to quote Aung San of Burma, 'angles to be straightened'. I would need a visa if I intended to remain in Thailand for longer than a fortnight and, more fundamentally, I didn't have anywhere near enough money for the fare. That was why I spent so long writing letters when we arrived in Hong Kong. Firstly I wrote to my cousin, outlining the problem and asking if I could crash out at his place for a few days when we returned to London. I knew he wouldn't object - he never does. What I neglected to tell him was that I needed to borrow an extra two hundred pounds so that I could afford a cheap flight back to Bangkok. Fortunately, as a result of those two lawyer-scamming all-nighters in Toronto, the funding difficulty never arose. Praise the Lord!

Once I knew I could pay for the flight, I confirmed an approximate date of arrival to Maalii in my second letter, which I posted in New York City along with a money order for the remaining ninety dollars from my poker gains. Simple, wouldn't you agree?"'

'Evidently,' Tim sighed, with heavy irony.

'"*On leaving Toronto, therefore, I knew for certain that nothing could stand in my way. The only other 'angle to straighten' was my eligibility to apply for an extended visa, which I duly obtained from the Royal Thai Embassy in London. Conveniently, the Embassy building is within walking distance of my cousin's place.*"'

Tim stopped the van at one of the many sets of traffic lights in the congested city centre, then shook his head pensively. 'He makes me sick, you know.'

'Because he sorted it all out so easily?'

'And without asking for help. At least now we know why he had to put his cousin in the frame.'

'There's more,' I said, shuffling the pages.

'Go on.'

'"*I left London last Sunday, having spent only five days with my cousin. He even gave me a lift to the airport–*"'

'I expect he needed to prove to himself that Lindsey was actually leaving.'

'"*The flight was quite arduous. There was a five-hour stopover in some*

obscure place in the Middle East, and we didn't land in Bangkok until ten on
Monday morning. Maalii was, of course, unaware that I had actually arrived.
Every day for four weeks, I wondered what our reunion would be like. When
I walked down Soi Phasuk towards her room, I felt as if I were experiencing
a drug-induced euphoria, whatever that feels like. I was practically shaking.
Only one of the girls in the entire block was home, sitting outside wearing
nothing but a flimsy bath towel. Nothing unusual there, I hear you say. It was
the pony-tailed girl with the enormous earrings. She flung her arms around
me and for a moment I didn't think she was going to let go. Maalii had gone
to the pharmacy, the one at which you had your films processed, so I left my
bag and ran along Sukhumvit to find her.

When I reached the top of Soi 4 I saw her stepping out of the shop. A few
seconds passed before she noticed me standing at the roadside. She bolted
straight across the junction and was almost run over by a tuk-tuk. We couldn't
contain ourselves. Two or three street vendors starting applauding and calling
out to us. The whole scene must have looked like something from an old black
and white movie. Rhett Corker starring in 'Gone With The Smog'! Naturally,
we ran back to Soi Phasuk, assumed the horizontal position, and didn't come
up for air until late afternoon. We have since cooled down a little and now it
feels as if I haven't been away.

Incidentally, your buddy Joel arrived, or rather, crash-landed, here a
few days ago. He was with some of his colleagues from the military, all
drinking themselves into oblivion and letting down what little hair they
have. By the way, when you met up with him a fortnight ago, I chose to stay
indoors with Nova simply in order to tell her of my intention to return here
and also to canvass her opinion. Angel that she is, she even offered to pay
for my flight.

We shall be taking the train to Krasang sometime soon, although we have
no fixed date in mind. Life is all very ad hoc, ad lib and add-it-up-as-you-go-
along. Just how I like it.

Finally, referring back to the beginning of my letter, please accept my apology for having been so secretive. I was reluctant to broadcast plans in case
they never came to fruition, which would have stung like hell. I guess I'm just
too proud. Enjoy the English winter, old fruits. L.C.'"

'We will, you bastard, we will.'

'And just listen to this for a post script: "Maalii was quite excited to hear
of all the other places we visited so, a couple of nights ago, I shaved her pubic
hair into the shape of North America. It was a geography lesson neither of us
is likely to forget. From Los Angeles to New York, I love every square mile of
her, particularly Arizona, where I have since spent many a depraved hour
exploring the Grand Canyon."'

'Very metaphorical,' Tim remarked. 'I wonder if he has discovered any other exciting landmarks. By the way, is that it?'

'Well it's six pages long. How much more did you want?'

'He didn't say when he would be coming home.'

'He did. He told us to enjoy the English winter, which implies that he won't be sharing it with us, and his visa could last for anything up to six months - possibly even twelve.'

We stopped the van outside a large, semi-detached house in a suburban cul-de-sac and jumped out, leaving the letter on the driver's seat. In a way, I was happy that Lindsey was where he so desperately wanted to be, but still felt deflated at the thought of not seeing him again until the New Year. At least he had taken the trouble to write.

I rang the doorbell, and a half-dressed woman old enough to be my mother, and with a colossal pale bosom threatening to explode through her blouse, appeared in front of us. We returned to the van and collected a small pine wardrobe.

'Where would you like it?' I inquired.

She raised her eyebrows. 'In the *boudoir*, of course. First door on the right.'

We carted it up the stairs, taking care as ever not to scratch the wallpaper, which was one of our trademarks, along with treading fresh dog dirt into shag-pile carpets.

'I'll turn the van round,' said Tim, wiping his hands on his jeans. 'You get the cash.'

The woman entered the bedroom behind me and opened one of the drawers in the dressing table. 'Ninety-five pounds, is that right?' she asked.

'It is, yes.'

I stood there awkwardly and watched her count out the necessary amount from a vast wad of notes.

'I hope I'm the first man you've had in here,' I joked, somewhat nervously.

'You're the first *man*,' she replied seductively, 'although I've entertained quite a number of *boys*.'

Having unintentionally identified her profession, and without managing to look her in the face, I took the money, bolted down the stairs and ran out to the van.

Tim gave me a strange look. 'What's wrong? She didn't try to eat you, did she?'

I told him what she had said and, predictably, he collapsed in a heap over the steering wheel.

'Let's get moving,' I said, with a mixture of impatience and embarrassment.

'Get back up those stairs! You can pay her with her own money!'

We set off again and rejoined the main road, giggling like a pair of ten-year-olds, although the incident was commonplace anyway. In truth, I had always lived for Saturdays and everything they had come to represent: good-humoured hours on the road with Tim, overexcited sports commentators on the radio, a possible bonus from his father on a good day and, every week without exception, a hearty supper cooked to perfection by his saintly mother.

By the end of the month, my routine had reasserted itself fully, and each week could have been superimposed upon the previous one right down to the minutest detail. Neither of us received any more correspondence from Lindsey, and my pile of foreign money remained undisturbed, gathering dust on the kitchen table.

Another typical delivery day came and went and, after spending the usual lazy evening at the McKees' house, sitting like dummies in front of the television, I boarded the bus opposite the railway station and headed for home, cold and alone.

It was generally well past midnight when I stepped off the bus on Saturday nights, and on this occasion even later than normal. The pubs that closed had done so, and, with the exception of the occasional Formula One minicab shooting past, there was scarcely a sound from anywhere. I trudged down the hill with my head bowed to shield my eyes from the rain, and my hands firmly embedded in the warm, dry depths of my jacket pockets.

As I turned the final corner I could see the cottage in darkness and, more ominously, the shadow of a man lurking under the porchway - my porchway as opposed to any of the nine identical others.

I then heard Lindsey's ethereal voice in my head: 'You're afraid of the dark, *aren't* you? Afraid of the dark, *aren't* you? Afraid of the dark ...' On and on it echoed. That awful, heart-clenching anxiety began to take hold. It was cold, even for late October, there were no lights on in any of the neighbouring houses, and the howling noises from the trees seemed to intensify with a little unsolicited help from my imagination. I held my breath and watched closely. His motive had to be criminal. That much was self-evident. But had he noticed me? Was he someone I knew? Was he alone? Were a couple of accomplices already inside my house?

The figure stopped moving. I proceeded cautiously on the opposite side of the lane. In a moment of pathetic optimism, I thought perhaps it was Lindsey, having returned home for some reason, inexplicable though that would have been. Moving closer, however, I realized that, whoever it was, he was considerably shorter. As I approached, he heard the sound of my footsteps and turned around sharply. It was the very last person I was expecting to encounter.

'How did you get here?' I asked, walking slowly towards him.

Tim looked blank for a few seconds, as if he did not know me. 'In the van,' he said, eventually, although his words were barely audible. He pointed tentatively around the corner of the end cottage where he had parked it.

'What's wrong?'

His eyes were glazed. He appeared to be looking over my shoulder, and seemed unaware that the rain was dripping from his hair and running down his cheeks like tears.

'What is it?' I persisted.

'I have something to tell you.'

I knew at once that this was not a joke. His vacant, paralysed expression was one I had never seen before - on anyone. Whatever he had to say, it could not wait until morning.

'Let's go inside,' I said.

I opened the door, walked into the front room and lit the fire. We sat down on the carpet and looked at each other. He took a deep breath and let it out slowly and loudly before speaking.

'At what time did you leave our house?' he asked.

'About eleven thirty.'

'Well, ten minutes or so after you left, we had a phone call.'

'From Lindsey?'

'Nova.'

'What did she want?'

He seemed either reluctant or unable to get to the point.

'Do you remember the day Jacques arrived home from his business trip?'

'Yes.'

'And we were all sitting around the breakfast table bitching about Erin?'

'I remember.'

'She killed herself this morning.'

I turned my head away and gazed into the flames in disbelief. Neither of us spoke for more than a minute, and only the partially muted sound of the wind bellowing amongst the trees outside disturbed the deathly midnight peace.

'Tell me the entire story.'

'I was–'

'The *entire* story. Don't miss anything.'

'All right, all right.' He warmed his hands in front of the fire then rubbed them vigorously together. 'I was in the bathroom when Nova rang. Mum answered it. To begin with, I thought she was phoning because I'd left some clothes in New York, but I knew from her shaky voice that something was wrong. She was so distraught, Jacques had to take over. That in itself was enough of a shock.'

'How did she find out?'

'Apparently, Adam called her two or three hours ago. It would have been about midday in LA. He was screaming at her down the phone and threatening to kill Lindsey with his bare hands. I didn't know this, but Erin had been prescribed antidepressants the day we left.' His voice softened to a whisper. 'I guess she must not have taken them, and so she just ... you know ...'

I tried to remain as rational as possible. 'Most bereavements lead to some degree of depression, don't they?'

'True, but Adam seems to think that, as tragic as it was, their mother's death on its own was insufficiently traumatic to make her end it all.' He looked directly into my eyes. 'The truth according to him is that Lindsey murdered his sister.'

'That's ludicrous,' I said. 'Words can't kill.'

'That's what Nova was trying desperately to tell him, but he wouldn't have it. He carried on ranting, determined that he would "track down the murderer" - an eye for an eye, as it is written in the Bible.'

'He's *mad*. If that didn't sound so disturbing, I'd laugh. Where was Jacques when all this blew up?'

'On his way back from Washington. He arrived back at the apartment to find Nova in tears. Adam happened to call again several minutes later. Unfortunately for him, Jacques answered.

'Then what?'

'Let me put it this way, Nova thought we might have been able to feel the earthquake on this side of the Atlantic. Jacques was incensed.'

'I don't blame him for exploding. After all, what was Nova's crime?'

He said nothing. It angered me to think that such an inoffensive being had been subjected to a barrage of gratuitous abuse, although I could have predicted that, given her nature, she would hurl herself in front of her brother. My sympathy lay only with her.

'How long were you speaking with Jacques?' I asked.

'Half an hour or so. I drove over as soon as I had put the phone down. I was surprised to find you weren't home yet.'

'The bus was late leaving Liverpool. When I saw a silhouette flashing about in the porchway I thought someone was trying to break in.'

For a moment we both laughed at my paranoia about burglars and the like, before our minds quickly refocused on his reason for having come round.

'You haven't told me how ...'

'How what?'

'How she, you know, did it.'

'That's the worst part.' He sighed and looked up. 'Shall I switch on the light?'

I had not noticed that we had been sitting in semi-darkness for more than twenty minutes. When he sat down again, the pallor of his normally ruddy face was more evident.

'Erin was supposed to fly to Edmonton with some college friends this afternoon but she backed out at the last minute. As far as Adam knew, though, she'd gone with them.'

'What did she do?'

'It's horrific. I keep thinking about it.'

'Is it really *that* bad?'

'It's the sort of thing that sticks in the mind for *life*.'

'I'm ready to hear it nonetheless.'

'The thought of it is just too dreadful to contemplate. I knew I wouldn't be able to sleep. That's why I came over straight away, instead of waiting until tomorrow.'

I handed him a small, half-empty bottle of whisky from the coffee table which Lindsey had once inadvertently left behind. He took a mouthful and grimaced. I was not entirely certain that I wanted to find out, but curiosity, responsible for both killing cats and bringing our species out of caves, prevailed.

'She drove east to a remote railway crossing–'

'Oh God!'

'And rested her head on the track.'

I raised my hands to my face and closed my eyes so tightly that they began to hurt. I felt cold and began to tremble. Tim turned up the fire thermostat even further. I automatically thought of what would have remained after the train had passed: the body of a wholesome young American belle, untouched apart from her head, which had been surely crushed into an unrecognizable, homogeneous mass of bloody tissue and tiny skull fragments. I could almost feel the pain.

'Does everyone know?' I asked him.

'Lindsey doesn't,' he replied, 'if that is what you are implying. He's oblivious to it all. By now he will probably have forgotten who she is - or should I say *was*.'

Past tense now, I thought. History. His choice of words, and the doom-laden way he spoke them, made it sound as if Erin van Bergen had been dead and gone for years.

Tim kept talking. 'Miles away in Thailand, he's probably happier than at any other time in his life, spending every minute with Maalii and constantly partying at the Plaza. He knows *nothing*.'

'Hasn't Nova contacted him?'

'How could she? He doesn't have access to a phone.'

'You're right. Still, Adam doesn't know of his whereabouts. That's the important thing.'

'I'm afraid he does.'

I wondered for a moment. 'How?'

'Nova told him,' he gulped.

'Christ! What made her do that?'

'Adam made sure he asked her before explaining his reason for calling.'

There was another silence.

'So he could be ...'

'That's right, on his way to Bangkok with the ultimate score to settle as we speak. That's why Nova was so hysterical.'

'Lindsey can take care of himself,' I said, optimistically.

'He could if he were aware of the story.'

It was all too much to absorb, especially in the middle of the night. We remained where we were, sitting cross-legged in front of the fire, trying to make sense of the sickening tragedy, and also figure out how we could inform Lindsey as quickly as possible - for his own sake.

'We can't *phone* him,' said Tim decisively, 'and a letter would take six or seven days to get there, which is too long.'

'In that case, only one other option remains.'

'Which is what?' he said.

'Either you or I will have to tell him in person.'

'You mean fly back to Bangkok?'

'What choice do we have?'

'Well, I can't go,' he said categorically. 'If you're serious, it'll have to be you.'

'I can't afford the fare,' I protested, but at the same time hoping he would hit upon a solution, 'nor could I expect your dad to allow me to take more time off work.'

'I could tell the old boy that you're ill, with flu or whatever, and you could consult the travel agent on Monday.'

'Are you serious?'

'Of course. When was the last time you took time off work due to illness? Not for well over a year.'

'Which would make it seem all the more suspicious.'

'Maybe, but you could be in Bangkok by the middle of next week.'

'But I've told you, I don't have the money.'

'You do, you know.'

'I *don't.*'

'You're forgetting something. What about all those dollar bills next to the fruit bowl in the kitchen?' he said. 'You could change them back into sterling to pay for the flight.'

The idea of returning to Thailand, for whatever reason, made me fizz with excitement, but Tim's endorsement alone seemed insufficient.

'How much do you have?' he persisted.

'I don't know. Four hundred pounds - assuming there won't be a currency devaluation on Monday. Better still if there is.'

'Let's count it, then. I'll lend you the remainder.'

He got to his feet and headed for the kitchen. I knew that the proposal was grossly unfair to his father, but the sudden prospect of seeing both Lindsey and Bangkok in a matter of days overwhelmed me to the point of blindness.

He re-emerged from the darkness of the kitchen and spilled all the notes and coins onto the carpet in front of me.

'Don't cash in the Thai money,' he warned. 'You'll be needing that.'

In total we counted the equivalent of three hundred and eighty pounds, excluding the Thai baht notes which I had originally rolled up and secured with an elastic band.

'I'm short of a hundred at least,' I pointed out.

'Don't worry, I can let you borrow that much.'

'Thanks, but I still feel guilty about deceiving your dad.'

'That's all right,' he insisted, rubbing his hands in front of the fire once again. 'I'll take care of him.'

'Well, it's nearly four o'clock,' I said wearily.

'Some night.'

I pulled out some old travel blankets from under the armchair. 'Here, sleep on the sofa if you like. I'm going up to bed.'

I left him to make himself comfortable downstairs, and then collapsed, fully clothed, onto the bed. I lay still in the dark, exhausted but unable to suppress my overstimulated imagination. I thought of the late Erin van Bergen, a girl whose eyes had once twinkled in the Californian sunlight but would do so no more; I thought of her brother, broken and delirious, in relentless pursuit of her tormentor; I thought of the Herculean Jacques, breathing fire in defence of the sublimely precious Nova; and, most of all, I thought of Lindsey himself, annexed in his brave new world which, rightly or wrongly, I now wanted to see again with my own eyes.

XXIII

'A youth to whom was given
So much of earth - so much of heaven,
And such impetuous blood.'

William Wordsworth (1770-1850)
Ruth

For the first time in my life, I was impatient for Monday to arrive. Sunday was my only free day of the week, but for once I was satisfied to dream away the daylight hours in solitude, walking along the desolate Marine Promenade, watching the occasional lonely boat sail jauntily up and down the Mersey estuary.

When lunchtime came around on Monday, I slipped furtively into town and made for the travel agency, where the original holiday had been booked. I emptied all my dollar bills and crumpled traveller's cheques from a large brown envelope onto the Currency Exchange counter and received in excess of four hundred pounds in return. I then shot across to an unoccupied desk and sat down opposite a prim female robot who was speaking on the telephone whilst simultaneously bashing details into her computer terminal. It was the very same woman who had arranged the marathon itinerary back in March - and the same woman who thought Bangkok was the capital of Iraq.

'Sorry to keep you waiting,' she said with a synthetic smile. 'How can I be of assistance?'

'I'd like to book a seven-day trip please.'

'Any place in particular?'

'Oh, Bangkok.'

'Bangkok.'

'In Thailand,' I pointed out.

'When would you be looking to go?'

'Right now.'

'Today?'

'Well, this week,' I replied desperately, and she began typing in Morse Code fashion.

I felt uncomfortably self-conscious, sitting there in my work overalls, clasping an envelope full of cash, planning to disappear to the other side of the world at a moment's notice. Perhaps she thought I was a fleeing fugitive, and was considering pressing the panic button or alerting the police. Then again, maybe she was not programmed to digress at all and therefore such lateral thoughts never even flitted through her mind.

'We'll be lucky to find anything for this week,' she mumbled, shaking her head.

I glanced repeatedly at the clock on the back wall as she investigated the various airline schedules and flight permutations. Even though I was impaled upon the desire to return to Thailand, I remained cautious about returning late to the warehouse.

Eventually, she located a solitary vacant seat. I sat up sharply.

'I can book you onto one of tomorrow morning's shuttles from Manchester to Amsterdam, connecting with the early afternoon flight which is scheduled to arrive at Bangkok Don Muang on Wednesday. That's the only available connection, I'm afraid.'

'Do it!' I replied, without thinking to inquire about the cost. In fact, it was at that moment that I realized my actual motive for returning. Incredibly, the furore surrounding Erin's suicide had become incidental; I just wanted to see Lindsey again.

'If there's any further information you need before we close this evening,' she said.

Please don't hesitate to contact me, I thought.

'Please don't hesitate to contact me.'

'Much obliged. Thank you very much.'

I crept back into work without raising suspicion and completed another unremarkable day, taking care to conceal my excitement but, at the same time, subtly making it known to everyone that I was beginning to feel off colour. Tim wandered in, not surprisingly, as I was about to put on my jacket and go home.

'What happened?' he whispered, eyes bulging. 'Did you book it?'

'I'll fill you in on the way home.'

I fastened my jacket and walked with him down the hill towards the station. The wind continued to blow cold, but it made no difference - I felt immune to it.

'Now, I've written a letter for you to give to Lindsey, explaining everything Nova told me.' He fumbled about inside his coat pockets. 'Also, I've a total of seventy pounds in Thai baht for you. Take my camera too. I'd like a picture of Soi Phasuk.'

'Why?'

'I can't really explain. It's like no other place on earth - those tumble-down shacks on one side of the lane and the railway line on the other.'

'Very well.'

'On second thoughts,' he said, correcting himself, 'miss out the railway line.' He did not have to explain why he would rather not look at it. 'And don't send any postcards, otherwise you might come home and find yourself out of a job!'

'I had thought of that.'

'Keep your face out of the sun, too. If you come back with a tan, you'll need a few more weeks off to get rid of it.'

'Good point.'

'Your trusty accomplice here will deal with everything else while you're gone. There's absolutely no reason for you to worry.'

Predictably, I awoke several times during the night, each time convinced that I had slept through the alarm. I eventually gave up and climbed out of bed at four thirty in the morning to pack the last of my summer clothes. As a consequence of my being too lazy to empty some of the items from my bag when I arrived home from New York, repacking did not take long.

At the unnecessarily early time of ten minutes to six, I slipped quietly out and locked the front door under the flickering light from the faulty lamp on the corner of the lane. It was a wonderfully unique time of day to be out on the streets, even in November. The pre-dawn calm was disturbed only by the faint sounds of the occasional vehicles passing along Seabank Road at the top of the hill, from where I had to catch the bus to Liverpool.

The local newsagent, an enormous man with thinning grey hair whom I had known since childhood, noticed me waiting at the bus stop as he opened his small shop to the world.

'Don't tell me you're absconding *again*, Phil,' he remarked softly, although the absence of background noise seemed to amplify his voice.

'Afraid so, Fergal!' I answered. 'Keep it to yourself, though. I don't want the cottage burgled for a third time.'

He raised a hand in acknowledgement, then picked up his bundles of newspapers by the knotted string and retreated into his den which was illuminated like a beacon in the morning mist. The smell of fried bacon tickled my face. A light was on inside the pebble-dashed cottage behind the bus stop. This tiny, insignificant corner of the borough was slowly returning to life, to face a day every bit as humdrum and predictable as the previous one had been, and as the following one would be.

I boarded the six-thirty bus and located the seat closest to the heater, keeping my jacket buttoned to the collar and withdrawing my hands into the fur-lined sleeves. Apart from half a dozen women, who looked like cleaners, sitting in silence at the back, the only other passenger was a middle-aged man on the seat opposite my own, who I knew worked at the bakery near to the ferry terminal. He gazed out of the window at the same rows of old houses and shop fronts that he had probably passed every weekday for most of his life. I observed his catatonic reflection in the window and contemplated for a few minutes: his routine was no different from my own, monotonous and totally uninspiring, but he was thirty years further down the slope. He looked like a man who was ready to commit suicide, only he was too paralysed by his own apathy to go through with it. Suicide, I thought. Erin van Bergen. The hideous details of her death resurfaced and refused to leave me alone until they had succeeded in making me wince.

In Liverpool, other buses, which were mainly empty, filed along Lime Street in front of the railway station, droning and belching fumes nonchalantly into the dawn air. As I walked up the steps to the concourse, as opposed to continuing up the hill to the warehouse, I could all but feel my life careering out of control. My fixation with joining Lindsey in Bangkok even outweighed the risk of being rumbled and then sacked by Tim's father; and I was able to suppress what guilt I felt as effortlessly as I had booked the flight.

No one saw me sneak into the station, apart from a tramp who was vomiting noisily into one of the shiny red litter bins; and the ironically-named 'sprinter' train to Manchester departed bang on time. I was surprised by the number of commuters leaving for their offices and factories so early in the day. Initially, I had assumed that those sitting around me all worked together, but I gradually came round to a more plausible explanation: their friendship resulted from having occupied the same seats in the same carriage for years. Indeed, they were no different from the man on the bus, or from millions of other 'train crews' throughout the world who assembled for the same few minutes each working day, acclimatized to their drudgery, and all betrayed by ideals that were never truly theirs to relinquish, less still fulfil. The individuals were different, some very much so, but the ritual was disturbingly similar. My second escape to the Far East was nothing but a weak rebellion against a clockwork life. I wanted, ideally, to be another Lindsey, steadfastly refusing to march to the beat of convention's drum, but in reality I possessed neither the intellect nor the single-mindedness necessary to break the shackles. He was so right: 'rut' was just an abbreviation of 'routine'.

My state of mind improved substantially when I entered the airport and strode down the sterile corridors towards the departures lounge. I was now only fifteen hours from the chaotic paradise that was Bangkok, and there were no obstacles lying in my path. I felt as free as I had ever thought possible. I enthused about hovering round the Plaza once more, wandering aimlessly between the novelty stalls on Sukhumvit Road and, above all else, seeing a rare look of surprise on Lindsey's face.

I spent three hours roaming in and out of the expensive duty-free shops at Schiphol, Amsterdam before calmly boarding the 747 bound for Bangkok.

The woman in the adjacent seat, who had never before ventured outside Western Europe, listened enthusiastically to my exaggerated anecdotes about long-haul flights and the wonders of the Far East, very few of which I had actually experienced. Still, in terms of travel, I considered myself to have come of age. I must have created the impression that jetting across the world was almost a way of life. Every so often, however, I could see Lindsey's smirking face, lingering like an unwanted conscience, amused but unimpressed by such pretentiousness. It was probably a symptom of childish excitement on my part, which I knew he would have realized, which made it all the worse.

The lights dimmed as the in-flight film began. It was the same one I had seen on the way to Bangkok the first time which was, incredibly, only seven weeks ago. The ten remaining hours became seven, then four, and eventually one, at which point I disappeared into one of the lavatory cubicles to change my clothes. I could not help but recall the memorably disgusting bus journey from Buffalo to New York City.

'Are you meeting someone at the airport?' the woman asked, when I reoccupied my seat.

'No, I'll need to take a taxi into the central district.'

'How long does that normally take?'

'About an hour.'

'That long?'

'Oh yes. The traffic congestion can be severe, even more so than in, for example, North American cities, and the geological composition of the land would render an underground transport system unfeasible.'

Even though what I said was factually accurate, I was doing it again: talking like the hardened globetrotter I was not. Before disembarking, I wished her well, in appreciation of both her friendly demeanour and the fact that she had refrained from reciting her life history, which I had come to learn was the authentic hallmark of an inexperienced traveller.

The immigration official, a pokerfaced man wearing the standard, tightly-fitting brown uniform, stamped 'Bangkok - Thailand' in my passport, right next to an identical one dated September the seventeenth, but made no comment on noticing that I had visited five other countries in the meantime. Evidently it was nothing extraordinary.

Outside, small clusters of people had accumulated around the exits, mostly taxi drivers touting for lucrative, early morning business. A couple of young Thai girls rushed in through the automatic doors, laughing to themselves, as I was leaving. They were just like the ones that worked at the Plaza. I was getting ever closer, and could now all but smell Sukhumvit's idiosyncratic mixture of motor vehicle fumes and the rich odour from meat satays being noisily barbecued by the street vendors.

I walked across to one of the drivers who opened his door for me without speaking. I climbed into the back and leaned forward between the seats.

'*Pai Suk-hum-vit, Soi Pha-suk!*' I said carefully.

'*Soi Phasuk? Ah, soi soong!*'

He understood, but then began to jabber away in Thai, unaware that the intelligibility of my request was merely the result of meticulous rehearsal during the flight. Had Lindsey been at my side, he would probably have struck up a decent conversation without thinking. Nevertheless, I was more than content to peer through the rose-tinted window and drift back to September.

We cruised along the expressway for half an hour before being confronted by the inevitable ocean of traffic. Instinctively, the driver turned off at the first available exit and, just like before, we snaked towards the central district along narrow side roads. I had paid the flat-rate fare, so his deviation was immaterial. If a similar detour had occurred in Manhattan, or London, it would undoubtedly have spelled trouble.

He tapped the windscreen to attract my attention and pointed straight ahead.

'*Sukhumvit!*' he called. '*Thanon Sukhumvit!*'

I looked over his shoulder and saw that we had reached the main road via Soi 3. As we crawled the remaining distance to the Expressway bridge, I caught glimpses of familiarity: the junction of Soi 4 with its petrol station forecourt on the corner, the numerous pavement stalls laden with counterfeit designer T-shirts and jeans and, finally, a dusty old lane which I had grown to love. The euphoria which Lindsey claimed to have experienced on his return now seemed perfectly natural.

We stopped by the side of the railway line at the Plaza entrance. All the bars were locked up apart from the nearest one, which was serving breakfast, and half a dozen of the girls were sitting idly at one of the tables, waiting for another wild day to begin. I climbed out and called to them, hoping that someone might have a good memory.

'Maalii Pasi,' I said. 'Where is Maalii Pasi?'

'Maalii?' said the one sitting furthest away. 'Me know. She live Soi Phasuk ... with *farang*.'

'Will she be there now?'

She simply shrugged, apologetically. 'Me don't know.'

'Thank you,' I replied, bowing my head a few times, and then headed for Soi Phasuk.

By the time I had carted my bags to the door to the first room of number twenty-eight, my face was dripping wet. I knocked hard and could see that it had been locked from the inside. I was relieved that someone was at home, but it never occurred to me that they might still be sleeping. It was, after all, only nine o'clock, and they did have a habit of not resurfacing before midday.

Just before I knocked again I heard a noise which sounded like someone fumbling for keys. The makeshift door opened very slowly and the unblemished face of Maalii's teenage sister appeared out of the darkness, looking drowsy and, at first, unsure as to who I was.

'*Sawat-dii khrup*,' I said, and smiled innocently.

'*Sawat-dii kha*. How are you?'

'Fine.'

She opened the door and let me in. She was alone, which made me feel worse for having disturbed her. As I sat down on the corner of the mattress, she dragged the fan clumsily across the lino-covered floor and positioned it in front of me.

'Thanks.'

'*Mai pen rai*. You come to see Lindsey, yes?'

'Yes, where is he?'

'He go with Maalii.'

'Where?'

'America.'

My heart rate doubled. 'Are you sure?' I gasped.

'Yes, they go New York. Lindsey have sister.'

It appeared that I had just travelled thousands of miles in the wrong direction.

'When did they leave?'

She began to chuckle. 'I am joking! They go Krasang. See Mama Papa!'

'When?'

'Yes-ter-day. I don't know when they come back.'

Her spoken English, along with her sense of mischief, had developed further since our initial meeting at the marketplace in Krasang, which was helpful, as I was straining to bombard her with questions.

'What are you doing here?' was the first that came to mind.

'I work bar at Plaza. Other girls go to work at big hotel in Phuket, so I work now, instead of them.'

'What about school?'

'Finished,' she said with pride. 'I no go school now. I work bar.'

She sounded thrilled that her days of compulsory schooling had come to an end, but I had a suspicious feeling that she would have remained in the classroom had she been able to scrape together the money. I also felt slightly ashamed, as I had quit school at the earliest available opportunity when an additional few years would have cost me nothing. What she had been tragically unable to afford, I had discarded voluntarily - as indeed had Lindsey, although he had contrived to further his education without having recourse to teachers.

'You want to go Krasang?' she suggested, having quickly gauged my state of mind.

'Yes, today.'

'Today? *Wan nii?* I come with you, yes? I come with you?'

I nodded. 'Of course.'

'We leave Bangkok tonight. Arrive Krasang tomorrow morning. You pay for me, yes?' she pleaded.

I smiled at her. If I could spend in excess of five hundred pounds on a return flight from England, then I figured that the cost of an extra rail ticket would be of negligible significance.

'I go shopping now. I go buy food, take to my mother in Krasang. You stay here - go sleep. I come back later.'

She undressed in front of me, right down to just a tiny pair of white briefs, and slipped into a bright yellow cotton blouse and black leather pants. Within weeks she had undergone the standard metamorphosis from school-girl into sexy temptress, and was now, undoubtedly, the focus of relentless male attention at the Plaza. In my eyes, that was all beneath her.

Before she left, I asked her if anyone had arrived in Bangkok in recent days in search of Lindsey but, as far as she was aware, the only *farang* he knew was Joel, with whom he had enjoyed the inevitably never-ending rounds of drinks at the fourth bar.

As soon as I was alone, I lay on my side on the flimsy bed and repositioned the fan so that it was blowing straight at my face. My initial belief that I would be capable of staying awake throughout the flight and then endure a full day in the Bangkok heat had proved laughably optimistic. I was utterly exhausted.

She returned before I awoke. I raised my head from the pillow and could see her sitting cross-legged in the darkest corner of the room, quite contented, tidying her clothes and scribbling in a large notebook. She may have been there for some time, not making a sound and selflessly allowing me the full benefit of the fan.

'You want go eat?' she whispered.

'Soi 2?'

'You want go Soi 2? OK, we go Soi 2. Lindsey also like go eat Soi 2.'

The second I stood up, she closed her book and collected her keys from the makeshift shelf next to the bed, which was littered with evidence of Lindsey and Maalii: a book of postage stamps, a pile of pound coins, an empty box of tissues and several loose photographs of decadent Plaza parties.

She padlocked the door securely and we set off along Soi Phasuk towards the main road. Once again, the young street children were playing football on the grass verge next to the railway line, which they probably did every day provided it was not raining. I recognized one of them - a skinny boy of about fourteen with buck teeth and sunken cheeks - and waved to him. He grinned and called out something I was unable to understand. Perhaps he was commenting on what appeared to be my instant acquisition of a new girl-friend, and a teenager at that. It would certainly have been natural for a boy of his years to be infatuated with someone like Auy. In fact, being in a posi-tion to ogle the Plaza girls may have been the sole criterion for their choice of playground.

She held my hand as we ambled along Sukhumvit past the T-shirt stalls. I had no idea what she was thinking, but I was not going to object, particu-larly as everyone seemed to be watching. We sat opposite each other at one of the small roadside tables and ordered the usual: chicken fried rice - it was the only dish with a Thai name that I could pronounce - and two glasses of icy grape juice. Eating at a pavement cafe, wearing summer clothes in mid-November made me feel that I was in breach of the rules, although I could not say whose rules they were, which amply demonstrated just how strait-jacketed my life had come to be. At least I was now able to see it.

From there we walked to the Plaza, where the bars had just opened and the resident crowd of female extroverts were loitering outside, shouting excit-edly to each other and debating which tapes to play on the hi-fis.

'Your friend go with Maalii,' one of them explained whilst wiping my face and forehead with a cold flannel.

'Yes, I know.'

'You want drink? You want beer?'

'Orange juice,' I replied.

'OK. I get you *oran joo*,' she said, and sprang up from her stool.

'Same Auy,' I added. 'Two oranges.'

It was a kind of bliss that I had never experienced before. This refresh-ing simplicity of life in the Soi Phasuk slum accentuated the blatant futility of western materialism - the blind, frantic pursuit of goals devised by the gods of avarice. I felt confident that, like the demobbed GIs, I would be able to live there on just a few bucks a week, buying food from the street vendors and living without the need to compete.

Knowing that it was hours before our journey was scheduled to begin, I was content to waste the afternoon hanging around at the Plaza, and Auy, ever perceptive, realized as much. At dusk, the coloured fairy lights, which were strung along the bars' wooden canopies, illuminated the Plaza walkway right up to the main road and gave it that same magical look I had originally noticed six weeks previously.

'Hey, limey Phil! Is that really you?' boomed a familiar voice from behind me. 'What the hell you doin' here?'

I swivelled round just before a large hand slapped me firmly on the left

shoulder. It was Joel, eyes as close together as ever, with a friendly but quizzi-
cal expression on his face.

'Good to see you,' I said, and shook his hand for the umpteenth time.

'Two beers, please!' he called, and grabbed a spare stool from the other
end of the bar. 'So ... couldn't keep away from these lovely ladies, huh?'

'I suppose not.' I saw no reason to explain about Erin's suicide and my
subsequent determination to find Lindsey.

'Where's your buddy?' he immediately inquired, prizing the tops from the
beer bottles.

'Tim? He's back home.'

'I meant that other scoundrel.'

'Lindsey?'

'He was sitting right here with me just a few days ago. Drunk as a
bastard, he was.'

'He and Maalii left for Krasang yesterday.'

'And doesn't he know you're in town?'

'Not yet. I'm taking the overnight train.'

'When, tonight?'

'Leaving at eleven.'

He looked down at his drink and picked pensively at the label on the
bottle. 'Tell me it's none of my concern, if you like,' he went on, 'but you sure
seem desperate to catch up with him.' He looked up at me. 'Liverpool to
Krasang is one hell of a distance. Does he owe you money or somethin'?'

'No, nothing like that. It's a long story. Do you really want to hear it?'

'Sure I do! There's never a dull minute with you guys!' He took a drink,
as if in preparation for a shock. 'If you're prepared to tell it...'

I began from when Tim and I had said goodnight to him after our evening
on Broadway, and explained about Adam's phone calls and the horrific way
in which Erin had taken her life at the weekend.

'Get away from here!' he gasped, at least three times, the accent on a
different word each time. 'That's some *coup de fucking grâce*, my friend. And
you're saying that all this has blown up since we were in Manhattan?'

'Every word of it.'

'Get *away* from here. And you think this asshole from Los Angeles is crazy
enough to come all the way out here in an attempt to carry out his threat?'

'I think he is.'

'What, crazy or an asshole?'

We both laughed for a moment and ordered more drinks, as if he needed
to dull his senses to digest the tale properly.

'Don't torture yourself over it,' he said coolly. 'If I see anyone sniffing
around, I'll say that Lindsey is out backpacking in the Burmese jungle.

Deterrents don't come much better than that. I know - I've been there.'

For some reason all conversation at the bar ceased at a stroke, and a faint vibration began to pass from the floorboards up through my feet. A few seconds later, a long freight train lumbered behind the bars with a deafening roar, causing the glasses to clatter together on the shelves. I watched each passing truck through a small hole in the back wall and pictured crossing the Kwai River, Lindsey cavorting half-drunk on the Forth Bridge and, mainly, a young woman for whose gruesome demise he was being held solely responsible.

Joel, as stunned as he was drunk, disappeared at nine thirty, but I made a point of telling him that I would be back by the following Monday at the latest, to be in good time for my return flight. Seeing him in Bangkok, New York, then Bangkok again within a matter of weeks seemed too absurd to be real.

Auy, whom I had not seen at the bar for a couple of hours, collected the money that Joel had left and took it to the till.

'We go now?' she suggested.

'All right. How much?' I asked, pointing to all the empty glasses and bottles.

She shook her head kindly without saying a word; Joel had thought to settle my bill as well as his own.

On leaving the Plaza we took a short cut back to Soi Phasuk, clambering over the broken wooden fence which separated the bars from the railway line. I shuddered as we stepped across the open track, and again, she took hold of my hand until we reached her room.

I collected the bags, into which she had stuffed miscellaneous scraps of seafood and a large bottle of mineral water, and waited for a tuk-tuk to emerge from the darkness. We climbed inside without my feeling the need to engage in that tedious posturing, otherwise known as bartering, with the driver. On this occasion, being wary of paying slightly over the odds amounted to a petty distraction. I felt more inclined to proffer a tip instead, so loose was my state of mind.

Auy smiled to herself all the way to Makkasan station. If anything, the place was busier than it had been during the daytime, when we had made the same trip in September.

'Is everyone here going to Krasang?' I joked as we marched across to the ticket kiosk.

'I don't think so,' she replied, jogging intermittently in order to keep up with me. 'Some go Kuala Lumpur. Some go Chiang Mai. Travel many hours.' I listened as she gabbled to the woman at the counter before turning to me again. 'You want air condition?' she squeaked with sudden enthusiasm, as if she had forgotten that it was available.

'Up to you.'

'Two hundred baht for air condition.'

I agreed and handed her the money for two first class tickets. It was still relatively inexpensive and, unlike in Britain, the fare included refreshments.

We slumped down in the smartest carriage which, conveniently, was nearest to the concourse, and watched as at least two hundred people passed noisily along the platform. There were young couples, single women harassed by countless small children, and old peasants struggling with battered luggage which would occupy as much space as themselves and which barely looked worth the effort. The whole scene resembled an enforced migration of the masses into the countryside, or even an exodus of refugees from a land ravaged by war. Auy studied them closely, still offering no comment, but it was hardly necessary; I had seen the same anxious expression on the faces of the other girls. Her determination to struggle free from the clutches of penury was quiet, but it was there just the same.

XXIV

'Men are but children of a larger growth.'

John Dryden (1631-1700)
All For Love, IV

At nine the following morning we pulled into Buriram station which, I remembered, was the one immediately before Krasang, and of a comparable size. Auy was curled up next to me, sleeping peacefully with her head nestling in my lap. I was reluctant to disturb her, but I was desperate to stretch my legs or, better still, stand up and walk around in the aisle. However, before I even considered shuffling around in the seat, a baby, being cradled by the woman opposite, began to cry and thereby unwittingly solved the dilemma.

Auy opened her eyes wide and looked at me. 'I am sorry,' she said, somewhat embarrassed by the position in which she had found herself.

I laughed and squeezed her hand gently, stretching my legs at the same time. 'It's all right,' I whispered. 'Stay where you are.'

She smiled and put her head back down. 'Thank you. You are kind man, Phil. You same as Lindsey. He take care Maalii. He love my sister very much.' She closed her eyes again. 'I know. She tell me.'

It was not necessary to disturb her as we were approaching Krasang station; she could sense where we were as soon as the train began to slow down.

The place looked surprisingly different in broad daylight. The surrounding land appeared not so utterly arid. Indeed, the trees were every bit as luxuriant as the ones that lined the Kwai valley. Down the slope at the back of the ticket office were a couple of rows of decrepit market stalls which I had not noticed in September; and on the platform thirty to forty villagers were waiting to be taken to Surin, the very end of the south-eastern line. Without really needing to look, I knew there was not a single *farang* anywhere, so I was ready to be scrutinized by numerous pairs of eyes the moment we alighted. It was the paranoiac's nightmare.

Once the train had resumed its journey with its characteristic din, we crossed the track and headed for Maalii's house, walking deliberately slowly in the blistering heat. After a few minutes, we left the main village thoroughfare and there it was, right in front of me: the broken-down shack which I had expected never to see again. As it came fully into view, I could see a cluster of five or six children playing by the side of the lane in the shadow of a small, skeletal tree. I did not recognize any of them until the smallest turned his head and looked straight at us. It was the inimitable, indomitable Chek, as filthy as before, wearing nothing but a pair of luminous orange shorts which almost came down to his ankles. Hand-me-downs if ever I saw any. He took a couple of steps towards us, gawped for a moment, then scrambled across the yard into the house, shrieking and hopping up and down as if his feet were being scorched by the dusty earth. A few seconds later, he reappeared and stared again, presumably to be absolutely certain that his eyes were being faithful to him. Once more, he retreated into the house. Then, just as we reached the top of the yard, he re-emerged, this time dragging a disbelieving Maalii by the hand. She was wearing the maple leaf T-shirt which Lindsey had bought in Niagara Falls.

'Hello, Phil,' she said, and her dark eyes smiled excitedly.

'Good morning.' I had almost forgotten how unfeasibly beautiful she was.

'Why you come Krasang?'

'To see Lindsey.'

She kissed me on the cheek and we followed her round the back of the house to a small, dusty enclosure at the edge of the rice paddy which constituted some sort of garden. Sitting there on linoleum mats were five or six more children, all watching attentively their very own god, who was performing sleight-of-hand tricks with several large, silver-coloured coins. He glanced up and sniggered to himself, as though he had been expecting me to show up all along but was amused by the fact that it had taken me so long. His face and arms had become as dark as the children's, and his hair, now considerably longer, was tied back with a length of old cloth. I waited for him to speak.

'So your passport has lost its virginity for a second time, has it?' he said. 'Have you come on your own?'

'Yes,' I replied, with Chek playfully snapping at my heels.

I walked over and sat down on one of the mats. Immediately, Chek followed and jumped onto Lindsey's back, clinging on with his hands and feet like an oversexed chimpanzee.

'Get away from me, you smelly little runt!' In a single movement he grabbed the boy around the waist, lifted him above his head and tossed him headlong into a pile of leaves.

'You're looking fit and healthy,' I remarked.

'I'm *feeling* fit and healthy. How about you?'

'Fine. Just great.' I tried to sound casual. 'It's nice to be back.'

He nodded slowly and looked down at his sun-tanned hands which were clasped gently together.

'Is anything wrong?' I said.

'I'm puzzled,' was his eventual reply.

Maalii appeared, carrying a handleless porcelain jug which was overflowing with cold water.

'Puzzled about what?'

He took a mouthful and passed the jug to me.

'It's a long, long way, Phil. Too far to come for no especial reason - particularly with it being yourself.'

His remark hurt me slightly, in a way only the truth could.

'Why is it?' I said, stubbornly. 'You know I love the place. Is that not reason enough to return?'

'Frankly, no. This is not like you at all,' he laughed. 'You've travelled six thousand miles to tell me something exceptional. It's just that I can't figure out what it could be. Would you have phoned if it had been possible?'

'Probably, yes.'

'Then why didn't you write?'

'Write?'

'You know, pen and paper.'

'Because–'

'Because that would have taken too long,' he surmised, raising his index finger to his lips. 'The urgency must have been too ... acute.' He began to look untypically concerned. 'Something's wrong, isn't it?'

Before I could begin my well-rehearsed explanation, Chek picked up a dirty bucket, which he had filled with dead leaves, and emptied it over Lindsey's head. All the children collapsed onto the mats, convulsed with laughter. Chek then flung his arms around Lindsey's neck and grinned obtrusively, showing his brown teeth which had probably not been brushed since September.

'*Rak khun!*' he chortled affectionately. '*Rak khun, rak khuuuuun!*'

'What does that mean?' I asked.

'He says he loves me! It's his devious little way of persuading me not to retaliate. I shall, don't get me wrong, but not when he's half-expecting it.'

Once the hilarity had subsided, Maalii waved all the children away and sat down next to us, equally keen to learn the reason for my unannounced return.

For what felt like the hundredth time, I recited the sequence of events beginning with Nova's desperate, late-night transatlantic phone call. He remained expressionless, although he shrugged his shoulders once or twice as he relayed the tale to Maalii in impressively fluent Thai.

'How did she kill herself?' he asked with sudden curiosity. 'Hah, don't tell me she drove all the way to Toronto and launched herself from the top of the CN Tower!'

'No, she threw herself in front of a train.'

He remained unmoved. 'How appropriate.'

'Why is it?'

'Crushed by the advance of reason,' he scoffed. 'Well, if she wanted me to feel guilty, she miscalculated.'

'Aren't you bothered?' I inquired as carefully as I could.

He shrugged again. 'What would be the point? I will concede one thing, though.'

'What's that?'

'I only had the nerve to lie down by the *side* of the track, so I suppose she outperformed me in that respect.'

I went on to tell him about Adam's outburst of fury and Nova's fear that he might already have set off for Thailand.

'So *that's* the reason you're here!' He stood up and began to laugh, which made me feel small.

'What's so funny?' I said. 'Do you know something I don't?'

He shook his head and walked over to a large bench where he had been sawing wood. He picked up some of the pieces and fastened them together with a couple of elastic bands.

'Let's get this straight,' he called, 'Nova thinks that our deranged Californian friend is ready to travel halfway across the world in order to put a bullet in my head, or whatever, and she managed to convince you and Sigmund. Is that right?'

'Yes, I suppose-'

'And you ruptured your bank account in order to warn me?'

'Yes, damn you!' I snapped. 'We were worried and so was Nova!'

'She worries about me too much. Always has. You could have written a letter and you know it.'

'We couldn't!'

'I don't believe you, Phil.' He sat down again and smiled. 'You were pining to see this place again, as you admitted only a minute ago, and were presented with a convenient excuse. That's how it sounds to me.'

'That's just your perception,' I protested.

He looked deeper into my eyes. 'So what were you pining to see? Me?'

I had to look away; his stare was too powerful to withstand.

'Whatever your reasoning, old fruit, I'm glad you're here,' he enthused, in a markedly less confrontational tone. It was his way of defusing situations and wrong-footing people so they could not then despise him absolutely, a tactic which was almost as annoying as the initial mockery. 'There's a multitude of things I want to show you,' he went on. 'Here, take a look at these.'

He dropped the pieces of wood onto the mat in front of me.

'What are they supposed to be?'

'Stumps! Cricket stumps, for the kids!' I made them yesterday evening. The little monsters sat and watched me for almost two hours.'

He began to explain in precise detail how he had fashioned them out of a single strip of wood which he had found discarded at the side of the lane.

'It was originally square in cross-section, so I had to chisel the corners to make it roughly cylindrical. Then I cut it into quarters - three pieces for the wicket, a smaller one to mark the bowling crease and the leftovers for the bails.'

'I'm impressed.'

'After that,' he said, running his finger delicately along the edges, 'I sharpened them at one end so they could be driven into the ground, and filed concavities into the opposite ends to facilitate accommodation of the bails.'

'Do you-'

'That's not all. Wait until you see *this*.' He returned to the bench and picked up another piece which was considerably thicker. 'One bat!' he announced with even more enthusiasm. 'I'll need to make the handle circular in cross-section then smooth the face with glasspaper - if I can get hold of some from the market, that is. I told the kids I would teach them how to play tomorrow. They can't wait.'

'Chek playing cricket, eh? Does that not make you nervous?'

'We'll only be using a rubber ball.'

'Good! If you let the little urchin loose with the genuine article, he might have someone's eye out.'

'Yes, most probably his own.'

'Well, I can't wait, either,' I added.

He had evidently dismissed Adam's threat as an irrelevance, which unsettled me even more. His proposed game of cricket with the children seemed infinitely more worthy of his attention. In fact, it was the only sport he truly loved, and there had been many occasions when I had known him to sit in front of the television from morning until dusk, absorbed by the mental and physical battles being fought out between batsmen and bowlers. As a schoolboy, cricket-watching had been his principal reason for truancy. He had frequently sloped into Nottingham on the bus and spent summer days watching test matches at Trent Bridge when he should have been cooped-up in class, such was his unyielding passion for what he called 'the paragon of cultural evolution, along with poetry and pure mathematics'. It was yet another subject which would lead to clashes with Tim who, in contrast, viewed the spectacle as 'an elaborate exhibition of organized tedium'. Unsure who to call a philistine, I tended to sympathize with them equally.

'Would Maalii's parents object if I were to stay for a few days?' I asked him.

'I don't think so. When do you have to return to Bangkok?'

'Monday at the latest.'

'So you'll be here for three nights.'

'How long will you be here?'

'Two months? Six months? As long as it takes.'

'Adam knows you're out here, you understand. He kept telling Nova that he considered your *game* to be unfinished.'

'I thought he had already lost. Besides,' he added with an icy glare, ' he couldn't harm me.'

I was not entirely convinced, but decided not to say anything further in case it irritated him.

'I need to go into the village in a minute to buy food for the day. And to pick up my glasspaper. Are you up for a walk?'

I quickly changed my shirt and we set off, leaving the girls to wash and scrub a basketful of children's clothes in two cumbersome lead bowls in the yard. Sensing the possibility of either Lindsey or I spending money at the marketplace, most of the children ran along at our side, shrieking, giggling and kicking each other's backsides which, in their world, represented a perfectly normal pattern of behaviour.

At the intersection of the lane and the main road was a muddy pond, about the size of a tennis court, where a group of teenage boys had stripped off their clothes and were splashing energetically about under the watchful eye of the morning sun. Whether they were practising swimming or simply bathing, I was not certain. Perhaps they believed that one came automatically with the other, although to what extent it did, I could not imagine.

The children ran along the pond's edge as a short cut to the road, leaping across puddles and slippery logs. It was no great surprise when one of them lost his footing and fell in up to his waist, and even less of one when I saw which of them it was.

'Look at the state of him,' Lindsey remarked, like some despairing mother. 'If there were a solitary pile of camel dung in a million acres of desert, he'd step in it.'

Chek waded out, laughing at himself as hysterically as all the others were.

Lindsey began to laugh along with them. 'He's unreal. He came with Maalii and me to do some shopping in Surin yesterday and somehow managed to lose his trousers on the train.'

'How?'

'Ask him. I get the feeling that all the villagers know who he is, and exactly *what* he is. Maalii reckons they watch him for entertainment purposes.'

'I can see why.'

We strolled on towards the market, past tiny, open-fronted shops and wooden shacks, in front of which peasants turned their heads as the mysterious procession passed by. Had I become a second Pied Piper, I asked myself, marching the children through their own village, or just another one of their number?

I could smell the food from the stalls long before we reached them. Lindsey wandered between the tables, bartering for cuts of meat and fresh vegetables which were displayed on newspaper and shaded by a large canvas canopy overhead. Of all the foods laid out, only the eggs were similar to anything sold in England, and most of those were a thoroughly repellent colour.

After he had bought what appeared to be enough to feed the entire village, he walked across to a corner stall and bought each of the children a small plastic bag containing apple segments and a brown sugar dip. The children lined up one after another and Lindsey handed each of them an identical portion, but not before they had expressed gratitude with the customary prayer-like gesture. They were, almost literally, eating out of his hands.

Lastly, we called on Maalii's elder sister at her table - the same jungle of precariously balanced tangerines and lemons which I had remembered so poignantly. The children, now uncharacteristically calm, followed us in single file, nibbling their snacks, like ducklings trailing along after their mother.

The preparation of lunch became the main event of the day. I sat outside with Lindsey and the two girls, washing battered pans, dishing out basmati rice and peeling an endless supply of raw vegetables. Unusually, it was anything but a chore.

At three in the afternoon I positioned one of the woven mats in the shade of a small but leafy tree then lay down and drifted away as the sun began to dissolve into the distant orange haze. It made me think of Lumpini Park again. The sleepy sounds of the occasional motor engine and children's voices echoed intermittently along the lane. The railway station was less than half a mile away, but not once could I make out even the faintest noise from a train rattling along the single track to and from Surin. Trains again. Erin van Bergen. Even in such a peaceful niche of the poor man's Arcadia, so far from everywhere, peace of mind eluded me.

The next voice I heard belonged to Maalii.

'Phil,' she coaxed, gently shaking me by the arm.

I opened my eyes and noticed that it was almost dark, although the temperature had barely dropped, if at all.

'Phil, you no sleep here.'

'Mmm ... why not?'

'Mos-qui-to!' she replied, arms extended horizontally at full length, implying that they were everywhere.

I followed her across the yard and into the house where Lindsey and her sister were sitting on the floor, talking quietly and leafing through a pile of papers which Lindsey had removed from his bag.

'Jet-lagged?' he said, then muttered several words to Maalii who burst into one of her fits of giggles.

'Now what's funny?' I said.

'Your hair is full of grass.'

I rubbed my head and brushed the mess onto the floor. I had a good idea who had put it there while I was sleeping, which was more or less confirmed by the fact that the little monkey was nowhere in sight.

Maalii pointed to my head. '*Pai amnam.*'

'What is she saying?'

'She thinks perhaps you ought to clean yourself up in the washroom. Your clothes will be full of little creepy-crawlies.'

'Perhaps the big ones in the washroom will see to them.'

'I'm sure of it,' he laughed.

'Mr. Darwin would have had scope for another lifetime's research in this place.'

I felt the urge to scratch myself all over, but resisted so as to deny them the opportunity to continue laughing. I could not tell whether the girls had understood my comment on the disturbing state of the washroom but, even if they had, I was certain that they would not have taken offence.

I felt much cleaner after pouring three or four bowls of cold water over my skin, although it was arguably psychological. Back in the main room I saw Maalii's old parents for the first time in six weeks. They smiled, politely but briefly, neither surprised nor particularly put out by my arrival. They left the room a minute later and I sat cross-legged on the floor alongside Lindsey.

'Are you sure they don't object to my being here?' I asked him quietly.

'I'm positive. In fact, they don't seem to care who wanders in. Yesterday evening, some crinkly old man whom Maalii had never even seen before, strolled in, had a wash, changed his pants then left without a word to any of us!'

'Seriously?'

'Of course. Oh, talking of old men ... I received this letter from Dr. King a few days ago. Here it is.'

He passed me a small, heavily franked envelope which bore the sort of elegantly flowing handwriting to be expected of a man who had been at school at a time when that particular skill had been considered worth being able to do well.

'I wrote to him as soon as I arrived back in Bangkok. I also enclosed a few photographs of the Kwai Bridge. I thought, being a war veteran, he might like them.'

'Thoughtful of you. Did you tell him about your *contretemps* in LA?'

'I didn't, and that's the principal reason I wanted to show you his letter. Listen to this part and tell me where you've heard it before.'

'I'm listening.'

'"*I found your sceptical attitude to the ultimate Big Brother most refreshing, particularly for someone of your age. I suppose religious faith can be described as a form of self-delusion emanating from three main sources: cultural indoctrination, psychological insecurity and the obvious one, scientific illiteracy. One by itself is sad enough, but a combination of the three must be as dreadful a mental tragedy as one can possibly suffer. Religion can become so consuming that some people's lives come to depend on it. The obvious danger is this: if one's faith disintegrates, one's life can easily do likewise.*"'

'Prophetic, wouldn't you agree?'

'Disturbingly so. Any other words of wisdom?'

'"*If one generation is brainwashed with the beliefs of its predecessor, then it will be condemned to bear the same prejudices, hence the perpetual insolubility of so many tribal conflicts. My friend, if there is an all-powerful entity, and he, she or it condemns me to the flames of hell simply because of my sinful tendency to insist upon sound physical evidence for what I believe, then I would be proud to burn.*"'

'He might be old,' I said, once he had reached the bottom of the page, 'but he's very articulate, and he seems to be particular about his choice of words and so on.'

He agreed. 'When I reply, I shall have to really be sure not to carelessly split any infinitives. I don't imagine he would enjoy witnessing the desecration of the English language.'

I changed the subject before he realized that I did not know what an infinitive was, split or otherwise.

'Nova was utterly convinced that Adam would fly out here, you know. Utterly convinced.'

'He won't come after me,' he insisted impatiently. 'As I said, some games have to be conceded. It'll dawn on him once his tears have dried, I'm sure.'

'Does Maalii know what happened?'

'No.' He then began to laugh. 'She thinks you've trekked all this way primarily because without me your life is a drag.'

'You told her that?'

'I couldn't lie,' he protested.

I assumed that he was joking. 'So what does she think actually happened while we were in Los Angeles?'

'Nothing to speak of. We wandered around, saw the sights but didn't take any photographs.'

'Well, that's a lie, is it not?'

He nodded and a more sincere expression spread across his face. 'It is, yes, but there's nothing to be gained by telling her, especially as there won't be any repercussions.'

'You hope there won't.'

'I'm certain of it - and I must say, you're beginning to sound as paranoid as my sister.'

He unzipped the end compartment of his bag and placed the sheets of notepaper carefully between the pages of his war book, *Railway of Death*, as he had done with Maalii's letter in the Niagara Falls cafe.

'The title of your book has assumed an extra meaning since you bought it,' I remarked, before he refastened the zip.

'I realized that while you were asleep outside. And since you seem unable to talk about anything other than the dead girl, there's something else you might be interested to learn.'

'What's that?'

He spoke briefly to Maalii. She picked up his bag and returned it to the bedroom, then sat down again at his side.

'Do you remember the morning we left Adam's place?'

I nodded attentively. 'It seems so long ago.'

'I never told anyone, but I whispered a few words to Erin as we passed at the front door.'

'I noticed.'

'I only meant it as a joke, for goodness' sake,' he said, as if, for the first time, feeling the need to protest his innocence.

'What did you say?'

'Here's a kiss from the antichrist.'

I was incredulous. 'What?'

'It was just a thoughtless, spontaneous remark.'

'I doubt she would have appreciated it. She may have gone to her grave believing that you were the Prince of Darkness himself - if she believed in such a thing.'

'I didn't mean it in a satanic sense. It just so happens that elements of our religious establishment teach us from a tender age that anything of an anti-Christian nature is inherently evil. It's a clever ploy to stigmatize non-believers. Still, it's all immaterial now, and I won't mention it again,' he said, troubled only momentarily by the girl's gruesome fate. 'We're about to call it a day,' he went on, and pointed to a shabby, awning-like extension which was tacked loosely onto the rear wall of the shack. 'You can sleep with Auy in there, if you like.'

'With Auy? Are you sure about that?'

'Yes, but some of the kids are in there, too, so don't get an erection - you won't be needing it.'

'Point taken. Goodnight.'

I pulled back the outer curtain to reveal a dilapidated mosquito net which had at least five sizeable holes at various heights. Instead of preventing the disease-carrying pests gaining access, it appeared that it would serve only to stop them getting back out. It might not have looked any different if it had been designed by the mosquitoes themselves.

The wild dogs' conversations in the paddies - either with their ancestors or each other - kept me awake throughout the night. Whilst Auy slept peacefully alongside the children, I thought about my carefree time in New York, particularly the warmth of Nova, my incomprehensible attraction to Krasang, and the numerous other ways in which my life had been illuminated as a result of Lindsey's unintentional influence. I did not - indeed could not - resent him for saying that in his absence my life amounted to so little. I resented myself because it was so evident.

XXV

'Still nursing the unconquerable hope,
Still clutching the inviolable shade.'

Matthew Arnold (1822-88)
The Scholar Gypsy

For almost three days, Krasang became my home. Each morning, Lindsey and I would stroll with the girls into the village to buy fresh food and then stop to watch the ten o'clock eastbound train pull into the station. Inevitably, and in spite of Maalii's protestations, the children tagged along, and worked themselves into delirium the moment it came into view on the horizon. It was not that they had never seen a packed train before, but simply because this was one of the most exciting events of their day. From a distance they peered through the carriage windows at all the people who had made the arduous ten-hour trip from Bangkok, fully aware that several years had to elapse before they would be able to investigate and appreciate the city's vices and mysteries for themselves.

I spent the afternoons helping Lindsey to orchestrate anarchic games of cricket with an increasing number of children on each occasion. I got the feeling that it would not be long before they began to pour in from neighbouring villages in order to take part. Never in my entire life had I seen a bunch of youngsters display such raw enthusiasm. They chased after the ball ten at a time, scuffing their bare feet as they slid recklessly into ditches, or disappearing into clouds of dust like jackals fighting over a carcass. Without doubt, the most hilarious spectacle was anything at all involving Chek. With each delivery, he would swing the bat in manic desperation, as if swotting a giant mosquito which was coming to bite him. Each farcical swipe would be met with squeals of helpless laughter from everyone, including Lindsey, which succeeded only in encouraging him on to greater depths.

Amid the chaotic scenes, Maalii would wander to and from the house, occasionally joining in the madness and constantly supplying us with buckets of cold water to drink and pour over our sweaty heads. Regardless of what she was doing, the look of admiration for Lindsey never left her face. It was an image which showed how inconceivable it would be for them to be apart for a second period, however brief. The bond between them was beginning to look impregnable.

Sunday was departure day and I could not help but think back to the previous weekend when Tim had helped plan my second trip. We ambled down the familiar, winding path to the station two or three hours before the westbound night train was scheduled to arrive. It was not necessary to say any goodbyes at the house, except to Maalii's parents - everyone else came along.

'You will come back,' said Maalii, who was watching as I gazed poignantly back up the lane.

'Yes, you return any time, Phil,' Auy added firmly. 'No problem with my family. You take train from Bangkok, then walk from station.' She smiled sweetly. 'You know Krasang now.'

We strode across the track and I followed Lindsey up the broad steps to the ticket office. A plump, friendly-looking woman, sitting behind the desk, sat up and smiled bashfully as he approached the window. He gabbled to her in Thai for a few minutes, laughing occasionally and at times making strange gesticulations. The second I reached for my wallet, however, he raised his hand to stop me.

'Let me pay for this, Phil. I owe it to you.'

'No you don't.'

'I think I do. You travelled thousands of miles solely to inform me of my impending death sentence. Your intelligence work may have saved my neck.'

'Are you serious?' I asked with suspicion, remembering his initial reaction to my arrival.

'Am I ever anything else?'

He picked up the tiny brown ticket from the plywood counter and said a very deliberate thank-you to the clerk whom he had impressed considerably. I was almost convinced that, had he asked for her hand in marriage instead of just a rail ticket, she would have been equally obliging.

'Third class all right for you?' he said.

'Actually, no. I'd prefer-'

'Don't worry,' he interrupted. 'It *is* a first class one. I know you won't be denied your precious biscuits and air-conditioning.' He cackled for a second or two, mildly amused by his ability to make me panic with such scant effort.

The train appeared on time at a quarter to ten. For once, the children remained subdued as its lights gradually illuminated the platform. I crouched down, put my arm around Chek's bony shoulder and squeezed his hand affectionately. He tugged at the tail of Lindsey's shirt and squeaked a few words.

'What is he trying to tell me?' I asked him.

'He says he doesn't feel as upset as he did the last time you left. He's convinced you'll be back soon. Anyway, whether you will or not, don't tell him. It would be cruel to shatter the poor kid's hopes.'

'I understand.'

'After all,' he added, stroking the boy's head, 'he doesn't have all that much to believe in.'

'What *does* he believe in? God? Fate? Anything?'

'He believes in me ... simply because he knows I'm here.'

I hugged the children almost simultaneously and gave a kiss to both Maalii and her sixteen-year-old sister.

'Goodbye,' said Maalii, 'for now.'

We all stepped back from the platform's edge as the train pulled in. Lindsey stared briefly at the unyielding metal wheels as they ground to a whining halt on the rails.

'Be happy, Phil. Write when you can.'

'Likewise,' I replied, and we shook hands in a consciously casual manner.

I climbed into the first class carriage and rolled down the window once I had located a vacant seat. A minute later, the train began to move and a row of shabby, underfed children waved goodbye from the front of the ticket kiosk. The smallest of them was cradling a small, home-made cricket bat - the undisputed jewel in his crown of pitiful toys.

The last voice I heard was Lindsey's: 'Enjoy your biscuits and air-conditioning!'

As he stood there on the platform, just another insignificant, dark-skinned shape in the shadows, I could not help but wonder when I would see him again, if ever. At least I had one final day in Bangkok, which I intended to cram with whatever I could afford.

I waited for the conductor to complete his rounds before settling down for the night; although that was not until we had arrived at the next station, Buriram, where another vast crowd, armed with cases, bags and boxes, had assembled on the platform. It seemed inconceivable that there could possibly be sufficient space for them in the second and third class carriages but, incredibly, and admittedly, after several minutes' chaos, we set off again, leaving the dimly-lit platform virtually empty.

The conductor took one glance at my ticket and shook his head sternly. 'Three!' he grunted, holding up as many fingers in front of my face and pointing towards the third class carriages at the rear.

After a few seconds of confusion, it became evident what he was trying to explain: I had succumbed to yet another of Lindsey's annoying little pranks. I handed the conductor an extra hundred baht in order to upgrade my ticket and thus remain where I was. To my relief, the first class carriage had not been fully booked, as then I would have been obliged to move into the packed lower class area and would not have appreciated the joke.

I closed my eyes and relaxed, knowing that wherever Lindsey was, he would be laughing to himself, if not with Maalii and the children too. It quickly dawned on me why he had been so keen to purchase the ticket for me in the first place: he knew I would be unable to decipher the particulars on it, as they were printed in Thai. I could understand, also, why the booking clerk, who had effectively collaborated with him, had found it all so entertaining.

The journey dragged like no other. Outside, one dark open space followed another, and there was barely a stir inside, apart from when the woman serving refreshments crept up and down the aisle occasionally, attending to anyone who was awake and awakening those who were asleep.

We eventually rolled into the city just before sunrise. Hundreds of dawn commuters were already loitering around the concourse and an army of slovenly teenage lackeys carted bulky white trays of fresh fish and vegetables to makeshift stalls nearby. I made straight for a vacant tuk-tuk and paid the requested seventy baht to return to the Plaza, although I knew I could not stay at Soi Phasuk because Auy had the room key back in Krasang.

The Plaza was deserted. Each of the bars was boarded and padlocked from top to bottom. The walkway was strewn with leaves from the creeper plants along with what remained of the previous night's litter. Until late afternoon, I knew there would be nothing there for me.

I decided to venture down Ploenchit Road, away from the familiar Sukhumvit district, and head for *Wat Phra Kaeo*: the Grand Palace which housed the two-hundred-year-old Emerald Buddha Chapel amongst its colourful array of national treasures. This was, ironically, the very first place we had intended to see on our scheduled visit in September.

I trudged sluggishly along the roadside, as always, to prevent my shirt becoming soaked with sweat. Even so, I seemed to make faster progress than the traffic, which was wedged together in typical jigsaw fashion. So much so, that if a motorist had offered me a lift I could legitimately have declined the invitation by claiming to be in too much of a hurry. Moreover, the absence of air-conditioning in many of the vehicles, particularly the grimy buses, made the suffering passengers look like victims of mildly sadistic humour.

Some other sights stung the eyes like tear gas. Young children with missing limbs were sitting on sheets of sun-dried newspaper, begging pathetically for 'pennies' on the dusty Ploenchit overpasses. Some had legs taken off above the knees, others scarred and flaccid stumps where arms used to be; and worst of all, one or two completely limbless and thus incapable of making the prayer-like gesture. There seemed to be some ghastly Orwellian rule of thumb in operation: four limbs bad, three limbs good. And no limbs at all being even better.

It was the first time I had walked Bangkok's filthy roads on my own, which seemed to signal to all the pimps and con artists that easy money was staring them in the face. If a look of gullibility did exist, it appeared that I had it. I recalled the short shrift which Lindsey had given to the drug-pusher in Toronto, as well as the mysterious package-bearing girl at Kanchanaburi Bus Terminal, and even the two Christian schoolchildren diligently canvassing in Lumpini Park. An unsolicited approach, I thought, warranted only a concise, unequivocal rebuttal, however convincing a disguise the leeches happened to be wearing.

After the third or fourth interruption, however, I was unable, or possibly just unwilling, to suppress my impatience. As I waited at the busy Krung Kasem junction, near Kasatsuk Bridge, I was accosted by two hungry touts, each carrying laminated photographs of semi-nude girls which they attempted repeatedly to push into my hands. I turned my back and prepared to cross the road. The shorter of the two grabbed me by the elbow and pulled me towards him. I lifted my arm angrily and accidentally struck him, my knuckles cracking loudly against the bridge of his nose. Instinctively, I gestured to apologize but my attempt at appeasement proved futile. Two other men, with whom they had been sitting, jumped to their feet and rushed across to join them. The one I had struck glared mercilessly then pushed me into the road. By now the lights had changed. I turned and dashed to the other side, forcing a tuk-tuk to swerve into the adjacent lane. The driver shook his head and looked at me in mild disgust.

'Wat Phra Kaeo! Wat Phra Kaeo!' I bellowed breathlessly, and climbed into his vehicle without even asking permission.

He set off, as hastily as he had stopped, leaving all four men mouthing obscene threats, in English, from the roadside.

I reflected upon my good fortune as my breathing slowed to normal. In an episode lasting only twenty seconds, I had escaped violent retaliation and possible arrest or, alternatively, becoming the victim of a road traffic accident.

The enclosed grounds of Wat Phra Kaeo provided me with a welcome sanctuary. I wandered freely among a mass of happy western holidaymakers, in and out of temples where shaven-headed monks in orange robes, some no older than the children of Krasang, sat in dignified solitude, peacefully practising their Buddhist meditations in full view of the crowds. In a way, I felt relieved that Lindsey was elsewhere; he would undoubtedly have looked upon the younger ones with pity, and at their mentors with undisguised contempt.

I stayed there until midday. Once I had bought a strange assortment of cheap souvenirs, I left the palace and followed an open road, lined haphazardly with fruit stalls, to Wat Po, home to the Reclining Buddha. From there, I boarded a small ferryboat and crossed to the west bank of the muddy Chao Phraya River, where the pyramidal Wat Arun, Temple of the Dawn, towered proudly into the bluish smog.

It was four in the afternoon when I finally returned to the east bank, having ploughed through three entire rolls of camera film. I ruled out the option of making my way back on foot for fear of further encounters with those whom it seemed sensible to avoid. Besides, I had been walking for too long. I left the jetty and embarked upon one last ride in a tuk-tuk. I paid double the normal fare in order to be shuttled back to the Plaza via an indirect, meandering route, and thus inhale one huge, terminal breath of Siamese heaven. In this city - of angels and other equally implausible contrivances - it was easy to travel from dawn until sunset but impossible to arrive. Of that, I was now convinced.

The Plaza was full of noise, bright lights and happy faces. The girls swanned from one bar to another, gyrating provocatively in an attempt to entice any strangers who cared to stray from the main road, as I myself had once done. Naturally, white men with wallets came, saw and conquered throughout the course of the evening. Some were content to drink away the hours in silence, whereas others disappeared back to four-star privacy with a willing female on each arm. This was normality, I kept having to remind myself - a simple equilibrium of supply and demand, just like any other. It did, however, convince me that prostitution was a way of life which I had no right to condemn. I understood, as did the girls themselves, that a more dignified, and less traumatic, alternative lay beyond their grasp.

Joel showed up at nine thirty, looking dishevelled and short of breath. 'So, how's Lindsey?' he puffed. 'Still alive?'

I laughed. 'He was when I last spoke to him. By the way, I owe you a beer.'

'Well, I ain't arguin'.'

Despite the fact that we were sitting next to the exploding hi-fi speakers, we managed to make ourselves heard.

'I wasn't sure you'd be here,' he said. 'What time do you have to leave for the airport?'

'In about half an hour.'

'So soon?' He picked up my rucksack which was lying by his feet. 'Is this *all* your luggage?'

'That's it.'

'In that case, I'll give you a lift.'

'Thanks. I didn't know you had a car.'

'I don't. I have a motorcycle. On these roads, Phil, cars are for people who don't mind spending every waking minute stuck inside the goddam things. I'm not kidding, this place makes Manhattan look like Montana, for Christ's sake.'

I found it impossible to relax, knowing how little time I had left. I had even begun to feel slightly nauseous. Another fifty-truck-long freight train passed behind the bars, crushing the rails into the creaking old sleepers;

and inevitably, during the minute's din, I thought of Erin once more, and the fact that only a week ago she had been still alive.

The bar girls wished me luck when we finally stood up to go. Some accompanied us to the main road where Joel had parked his bike. I handed one of them my remaining Thai money, coins included, which amounted to just short of fifteen hundred baht, or forty pounds sterling.

'Give this to Lindsey,' I instructed her. 'He might need it.'

'Yes, me understand. Me give it to him.'

'Don't give her your escape money!' Joel blurted out suddenly.

'Escape money? What's that?'

'You know, airport tax.'

'Oh, that's in my passport wallet.'

'Just as well it is, otherwise you would have to stay here forever!'

I smiled, in a miserable sort of way, and waved goodbye to the girls who were prancing about under the expressway flyover in time to the music which they could barely hear for the traffic din. It was exactly how I wanted to remember them: joyful and oblivious.

Joel wove his way across Sukhumvit and opened the 750cc throttle. I tried not to dwell upon the fact that neither of us was wearing a crash helmet, particularly when we were speeding between lanes and leaning into bends at forty-five degrees. Consequently, we arrived at Don Muang in plenty of time. Having passed through several other airports since my departure, I had forgotten how closely the place resembled a cattle market. Even as late in the evening as this, hundreds of travellers packed the check-in area, some impeccably calm, others barking furiously at the desk staff who were, it appeared, exclusively to blame for the passengers' lives being complete misery.

'See you next year,' said Joel, holding out his hand.

I shook it firmly. 'I hope so.'

'Either here or in Manhattan. I don't mind which.'

I proceeded to the gate and instantly switched my thoughts to what lay ahead: an unauthorized bank overdraft, a cold cottage, and a loyal employer whom I had selfishly and shamelessly deceived.

XXVI

'Now the peak of summer's past,
the sky is overcast
And the love we swore would last
for an age seems deceit.'

Cecil Day Lewis (1904-72)
Hornpipe

One of the most deflating characteristics of air travel, so I had been assured, was one's emergence, alone and exhausted, into a packed arrivals hall only to discover that not a single face in the entire expectant crowd was familiar. Fortunately, leaning against the wall at the back of the lounge at Manchester Airport was someone I recognized straight away.

'Thanks for taking the trouble,' I said with relief.

Tim smiled briefly. 'My pleasure. I've taken the day off work and the old boy let me borrow the van.'

'How have things been at home?'

'I'll explain everything once we're out of here.'

His words sounded ominous. We climbed the stairs to the short-stay car park, neither of us uttering a sound. I could sense that something was troubling him; he had not dragged himself out of bed early and disrupted his week's routine at the hospital primarily to save me the cost of a rail ticket.

'*Snow?*' I protested, looking out on to the road.

'Afraid so.'

'Since when?'

'Yesterday, although it's not too deep in Liverpool.'

'It's still November, for Christ's sake.'

'Not for much longer.'

I slung my rucksack into the front of the van and jumped inside, shivering uncontrollably. He started the engine and sighed loudly, his breath as visible as cigarette smoke.

'Where shall I begin?' he muttered.

I said nothing as he reversed out of the sheltered parking bay and turned on the windscreen wipers.

'Nova called again yesterday evening.'

'How is she?'

'Anxious.'

'How bad?'

'Bad. Jacques contacted his company's main office in Los Angeles on Monday. Adam hasn't been seen there since the previous weekend. Apparently, he told one of his secretaries, presumably in confidence, that after the death of his mother, and now his sister, he had only one thing left to lose.'

'I don't suppose she had any idea what he meant.'

'Have you seen him?'

'Adam? No. And so nobody knows his whereabouts.'

He shook his head pensively. 'Jacques phoned every one of his business associates across the whole of North America, virtually every state capital, for Nova's sake, but it was a waste of time.'

'Did you tell Nova that I'd returned to Bangkok?'

'I did. She was grateful that you'd gone, as well as surprised.' He looked at me out of the corner of his eye. 'I assume that *he* is keeping well.'

'He seems happy.'

'How does he feel about all this?'

'He doesn't *feel* anything.'

'I thought not.'

'And why should he?' I said pugnaciously. 'Adam can't trouble him.'

'How do you know?' he snapped. 'You seem to share Lindsey's own view that somehow he's untouchable.'

'He is.'

'We shall see,' he replied, looking appalled by what I had admitted.

Thick flakes of snow began swirling in the headlight beams like particles in a vortex as we crawled along the inside lane of the motorway. Visibility was gradually worsening. I could not recall the last time snow had fallen so early in the season.

'Thanks for misleading your dad, by the way,' I said, breaking the silence. 'He doesn't suspect, does he?'

'Suspect? He knows.'

'What?'

'He knows where you've been - and why.'

I twisted myself round in the seat to face him and began to hyperventilate a little. 'How did he react? How did he find out? How-'

'He overheard me talking to Nova on the phone, and I let it slip.'

'And dropped me right in it! What a blockhead!'

'I know, I know. I thought he was in the garage. Careless of me, I admit.'

'So what did he-'

'There's no need to panic.'

'Not for you, maybe.'

'Well, let me put it like this: he isn't half as angry as he was.'

'And how angry was that?'

'He said he was going to have your nuts for doorstops!'

'It's not funny.'

'Leave off. If you think he would never have found you out, just look at the colour of your face in the mirror. I told you to stay in the shade. You look like Al Jolson.'

The apparent security of my job provided no compensation for my sudden feelings of guilt. The prospect of looking his father in the eyes rendered me incapable of focusing on anything else. I appreciated the fact that trust was like a plant cutting: it would always wither far more easily than it took root initially. My apology could never truly be enough.

We arrived at the cottage shortly after nine o'clock. A collection of utility bills, along with what looked like a 'thumbscrew' letter from the bank, lay scattered on the doormat, and the front room was so cold I considered opening the windows to let in some heat. Worst of all, I noticed that, although I had switched off the electricity prior to my departure, I had forgotten to open the fridge door. Consequently, the two of us spent a miserable half-hour scratching at tenacious, mouldy residue which had accumulated all over the panels inside. I could hear Lindsey's mocking laughter echoing throughout the kitchen, and its annoying presence outlived that of the mould itself.

The problems at work were thankfully short-lived. Mr. McKee's displeasure resulted not from what I had done, but from my having lied when the truth would have sufficed. His leniency was not something I deserved.

The icy conditions persisted into the first week of December. Each bleak, heartless day consisted of nine or ten hours at the warehouse followed by a quiet evening alone at home reading books which Lindsey had borrowed, on a permanent basis, from the library. As each day passed, I was spending an increasing amount of time thinking about him, and whatever he might have been doing on the other side of the world. The more heavily the snow fell, the happier I became. The disruption of normality excited me, even if it resulted in a mere ten-minute delay returning home on the train. I appreciated nature's blind interruptions to my monotonous schedule more than ever.

Delivery days became understandably hectic as the mad season approached. Sales were increasing steadily, which pleased Mr. McKee to the extent that my misdemeanour became irrelevant, and the traffic on the city roads began to resemble Bangkok without the tuk-tuks.

On the penultimate Saturday before the Christmas holiday week, I had no choice but to leave for work as early as six thirty in the morning in order to load the van with an additional assortment of boxes, mostly containing idiot-proof self-assembly units which were not really idiot-proof because some idiots were ingenious.

The sound of the telephone startled me at twenty to eight, just as I had completed the extra jobs. I darted across the showroom and into the office without stopping to switch on the lights. I presumed that it would be Tim, calling to say he would be late, as he often was.

'McKee's Furniture Warehouse. Good morning.'

'Phil, I'm going to be late.'

'I guessed that. Don't worry, everything is loaded. What time will you be here?'

'Give me half an hour. By the way, a postcard has just landed on the mat. I'll bring it with me.'

He hung up before I could ask who had sent it, but I was confident that it would be from Lindsey, back in Bangkok for more Plaza parties.

A full hour later, Tim sauntered in, still drowsy and stuffing his fat face with a bread roll, his cheeks bulging symmetrically with each bite.

'Have you brought the postcard?'

He nodded and pulled it from his jacket pocket. 'Make of it what you will,' he spluttered. 'I'm damned if I can understand it.'

He passed it to me somewhat dismissively and filled the kettle with water. I switched on the main lights. On the front of the card was a flattering picture of the River Kwai Bridge, and just visible in the bottom corner was a floating restaurant where I had once eaten breakfast.

The other side read:

> *Somewhere in Thailand.*
> *8th December.*
>
> *The end-game commences!*
> *Knight's pawn has just blossomed into a queen,*
> *And a magnificent one at that.*
> *Checkmate in four moves.*
> *It has to be so.*
>
> *Elsie and Maalii.*

'Elsie?' I said, looking up at him.

'LC - his initials.'

'Oh. What is he telling us - or not telling us?'

'As I said, I haven't the first clue. Why compile a cryptic message if the recipient is unlikely to solve it? Pointless.'

'If he believed that,' I argued blindly, 'he wouldn't have wasted his time writing and sending it.'

'So you think he expects us to understand him? How?'

'I can't play chess,' I said. Once again, I could hear Lindsey cackling inside my head. 'But you can.'

He handed me a mug of steaming coffee and reread the message. 'Well, *Knight* is his middle name. I believe Nova has it, too.'

'He has never broadcast it.'

'Would you?'

He folded the card in half, unimpressed by the whole thing, and stuffed it back into his pocket. 'If this is the latest chapter of this cat-and-mouse posturing with Adam then I don't want to know. There are more important things to worry about.'

Despite the fact that the card's meaning eluded me, I was convinced that Lindsey had begun to take the threats seriously. I could, however, see that even in doing so, his confidence in his safety remained intact - as, of course, did my own.

All day long, as we criss-crossed the city listening to the radio commentary of the FA Cup ties, I tapped Tim's considerable knowledge of the game of chess: the defining characteristics of each piece and examples of tactics and strategy, not that I could comprehend even the most fundamental aspects of the game. Predictably, my persistent questioning and inability to grasp the basics impressed him about as much as the card itself.

'Change the bloody channel, will you?'

'Sorry.'

'Listen, if clever-arse Corker has to spend the rest of his life checking behind doors, then that's for him. It's no more my concern than it is yours. But, while ever his belongings remain at our house, he ought at least to have the courtesy to let us know what his plans are.'

'Perhaps he *has* let us know,' I teased, referring to the card again. 'He might simply have overestimated your capacity to reason, that's all.'

'Piss off.'

There followed a comfortable silence which lasted about two minutes.

'Did you say the rook was shaped like a horse's head?'

'Phil!'

I continued to annoy him, in a playful way, until we arrived back at base at six in the evening. In truth, though, I knew precisely where his tolerance threshold lay, and he, in turn, knew that I would never intentionally cross it.

I spent that night at the McKees' house, sleeping, or at least trying to do so, in the tiny boxroom which Lindsey had occupied, free of charge, for most of the previous eighteen months. The temperature outside had fallen below zero for the fifth consecutive night and, typically, Tim's mother anticipated and appreciated my reluctance to return home in the cold.

Lying undisturbed on the dressing table were a few of Lindsey's possessions: a silver-cased pocket watch which was a treasured memory of his late grandfather, three chewed-up paperbacks - a biography of the great Sir Donald Bradman and a couple of old Steinbeck novels - and a faded photograph of a youthful Nova, smiling that dreamy smile of hers, her eyes shaded by a wide-brimmed, straw hat. I looked at the picture. I wanted desperately to ease her crippling anxiety but, in reality, only one person stood to achieve that, and, as far as I was aware, she had not heard from him since September.

The Sunday morning sky was the purest shade of blue; the look of midsummer was betrayed only by the nakedness of the plane and poplar trees and gritted patches of snow which decorated the pavements and gutters.

I struggled downstairs for breakfast, half-dressed, at twenty past ten. Tim was sitting on the hall carpet with his back against the front door and the phone sandwiched awkwardly between his left ear and shoulder. He glanced up at me, eyebrows raised, and pointed repeatedly at the earpiece.

'Is it Nova again?' I whispered. 'Let me speak to her. Let me speak to her.'

Without bothering to get up, he handed me the receiver and yawned loudly.

'Hello ...'

'Well, old fruit, was my bed comfortable enough for you?' said an unmistakable voice at the other end.

Tim stood up and disappeared down the hallway and into the kitchen, closing the door behind him. I was now alone with the voice.

'Where are you?'

'You tell me.'

'Back in Bangkok?'

'Not even close.'

'Where?'

'Heathrow.'

'You're in *London*?'

'Full marks.'

'When did you arrive?'

'An hour ago.'

'What about-'

'Hold your fire. I don't have any more change. I'll explain what has happened when I arrive this afternoon.'

'At what time?'

'Between two and three o'clock.'

'Tell me what has happened! Lindsey!'

The line went dead. I reluctantly replaced the handset and opened the door to the kitchen where Tim was sitting at the table with his mother.

'Good morning, Phil,' she said sweetly.

'Good morning, Maura.'

'What did he say to you?' asked Tim, in a tone designed to mask his curiosity.

'Very little. He'll be here between two and three.'

My elation was tempered with apprehension. Lindsey had left Thailand long before the expiry date on his visa. I could think of just one possible reason for his premature departure.

From one o'clock onwards I sat opposite Tim at the dining table, sifting purposelessly through the encyclopaedic Sunday newspapers, and stopping to peer under the net curtains whenever a bus passed along the avenue. At twenty-minute intervals I waited until each one had moved off, to see whether a tanned figure armed with a worn-out travel bag had appeared at the roadside.

By four thirty, Tim was becoming restless. 'London to Liverpool takes three hours. What is he playing at?' He folded his arms impatiently. 'I do hope the phone call wasn't another of his stupid pranks.'

'I doubt it.'

'Oh really? How can you be sure that he wasn't phoning from abroad?'

'Dial one-four-seven-one.'

'I already have.'

'And?'

'Nothing.'

I thought for a moment. 'He was telling the truth,' I insisted.

'How come?'

'Because he must have realized that, the second he hung up, your mum would set about preparing an extra dinner. He would never inconvenience her - us, perhaps, but not your mum. Never.'

Before I had time to doubt myself, a black cab appeared and pulled up at the end of the driveway, spraying snow onto the pavement with its dirt-splattered wheels.

'Here he is ... and about time too,' he muttered, gathering together all the newspapers. 'Get the door, will you, Phil?'

I jumped up and leapt hastily towards the porch without moving the chair, causing it to topple backwards into the curtains. I opened the front door and watched as a dark figure, wearing the familiar brown leather jacket, climbed majestically out of the nearside of the cab. For a moment, I was unable to do anything but stare in utter disbelief, but understood at once why he had returned prematurely. The figure turned round and smiled at me, her long black hair falling freely across her face.

'His extended visa has evidently served its purpose,' I said to Tim, who was now standing behind me.

An equally dark shape eventually emerged from the other side and slung a couple of bags over his shoulder as the taxi moved off.

'Sorry we're late, gentlemen!' he called.

'What happened?'

'We took a detour. I needed to drop in on my cousin again.'

I pulled Maalii towards me and held her as closely as I could, her slender frame lost under several layers of Lindsey's clothing. Naturally, freezing temperatures and snowdrifts were as alien to her as Thailand's stifling humidity had been to us.

Tim's parents joined us in the sitting room which was filled instantly with affection and wild laughter. The sight of Lindsey and Maalii perched side by side on the sofa possessed a surreal quality. They appeared to have pooled their physical characteristics in order to converge upon the same hybrid form: he with dark brown skin and long hair, and she with a fixed expression of unshakeable composure. To love each other was to look like each other.

'You have received the postcard, have you not?'

'Yesterday,' I replied.

'Just in time.'

'Although neither of us managed to decipher your message.'

'I realized that as soon as I saw your faces outside. I thought *you* would have liked it, Tim - having all the analytical faculties of a psychologist.'

'Go on, then, explain it to us.'

'I was telling you that the British Embassy in Bangkok had approved Maalii's visa application and that she was coming home with me.'

Tim remained puzzled. 'How?'

'Think about it. In chess, every pawn begins the game by moving slowly and predictably. If, however, it succeeds in negotiating a tortuous pathway in accordance with a peculiar set of conditions, it becomes a queen, and is then endowed with freedom of movement.'

'How very imaginative you are. But don't forget, a fool can ask more questions than a wise man can answer. What about the rest of it?'

'Well, the two of you, not to mention my dear old guardian angel of a sister, have made it abundantly clear that I ought to be concerned for my own well-being.'

'Don't you think that's justifiable?'

He shook his head in his usual complacent manner. 'Not really, but I had to put Nova's mind at rest.'

'And what were the so-called *moves*?'

'Krasang to Bangkok, Bangkok to London, and London to Liverpool.'

'That's only three,' I said.

'Pardon me?'

'I said, that's only three. What's the fourth?'

'The fourth?' He sat back and began to caress Maalii's forearm. 'Back to London.'

'You're returning to London? When? And why?'

'After Christmas.' He looked at me with a sincere, even apologetic, expression. 'My cousin has agreed to let us both stay at his place for the foreseeable future.'

'Rent-free?'

'Of course.'

'So you'll be within walking distance of Lord's Cricket Ground. Convenient.'

'Isn't it just? Secondly, our homicidal friend from Los Angeles won't be able to find me there. And finally, London is more cosmopolitan than anywhere else in Britain. As well as losing ourselves in the crowd, we might even be able to find a Thai midwife.'

'Why?'

'Three guesses.'

Maalii seemed to realize what he had announced to us the second I looked at her, as if she had been able to follow the entire conversation.

Tim laughed a little and shook his head. 'Any more surprises, Elsie?'

For the rest of the afternoon and throughout dinner, we listened enthusiastically to Lindsey's ambitious plans - for Maalii, himself and their unborn child. I was disappointed that it was not his intention to stay in Liverpool, but at least London was far more accessible than either Bangkok or Krasang.

It eventually occurred to me that all he had said and done since jumping unexpectedly off the train at Hammersmith station had been not only logical and far-sighted, but also totally honourable. I even managed to forgive him for the rail ticket episode in Krasang.

'How was Chek when you left?' I asked.

'Philosophical, although his little eyes filled up when the train pulled in.' A rare perplexed look washed over him. 'I'd never seen him cry before. I assumed that the silly grin was a permanent fixture.'

It seemed to have made him appreciate that, despite Chek's quirky ways, he was still just a small boy, tortured by the same fears and weaknesses as any other.

'Did you say when you would be returning?'

'It wasn't necessary. I told him I would be watching over him from up in the sky, guiding him through each day and helping him to pick himself up every time he fell to the ground.' He restrained a sly grin. 'I only pray no one fills his head with religious nonsense while I'm away.'

Tim looked up. 'I don't imagine he'll allow anyone to contradict the things you've told him, however audacious. Give me the child for the first few years, and I'll give you the man. That's how religions get started.'

Not surprisingly, Chek's engraved pebble was still hanging conspicuously around Lindsey's neck, but was now threaded on to a fine gold chain instead of its original length of dirty string. It was definitely there to stay.

'Incidentally, has the pub at the end of the avenue been demolished?' said Lindsey, quite suddenly.

'What? No, of course it hasn't.'

He winked at me. 'That's tonight pencilled in, if no one objects.'

Tim followed me upstairs when I went to collect my overnight belongings from the boxroom.

'What's the matter?'

'Doesn't anything strike you as odd?' he inquired, gently closing the door behind him.

'About Lindsey?'

'About either of them.'

I paused to think. 'Not really.'

'Open your eyes, Phil!' he hissed. 'Two air tickets from Bangkok to London would have cost hundreds, and then there were the rail fares on top of that!'

'What are you saying?'

He shook his head slowly. 'Don't you ever wonder where all his money comes from?'

'What business is that of mine?'

He was beginning to analyse me. 'Can you not bring yourself to believe that he might well have stolen it or, even more likely, conned a few gullible tourists?'

'No I can't.'

'You mean you *won't*. And how do you suppose he wangled Maalii's visa? They aren't dished out willy-nilly. Most applications for girls like her are rejected, in case they end up walking the streets over here instead of over there.' He breathed deeply. 'Anyhow, whatever tricks he pulled, I fear he may finally have met his nemesis.'

'Who?'

'Maalii,' he whispered.

I pointed to the seat of his pants. 'You're talking from here.'

'Am I, Phil? Am I?' His voice softened when we heard footsteps on the stairs. 'Can you be certain she's pregnant? Or that she loves him at all?'

'For God's sake, why else would she be here?'

'For a better life? To transform herself from a mere pawn into a queen? Could it not be the case that she is actually more shrewd and more devious in her little games than even he is?'

'You're being ridiculous. If anyone attempted to manipulate Lindsey he would sense it instantly ... and the subsequent retribution doesn't bear thinking about.'

He grabbed my shoulders to make me take notice. I could not believe the intensity of his feelings.

'You're becoming more obtuse by the day! Have you forgotten what Erin said at that Italian restaurant, about *oriental sex-kittens* routinely fleecing western travellers?'

'Those girls are victims, not bloodsucking opportunists. Erin knew *nothing*.'

'You're blind! She might one day be proved right in everything she said ... not that she will ever know, of course.'

'You criticize Lindsey for being cynical, and you're just as bad.'

'Cynicism is just an unpleasant way of expressing the truth - remember? He said it himself.'

He looked at me in disappointment before going back downstairs. I straightened the room and kissed Nova's picture before joining him and the McKees in the sitting room.

At eight o'clock we wrapped up and trudged through the ankle-deep snow to a public bar which was widely regarded as being one of Liverpool's finest. It was not entirely coincidental that this was one of a dwindling number where the walls did not tremble to the beat of Patpong-style music. The sound of Scouse voices, joking, teasing and digesting the previous day's football results provided the place with the authentic essence of an unspoiled community. Dear old Mr. Leonard, the ever-agreeable landlord, greeted Maalii with his unique blend of warmth and courtesy, and Lindsey with a spontaneous witticism about the unchecked length of his hair.

'It's good to see you again,' he said, handing over a generous measure of single malt to a favourite member of his flock.

Lindsey reciprocated his affection: 'Likewise, Tom. Cheers.'

The four of us huddled round a small table in a quiet corner and reflected upon the previous four months. For the first time ever, September had marked the beginning of a memorable chapter in an otherwise bland life rather than its unwelcome conclusion. Regrettably, however, it felt as vague and remote as the Septembers of my early childhood. My prediction that the future would be profoundly affected by the holiday had proved accurate, if only as far as Lindsey had been concerned. As for Tim's knee-jerk doubts about Maalii's integrity, I thought they were just plain ludicrous. He was seeing only what he wanted to see.

'Something I almost forgot to ask you,' I said. 'Did you get the money I gave to the girls at the Plaza?'

Lindsey looked bewildered for a moment, then smacked his lips and shook his head. 'Did you honestly believe they would hand over money they knew I wasn't expecting?'

'I never even considered that.'

'Thanks all the same,' he added, 'but don't be disgusted or angry with yourself. Think of it as a selfless act on your part rather than a naive one.'

'Very well.'

'Incidentally, who took the money?'

'The very small one with the cropped hair.'

'Her name is *Wanpen*. Don't resent her either.' He then sighed sympathetically. 'At least the poor girl won't have needed to open her legs for a few days.'

Tim interrupted without looking at anyone. 'He's right, Phil. You can't blame her for cheating you. She's nothing more than a slave to her own ruthless nature.'

Maalii looked supremely content, albeit eyeing her strange surroundings with private curiosity. She gazed with wonder through the window at the falling snowflakes as if she were an art critic admiring and analysing an unusually stunning portrait. Lindsey was looking at her in a similar way.

'Whose round is it?' I asked.

The inevitable response followed. I returned to the bar where some middle-aged men were standing with their wives, as smartly dressed as they knew how, and laughing amongst themselves. They, too, were about to settle in as the evening chill tightened its hold.

As I waited, clutching a ten-pound note which I had had to borrow discreetly from Mr. McKee, I leaned lazily against the bar and scanned the far corner of the carpetless tap room, where three contrasting individuals, whose friendship I valued more than anything, were conversing leisurely together.

On a small stool with his back to me sat Timothy McKee: a brother in all but name for almost twenty years.

Seated directly behind him was the now serene Maalii Pasi: a young woman who would dominate the dreams of most red-blooded males, but who was about to fulfil those of just one.

And, at her side, the infallible Mr. Lindsey Knight Corker: a man whom I could picture crossing the mile-wide Mersey on foot. Inside my head, however, I could hear my mother's voice, now as faint as a dying whisper, wrongly insisting that I had become too deluded to visualize the alternative.

THE END

AUTHOR'S NOTES

All the characters in this novel are fictional and bear no relation whatsoever to any persons living or dead. The locations, however, are real and have been described as accurately and as honestly as possible.

Title Choice

The book's title was taken from *Galileo*, by the exiled German poet Bertolt Brecht (1898-1956), whose other works include *The Threepenny Opera* (1928), in collaboration with Kurt Weil, *Mother Courage* (1941), and *The Caucasian Chalk Circle* (1949). The relevant dialogue, from Chapter 13, begins with one character, Andrea, lamenting:
>'Unhappy the land that has no heroes.'

To which Galileo replies:
>·'No, unhappy the land that needs heroes.'

Its use is, above all, a reference to the book's principal theme of misguided reverence - Philip's ever-growing obsession with Lindsey (despite the words of his own mother which Lindsey himself endorses), Chek and his peers as Lindsey's credulous 'disciples' and, most contentiously, Erin's unhealthy, and eventually lethal, dependence upon a brittle Christian faith.

Masonic Metaphor

The story's first lines - 'Worship and idolatry ... temple of insanity' are a loose paraphrase of the Freemasons' 'Second Degree' ritual, which states that:
>'B--- and J----- were the twin pillars which stood at the porchway or entrance to King Solomon's temple.'

I have withheld the two names in order to avoid the risk of incurring the displeasure of their organization. That said, much of the information regarding their secret workings is freely available from major libraries, particularly in a couple of infamous journalistic exposés compiled by the late Stephen Knight.

A Street in Bangkok

Soi Phasuk no longer exists in its entirety. Pronounced Saw'-ee Pah-sook' - 'Soi' meaning 'lane' - it was originally the very first of over a hundred such lanes emanating at right angles from Sukhumvit Road in the central district of Bangkok. Its decrepit, wooden dwelling-houses were demolished in 1994, and the road itself has since been widened and restructured in an attempt to ease the ever-worsening traffic congestion on the Don Muang Expressway. Nevertheless, I doubt that the changes will bring any subsequent benefit in the long term.

Buckskin Joe's Village, to which I referred simply as 'the Plaza', was also rumoured to have been earmarked for demolition when I last visited the city. It seems unlikely, therefore, that the area will retain much of its original character.

Memoirs of Death

The fictional book title *Railway of Death* (see Chapter XVIII) is based upon *Death Railway* by Cornelius B. Evers, who was a Lieutenant in the Royal Dutch Army before becoming firstly a PoW, and following that a War Crimes Investigation Officer. To anyone who may be interested in the history of World War Two beyond the speculative musings of armchair historians, I would recommend it wholeheartedly. The 'extract' quoted in Chapter VI is of my own hand, although I would like to think that its sentiment would be viewed as accurate by both the veteran Lieutenant himself and all the other allied servicemen who remember the dark days of 1942-3.

The book title *Contemporary Asian History* (see Chapter VIII) is also fictional, and bears no relation to any other publication bearing that particular title.

Bridge on the River Kwai?

The title of Pierre Boulle's classic 1952 novel *Bridge on the River Kwai* is, in fact, a misnomer. The 'Death Railway' does not cross the River Kwai at all, and never has. The bridge was actually built across the Mae Khlong River, of which the 'River Kwai' is but a small tributary running parallel to, but at no point passing beneath, the track. In order to resolve this nomenclatural problem, the Mae Khlong was renamed *Kwae Yai*, which translates as 'large tributary', so that the 'River Kwai' could legitimately retain its world-famous name.

Patpong, Past and Present
Bangkok's 'notoriously X-rated' Patpong strip, situated between Silom and Surawong Roads, is not what it used to be. To any of you - men, heterosexual - who, having read this book, are now hastily planning a holiday with a difference, you would be well-advised to readjust your sights. Travel journalist Steve van Beek, who went to work in Bangkok on a fourteen-day assignment in 1969 and is still there to this day, explains:

> '(It) used to be a hell-raiser's haunt with bargirls and booze and rough and tumble males from around the region. The street now boasts a Christian book store, three restaurants, a discotheque and a pharmacy.'

Bangkok by Steve van Beek was published by APA Publications (Hong Kong) Ltd. in 1991, and became my traveller's 'bible' from 1992-4.

Holy Duplicity
Overpopulation is one of the most worrying (and overlooked) problems facing our world. Many cities - disturbing examples are Sao Paolo, Mexico City and Calcutta - are experiencing a prodigious escalation in population density which shows no sign of waning. Indeed, the population of some cities is set to double within twenty years. Plainly, as the earth's resources are finite, the Malthusian ceiling will eventually be reached and, consequently, something will have to yield, probably in the form of mass starvation, famine and war. (One has only to recall what has repeatedly happened in Africa in recent years to see that this is true. Do your eyes not fill with tears whenever you see Michael Buerk's 1984 'Band Aid' report from Ethiopia? Mine do, even now.)

Fortunately, there are three possible remedies for this dangerously unsustainable rate of population growth:-
1. The immoral option: rapidly increase the death rate to compensate, and thus establish a manageable equilibrium;
2. The fantastic option: locate and then inhabit another planet that is sufficiently compatible with our own biological specifications ... and then another ... and another etc., at an ever faster rate;
3. The practicable option: reduce our overall rate of reproduction by the widespread use of 'artificial' methods of birth control.

An easy choice, I am sure you will agree. But consider this: suppose the dictatorial rulers of just one group of people successfully instil into their flock the notion that the use of such methods of contraception somehow constitutes a breach of moral law, then not only would that be tantamount to gross irresponsibility, but it also follows that, other things being equal, there would be a net increase in that group's own numerical proportion in subsequent generations, at the expense of all the other groups. More of them, fewer of everyone else. Such a policy could lead to world domination. How unintentionally convenient.

It does seem somewhat paradoxical then, that, after having spent most of the last hundred and forty years denying the authenticity of orthodox evolutionary theory, the organization to which I am alluding relies upon a variation of those same Darwinian parameters to further its own cause! Duplicity could never be as pure as this.

The Trouble with Religion
Even before the book's final draft had been written, in September 1998, several critics took offence at some of the irreligious themes running throughout the story. I am pleased to report that, deserved or not, a good deal of it was reasonable and well-researched. The rest was a sour mixture of the muddled, the meaningless, the hateful, the patronizing and the utterly incomprehensible. (One critic managed to include the whole gamut.)

The concepts of freedom of speech, expression, movement and assembly are rightly cherished throughout the civilized world. Our rights to each of them have been defended with bravery, often involving massive human sacrifice and environmental devastation, on countless occasions in recent history. As we enter the new millennium - 1st January, 2001- they will doubtless continue to be so. The more fundamental notion of freedom of *thought*, however, is, in my view, nowhere near as self-evident as many social scientists would have us believe. This assertion may sound absurd, especially when applied to countries in which personal liberty supposedly flourishes, but I am convinced that it remains undeniably true.

Allow me to explain. The genetical (neo-Darwinian) theory of evolution by means of natural selection - meticulously expounded in 1930 by the pioneering mathematician Sir Ronald A. Fisher - constitutes the backbone of biological philosophy and probably always will. In short, all members of all species on earth are products of their own particular genes, having evolved against the odds over billions of years.

In light of this, it is now generally accepted among scientists that animal behaviour is, in a statistical sense, genetically biased. A bee's readiness to sting, for example, is determined not by virtue of its acquired intelligence, but merely as a result of its genetic programming. Genes provide a modifiable bias for human behaviour, too. The simple truth is: the DNA in our genes strives to maximize only the differential probability of its own propagation, hence the term 'selfish gene', first coined by Richard Dawkins, Professor for the Public Understanding of Science at Oxford University, in 1976.

Thus freedom of thought is, in effect, compromised before we are even born. The Freudian concept of the *tabula rasa* - literally, 'scraped tablet', meaning that none of our behavioural traits is inherited - is, frankly, pure nonsense. Edward O. Wilson, Pellegrino Professor and Curator in Entomology at Harvard University, exposed this fallacy very forcefully in his influential 1975 publication, *Sociobiology: The New Synthesis*.

Our own species, *Homo sapiens*, has evolved the ability to rebel against its own genetically-based tendencies. When we use contraception, for example, we are thwarting our DNA and thus denying it the opportunity to transfer its specific digital code into the next generation.

Human beliefs, too, possess an hereditary component. For example, when young people vote in elections for the first time, they often show allegiance to the same political party as their parents for no more profound a reason. They are not obliged to follow their parents' lead, but evidence shows they often just do.

There are other, far more disturbing ways, however, in which freedom of thought is violated by these *pseudo-genetic* factors - or perhaps I should call them 'cultural parasites'.

For example, in Somalia, young girls are ritually circumcized, frequently without anaesthetic. There cannot possibly be any moral justification for this, but it happens nonetheless. Why? Because the girls' mothers were subjected to the same barbaric treatment, and their grandmothers before them, and so on. Now, anyone possessing even the tiniest amount of compassion would condemn the practice as either backward or just plain evil, and yet it persists to this day, purely as a result of blind adherence to tradition. Let us be unequivocal: mutilation is mutilation, regardless of its *raison d'être*.

The limitation to our freedom of thought is, to some extent, therefore, inevitable. I can accept that. It must be stressed, however, that just as genes can be overcome, so can these cultural parasites, but the first step is to recognize them for what they are.

The least contentious premise for the mystery of the origin of life must be: simplicity precedes complexity. It is a view that is widely proclaimed in a variety of different ways by the intellectual *cognoscenti*. Daniel C. Dennett, Distinguished Professor of Arts and Sciences and Director at the Center for Cognitive Studies at Tufts University, Massachusetts, is one of its most eloquent exponents. I shall try to outline the general theme as concisely as I can, and as well as my limited knowledge permits.

For example, individual stones precede buildings; the existence of atoms must have preceded the formation of complex molecular structures such as DNA; musical notes precede chords which in turn precede compositions; and the twenty-six letters of the alphabet precede the organized text of a novel or poem. Some of these conversions, although non-random, take place without conscious thought or planning - our evolution being the most striking example.

An omnipotent (all-powerful), omnipresent (all-seeing), omniscient (all-knowing) supreme being would represent another example of complexity - mind-boggling complexity! - but where is the necessary preceding simplicity in this case? There is none. The idea contravenes the logic, does it not? The argument that living creatures as complex as ourselves were designed and created by an already-complex artificer is transparently circular and therefore solves absolutely nothing.

To put it another way: 'Who made God?'

This childishly simple question seems to represent 'checkmate' for creationists. (I have a penchant for chess analogies!) Explaining the origins of the very simplest - that is, *prokaryotic* - life forms is difficult enough, but the idea of intelligence, and subsequent engineering skills, having been present since the beginning of time, really would take some explaining. 'God was always there' is, as far as I am concerned, a feeble cop-out and an insult to truly honest intellectuals such as Graham Cairns-Smith, whose book *Seven Clues to the Origin of Life* (1985) is, to my mind, infinitely more credible.

Still, in spite of such a fundamental flaw in the god-derived view of life, not to mention a woeful lack of evidence, the notion of the existence of such an illogical entity remains one of the most widely accepted fallacies ever peddled. The reason for this seems obvious: 'God', like various other irrational, pre-Enlightenment concepts, has been successfully transmitted, pseudo-genetically, from one generation to the next, beginning in an era of universal ignorance. Moreover, throughout the past two thousand years, say, the questioning of religious doctrine has been widely discouraged or even expressly forbidden - a damning betrayal of the fragility of its tenets. The Roman and Spanish Inquisitions, threats of 'eternal punishment' and 'hell fire' to children, and even the banning of the teaching of evolutionary theory in schools of the southern US, all contributed to the successful propagation of Christianity. Without such enforcement, the creed would surely have perished long ago. (You need not take my word for this. Instead, I would gladly refer you to *All in the Mind* (1999) by Sir Ludovic Kennedy - a convincing, and yet touchingly personal, advocacy of informed atheism.)

My conclusion is as follows: for God to 'live' - that is, in the minds of the faithful - dissent can never easily be tolerated. I can think of only one reason for this: it endangers God's metaphysical 'survival'.

Permit me to digress into superficiality very briefly, in order to dismiss the ridiculous concept of Divine Revelation. As a former medical student, I frequently heard the term *schizophrenia* defined as being:

'mental fragmentation resulting in, amongst other symptoms, an inability to differentiate internal from external stimuli'.

What that means is: schizophrenic sufferers often believe, quite adamantly, that the voices they hear inside their heads actually originate from elsewhere - the house next door, for instance, or the television, or even outer space. The eminent American psychiatrist, Dr. Thomas Szasz (1920-), famously wrote:

'If you talk to God, you are praying.

If God talks to you, you have schizophrenia.'

Or are these people simply deluding themselves? You be the judge.

In schools throughout the United Kingdom, children are required by law to engage in acts of worship to this non-evident being - every day in the most unfortunate cases. They are offered little choice. I agree, their parents may object, but how can the children defy both their parents and the school?

In terms of worship and idolatry, the personality cult of Jesus Christ (c.5BC-33AD) bears a disturbing resemblance to those of several other dead heroes. I offer four examples:

1. Elvis Presley (1935-77): 'Presleytarian' churches now exist in southern parts of the United States and already attract thousands of devout worshippers.

2. Eva Peron (1919-52): According to some officials in Buenos Aires, the General's wife 'passed into immortality' after her forlorn battle against ovarian cancer.

3. Kim Il Sung (?-1994): Propaganda was rife after the death of the 'Dear Leader' that, instead of having being born the son of a peasant farmer, he in fact 'descended to earth on the wings of a dove'. South Korean sources have asserted that the latter explanation is the one routinely instilled into North Korean schoolchildren.

4. Diana, Princess of Wales (1961-97): Since her premature demise, the 'People's Princess' has made many a miraculous 'appearance' throughout the world.

The comparisons are unnerving, are they not? In fairness, one might argue that it would be unlikely that any of the aforementioned icons will achieve the dizzy level of adulation afforded to Christ, and I would not disagree. But is this simply a reflection of the fact that superstition, colonial conquest and despotism were more widespread, and rational analysis less stringent, hundreds of years ago? The list is endless. Perhaps I ought to have included the flawed protagonist in this novel.

We now enter the 21st century. Gods and idols have been superseded by rationalism. Logic, mathematics and science by their very nature provide us with worthy answers to the profound questions we are entitled to ask. Blind instinct, emotion and religious faith do not, and cannot. There ought to be no place in our lives for supernatural myths masquerading as absolute truth, or mindless traditions being perpetuated down the generations like defective genes. Cultural parasites such as these deserve to be driven to extinction. If, as I believe, we owe everything to our children, then I would argue that maximum freedom of thought, vital for their psychological well-being, ought to be at the top of the agenda.

One final note on this rather depressing subject: since I began work on the initial drafts, in February 1995, friends and foes alike have warned me of the existence of an archaic law governing something called *Blasphemous Libel*, which concerns offensive material about the Christian religion. What they have been unable to point out, however, is what would actually constitute illegality and, of course, whether this book crosses the line or not. We shall see. In any case, I kept asking, how could it be possible, legally, to libel a dead man?

The Colour of Love

I would like to stress that, in view of the storyline, I am not making some sort of tacit suggestion that all sexual relationships between western males and oriental females - the reverse situation is rare - are born of dishonesty and ulterior motives, but crucial factors underpinning some such liaisons would seem difficult to refute.

For a start, social security systems in many Asian countries are either underdeveloped or non-existent. This, coupled with rapid population growth and subsequent rising unemployment, compels teenage girls from rural villages to head for the cities in search of jobs for which they have neither the necessary educational qualifications nor any relevant experience. Most jobs require at least a reasonable command of English.

What often follows is unbearably tragic. The girls - and sometimes boys too - are forced into the same dilemma that William Shakespeare assigned to poor old Hamlet: to be, or not to be. In their case, the opening line of that often-quoted soliloquy translates as: Prostitution, or destitution. That is the question, and what a choice to have to make. Inevitably, cities such as Bangkok and Manila have experienced a relentless influx of undeniably beautiful young girls clamouring for a limited number of casual, poorly-paid jobs in seedy bars, supplying mainly western men - or *farangs* - with food, drinks and anything else that might earn them some money, however degrading. The scenario smacks of Darwinism, and, as we know from the way Darwinian competition governs the natural world, there is no foresight, no justice, no compassion and, of course, no safety net (for the girls). As in nature, it is survival for survival's sake.

The bar owner's principal objective is, patently, the maximization of profits, and this can be achieved only by employing girls that are both very pretty and willing to do absolutely anything for their 'clients'. Relentless competition ensues, and only the 'fittest' (most productive) girls 'survive' (remain in employment).

In reality, those that do manage to get by do so in true Darwinian fashion by successfully adapting to the demands of their environments - that is, by devising the most effective ways of separating *farangs* from their money. Morality, as defined by our attitudes I might add, does not enter into it. Nor could it, for too much is at stake. Consequently, such wallet-raiding strategies are often ingenious, highly devious and in some cases downright criminal. (I once saw some insightful graffiti daubed across a toilet wall in a dive bar in Chiang Mai - don't ask what I was doing in there - which read: 'I love Miss Siam'. Underneath, some wise old scribe had added: 'He'll learn'.)

This forms the basis of Tim's wary remark at the end of Chapter II about the bar girls' 'survival' in employment at the Plaza being 'no accident'. Richard Dawkins, making a not dissimilar point about Chicago gangsters in *The Selfish Gene* (1976), wrote:

> *'... you can make some inferences about a man's character if you know something about the conditions in which he has survived and prospered.'*

Long-term, and long-distance, relationships, then, often with more than one man at a time, become commonplace, and marriage to a *farang* can sometimes represent the 'Holy Grail' for all the wrong reasons.

There is, however, another side to this unfortunate equation. The males are not exclusively the victims, far from it. Just as he is exploited for money, she in return is exploited for sex - and to a similarly ruthless extent. The sight of a stunning, sable-haired, teenage waif walking hand-in-hand with an ageing, overweight, sunburnt *farang* might seem bizarre but it is nothing unusual. It is the same old tale, but with elaborate undercurrents. A cynic might respond here by asserting that any relationship is merely a vehicle for mutual exploitation, but in this case one does not need to be too cynical to believe this description to be fair.

As a result, western males risk 'following their dicks' into a world of debt and venereal disease, and young females frequently become the victims of appalling degradation. The fact that Aids amongst the girls is alarmingly prevalent sums up the whole unfortunate business. What price political willpower, I wonder?

Shooting the Messenger

Regarding the reference to Bangkok's poor amputees (see Chapter XXV), the important point to remember is this: since greater physical debilitation tends to generate more sympathy, and with it more money, then, logically, this will precipitate a worse overall level of mutilation. It is a truly abominable fact of life that, in some parts of the world, destitute parents are prepared to amputate the healthy limbs of their own children in order to increase the efficacy of begging and hence raise their standard of living. I have seen all this with my own eyes, and it will haunt me while ever my memory remains capable of bringing it back.

Again, though, several high-minded correspondents have complained about my having referred to such an unpalatable truth. According to some, my description could be construed as a slur on a number of nations whose governments are (I am told) addressing the problem with the urgency it demands, and I must therefore be a racist! Furthermore, one individual claimed that my own prose style painted 'a simplistic and jaundiced picture'.

So what? Why should either neo-McCarthyism - a.k.a. 'political correctness' - or one's limitations as a fledgling writer negate the need for such tragedies to be reported? Evidently some people have different priorities from my own.

Mariner's Cottage

Philip Gainsborough's cottage is based upon a three-storey, listed building on Mariner's Road, New Brighton, where I myself lived from March 1991 to June 1992. Unlike the shacks on Soi Phasuk, it is still standing.

Paul Spradbery
Wirral

December, 2001

Acknowledgements

I should like to pay a sincere tribute to a number of individuals who provided support, encouragement and tolerance - mainly tolerance - as this book very slowly took shape, beginning with its conception at 2994, Oslo Crescent, Meadowvale, Ontario during the autumn of 1994.

If the apprenticeship for writing is reading, then it is only proper that I offer thanks to those who have, through the years, ensured that my birthday presents have come from one bookshop or another. In particular, I should like to name Ian and Pamela Hall for kindness not always deserved.

My love to Mike and Angela Winch - in appreciation of theirs given unreservedly to me.

To the enigma known to me as KJW - I will always think of you on your birthday, 8th October.

Thanks also to David Hall, John W. Steele, the late Bryan Littlewood, Stuart Whatham, Kia Pheng Tan, Dr. Derek McCartney, Rashmi Shah, Judith Bell-Taylor, Robert J. Wilkinson, the Andover clan from Andover, Pauline R. Summerfield, Col. Brett 'Steve' Donkelbarger, Bill 'the biologist' Keig, John and Shirley Bowers, my friends at the Machim Apartments, and Sue Fletcher and the girls at the place that no longer is.

To J (1993) - I know you are mine.

Special thanks to Yvette T. Thomas - for opening all the windows.

Finally, to my mother and father - in appreciation of something unique which happened, not all that far from here, many years ago.

Few of these wonderful people will be the least bit surprised that I did not always follow their advice.

Paul Spradbery
Wirral

December, 2001